FINDING LADY ENDERLY

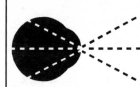

This Large Print Book carries the
Seal of Approval of N.A.V.H.

FINDING LADY ENDERLY

JOANNA DAVIDSON POLITANO

THORNDIKE PRESS
A part of Gale, a Cengage Company

Farmington Hills, Mich • San Francisco • New York • Waterville, Maine
Meriden, Conn • Mason, Ohio • Chicago

LIBRARY OF CONGRESS CIP DATA ON FILE.
CATALOGUING IN PUBLICATION FOR THIS BOOK
IS AVAILABLE FROM THE LIBRARY OF CONGRESS

ISBN-13: 978-1-4328-7064-5 (hardcover alk. paper)

Published in 2019 by arrangement with Revell Books, a division of Baker Publishing, Inc.

Printed in the United States of America
1 2 3 4 5 6 7 23 22 21 20 19

Finding Lady Enderly

1

I do not truly wish for all my dreams to come true. After all, nightmares are one type of dream.

~ Diary of a Substitute Countess

Spitalfields, London's East End, 1871
For one blessed moment I was beautiful. The flickering gaslights of Church Street illuminated my reflection in a window, and I gasped at the vision of loveliness framed on the grimy pane of Bryn and Saunders Textiles. I paused and twirled my hair up, looking with wonder at the whole of me in this luscious borrowed gown — shapely, trim, and utterly feminine. For the first time in my life, my willowy body was fitted in a garment with shape and form.

Mercy gracious, I looked like a normal woman.

A flash of vanity lighted my heart, but it was snuffed by chilly fear a moment later.

The grim reflection of a fine-suited gentleman lurked behind my image in the window, moving steadily toward me. He must be coming for the gown and shoes.

With a shiver, I dropped my upswept hair and slipped into the shadows of the building, heart thudding with powerful force as I hurried away. The stranger's shoes clicked on the damp street behind me, splatting over little rivulets of rainwater as they moved toward me with purpose. I had only meant to borrow them and return them before they were missed, but what could I do now — strip down to my dirty chemise and run through the streets?

"You there." His low voice thudded through my senses, sparking me into action.

I sprinted past my rag cart and down a narrow, unlit street. I never should have touched the thing. The gown had been lying across a chair in the Hollingsworths' laundry cellar, and the maid had left me alone with it while she'd gone to fetch the castoffs for me. Once I glimpsed the ivory organza, and the little jeweled slippers cast under a stool, I hadn't the strength to leave them alone. I'd intended to return them within minutes. An hour at most.

Yet there was no point in stopping for explanations, for I was a rag woman, as much a castoff as the rags I peddled. People called me Ragna, a cruel twist on my real name, Raina. I sprinted with all my might, loose rocks skittering under my feet as I hurtled through the shadows, dodging the yellow glow of streetlights. I stumbled as one of those ridiculous slippers came loose, and I kicked it off, darting on one shoe and bare toes into the first alley I saw. I stumbled into the dark and *thunk* — my shins collided with something wooden, sending me sprawling over the broken cobblestones in a pile of crinoline and mud.

Miserable crates.

My pursuer turned the corner into the alley too, and I glanced back to find myself in a dead end with walls surrounding me on three sides, the man blocking my only escape and closing the distance between us. Cornered, I wrenched the other jeweled shoe off and held it aloft. The long, dark shadow of the man approached with steady confidence, and I realized he'd kill me and *then* drag my dead body to the constable. Defeat stole over me as I gripped the accidentally pilfered shoe. I'd survived twenty-two years in this slum, fought off every evil around me like a cornered tiger, only to be hanged for this — a mere moment of weakness.

I scrambled back into the alley's shadow as the steady rhythm of his approaching footsteps continued. Rooted to the spot by fear, I prayed to God that the foreboding stranger who most certainly did not belong in this section of London would simply ignore the pile of finery tangled in long limbs and move on.

Yet it seemed God had other plans, for the man strode through the dark right up to me, the tips of his shiny leather shoes coming to a stop before the hem of the once-white gown. I looked up into the first face I ever remembered seeing inside of Spital-fields as the gaslights along the main street highlighted his confident features. Fear drowned my voice into silence as the fine gent crouched before me with a conspirato-rial smile and held out the shoe I'd abandoned.

"Pardon me, have you lost a glass slipper?"

Shock pulsed through me. His handsome blond curls caught the moon's glow as a smile warmed his face. I forced myself to breathe.

He reached toward my dirty bare foot and his nearness sent me scrambling upright, leveling a glare at him as I brushed smudges of mud off my bare arm.

Men grew uncomfortably brazen as the sun set over this cramped little section of town. Did he think his fine appearance would earn whatever he wanted from me? "Thank you kindly for the shoe, sir, but if you'll excuse me." I felt the sting of my words, but I'd lived long enough to know that kindness from strangers must be clearly snubbed. Anything less would find a girl helpless and ruined.

"You are excused." But he merely rose to stand before me, remaining in my path with his arms crossed over his chest. He tipped his head and smiled down at me. "Are you all right, then? No harm came from your tumble?"

"Perfectly well, thank you." I smoothed the limp dress over my body and attempted to duck around him, but he stepped easily in front of me.

"If you'll give me but a moment, I believe I can help."

Help, indeed. "You're blocking my way."

"Or perhaps enticing you to take an entirely new one." He lowered his voice. "No woman ought to live this way."

"Hoping to save the lot of us poor folk, then? That'll take a fair bit of time, sir, and all your fortune." I watched him, breathing hard and poised to escape this odd encounter at the first chance. Whatever it was he offered, it could hardly be chivalrous.

"Won't you give me but a moment of your time? I only wish to help, and I've a splendid opportunity in mind."

"I'm not in need of one." I shoved past him and limped toward the main street on two sticks of throbbing pain but my chin up, leaving this darkly clad stranger with as much conviction as any high-bred lady might. When it came to these sorts of men, don't run and they won't chase — every Spitalfields lass knew the rule, but this was my first chance to test the old adage.

But even as I walked away, the word *opportunity* settled into my mind and ignited a bloom of fanciful notions. They came almost unbidden, for I had been born with both a spirited imagination and a life that demanded regular escape into it.

I slowed and snuck another glance behind me. The odd stranger appeared both sober and sane. His trim gray cutaway coat with perfect black buttons contrasted sharply with the surrounding grime and decay, and made me both suspicious and fascinated in whatever drove him to continue pursuing me.

I strode on with my head high, some wicked part of me willing him to catch up and quench my curiosity. A few paces later, he did at least grant the first part of that wish. His shoes *splat-splatted* over the rain pooled in the ruts of the cobbled road, and he again stepped before me, halting my progress. "I noticed you did not say no." The defined *M* of his upper lip uncurled into an enticing smile as he held out the little jeweled shoe.

"Only because I cannot bring myself to take you seriously."

"No, it's more than that. Admit it — some little part of you desperately wants to hear what sort of adventure this stranger is attempting to offer you."

I dropped my gaze, for surely my entire personality must be in vivid display upon my face. How else could he have spoken so directly into my secret heart? His smoothly spoken word "adventure" inflamed a desire in me so great, it tempted me to cast aside everything I knew and follow him.

"I've passed hundreds of other women in need before now, but you're the first to catch my attention, to inspire me to do more." He paused when I remained silent, cocking his head at a charming angle. "You seem to doubt my sincerity. Shall I tell you more specifically what I find so enchanting about you?"

The dress — it must be this magical dress. I touched its wilted skirts as my fickle heart struggled to remain aloof. "I'll not believe you. You're either lying or . . . or mad."

"What a monstrous thing to say to someone who's just paid you a compliment." He offered his arm with a smile. "Your punishment is that you must endure my company for the duration of your walk home."

Unease sliced through me at these words and I stepped back. The man would not come near the flat occupied only by myself and an elderly widow. "I bid you good evening, sir." Tingling with fear — or maybe excitement — I turned, but he laid a hand on the wall to bar me from leaving. The effect was surprisingly arresting.

"What if I could manage a respectable position for you at a magnificent estate, among the finest gowns and fields of flowers, and all you had to do was come with me and step into it?"

His words pulled at me at the heart level, where a love of beauty was buried, yet I resisted with all my might. If only he knew how he tortured me. "I couldn't simply walk away from —"

"From what, all this?" He spread wide his arms in the dank alley thick with the odor of trapped moisture. "Come, what would you be leaving behind, truly? Have you a family at home? A respectable man waiting for you?"

In an instant, images of the man I loved engulfed my heart with a familiar pain. My mind saw him as he was years ago, swinging upside down from a rusted stair rail, fueling our lives with music and joy, saluting his farewell with a lopsided grin from the *Maiden Faire* as it sailed into the fog. That dear face and the marvelous personality behind it, forever gone with the sunken ship.

Oh yes, I had a man. A splendid, big-hearted, gallant one who was no less mine simply because he was dead.

But that wasn't what he meant, of course. I fisted my hands against the wall and forced myself to answer over the wave of fresh pain. "I suppose not." My parents were dead, all my older siblings long gone from Spitalfields, and my younger brother Paul was stationed somewhere in the West Indies with no desire to return.

And why would he? Nothing about Spital-fields could ever feel like home, even to those who lived here. Even my rag cart was now lost to me, abandoned in my haste. I studied the man's waiting face, tempted to cut the slender threads that bound me to this place and walk into whatever it was he

15

offered. I cradled the idea in my mind even as I searched feebly for reasons — any reason — that I should refuse him.

His smile revealed perfect white teeth. Too perfect. "Have you ever heard of Rothburne Abbey? It's far from here, where green fields spread out like gentle carpet and flowers bloom on every doorstep. The position pays one hundred a year."

I coughed. *"Pounds?"* My brain immediately sifted that sum into a thousand possible uses. First, I would have the pure pleasure of writing to Paul that he could keep the pittance he sent me out of his pay, that his sister was finally earning her independence and would no longer be his burden to bear. "I'm naught more than a rag woman, you know."

"I see so much more in you, in that restrained fire in your eyes, that poise in your spine, and I see what could be."

My lashes fluttered at the weight of the temptation before me. I could work endlessly and never see reward, or I could step into this opportunity and fill both my pockets and my soul. Still, anything that seemed too good to be true usually was.

"At least come see it. You owe yourself that much. You already know what it is to be here, barely surviving and cowering from

16

every stranger. Empty pockets, empty belly, empty future. There's so much more you can do with your life."

I stared at him as a parched person eyes an icy lemonade.

"Now that I have you sufficiently intrigued, I'll leave you to your normal routine and see if you still find it worth holding so tightly. Tomorrow morning I'll be at the train. I pray the night will not torment your mind to a great degree with indecision." With a sweeping bow, he handed me the little jeweled shoe, replaced his hat, and followed his shadow back into the darkness from which he had come.

A powerful shiver ran through me. I slipped on the shoe and paced home, my sore feet crossing back and forth over the drain gutter running down the center of the rain-drenched street. All manner of rationalizations flooded my tired brain, tugging me this way and that.

Soon I ducked beneath the flapping sheet strung across my alley and stood before the broken shutters and ugly chipped brick of my tenement building. I was hemmed in with no evidence of God's creation around except the starless sky above, but it was my life. My reality. What right had I to hope for more?

With a sigh, I lifted my skirt to climb the steps and glimpsed the jeweled slipper he'd left with me, inviting me into a Cinderella story. I found myself surprisingly immune to his charm on the whole, having already spent my entire heart on one man with no desire to retrieve it, but the hope of his offered adventure flared through my heart. I looked up and suddenly my building seemed ten times more wretched and grimy than it had when I'd left at dawn. With a whole world of possibilities offered to me outside this cramped district, it suddenly felt impossible to remain here.

I settled before the open window that night with a view of the distant train station, churning the decision through my mind. If I left, that meant admitting Sully wasn't coming home. His ship was gone and my Sully with it. He'd be my most treasured memory, captured in my mind like a miniature in a locket — his wide smile, the jaunty blue cap he always wore. I'd made it for him in return for him teaching me to read so many years ago, and he'd worn it so often it seemed a part of him.

"Hello there!"

I jerked as Widow McCall's voice carried through our flat from her curtained-off cot, and I swiped madly at my tears.

"Oh, and look at you, lassie! I've never seen you looking so fine, even if the gown do have a bit of extra trimmings to it." Her shrunken form sailed through the room to finger the mud stains on the lovely skirt, and the frown that contorted her warted features made me smile. "And just what is my li'l lass doing out after dark? Only God is invincible, you know. Ach, you and trouble ought to be the closest chums, the way you always go together."

"This time my trouble may have brought about some good." I unleashed the tale, and with every turbulent sentence, the encounter seemed more unbelievable. I told her about Rothburne Abbey and showed her the little slippers, wondering if I'd stumbled into the pages of a fairy tale on my way home. What other reason would a gentleman have for imploring the woman who sold castoff rags to follow him to a life of splendor? It wasn't as if I even had experience in service or letters to recommend me.

"I shouldn't do it, should I? It's too odd. Too risky."

Her eyes glistened. "Precisely why you should, love. This place holds you in its grip, but it doesn't define you. It's as if fate is plucking your pretty little self out of this mess and placing you where you belonged from the start."

"Oh no, I —"

"Now, now, don't argue with an old woman. I have eyes, don't I?" She reached out and rubbed the ends of my curls between her gnarled fingers. "A sort of queen is what you are, stepping through the rubbish like you was balancing a crown on that pretty head of yours. I suppose it's in your blood, being one of them wealthy Huguenot silk people."

"That's long past. We've been nothing but rag vendors since I was small." It was the cost of progress. If only those merchants who'd begun importing silks knew what their prosperity had cost an entire community of local artisans. The Huguenots were no longer a respected immigrant community spinning silk from behind tall, sunny windows. I barely remembered what it was like to wear ribbons in my hair as I recited my lessons in the schoolroom. We'd never been as wealthy as our ancestors, but we'd been respectable.

"Ah, but you've got a touch of the old blood in you, coursing through like a vein of gold. The way you talk, the look of your face . . . There's something noble about you, lass. Finally someone else stood up and took notice of it too, and you'll not refuse the brilliant man who's had the sense to see it." She lifted sharp old eyes to meet mine. "I'll miss you something fierce, but don't you ever come back. You've always belonged somewhere better'n here."

I frowned. "What do they want with the likes of me at an abbey, anyway? It's an odd place to find a position."

Her eyes sparkled beneath the frizz of gray hair. "Did Abraham require the good Lord to give him a description of the place where he was being sent? You'd best go and find out."

When she took herself away to her little cot in the corner again, I turned back toward the distant station where I was supposed to meet the mysterious man on the morrow. For years that station had symbolized the hope of Sully's return, but now it meant the opposite. Leaving on that train would sever the last connection we had — a lifetime of memories in Spitalfields. Could I give up that dream to risk another?

It struck me then that I'd never see on his face the great love he wrote of, never hear him say it in his own voice. For years we'd been the best of friends, and somewhere along the way I'd fallen deeply in love with the man so full of life and music, but I

21

hadn't dared to hope he'd return it. Until he left for sea after a row with his father and the letters started to come.

Oh, those letters!

Once again I drew them out of the little broken place in the wall and flipped open the first, sinking back against the blanket in the windowsill.

My dear Raina, it began, and that was enough to saturate my heart, for his every action since I'd known him had proven I was exactly that. He was one of the few who called me by my true name, and his use of it always touched me. The rest of the letter was doused with words from a passionate heart that had lain hidden behind the playful, lively exterior I'd always known. Why had he never spoken these words aloud before he'd left? He couldn't have feared rejection from me, for I'd loved him fervently before I even understood what the word meant.

What would I do, come morning's light? I could go two ways — one was bleak, offering nothing, and the other was beckoning me away to adventure, which had been my weakness since childhood. It lured and fascinated me, causing me trouble and constantly disrupting the ruts of life. Though now there was no Sully to rescue me from my scrapes.

But neither would there be if I remained in Spitalfields, pining away after his memory.

So it was that I found myself taking one final walk through Spitalfields the following morning as the sun dawned over a new day and a new life, a limp carpetbag swinging against my leg, anxiety and excitement chasing each other through my veins. I slipped the carefully freshened gown and slippers back into the laundry cellar of Mrs. Hollingsworth and turned toward the station. Widow McCall had made the situation seem so natural, almost inevitable, but now that I reached my destination, the oddness of it all pricked me again.

As the sun heated my skin, I stood on the platform until the throng of travelers parted to reveal the stranger who had slipped into my life and upended my future, and I tensed at the sight of such a finely dressed man smiling at me. What was that odd sensation he elicited in me with a mere look? I couldn't tell if it was thrilling or scary. Either way, it was addictive.

He strode over and, with a small smile of victory, scooped up my bag. As I watched him stride away with everything I owned, panic unfurled inside. I hugged my patched old shawl about me, a tangible reminder of who I truly was, because it seemed I'd forgotten. I dreamed so often of normal clothing and a world of acceptance, but I still awoke every morning — including this one — as Ragna the seller of rags.

Yet this gent wanted me. Quite ardently. Something was not right.

I caught up to him as steam huffed from under the train. "I don't even know your name."

"It is Prendergast. Victor Eugene Prendergast. I am the private solicitor for Rothburne Abbey." He considered me with amusement. "Would you also like to see my character references?"

I looked up into his tolerant face. "What is Rothburne? What could I possibly do at an abbey?"

"It's a monastic fortress renovated into a private estate. It's now the country home of the Countess of Enderly."

A countess. He wished me to work for a countess? I pressed my lips together and watched hundreds of more appropriately dressed people swarm onto the train ahead of us, wondering again why he'd insisted on me. With one more powerful billow of steam pouring across my vision, I followed him and glanced back for the last time at every-

24

thing I was leaving behind.

"Final boarding!" A red-coated man hung out of the door of the train car before us, urging us on.

I hesitated, waiting for the steam to clear for my final view of home, but my new employer tugged my arm. "Come, Cinderella. It's time to go."

"Raina. My name is Raina."

When I glanced back at the station again, uncertainty weighting my steps, a blue cap descended into the billowing steam farther down, black boots landing firmly on the solid wood platform. Heart exploding in my chest, I braced myself against the doorway, willing the steam to clear so I could see who it was. It couldn't be him, but I simply *had* to know before I left. Through the haze I saw a lanky, energetic sailor with a coat tossed over one arm, bag in hand. How well I knew that stance — but it was impossible. Impossible! If only I could see his face.

"Doors closing."

I gripped the metal bar, but strong arms guided me into the train car. "Wait! Stop!" The chaos of the station drowned out my voice as I resisted.

Another billow of steam, and the blue-capped man turned at the commotion I made. I strained for another glimpse, but before the steam cleared, the arms yanked me in and the train door shut and latched before my face.

2

I have a great many adventures simply because I have always feared regret more than failure.

~ Diary of a Substitute Countess

I clutched the edge of my seat and rested my forehead on the shuddering train window. It wasn't Sully. *Wasn't.* Months ago I'd seen the notice in the paper about the storm they called the "Great Gale," and my trembling finger skimmed down the list of lost ships until I spotted it — *Maiden Faire.* I forced myself to recall the sight of that name. The ship had gone down, and with it, Sullivan McKenna. My Sully.

How foolish to risk everything for proof that the stranger at the station was not him. There were plenty of men in the world who owned a bright blue wool cap. Sully was dead, and I was merely nervous.

Yet I resented my new employer's slight

coercion. Catching sight of my carpetbag — *my* bag — in the stranger's grasp, I snatched it away and held it close, the sound of crinkling letters inside calming me.

He shifted in his wooden seat. "You are cross with me."

"You wouldn't listen. I changed my mind, but you forced me onto the train."

He flipped out a newspaper and scoffed. "What a terrible word for it — *forced.* I tell you, it was merely a misunderstanding. I thought you were dallying and might miss the train, and we wouldn't have caught another until the evening. Surely you can understand my position."

His cool words swirled anger and doubt into a vague apprehension, and I didn't know what I believed. Perhaps if I could just be certain about that stranger. As the long, low whistle sounded and we approached the next station, I sprang up but the man stood and braced me as the train shifted.

"Come, take your seat before you fall across the aisle. You haven't a shilling for return fare, anyway."

I gripped the seatback in front of me. "Can you not spare the little it would cost to return me?"

"Certainly not." He tensed as the train

jerked to a final stop. "I could, but why ever would I pay for what I do not want?"

"Gentlemanly regard for a lady."

He puffed out a breath and turned that warm gaze on me. "It is my regard for you that makes me so insistent. I believe this will be a chance of a lifetime for you, even if you cannot see it. Return now, and you'll forever be the rag lady, scorned by all decent society and even by most in Spital-fields. Besides, what are you returning for, anyway?"

A ghost. I clutched the seatback. I had to get on with the business of living at some point, or I'd go mad, seeing blue caps and fiddles everywhere.

His voice tugged at my attention. "Try it for one day. If you cannot bear the beauty and gracious lifestyle, if Rothburne does not sweep you up in its charming spell, you may return tomorrow — with a few far-things in your pocket for the trouble."

I shifted back into my seat — for now. Conceding a battle didn't mean losing the war, and I always won when it counted.

"I can only help you if you let me."

"You don't know me from a rock in the road. Why, I could be anybody. I'll have you know I've been to prison."

He merely cast a tolerant smile in my

29

direction, as if we were playing cards and he could see through the back of every one in my hand. "And what happened? It must not have lasted long."

I hung my head. "Just the night. My fines were paid by morning."

"Let me guess. A misunderstanding in which no one believed the rag woman, and she was arrested. Someone who knew better came to get you, and you haven't been back since."

I blinked as he so coolly put my past before me with casual indifference. It had been a moment of foolishness, as so many of my mishaps were, and I hadn't even set out to steal. Unless one counts pilfering trash. What I'd mistaken for piles of castoffs left just inside the woman's laundry cellar for me to collect had been her maid's laundry set there while the woman returned for some forgotten thing.

He winked and settled back. "Come now, where's that contagious sense of adventure? If you must leave, I'll pay for you to return and replace that cart of rags you were forced to leave behind. I'll even give you a beautiful dress of your choice. You'll have spent a day or so away from that sordid slum and come back the richer for it."

A new dress. I could return in style, and if

that blue-capped man did turn out to be Sully . . .

Ah, how my imagination ran away with me. Reality twisted my insides again. "Why in heaven's name would you do all this for me?"

He lowered the newspaper and studied my face in a probing way. "Because I see more in you, Raina of Spitalfields, even if no one else — including you — does. I earnestly hope to change your mind."

I leveled my gaze to evaluate his sincerity, but his smile pleasantly veiled everything he didn't wish me to read. I crossed my arms. "I suppose I have no choice."

I turned away then, and for hours I stared out the window in bitter silence, refusing to give him the satisfaction of having a willing companion. His punishment went unnoticed, however, as he'd given himself over fully to his newspaper. Even when we reached the neat little brick station called Havard Joint, he merely tucked his paper under his arm and extended a hand to help me disembark. Again the swirl of tension rose as I touched his hand, and I wondered if this was romance . . . or imminent danger.

I primly settled my fingertips on his hand as if I were a lady and allowed my tired self to be led down the steps and over to a sleek carriage that stood amid the dust and steam from the puffing train.

"Here awaits the carriage that will carry you into the grandest adventure of your life."

After the first few tense moments in the conveyance, a powerful exhaustion over-whelmed me, temporarily banking the fires of curiosity and excitement. I hadn't re-alized I'd fallen asleep until my companion poked me awake with the same jolting insistence with which he'd disrupted my life.

"I didn't want you to miss your first glimpse of it. Quite breathtaking, except when viewed through your eyelids." His charming smile was the first thing to come into focus, then the entire satin-lined coach around him. Tassels hanging from velvet curtains bounced and swayed as we trav-eled, and I pushed up, wiping away a trace of drool from the corner of my mouth. Certainly, I was proving myself fit for fine life.

How long had I slept? I glanced out the window. Orange glowed across the sky as the setting sun gave up its grand finale of light and sank into the green fields spread out before us. I tipped my face out the window to cool it with fresh breeze, taking in an earthy, rich smell of clean air, and the colorful scenery burst upon my vision with all the enchantment of my grandest dreams.

A line of trees passed as we traveled at a leisurely trot up a long lane. Slightly wild gardens spilled across an expanse of green grass dotted with bright red poppies, together seeming more like art than outdoor growth. They were so much more thoroughly *red* than I'd ever imagined. Perhaps a brief holiday here would not be entirely miserable. I would take a handful of poppies home to liven the flat. My face grew warm when I noticed Victor Prendergast watching my childish delight with amusement.

I sat back and frowned at him. "Poppies don't grow in the autumn." As if challenging him to prove that this was not a dream.

"They're a fall breed. The gardener takes care to have a full range of color for as much of the year as possible. Quite wonderful, isn't it?"

I was searching for things to be amiss, that's all. It was foolish, really. The place was as real as my rags and this was no dream.

When I shifted my gaze farther up the lane, it fell upon our destination — an enormous stone palace of a house that inspired all the awe an abbey was meant to instill in its deeply religious inhabitants. Endless stone buildings rose triumphantly to latticed tops that gave it the look of a castle that had emerged from the earth and rocks around it.

The carriage delivered us around to the west side of the building before a long wing with rows of unimaginative square windows set in immaculate brown stone. The setting sun bathed the windows in a golden glow that gave a bit of splendor to the otherwise practical things. Mr. Prendergast tossed me a heavy hooded cloak, but I shook my head. "It's a fine night to run about. I want to feel the fresh air on my skin."

"Put it on to conceal yourself. You deserve a grand entrance when you are refreshed — and relieved of the dust of poverty that covers your true beauty."

I turned in the shadows to hide my heated face and looked down at the drab garments that draped me in the reality of who I was. I peddled rags, dealt purely in castoffs, and his compliments felt foreign. Misplaced.

False.

Yet I did not dwell on it. Draped in the borrowed cloak, I stepped from the carriage with his assistance. The driver was already walking toward the stables for someone to attend the horses, while my new employer hustled me toward an ancient wood door with his arm about me, as if shielding me from rain even though the evening was clear. Once inside, I peeked from under the hood into my adventure — a long white-washed hall in which everything was arched, from the windows and doorframes to the ceiling itself. No adornments interrupted its gleaming purity.

"This was the monks' dormitory. It used to be the servants' quarters until the previous owner created a separate wing for them in the main part of the house." Prendergast guided me into the second doorway and shut the door behind us, cutting off the richness of life and freedom that stood just outside. He slid a long wooden arm across the door to secure it and turned to me with a contented smile. "There. Now we shan't be disturbed."

I pulled the cloak tighter about me as he approached, and the familiar fear stole over me. I wasn't about to be another Jane Clousen if I could help it, even if this was a wealthy estate rather than a print factory and a gentleman stood before me instead of a stuffed-shirt printer from Greenwich. No matter how it felt when we'd arrived, this place was no different than Spitalfields, because the entire world was the same. No, *men* were. I searched for that dull glow of hunger in his eyes as he neared, and a slender blade of fear sliced through my sense of adventure, leaving me longing for a homebound train. For Sully.

I backed until I found myself against a textured white wall with nowhere to go as he bent to light a lamp. It occurred to me then that there were fates worse than Spitalfields and fortresses more dangerous than the open streets. If escape became necessary, and I feared it might, I'd have to accomplish it on my own. "I do hope you were sincere in your offer to return me tomorrow."

He glanced my direction with a smile after replacing the glass over the lamp. "Only if I cannot change your mind before then." He stepped back, folding his arms across his chest to look at me. "I'm certain I won't have to do much convincing to keep you here, because you will find this beautiful place suits you. There's something naturally charming about your bearing, your very face."

"I am Ragna the rag woman." I forced out the words claiming the identity that, for once, felt like a protection.

A quick smile twitched his mouth to the

side. "On the outside, perhaps. I believe you're something else entirely past that ragged exterior. Give me but a day and I shall change the outside to match, and you'll be the most splendid beauty in all of England." With a wink, he turned toward a partition closing off part of the room. "There's a bath readied for you behind the screen, although I imagine it's cold now. You'll find something clean to wear on that bed, and a dinner tray will be sent."

"What'll my duties be, if you please, sir? Do I start tomorrow?"

He watched me with his now-familiar smile of warm amusement. "Absolutely. At first light, you shall begin a whole new chapter in your life." He moved toward the door. "In the meantime, content yourself with your bath and dinner. Only, keep to this room, if you will. Parts of the abbey renovations are not complete, and I wouldn't want you coming into danger just as you're about to step off into this grand new life." With a charming wink, he slipped from the room.

After a few moments of staring at the door, I began to peel off the layers of rags until there was only me. When I went to stand over the still water, that new nameless person looked back at me, for I looked nothing like the rag woman now. Without the many layers of rags overwhelming my frame, my eyes were what stood out the most. Blue with dark edges and a lash-fringed upward slant, they sparkled in a feminine manner that pleased me.

I washed as requested, scrubbing in the tepid water with eager delight as it refreshed my skin. I dressed in the fresh chemise and fawn-colored muslin laid on the bed and eagerly consumed the food that had arrived while I was in the bath, but a powerful curiosity drowned out the second command — that of remaining in the room. Forbidding me to leave nearly ensured I would.

As I stood in that quiet little room with the borrowed garments hanging against my freshly scrubbed skin, my uncontrollable sense of adventure returned, and I felt like a shiny new girl on the cusp of experiencing something wonderful. I snuck out and looked about.

My uncertain footsteps echoed in the empty space, nerves as skittish as an alley rat as I slipped down a narrow wooden stairway at the end. I felt my way along the curving wall in the dark until I reached the bottom and walked into a hall glowing with a silvery blue moonlight that streamed through a wall of greenhouse windows.

"Mercy gracious," I mumbled to myself. It was an entire garden right in the house!

The long hall was lush and alive with plants and flowers that climbed up from all sides, and I could imagine the queen walking down this red-carpeted passageway for her coronation.

Driven forward with a sense of expectancy for what lay in the rooms beyond, I passed through the door at the other end and down another hall into a large, domed space heavy with an air of moisture and neglect. My heart caught in my throat at the sight of an old, decrepit chapel left to rot, with dust wrapped thick and gray over the dark wood pews and rails, and a massive organ that hadn't been touched in decades. Its tall gold pipes hung at odd angles like broken teeth.

How terrible the former inhabitants would feel if they could see what had become of so sacred a space. One could sense the presence of a thousand prayers lifting into this room, and though the men uttering them had departed, there remained an air of sacredness here as if their pleas had lingered, the atmosphere still charged with God's presence.

Standing in the center and looking up into the great dome, I felt a breathless wonder that was at once delightful and frightening fill my chest. I hurried through the hushed space to the next room and found myself in the dark. Crossing to the tall windows and inching back heavy drapes to let in the moonlight, I turned and gasped at the chaos and ruin of what was once a great library. Heavy books lay open in dusty piles about the fringes of the neglected room where they'd fallen out of the crumbling old shelves lining the walls. Three crooked sliding ladders hung listlessly from metal brackets.

Was this the same house to which I'd arrived with the tree-lined drive and stately towers? The eeriness of the space in which I now found myself deeply bothered me and drew me, like a disaster from which one could not turn away. I walked several paces into a narrow, arched hall also lined with debris and aching of neglect but paused when distant voices floated toward me. The arresting voice of Victor Prendergast pricked my ears.

"You needn't worry over me, Bradford. I've only been out fetching a little surprise for our dear countess. I have it on good authority she'll be arriving on tomorrow's train, and she does expect her little amusements."

So, I was to be an amusement for her.

Perhaps he intended me as her companion. But even that made little sense.

Another deep voice responded. "If you please, sir, what might her favorite flower be? I'll have my staff fill the house with cut arrangements in her honor."

"Red poppies," I breathed to myself, closing my eyes and swooning with delight as I recalled the bursts of petals that had so captivated my soul on the drive up the lane. They would most certainly be my choice.

"I believe red poppies are her special favorite, Bradford. She'd be pleased to see fresh vases of them when she arrives."

I sucked in my breath, touching my fingertips to my smiling lips. To think I had something in common with a countess.

"It shall be done, sir. I'll have them arranged all over the house. Lady Enderly's arrival is a day worth celebrating."

I turned and walked back into that forgotten relic of a library, away from the voices so I would not be discovered. Perhaps the lady of the house would recognize in me a shared love for beauty and ask me to help with the garden's design. What a delightful position that would be.

Yet there was a chance I'd decide to leave on the morning train if I took my would-be employer at his word. Or perhaps the afternoon train would be more suitable, for I would surely be awake long into this night, even after I'd convinced myself to return to that dim little room and attempt sleep. It would also allow me a chance to glimpse the great countess herself — from a distance, most likely, but close enough to see her lovely gown. What would such a woman wear? Silk or organza? Perhaps an enchanting combination of both. Something in red like her poppies?

Turning about to take in the room still grand even in its disrepair, I caught sight of a rich wood frame with ornate carvings and a portrait mostly covered by a dust sheet. Was it her? Would I have a glimpse of the great countess? Golden waves of hair twisted down over a rich red sleeve in the exposed edge of the painting, the sight of which enchanted me. She stood in the midst of a garden, a parasol swung low to the ground behind her. I strode across the room, drawn by an invisible force toward this woman with a gown lovelier than the flower we both favored. Would her face be as splendid?

I reached up and tugged free the coarse material draped across her portrait. With a puff of dust, the cloth fell to reveal an image so shocking it left me breathless. I stumbled back, unable to take my eyes off those of the woman looking back at me. They were the same eyes I'd glimpsed in the still waters of my bath, the eyes I'd seen in hazy mirrors all my life.

There on the wall hung a portrait of someone so startlingly familiar I felt as though I was staring at my own face.

3

Even the most luscious gowns were once raw threads on the floor of the spinning room.

~ Diary of a Substitute Countess

When I awoke in the stale little room of the monks' dormitory the next morning, every one of my belongings had vanished. My pile of rags, the carpetbag I'd abandoned by the chair, even my shoes had all disappeared as if they'd never existed in this new world, and it unsettled my sleep-clouded mind. I sat up and looked around the dawn-soaked room. What was reality, Rothburne or Spitalfields? Had my ragged belongings and the old carpetbag even existed at all?

In the place I could have vowed I'd left my bag stood a smallish stateroom trunk with metal rivets and leather straps. Panic curled through me as I rose and plodded in bare feet over to this foreign case. Had I been caught in a strange dream? I triggered the latches and lifted the lid to reveal the most lovely wine-colored serge traveling garment. I lifted the bodice and held it up to myself, fingering the luscious velvet trim.

A knock on the door startled me. I dropped the garment and slammed the lid shut.

"I'm wondering if Cinderella is at home. Might I come in?"

Victor Prendergast. I yanked a worn cotton gown from the wardrobe and tugged it on over the borrowed chemise I'd slept in, taking the time to fasten it in front before hastening across the room. Trembling, I inched open the door. "What's happening? Where are my things?"

"Why, they're in your trunk, my lady." He gestured toward the steamer, watching me with gentle amusement, arms folded over his chest. "No rescue would be complete without giving you the items you needed for your new life."

I stepped back to look over my rescuer, eyes wide as images of that portrait loomed in my mind. "What exactly have I been brought here to do?"

His steady gaze remained on my face. "You must know by now that I didn't just happen upon you in Spitalfields last night.

45

I'd seen you before, more than once." He stepped into the room and shut the door, leaning back on it. "I also saw the way those men jeered at you from the docks and the carriage that nearly ran you over in the street. Not stopping, not recognizing anything of value from the one so wonderfully different from them. Forgive me, but I could not erase you from my mind. It grew into a fabulous idea, and I couldn't dismiss how perfectly suited you were to Rothburne, to a very specific role." He seated me on the cot as he sank into the chair before it. His earnest eyes bore into me. "I've rescued you from the terrible squalor of London's East End to give you an opportunity, a most fitting position — *the Countess of Enderly.*"

I blinked as his revelation dangled in the air between us, and nearly laughed in his passionate face. Me, a countess! Was the man sane? "I believe that position is taken, sir."

"Hear me out." He moved the chair closer. "Lady Enderly is of a delicate disposition, and she wishes to rest after sailing to the continent and to India, but a woman such as she can hardly just disappear. Which is where you come in." He took my hands and lifted his wide, glittering smile, as one who feels the brilliance of his plan. "You have the privilege of borrowing her remarkable life for a time and living as fully and richly as you've always wanted. Lavish gowns, grand estate, fine food . . ."

I looked away, cheeks burning. Did he truly think me so easily tempted by finery simply because I was poor? "The woman ought to take her rest, then. A holiday by the sea. No need for a replacement."

"But her life is somewhat public, you see, and she desires that no one know of this. Everyone is entitled to a little privacy, especially when it comes to one's health. Consider what this would do for her, what it would mean."

I rolled my eyes. "The world won't miss one noble lady for a short time." I felt little pity over a countess drowning in her social duties. Had anyone stepped in to ease my own *maman*'s burden of true work before it killed her? And she, only seven and thirty at the time. She could have had so much life if poverty had not wrung it out of her.

A knock at the door cut into the conversation, and Mr. Prendergast spun to beckon in a short woman in a hooded cloak, who bustled in with two large baskets. "Thank you for coming, Esmerelda. She's over here."

"I haven't decided to stay yet. You did

promise to take me back today if I wished it."

He smiled at me with amusement. "That I did, my lady, but I never said *when* today." He leaned close. "Allow me a chance to change your mind. Meet Esmerelda, a brilliant woman from the next shire who will be touching up your appearance with a few aids."

"I'm not vulgar enough for cosmetics."

"Most ladies wear them." His dark eyes gleamed. "It's only vulgar if they admit to it."

"I doubt I'll see the position any differently from behind a few cosmetics."

"Not the role, but *you.* Under all those rags, there's a radiant woman who burns too brightly for the world of Spitalfields. And I'm anxious to let her come out and live."

Emily Brontë. He'd quoted Emily Brontë to me . . . and well I knew that quote. What other rag woman did?

"Come now, won't you humor me?"

I sighed. I could say no in a beat to forceful or angry insistence, but this gent's agreeable charm, his engaging nature that filled the air, warmed right through my defenses. I glanced at the basket of bottles and brushes, intensely curious what she'd make of me with them.

I grew stiff from sitting on the stool.

"What wretched-smelling water." I coughed as the stench of the clear liquid being swept over my face by the squatty little woman spiked up my nostrils and made me woozy. I already had an unnerving wooden instrument strapped to my back to straighten my posture, and this noxious aroma was too much.

Victor Prendergast smiled from his shadowed corner of the little room where he'd witnessed this torture session for at least three quarters of an hour. "It's ammonia. Clears the skin and lightens imperfections."

I coughed again as the woman stoppered the little bottle and turned to rummage in the nearby basket full of jars and tins. "So when you told me I was perfect for the position, what you meant was *nearly* perfect."

"You do bear certain traces of . . . privation. But those are easily concealed." He moved away from his wall and strode closer, circling me on my little stool in the middle of the room.

"It is uncanny, though, how little we must do to change your appearance. Never before have I seen a working-class woman with such a fair, unblemished complexion. How have you managed to remain so pure and white?"

"Sickly and sallow, you mean? A severe lack of sunshine and leisure will do it every time. You'd be white as a ghost too if you spent all the daylight hours in a dark little flat, piecing together other people's rags." I grimaced as the gruff woman dipped two fingers into a jar of cream and smeared the stuff on my face. The surprising coolness made a pleasant contrast to the sting of the ammonia and calmed my irritability for the moment.

The man's eyes sparkled in the dim room. "You're as amusing as you are lovely. What a creature."

Heat crept up my neck. How did he always do that? Somehow his words, his direct gaze, filled the millions of little cracks chipped into my heart in my two and twenty years as the rag woman. I hardly noticed them anymore, until I felt them being filled so thoroughly now.

"No smile." These were the woman's first words to me, and instantly my face melted into a neutral expression.

Prendergast's smile only widened. "Don't take it to heart, love. She knows what she's about."

"Smiles make creases." Her hoarse voice

50

continued. "Powder settles in creases and makes them worse." The woman's thick eyebrows nearly met in the middle, her frown deep and constant as she hovered mere inches from my face, smoothing cream over every surface.

"Is all of this necessary?"

"Well, we haven't time to give you consumption. That'd be the best way to achieve the right complexion, but we'll settle for this."

"How decent of you."

Soon the little woman stretched the screen across the room to shield me from Mr. Prendergast as she helped me dress. Unceremoniously stripping me of the cotton gown, she smoothed the chemise and covered it with crinolette, petticoats, and a snug corset that gave my figure a surprising strength and elegance. Far from the restrictive discomfort I'd expected, the support and natural poise offered by the stays felt wonderful.

She hoisted the skirt over my head, letting it float down like flower petals around my frame, then wrapped the bodice around my torso, crossing it in the front and securing it in back. As she twisted and pinned my newly smoothed curls into place, lifting them off my warm neck, I gasped in pain with a few tugs and twists, but soon she had everything resting comfortably on my scalp with only a slight throb from my poor head that was unused to such treatment. The oils she'd used on my hair gave it a healthy sheen.

When she had finished, she shoved the room divider back into its folded position behind me with a few grunts. There I stood, staring at the woman in the mirror before me, and it seemed the cosmetics had seeped through my skin and into my heart that had never expected to possess such beauty. I turned to face Mr. Prendergast where he lounged in a chair, rolling a pocket watch across his knuckles. The watch clattered to the floor. His look of boredom melted into pleasure, and he rose as if the sight of me compelled the gallant gesture.

I focused on breathing, in and out. In the continued silence, my skin warmed under the layers of tight clothing as dust sparkled in the sun pouring through the high window.

"Now," he whispered, taking my hands with a gentle touch. My pulse thrummed against his fingers. "Do you see what I see?"

He turned me to face the mirror, his hands gently bracing my shoulders. His words, his low voice, stirred something deep inside, for I *had* seen. I'd expected the

change to be drastic, my face unrecognizable, but instead the woman's efforts
seemed to merely uncover the woman who
had been buried, drawing hidden loveliness
to the surface and swathing it in silk and
scented oils. She'd brushed and polished
me into a far better version of myself.

"Perhaps now you will believe me, Raina
Bretton, when I tell you that you were created for something more, something far bigger than piecing scraps together and selling
rags in alleys."

My stomach knotted. "It feels so odd. All
of this. It can't be right if it makes me feel
this way."

His soft chuckle smoothed over my nerves.
"Is it truly so foreign to have what you
desire? Don't worry, you'll grow accustomed
to happiness if you give it half a chance."

I spun toward the window, raising my
chin. "I know my Bible, sir, and it tells me a
lot of other things I should be before
'happy.' "

"One of *those,* are you? Perhaps I can
speak your language. Do you recall the story
of Esther? How brave she was, taking on
the role of queen even though she was
naught but a poor Jewish woman. She used
her beauty to great advantage — not for
herself, but for her people. She saved them,

and you can do the same."

"What, rescue a silly noble woman?"

"You're thinking too small, love. In this new position, what might you change in that little flat you left behind? Maybe all of London's East End. And you can afford to think of your own too. How many brothers and sisters did you say you had?"

"I didn't, but there are seven."

"Seven. You can change their lives for the better, or entire districts for that matter, by merely becoming 'queen' for a time. Think what you could do with that sort of influence, the resources at your command. What would you change first? Whose life might you better?" He stepped closer, his minty breath fanning over my face. "What a waste it would be, that adventurous spirit tucked inside a beautiful woman, all rotting away under a pile of rags and poverty. You could be so much more if you only had the courage, recognized what was inside you."

This stopped me cold. His impassioned words had burrowed through an unseen crevice in my high wall of defenses and reached my heart — my heart that had ever swelled to pour into something bigger than myself, for my life to have a far-reaching impact and deep meaning. Only then would I be more than Ragna the burdensome rag woman with the empty life and empty coin jar.

"You could have such a remarkable influence. And all you need to do is —"

"Lie." My breath came hard and fast.

His face looked pained. "I'd never ask you to do such a vulgar thing. Have I asked you to tell one single person you were someone you were not, to say one untrue thing? Even Esther changed her name when she entered the palace. All I've asked you to do is waltz into the abbey dressed this way and allow everyone to draw their own conclusions."

I didn't speak. I couldn't. His words dulled the edges of my conscience, and that felt dangerous. It seemed wrong, or maybe just too good to believe. He alone had seen in me what I wanted to be and tempted me by breathing life into that far-fetched dream.

"Come now, be reasonable. Are not actors paid to do such a thing? All those men and women of the opera stand up on that stage in costume and let their audience pretend they are someone else. For pity's sake, everyone you meet is acting — as Shakespeare said, 'All the world's a stage, and all the men and women merely players.' Only, this acting position will also be more than fantasy — it will change lives. Imagine what you could do with the influence of a countess."

I already was.

He massaged his jaw with one hand. "Look, I'll offer you this. Try it for a time. You're already committed for the day. If your conscience still troubles you, I shall return you to Spitalfields with a gown as promised and allow you to waste your life away there."

I looked directly into his clean-shaven face. "You'll take me back as soon as I request it?"

His lips spread into a grin, as if he'd known all along I'd agree. "That very hour. Come now, it's time to go."

"Where?"

"You must make a grand entrance, coming from the train station. A lady would never arrive home unannounced."

More deception. "I'm not sure I can be convinced to stay."

He cast a knowing smile my way. "We shall see."

4

When amongst strangers, one can either
fear the unknown or be exceedingly grateful for a blank slate of possibilities.
~ Diary of a Substitute Countess

Sullivan McKenna whipped his fiddle and
bow up above his head after his song and
took a deep bow inside the straw-covered
stables. A smattering of applause met his
ears, followed by a bit of laughter that
warmed his merry soul. It was a fine day
when his playing could liven the hearts of
strangers, and he'd always believed it had a
nearly magic ability to do so. Even without
words, music was contagious.

He smiled at the little crowd of amiable
servants who looked on, hanging off the
hayloft and standing amid the straw, and
breathed in the raw, earthy aroma of a farm
that matched the people. What a jolly place
this seemed to be.

As the servants turned back to their work with chatter and laughter, Sully addressed the man who was clearly in charge. "I'm hoping you can help me. Looking for a lass who might be about these parts."

"Irish, are you, boy?" The weathered old stable master stepped forward and shoved his rake into a pile of straw.

Sully shrugged with a lopsided grin. "I'm a patchwork sort of fellow, with scraps of this and that all sewed together. Me mother was Irish, but me father's a good old Brit."

"I thought I recognized a bit of the brogue. So who can we help you find, good man?"

"A Miss Raina Bretton. She's a friend of mine from back home. She'd have come to work here as a scullery maid or maybe a seamstress."

"It sounds familiar, but I can't say I've met anyone by that name. I'll be sure to pass her a message if I do, though. Care to leave a word for her?"

He hesitated, kicking at the straw on the stable floor. A deep breath filled his senses with the scent of livestock and moisture. "Would there be someone else I could ask, maybe up at the house?"

"Lucy," he called over his shoulder. "Is there a new girl up at the abbey?"

"No sir, not for some time now. Heaven knows we could use another one or two in the kitchen with the mistress coming, though."

The man shrugged. "If anyone knows, she would. She's the daughter of the house-keeper and her ears are the sharpest in the place. No one so much as eats a tart below stairs without her knowing it."

"You're certain?" Sully met the frank and gentle gaze of the stable master. "She's gone from home, and I heard she was headed to this very place. This here's Rothburne Abbey, isn't it?"

"That it is, son." Pity softened his features. "Perhaps your girl changed her mind. Women often blow hot, then cold, you know, changing their intentions without a word. Perhaps it's best to move on."

"Aye, that they do." Not his Raina, though. When she set about to do some-thing, she saw it through, even if it nearly killed her — or more likely, him. "Thank you kindly." His mind hummed with ideas even as he turned and exited the barn with a wave, swishing straw under his boots. Hesitation weighted his steps, making him less than anxious to depart. Once he left, he had no leads. Old Widow McCall had been certain about the name too, and she'd remembered clearly that it had been an abbey.

But what could he do, stand about hoping for a glimpse of her? Slinging his worn sack over one shoulder and dangling his fiddle in the other hand, Sully traipsed across the yard, staring toward the sun burning orange and yellow above. All that was left to do was return to Spitalfields and hope she came back, but he knew in his gut that she wouldn't, sure as he knew the grass was green and the ocean deep. An odd fear crept deep into his bones the longer he pondered it all.

He could still picture the little waif of about ten years whom he'd rescued from the bell tower of his father's church. It was his first glimpse of her. Such an eager little thing she'd been, breaking into the building at night and dragging a heartsick old widow up into the tower just to get her as close as she could to the stars. It was weeks after the funeral service for the woman's husband, and everyone else in the neighborhood had moved on from the distraught widow's grief. Despondent and unkempt, the woman had become nearly as dead as her husband, but little Raina was not ready to give up on her.

"She's simply got to see them," she said

about the stars as he'd gripped her arm to keep her from plunging into the Thames below. "All at once, to take in their full beauty." She claimed there was something healing in immense loveliness, because when they took their eyes off the ugly, chipped old buildings hemming them into Spitalfields, there was a great, wonderful world out there that offered many a reason for living. Man's feeble work was destined for decay, but God's starry skies reminded them of the eternity they had before them, just beyond the reach of this earth.

He tried to persuade them to come down, but instead she convinced him to delight in the stars with her, and it had burst his world wide open. She helped him look up from the daily grind and see the beauty in anything, from a star-studded sky in the slums to a lovely soul buried within a forgotten widow, and it had formed the basis for the longest, deepest camaraderie he'd ever known.

Yet perhaps she wanted it to stay that way. He should have told her the way he felt in person so many years ago when they ran about together. He nearly had, more times than he could count, but when he'd looked up into those storm-blue eyes, her ready smile had knocked the words clean down to his toes and back to his brain in a muddled mess of nonsense. The risk of this enchanting, full-of-life friendship becoming marred forever by his declarations of love stopped him from voicing them to her, even though they shared most everything else.

"Hey there, lad." The stable master called out to him, and he spun to see the man jogging toward him, one hand held high.

Sully paced a few steps backward, then stopped, waiting for the man to catch up.

The older man huffed to a stop before him and dug through the pocket of his oversized coat. "You Sullivan McKenna, by chance?"

He raised his eyebrows, anticipation tightening his chest. "Aye, that I am. What do you have there?"

He held up a hand and wheezed, hands on his knees as he caught his breath. Finally he straightened. "I remember where I heard that name." The man held out the charred remains of Sully's very own letters to Raina. "Had these in the stable. The missus wouldn't let them be destroyed, so certain she was that there was a story to them. We couldn't make out most of what they said, but it struck me that they must belong to your missing lass. Raina, it says here on the front. Isn't that the name you gave?"

She *had* been here. Breathless, he accepted the letters whose burnt edges flaked against his touch. There they were, these letters, his heart poured out on the page — and torched. He turned away, unable to bear the sight of his honest words cast aside like fish guts. She'd never been able to write back, with him sailing from port to port, so he had no idea what she'd thought of his declaration.

Raina, my Raina.

He reached up to pull off the blue cap she'd made for him so many years ago and looked at the careful stitching. No matter the storms threatening to snatch the thing from him on the ship, he'd kept that hat firmly fixed on his head — and its lovely creator filling his heart to bursting.

He forced himself to glance down at his cast-off letters, running a finger over them. Any way one looked at it, this sight was not a good sign. "Where did these come from?"

"The rubbish pile, out in the field. The maids bring it out by the bucketful from the abbey, and we burn it when it's full."

Sully glanced up at the castle of a house in the distance, its perfect stone walls guarding some mystery about the woman he adored. What had happened here?

"The scullery maid brought this load out with orders to burn it straightaway. It was left behind by some wandering vagrant, they said, and they were afraid of disease and such. There's something odd about the whole thing, if you ask me, though. I probably shouldn't be giving you these, and I fear I'll see trouble over it if anyone finds out." He glanced out to the field at a little cluster of cottages. "But I'm more afraid of what my wife would do to me if I didn't."

Sully grinned at the stable master.

"Can I offer you a place to spend the night? My missus would love to host the man who wrote those letters. She might not let you sleep much, once she finds out who you are, though."

Sully shook his head, cringing at the notion of exposing one of his deepest hurts to a nosey housewife when he had barely begun to share them with Raina, yet his mind was a blank as he tried to fathom where he might go next. He sighed. "I should see if I can catch a train back to town and join another ship crew. Thank you for everything, just the same." He tipped his cap and swung his bag over his shoulder, marching toward the drive.

"I do have one other suggestion for you." The man's voice carried over the tall golden grass bowing in the breeze. "If you've nothing else to do with your time."

64

Sully took a step back toward the man, prepared to say yes to whatever it was if it gave him the chance to remain. He'd ask every person in the household about her, hunt down every clue until he found the truth. It wasn't in Raina to disappear from her whole life the way this man suggested, but it certainly was in her to find trouble, and it seemed she had.

And just like always, he'd be there to swoop in and rescue her.

5

Just because it's who we have always been, it does not mean it's who we were created to be.
~ Diary of a Substitute Countess

The second time I rode toward that grand house, I was shaped into an entirely different person. Torso erect against firm stays and hair piled in graceful coils about my head, I couldn't help but feel every inch a lady. My skin felt fresh and alive, tingling with all that it had undergone that day, and my hair was clean and soft, loose curls framing my face. I'd never realized how much grime had layered my skin until it was removed and replaced with creams and powders.

Perhaps this truly was all of God, for it seemed he specialized in the extraordinary. Sully was always telling me that, and he had been the vicar's son. He knew everything about God. How I wish I did too, especially in moments like this that were foggy as the London air over the Thames at night. No matter how much I pored over Sully's Bible, God remained a mystery, an enigma as far from my grasp as the mansions of Mayfield Square. They were a mile from Spitalfields, but an ocean away from my life.

"There's just one more piece to cover before you can be presented at the abbey." He then poured out to me the details of the woman I was supposed to embody. Lovelyn Rumilla Margaruite Shaunghess, Countess of Enderly, was bright and graceful, a soft glowing light of regal poise and graciousness — and utterly benevolent. Like an angel of mercy, she cast about her considerable influence and fortune to help those who needed her. India, Africa, even London's Whitechapel district saw help from this magnanimous woman. She was everything I'd always wanted to be if I were cut free from the poverty that had stunted my life.

"She is confident, but not outspoken. Beautiful, but without airs. She is, in every way, a most compelling and accomplished lady."

I turned my flushed face to the window and caught sight of my reflection. "I won't fool anyone. Won't the rest of the staff know straight off that I'm not her?"

He smiled under the shadow of his hat. "Not unless you tell them. I don't believe she has ever made the time to visit this particular estate."

"Where does she live, then?"

"She spends much time abroad, involved in great charitable endeavors and adventures of various sort, but she keeps a house in London."

"So the abbey has sat empty all these years." That would explain the neglect I'd seen.

"Not exactly. The former owner began renovating the abbey into a manor house, but he didn't complete the project before life and old age cropped up. Rothburne has become a sort of escape for whoever needs it, complete with a year-round staff to keep it running. There are often cousins or acquaintances about, using the place as a stopover in their travels, or a disgraced nobleman needing a reprieve from the public eye. The earl visits regularly but keeps to himself. He's a rather surly sort, so this is a fabulous hideaway for him. It's a marvelous source of income, with many tenants farming its lands and paying you for the opportunity to do so."

"How kind of me. I hope I'm a good landlord."

The stately abbey came into view then, majestically tall and adorned with garden hedges and windows that promised hours bathed in glorious sunlight. I gasped, my gloved hand covering my mouth. I'd barely gotten a glimpse of it the other day as we'd been delivered directly to the old dormitory wing. To the far left, a sparkling blue pond cut into the spread of green grass, and a haven of nature beckoned to me beyond it.

He smiled, enjoying my reaction. "Just look at it — an incredible gem hidden away out here among the wildflowers, ready to be plucked from ruination and neglect and, with just a little help, made to flourish. Just like its new mistress."

His wink flustered me. "I'd be a closer match to the mess of wildflowers just beyond the mews, sir."

Then we rounded the curve toward the house and slowed. I sank back into the plush seat as an army of liveried servants watched us approach. Here was my first test, and I felt sorely unprepared. He'd made it seem so easy, but how would they not know? Surely something would give me away.

"Don't look them in the eyes." Prendergast lowered his voice as the carriage slowed before the arched entrance set into a tower. "They'll think it odd. Simply bow and smile as if you're the queen greeting her subjects and go along inside. Walk with slow grace, as if wading through water. The only task before you now is to be seen, be poised, then be hidden in your chamber. And try not to say a word until we've polished your speech."

I couldn't stop trembling. Lady Enderly wouldn't have trembled. "I'm not a queen."

"Queen Esther then." He shot the words out in a low whisper as the driver came 'round for us. "Be Queen Esther. Just hold your composure until you're alone in your suite of rooms and keep your tongue in your head."

Lifting my chin, I took the driver's hand and stepped down onto crushed gravel, glancing at the two long rows of servants watching me with expectancy. The fine gown embracing me brought a weighty peace to my body as I strode toward the house. Birds trilled, wings whipping the air as they flitted about the expansive estate so far removed from the chaos of city life. With poise created by tight lacing and a hat angled smartly on my head, I glided up the drive as if wading through imaginary water,

70

yet my heart pounded madly beneath my traveling gown. The pond on my left would be the perfect place to practice wading. If only I were swimming in it now.

A tall balding man with an affable face stepped forward and bowed. "Welcome to Rothburne, your ladyship."

"Burt Bradford, butler." Prendergast gave a slight head bow to the man. "He's kept the place running for you quite well."

"Mrs. Langston, the housekeeper, and I would like to meet with you to discuss your stay when you find yourself available."

Prendergast opened his smiling mouth to answer. Before I knew it, my response rolled out with the smooth edges I'd used to read high-brow poetry with Sully in terribly dramatic voices on the tenement steps. "Wonderful idea, Bradford. I believe my schedule has an opening at ten in the morning, on the morrow. Would that suit?" I softened the dramatics, and it came out with surprising elegance and flavor.

The utter shock that paled poor Prendergast's smiling face was nearly my undoing, for once I'd rendered the man speechless, I dearly wished to have a great laugh over it.

To my delight, Bradford smiled mildly as if my imitation of all the ladies and lords I'd met rang true to what he expected. "We will make anything suit, my lady." A formal bow punctuated the end of his statement.

Before I had to decide what to do next, a hand guided me forward with gentle pressure on my arm. Chin lifted, I cast a lofty, distant smile to no one in particular and walked toward the house. Like a rolling ocean wave, each servant dipped in a bow or curtsy as I passed, no one looking me in the eyes. The effect of my presence on these strangers buoyed my confidence tenfold. He'd been right. It was working. All was well.

No, all was *amazing.*

Then suddenly it wasn't. I straightened and my keen eye registered a glimpse of dark hair that jarred me with its familiarity. My heart shuddered. I saw only a trace of his profile farther up the row of servants, but there was no avoiding him. I stilled the tremor in my stomach as my guide introduced the rest of the staff but none of the names remained with me.

Suddenly made awkward by my jittery nerves, I kicked out my skirt hem with each step, focusing all my energy on not tripping, yet fearing it was inevitable. My heart fluttered uncontrollably and I wondered what would become of me if I dropped dead just now. Would that great God Sully spoke of laud my courage or rail at my deception?

But when I neared the servant who'd caught my eye, I looked upon a completely foreign face whose only similarity was dark hair and eyebrows. A glassy, benign expression replaced the jovial one I would expect from the man I knew, and features quite different than Sully's stared back at me. Relief and utter despair pulsed through me, and I forced my quivering limbs to carry me forward past this servant introduced as the footman.

It must be my overly sensitive conscience making me believe I saw him everywhere. He never would have liked this plan, and well I knew it.

I passed under a tall stone corridor, swept up the three flagstone steps, and into the square tower. The abbey opened into a magnificent entry space with two-story leaded windows and a great chandelier gleaming over gray-brown stones. Vases of red poppies contrasted with the ancient building that seemed to ring with the somber utterances of the monks who had once inhabited the place. A bit like a crypt, but still grand in its own austere way.

So this was the countess's abbey. With Victor Prendergast caught in conversation outside, I wandered through the arches to the left and down a wide tiled hall. Candle-light from brass chandeliers highlighted the dark stones of the walls. I jumped at the sight of beady little eyes staring at me from the shadows, but found it was only a statue of some small creature on a shelf recessed into the wall. Not quite gargoyle, yet not at all angelic, the being seemed to be both growling and leering.

I lingered in the hall until I heard Prendergast's voice as he entered the house with the butler and strode down a different hallway. I had to retrieve my carpetbag still, and Sully's precious letters would be the perfect end to this day. Yet when I found Prendergast in a study near the front, my question was met with awkward silence. The tall man seemed so small in that room of elegant, gilded-edged doors and velvet-draped windows. "You've no need of your old things now, have you? Certainly you cannot wish to wear those rags when you have —"

"It isn't the rags, Mr. Prendergast. I have other belongings in the bag, and they are very personal."

He studied my face, the power of his gaze once again arresting me. "That is precisely why we had to be rid of them. What do you think would happen if they were found?"

Panic tightened my chest. "What have you done with them?" All those letters — my beautiful letters full of Sully's affection. They were the only love letters I'd ever had. I studied the man's profile with a fierce disgust that would not be contained, as if he'd been personally responsible for the Great Gale that had torn Sully from me.

His tense jaw twitched, and he looked over at the ancient wall mural to my right. "I disposed of them." He turned to leave, disregarding my anguish.

I marched toward him. "How dare you —"

He spun with a powerful flare of anger and grabbed my arms. I glimpsed behind those wild eyes all the violence he was capable of, and it terrified me.

"Let me remind you only one of us is in charge of this operation, and it isn't you." His terse, low words stabbed at my senses. "Carrying on this way will bring every servant in this house running, thinking you've gone mad. They'll soon know the ugly truth — which will be whatever I tell them — and they will ship you out, or worse. Your things are gone, and so is your old life. It is in your best interest to control yourself, and I implore you to do so by whatever means necessary."

"You're keeping me prisoner." I steeled myself and spoke the quiet words like a challenge for him to deny.

He stepped back, releasing me, yet his gaze did not. His low voice wrapped around me tighter and tighter, cinching about my throat until I couldn't swallow. "Walk home if you wish. I won't prevent you. It's over one hundred miles and will take you the better part of a week, but by all means, you are free to take your chances among the ruffians between here and town." His bright eyes snapped. "Just remember, the world may not miss one more noble lady, as you say, but even less will it miss yet another penniless waif." His jaw twitched. Even the muscles in his face were hard as rock. "Do not wear out your favor with me, Countess, for you won't like what you find beneath it."

I stiffened, but a distant sound stilled the fight in the Spitalfields lass. The happy squeaks of a fiddle drifted in through the open window, seeping into my tense muscles and loosening them in spite of myself, flooding me with precious memories in the midst of the chaos about me.

My heart had exploded, hadn't it? Exploded and left little pieces of Sully all over for me to find in random places. Maybe it was God's way of comforting me. That stranger in the blue cap at the station, the dark-haired footman, and now the fiddle music. Perhaps I was losing my mind. Or perhaps . . . *perhaps* . . .

Prendergast moved closer to me than any man except Sully had ever stood. I could feel the warm breath from his flared nostrils. "I do not tolerate mistakes, even small ones. No one must even guess at the truth, or it'll all be over. You must release every part of your past, as if it never happened. Is that understood?"

I forced a swallow and nodded as the sounds of the violin continued to drift through the open window.

Yet I wasn't entirely sure my past would agree to remain hidden.

6

Every new day chips away at the person we were, slowly revealing who we were always meant to be lying dormant beneath.
~ Diary of a Substitute Countess

"This is your suite, my lady. I hope we've readied it sufficiently. Your orders were carried out to the letter."

"Thank you, Bradford." I shifted under the weight of this new order-giving persona and smiled at the butler. He'd come to my rescue when I'd wandered into the salon on the second floor and kindly shown me to my bedchamber. One needed a candle to proceed through the dim hallways anyway, he'd said with a gracious smile.

Now he placed a hand on the door latch but paused, thoughts churning behind his shadowed face. "I wanted to express, my lady, on behalf of the entire estate, that we are gratified at your presence among us. We all wish you to know that we are always available should you need us. For anything at all." His words, heavy with deeper meaning, descended into my deepest nerves and left them unsettled. "The earl is well known to all of us, and very little would surprise the abbey staff. Just know you may call upon us for anything."

I forced a smile, steeling myself against the guilt that gnawed at me when I looked into this servant's kindly face. I hadn't spoken one untrue word, as Prendergast had promised, yet the weight of deception settled heavily on my tender conscience, especially in the presence of this gentle giant who meant to be my protector.

Before I could respond, his placid smile smoothed right over the memory of those weighty words as if they'd never been spoken. "Tea will be ready shortly. Shall I send someone to help you dress?"

I exhaled. "Yes. That would be lovely."

"I'll see if I can find Miss Simone."

When I did not readily answer, he supplied the information. "Simone Bouvier, your personal maid. Your estate manager took the liberty of hiring her, at Mr. Prendergast's suggestion, when he heard you would not be bringing the one you employed in London. We hope she meets with your approval."

"You needn't worry."

Mercy gracious, I have a lady's maid.

Bradford pushed open the doors and departed with a bow. Then with a pounding heart, I stepped into a haven of dreams, a large lamp-lit room that glowed pink and gold with a canopied bed, fringed drapes, and three tall bay windows overlooking a spread of flowers. Sunlight glowed through sheer embroidered curtains. Beyond a doorway to the left stood a generous dressing area with mirrors at every angle and a wardrobe standing poised and ready to offer me any number of beautiful gowns.

Perhaps this was what Prendergast had thought would convince me to remain. I must admit, his wager had merit. "I must've died and gone to glory." I mumbled the words to myself as I walked with wonder into the space. I turned to take it all in, my mouth hanging slack.

"Good evening, my lady."

With a start I turned but saw no one. Then the shadows shifted and a woman in gray separated herself from the darkness on the fringes of the room. Her piercing hazel-flecked eyes narrowed as she examined me. No older than thirty, she looked as though the world had tight-laced her life as efficiently as the bodice of her gown constricted her slender frame, yet her lovely pearlized face was barely touched by age. She glided toward me, that severe woman full of haunting beauty, and I wondered the reason for the immediate dislike evident on her face. "Welcome to Rothburne, Lady Enderly." The staccato rhythm of her words carried only a faint hint of her French origins that had been smoothed and faded by time.

"Who are you?" Or *what,* perhaps, for she hardly seemed human.

"Simone Bouvier, my lady." Her lips curved up in a smile that did not alter the rest of her face. "I am glad to see your suite pleases you."

I blushed to realize she'd seen me gaping a moment ago. "I've not been here recently, so it feels new to me." True words, yet slightly deceptive. My grasp on integrity was becoming looser by the minute in this place.

She passed before a delicate oil lamp, and the glow illuminated a surprisingly appealing face with sharply intelligent eyes under dark lashes, all framed by thick ebony hair twisted back into a chignon against her neck. I searched her countenance for help, but her face was curtained like a house closed up against intruders. She glided forward and paused to examine me with a delicate frown. "Blue." That icy voice, so quiet and severe. "Your eyes are blue."

Her tone nearly compelled me to apologize, but I held my tongue. I was supposed to be the mistress of this house.

"I was told green. I had an emerald gown readied for tea, but I suppose we can make do with one in another color."

"Formal tea isn't necessary. I'd like a chance to rest. Perhaps I can simply take it in my room."

Her perfect little lips turned up in a smile. "I am afraid you are not afforded such luxuries, my lady. Your status entitles you to a great many amenities, but freedom is not one."

I stared at this unusual woman who managed to be condescending without uttering a single rude word. "Why shouldn't I have a night to myself if I desire it?"

"You have a guest tonight who insists on meeting now."

"Guest?" I nearly choked on the word. Did Prendergast know of this? "Who is it?"

"The earl's cousin, Philip Scatchard."

I pressed my fingertips into my forehead. "Can we not send him away until I'm rested?" Or gone, as I would likely be soon.

"I am afraid not, my lady." But the gleam

in her eyes told me she was anything but regretful to refuse my request. "He would not allow it." She turned to lay out white undergarments from the drawers, piling them on the bed. She paused to consider me as I clung to the back of a chair. "Are you ill?"

"I'm merely adjusting to . . . everything."

She eyed me. "The abbey must be quite a change of scenery for you."

I ducked from under her razor gaze and made my way to the wardrobe. Inching it open, I ran my fingertips along the gowns worth more than my very life and stopped at a vibrant blue affair with sweeps of lace across the skirt. I let my fingers indulge in the fabric. "This will do nicely." I attempted to add an edge of authority to my voice, but it seemed impossible in her presence.

I stood perfectly still on the dressing room stand while Simone fitted the layers of stays and crinolette, then hoisted the frock over my head and let it fall in soft layers of material about the frame, bracing myself against delight. How would I ever return to my sodden pile of rags after this? Layer after layer wrapped smoothly against my body until I felt lightheaded from standing so long, but the result was splendid.

"He's asked to meet you in half an hour.

Shall I tell him you'll be down then?"

"Of course."

She left, closing the doors behind her. I now only had a matter of minutes to convince myself that I was Lady Enderly. It was when I passed the little secretary in the corner that an idea struck. There on the wood surface sat a tray of vellum writing paper embossed with the countess's elegant name. *Lovelyn Rumilla Margaruite Shaunghess.* Sliding into the chair, I dipped the pen in the inkwell and tapped the end of it against my jaw. What would her voice sound like? What opinions might she have?

With light strokes I began writing a diary entry as if I were her, summoning my idea of her voice and tone as the words spilled forth onto the page.

Here I sit, in the world's most dreary old abbey, and I cannot help but wonder if it is perhaps haunted.

The marks of ink became bolder, darker, and my thoughts flowed as I wrote, the persona taking shape and solidifying in my mind.

What a shame that rest and boredom must coexist, but it seems I am trapped here for a time, and I must grow to like the place. They say a house is a reflection of its mistress, and I wonder if I'm truly as intimidating and cold as the place suggests.

I wrote this way for a full page and set the paper aside to dry. Courage and hope wavered against traces of doubt. An odd sensation swept over me as I stared at my writing with the other woman's name printed across the top.

Then I drew out another page, my thoughts racing. The only way I knew to deal with my conscience, which rang with the underlying air of deception about this situation, was to discover noble reasons for my decision that balanced out the doubts. Change would come through my hand, as Prendergast promised, and it began now, with one very important business. Lifting the pen and adjusting the blotter, I began my first missive as Lady Enderly.

My Dear Mr. Crawley, I wish to bring to your attention the deplorable lack of regulations I have seen in your establishment . . .

My pen raced across the page as I scrawled my strong feelings toward the owner of the textile factory that had sucked the life from Mother. He hadn't even paused production for the accident that nearly took her life years ago, and it was time he felt the sting of his carelessness. It would no longer help my dear *maman,* but it might save someone else.

It was a thrilling sensation, putting those strong words onto thick vellum paper and sealing it with the family crest in wax. It might do nothing, but it felt wonderful. I wrote another letter and another, my sense of justice quenched by the words flowing onto the page. All too soon, a knock sounded on the door and my aching hand dropped the pen. I rose and left the bedroom, ready as I'd ever be to meet this cousin.

I trailed my fingertip along the polished railing to the bottom of the grand staircase and paused to listen for this guest.

"You're late."

I spun to face Prendergast, lurking just behind me in the shadows of the stairwell. I grabbed the stair rail behind me and forced steel into my trembling voice. "You didn't tell me about a guest." He stepped toward me into the little circle of light from an overhead chandelier. "How will this cousin not spot a fake?"

I looked up into his face and paused at the change there as he watched me. All that bold assurance I normally found in his countenance had melted to utter astonishment. "I'm beginning to think you're not." He stared at me long enough to make my skin heat, drinking in every inch of me with a gaze that penetrated too far. How different he seemed than in the library. Gone was his anger, but his piercing stare still left me feeling exposed, vulnerable.

"I'd planned to work with you much longer before this moment, but we can make do for a short appearance. Fortunately this visitor is not a frequent part of your life, so he won't know the difference." He moved closer and lowered his voice. "His name is Philip Scatchard. He manages this property and another one south of Kent, belonging to an uncle."

A door slammed and a male voice sounded in a nearby room.

Prendergast leaned close to whisper. "He will have no reason to doubt you, correct?"

I shivered and nodded.

"Move with grace and command as the mistress of this house. Chin straight, shoulders low, even voice. Not a hint of surprise at anything he says."

Dread rolled through my belly for what

this cousin might reveal.

The butler scuttled past us into the room and left the door ajar. An assertive voice echoed out from beyond the double doors. "Good day there, Bradford. Now tell me, where is that basest of creatures hiding out?"

My skin went clammy. "Is that the cousin? Who is he talking about?"

"You." Prendergast shoved me toward the door, his terse whisper drifting into my ear. "He has a great deal on his mind to go along with that chip on his shoulder and he despises you immensely."

I jerked out of his grasp. "How do you expect me to face a man like that?"

"You can, and you will. Go in there with the same gumption that made you face a stranger armed with a jeweled shoe and give him what for."

"But he hates —"

"Breathe." He demonstrated with deep breaths. "Courage in, doubts out. In and out. Again. That's it, puff up your chest a bit. Emotion descends onto us faster than reason, so you must subdue the one and wait for the other. Remember, he manages the property, but you control the estate. Keep him in his place. There, now off you go."

With a quick pat to my shoulder, he

shoved me through the double doors, and a spirited gent spun to face me with wild, glittering eyes underscored by violet half circles. He stalked toward me. It was too late to retreat, although it seemed my voice already had. How fleeting was this new-found courage. *Father God, give me strength like you always did in Spitalfields, because once again I'm in the lion's den. Watch over —*

But did I truly want him watching me right now? I cringed at the notion as my heart pounded and pushed it aside. We'd discuss everything at length once this was over.

"Ah, there she is, in the flesh. Or the scales, perhaps." He stood too close and looked me over from hem to hollow with the most compelling, deeply shadowed look. It sliced through me as Victor Prendergast's had in the alley but was strengthened by a burning hatred smoldering below the surface.

I backed up as if it might scorch my gown. "Good evening, Cousin Philip. Would you care for tea?" Wasn't that always the first thing a lady asked her guest? I dipped my head to avoid his burning gaze and strode to the tea cart.

He held up his glass half full of amber liquid and took another drink. "How becoming you are, even in that puff of finery."

I paused, breath caught in my throat.

"I'm not sure whether to admire you or go on despising you. A little bit of both, I suppose."

Despising me? Curiosity teased at the edges of my nervous mind. Perhaps it was the challenge or the desire to please, but I had a sudden longing to understand the reason for this man's bitterness and change his mind, make him like me — or rather, *her*. The mysterious Lady Enderly.

He swirled the drink in his hand and drained it, studying me with a mix of contempt and disbelief. "I can't help but wonder at how very different you seem."

I tensed as he poked at my delicate façade, glancing toward the door to see if Prendergast had heard.

"Too bad all that comeliness is deep as a puddle." He turned and scowled at a young maid hovering inside the door. "You've brought the tea, haven't you? Now go."

I stood between them, my spine straightening with the steel of a Spitalfields girl. "Let me remind you that you are in my home."

His eyes flashed. "No reminding needed."

He truly was boorish. "Sugar?" I moved to the cart and held up the silver dish with a smile. "Seven or eight helpings might be a start."

He scowled and drank the offered tea in two swigs without sugar, slamming it down on the cart beside his empty glass. I met his gaze when he looked at me again, but each passing second ticking by on the ivory mantel clock eroded my bravado.

A light knock on the doorframe broke the tension and I exhaled in relief. We both turned to see Bradford in the doorway. "When you have a moment, Mr. Scatchard, there's a man here to meet with you."

"By all means, Bradford, send him in, and bring another tea setting. Or perhaps something stronger." He held up his empty glass. "I like that Bradford. He appears when he's needed and otherwise you never see him."

I replaced my cup on the cart, eyeing my escape through the double doors. "I'll leave you to your meeting, then."

"Not so fast," he called after me as I strode away. "I still have a bone to pick with you, Lady Enderly. Quite a few, in fact."

I paused a mere three feet from the double doors welcoming me into the safety of the hall, fisting my hands. "Since we have a visitor, perhaps we can leave all the bone picking for a private conversation at the evening meal. I'll return then." Unless I managed to escape before it. Without giving him another chance to argue, I sailed on. Had I succeeded or failed? It was impossible to tell with such a man, but I certainly felt anything but victorious.

I clung to the last shred of poise left to me as I escaped this hateful cousin and passed into the dim hall, but even that confidence snapped as I rounded the corner and my shaky steps caught my hem to send me sprawling on the tile floor.

With a quick glance back to see that Cousin Philip was still engrossed in rummaging through the teacart offerings in the distant room, I adjusted my skirt and prepared to stand. In the hush of the dim hall, a tall, trim servant knelt before me, hand extended to help me rise. An aura of tenderness exuded from the man in a way I sensed without even looking up at him. I laid my fingertips on the warm, open palm, and the gentle grip sent my heart fluttering with the shock of recognition that vibrated through my body. I knew this touch.

I rose and looked up into the kind eyes that had smiled down at me countless times, watching shock fan out over the dear face of my very own Sully.

7

Some memories are far too precious to leave in the past. A woman must take them along with her to light up her uncertain steps into the future.
~ Diary of a Substitute Countess

"What have we here?" Philip Scatchard's voice intruded upon the moment before any explanations could be given, any words exchanged. He strode out into the hall with his arms crossed as I steadied myself. This cousin would have me arrested if he found out, wouldn't he?

"Just a misstep." Moving back, I smoothed my skirt and lifted my eyes to meet the lively, boyish face I had memorized with painful clarity.

Shock had stilled his tongue. I was unprepared for the avalanche of emotions that pummeled me as I met Sully's bright countenance, from amazement and wonder to utter fear for what would come next. My heart pounded, and what I truly wanted in that moment was for him to wrap his arms around me and hold me up as my knees seemed to be unable to do. All that my tangled thoughts could form was, *He's alive. He's alive!*

Sully stared openly, making me highly aware of the drastic changes in my appearance, from the necklace suddenly pulling at my neck to the shoes that pinched my feet and the tight-laced corset hindering my breath. I forced a gulp as heat gathered beneath my layers of garments, and he continued to stare, shock radiating from his honest face.

"Fortunately this man has come to my aid."

"And who might this fine gent be?"

The butler stepped forward. "It was the stable master who brought him to my attention, sir, suggesting him as a second footman. He has roughly the same coloring as Duncan."

Duncan, the first footman. I recalled my moment of panic upon arrival when I'd spotted the man in the lineup of servants.

Cousin Philip turned to me with a smile. "What do you think, dear cousin? Shall we install him at Rothburne?"

I looked at my dear friend and realized we'd come full circle. How well I remembered the times Sully, as the respected son of the parish vicar, had stood up for the rag girl he'd befriended against the wishes of everyone he knew. He'd always been prepared to fight for my honor to anyone who demeaned me — including his father. Now I stood in the lofty status, looking down upon him as a common man seeking a position, and I could hardly do less than he'd done for me through the years.

Yet how could I maintain my charade with him about? Even now his presence left me shaky and uncertain, unable to hold together my delicate poise.

As he watched me, Sully's grip on his hat could have snapped a heavy branch from the looks of it, and his suspenders swelled in and out against his chest with each heavy breath. I'd day-dreamed often of laying my face against that very chest, of feeling the beating loyal heart of this man I knew so well, and now he stood before me and I couldn't be near him — couldn't even acknowledge him as anything but a stranger. The torture was more acute than his absence.

"Well?"

I ripped my gaze away and folded my

hands before me. "Do we need a second footman? Isn't one enough?" I crossed into the drawing room to voice my thoughts out of Sully's hearing. Cousin Philip followed. "There's such a roughness to this one, a ragged appearance that doesn't fit at Rothburne."

"Appearances can be changed on a whim." He frowned. "The truth is, he's perfect for the position, and he's *here.* I know you don't involve yourself in the details of your country estate, but you must know how hard it is to convince reliable help to come away from town of late, and he's willing."

"Thank you kindly for the offer, sir, but I believe I'll be on me way." Sully spoke from the doorway, his gaze narrowed on me. "I have a rule, see. I never go where I'm not wanted." The blue hat slipped from his hand, and my heart dropped with it, down into a shattered mess on the floor. I retrieved the cap by instinct.

Sully spun on his heel, but desperation propelled me forward, hand outstretched to offer the hat. "Wait." *Please take it. Please.* If he walked out the door, heart broken by me, he'd be on the first train to someplace I'd never find him. I knew Sullivan McKenna, and he did everything in absolutes.

All three of them turned to me, Sully

poised in the shadows of the doorway with hurt darkening his features. How dangerous it would be to have him so close, yet when it came down to it, the notion of him leaving again, possibly disappearing for good, nearly suffocated me.

My impetuous side overruled, as often happened. "Perhaps I spoke too soon. One can always change clothing, after all."

"It does make quite a difference, doesn't it?" Sully eyed me as he accepted the hat but did not return it to his head. "Without them fine things you'd be just like me, wouldn't you? And that would be a pity."

Silence thickened in the room and his quiet words tensed the muscles along my back. The vague guilt I'd felt at my questionable decisions solidified into heavy shame. We stared at one another, our gazes locked, an ocean of tension between us. I remained stoic by sheer force of will, swallowing the lump bobbing in my throat.

A few popping claps from Philip Scatchard broke the tension. "Well done, my man. I insist on you staying now. I need someone besides myself who will speak this way to my dear cousin, and none of the other servants have the gumption. Or the foolishness, perhaps."

"It's never foolish to say what's true."

Cousin Philip's eyes sparkled. "I do believe you'll get on well here."

As dinner unfolded that evening, I was reminded of how easily I could ruin everything. A long table separated me from this cousin so full of mysterious hatred for me, and a large silver vase with red poppies stood between us, but he lifted his condemning gaze to me when I eagerly accepted a little bowl of plum pudding.

"I'd heard you couldn't tolerate the stuff."

Without hesitation, I released a gracious smile across my face. "I simply will not let you best me, even in so small a matter. You see? I am aware of your schemes, Cousin Philip, and I've set my mind to thwarting them. You'll have to try harder to upset me." I dipped my spoon into the delectable pudding and nibbled its creamy deliciousness. I grimaced as the plum flavor tickled my senses, pretending to merely tolerate the delicious treat. Cousin Philip frowned.

Sully and the first footman brought us platters and bowls of steaming food. How quickly he'd been adopted into his new position. Every time Sully neared, I looked away to control the quick bloom of fear. When did he plan to say something? The moment must be coming. Through the entire dinner, however, he spoke not a word to either of us. I felt his gaze upon me, but he said nothing to give me away.

I had slipped into cautious relief when I lifted a water glass from Sully's tray and spotted a tiny scrap of paper beneath it with that familiar handwriting staring up at me. I clamped the note to the base of my cup with a trembling finger as I accepted the drink and kept it planted there. Though my throat burned, I refused to take even a single drink under the cousin's watchful gaze.

When Cousin Philip turned to speak to a footman, I slipped the paper into my lap and looked at the single word written there. Although it wasn't a word at all. *JA:MP 386,* it said. My heart fluttered — it was a childhood game of ours, a treasure hunt through literature as he taught me to read. The JA would be Jane Austen, and MP must be *Mansfield Park.* I quickly covered the paper again and returned to my food.

With every quiet moment that passed, my muscles loosened. I watched Sully through the fringe of my lashes as he piled Philip's dishes onto a tray. He glanced at me as he turned to leave the room, and for that frozen moment I was aware only of my thudding pulse and the dryness of my throat. I exhaled when the door closed behind him, tension melting from my shoulders.

After the meal, which had unsettled my stomach with its richness, I made an excuse to visit the abbey's new library, a fresh and modern room so different than the ruin I'd seen that first night. I pulled down *Mansfield Park,* flipping to page 386 with eager fingers. A single line had been underlined in pencil: "I was quiet, but I was not blind."

My fingers trembled under the book's cover. I gulped in vain several times, trying to dislodge the lump in my throat. Closing the volume and replacing it on the shelf, I wandered the halls to steady my nerves. I had to find him before everything erupted and figure out what to do.

As the bold, red sun descended toward the horizon that night, I smoothed my thumb over the familiar surface of my Connemara stone I had plucked from the still-warm ashes beside the abbey. Everything else I owned had been consumed by flames, yet this rock remained, ever present, ever the same.

Much like the man who'd given it to me.

I lifted my gaze toward the barn as I approached and listened to Sully's music. The lively melody blended with the snap of an

open fire and the stomp of his listeners'
boots. I had to steel myself against clapping
and spinning about with the vivacious fiddle
music that wafted through the cloud of
dread around my mind. Slipping across the
yard when a smattering of applause
sounded, I flattened myself against the side
of the barn with pursed lips and listened to
the voice that was so familiar to my heart as
he began the next song.

"Nigh on fifteen years ago
a lass so hapn'd on me.
Not so much upon my path
But on my heart, where she
Left her mark, but did depart,
Gone far away from me.

"I cannot blame her,
For I'm no tamer,
Having left her for the sea."

Laughter and clapping popped against my
fragile senses as I closed my eyes to absorb
his version of our story. As the notes length-
ened into the somber music that always held
me captive, I sank into the bliss of the moment, forgetting what I must do and who I
must be, and all the worries that came with
it. My breath evened and my pounding

heart slowed as a lyrical ballad wrapped itself around me and soothed my tension. Then when my mind had settled into a pleasant trance, the music stopped.

Sully's voice broke through the night. "Beg pardon, but I believe someone's calling for me."

His footsteps swished through the grass, and I panicked, nails digging into the paint on the stable wall. He must have seen me. Hoisting up the hem of my gown, I sprinted for the cover of shadows ahead, hoping I wouldn't suddenly find myself stepping off into a small pond. Slower footsteps clicked on the patio pavement in the distance and a door shut — Prendergast?

I hurtled through the dark toward an amply lit garden and dove behind a hedge. I tucked myself into the little shrub alcove and hugged my knees to my chest, my back to a stone garden wall. Hand to my pounding heart, I waited until footsteps thudded against the path. Then he was there, whispering my name on the other side of the wall.

"Raina." Footsteps shuffled closer. "Show yourself, Raina Bretton. I'd recognize that panicked sprint anywhere. Heav'n knows I've seen it enough times in me life."

I leaned hard against the chilly garden

wall, imagining what would become of us if Mr. Prendergast discovered us this minute. Someone besides Sully was out here, likely looking for me. "Stay where you are. We cannot let anyone see us talking." This man to whom I'd once told my every secret had suddenly become my biggest one.

Then came those familiar little puffs of breath that meant a lecture was forming.

"Before you speak, just know there's a reason for all of this."

"There always is. Don't mean it's a good one, though."

"Sully, what happened to you? How are you . . . alive?"

"I was born that way, wasn't I? Now stop putting me off. It's time for answers, Raina. Why are you doing this?"

"No, *you* answer." My words fired out in an angry whisper. "Do you have any idea what you've done to me for months?"

"All I know is I left a wonderful lass behind in Spitalfields with a promise to return, and I've no idea what happened to her."

"She left." I clasped the little stone in my palm. "Her last reason to stay was drowned on a ship in the Great Gale." I took a shaky breath. "Yet you're alive. How are you alive?"

"I was never drowned. Where'd you come by a fool notion like that?"

"Oh, just the death notice that appeared in the *Penny Newsman.* Three ships sank, including the *Maiden Faire,* and all hands were lost, it said, in black and white."

"Well, I wasn't on it. I haven't been on the *Maiden* in months. They must've forgotten to take me off the ship log."

"Forgotten." I closed my eyes, my breath coming hard and fast. It had been a mistake. A senseless, unpardonable, cruel mistake. A clerical error that had shattered my heart and left the pieces scattered among the rubble of Spitalfields. The enormity of everything settled on my chest like a rock, forcing all air from my lungs and thoughts from my brain.

"Stop changing the subject. You always do that." He jerked against the bushes. "Tell me what in heaven's name is going on."

I cleared the fear coating my throat and forced out a quick explanation. "It's a ruse. I'm to pretend to be this woman who looks exactly like me. That's all. They want me to attend social events as the Countess of Enderly and go about her estate as its mistress for a time to give the real one a small break."

"Break?" He snorted, cutting me off

before I could tell him I was thinking of leaving. "None of the rest of us sees a break from life, and I can guarantee there are a thousand men on the docks who work harder than she does. Of all the foolish —"

"It's hardly foolish to help those in need." I couldn't keep the snap from my voice. "No matter how I do it."

He grumbled in his usual way, kicking at a bush. "If only God saw fit to give both beauty and sense to the same woman." He sighed again. "Do you really believe you're helping this woman? There's something more to this cockamamy scheme, and I think you know it."

Before I could correct him on who I meant to help, distant footsteps crunched on gravel.

"You don't have to help me." The sharp words smarted on my lips.

He shifted, the darkness thick with unspoken thoughts. "You know me better than that."

His words smothered my exasperation like a gentle blanket, and I squeezed the stone I'd rescued from the ashes. "A glutton for punishment, are you?"

"I must be, to follow after you all the time." He heaved a sigh. "Only you would drag me to such a creepy, broken-down . . ."

"You've not seen my suite of rooms. A canopy bed, soft carpet, and at least thirty mirrors in the dressing room. I've never seen the like."

"What does a woman need with thirty mirrors? You've only got one face, haven't you?"

I pinched back a smile and closed my eyes as his simple words rolled over my heart. Sully, dear Sully. The same as ever.

And he was here. For me.

"I missed you something terrible." I breathed the words past the lump in my throat and rose, threading my hand through the shrub.

"I missed you worse." His warm one grasped it on the other side. "Come away with me. Right now. You know this isn't right if you have to go about it this way."

My heart thudded as his words echoed my own convictions. Yet my upper arm still ached from where Prendergast had grasped me. "I'm not sure I can simply leave."

"You're afraid, aren't you? Afraid to leave. Even more reason — Raina, we *must* escape while we still can. Let me help. We can get out together."

"He promised to take me home if I stayed the day. Look, the day is over and he'll have to return me soon."

"Do you truly trust the man? Do you?"

I couldn't answer.

"He'll only make it harder to escape with every hour you spend here. You must come with me."

"He'll come right back to Spitalfields looking for me. It's where he found me to start."

"We're not going back there." He paused. "I've got to find someplace new anyway."

Dread tightened my chest. "Oh Sully. It's true, isn't it? They said you were suspected of mutiny before the ship went down, but I thought it merely a rumor. Tell me it was a mistake."

He shifted against the shrub. Exhaled. His voice softened for a brief moment. "No mistake."

And those two words told the entire story, because my heart that had loved Sully for years could fill in the rest. He was a rescuer, both for me and anyone not able to help themselves. "Was the captain that wretched, then?"

"A tyrant. He threw sailors overboard at the least sign of disrespect — young lads who'd barely begun their lives were cast out like rubbish. I couldn't stand for it. I rallied the men together."

An uprising against the authority, a rallying of the abused men, led by him yet spiraling out of his control, and ending in . . . I lowered my voice. "Did someone die?" I held my breath as I waited for the reply.

"Two sailors and the captain's brother. Not by my hand."

Yet he would be blamed for them if he'd rallied the men who had ultimately done it. I shuddered. At times our greatest strengths become the rocks that trip us up.

"Raina . . ." His voice was soft, pleading for me to understand.

And I did. I always did, because it was Sully. He couldn't *not* be the rescuer, and I loved him for it. "It seems we'll both be in hiding. Might as well do it together."

He let out a gusty breath of relief. "We'll go tonight."

"I'm to meet with Prendergast in a few minutes. I should keep the appointment, then we can escape without anyone missing us for several hours at least."

"I suppose. All right, I'll go fetch my things. Meet me at the end of the lane in an hour." With one last exhale, he sprinted away, gravel popping under his boots. In his absence the air chilled considerably.

The chorus of night critters swelled, and I lifted the Connemara stone up to the light cast down from the great house. He'd given

it to me the first time his father, the Spitalfields parish vicar, had chased me away and
declared me unfit to associate with his son.

I couldn't have been more than ten years
old at the time, but I felt that moment
keenly even now. Unwilling to cause my new
friend trouble, I gave up Sully and his
delightful reading lessons. Yet Sully, my dear
tenderhearted Sully, had found me and
pressed this stone into my palm, vowing to
continue our lessons. "It's Connemara
marble from Ireland, solid and meant to
handle anything you put it through. You see,
it isn't going anywhere. Just like me." His
fingers had folded mine around that
smoothed marble oval, and he sealed his
promise with a warm smile. I held it every
time I needed to recall the solidness of his
friendship, for precious little in my life had
been stable. "Every adventurer needs a
rescuer, and I plan to be yours." I closed
my eyes and pictured his face, listening to
the gentle noises of nighttime in the coun-
tryside.

After a safe amount of time had passed, I
tucked the little stone into my sash and
rose. I would leave as many of the countess's
things behind as possible so I could not be
accused of stealing, yet I hadn't even my
own clothing left to me. I stepped forward,

using only the light shining down from the house. I would have to fashion something —

My foot caught. I flailed, tumbling forward in the dark and landing beside a pair of gentleman's shoes.

Mercy gracious, the end has come.

"Falling at my feet now, are we?" The deep voice of Victor Prendergast rolled through the empty garden. "I'm flattered."

I struggled to stand and glared up into his face. I would not let him make me afraid. "It's a wonder your head fits through door-ways."

He chuckled and tipped his head to study me with amusement. "I will so delight in having you about the abbey for a time. It won't be so bad, you know."

I stiffened, weighing my options. "I must bid you good evening, sir." Mustering false confidence, I gave him a nod and brushed past with two long strides.

"You do love him, don't you?"

I froze on the path, my heart wilting down to my toes. He *had* seen us.

"Don't look that way, love." He approached from behind and traced the line of my shawl-covered shoulder as if he touched my bare skin. "This is a fortuitous turn of events for you, I promise. Your beau happens to be in a spot of trouble with the law, and I happen to be a first-rate solicitor."

I turned to look at his grinning face with loathing. "We don't want your sort of help."

"Oh but you do, my lady. You may not wish for a cunning and somewhat underhanded ally, but you most certainly don't want that type of adversary, either. Believe me, I'm the worst sort to have. And I have the tendency to get my way."

I hugged my wrap to myself. Then I felt the Connemara marble in my sash. "Find yourself another rag woman to lie for you." Bowing my head and striding away, I was stopped short as Prendergast stepped firmly in front of me, his face coming near mine.

"I warned you not to make an enemy of me, Countess. It won't end well for you."

I tensed under his wicked gaze and looked toward the stables where Sully had disappeared.

"Play the part, and he gets all the help he needs. If you refuse, it'll be nothing to lock you in the keep tower for a few hours and ensure it's the constable who meets him at the end of the lane in an hour instead of you. I'll make certain you're present to watch him hang too."

Panic flashed hot and cold over my skin. The threat rained like acid over my wounded heart that was still freshly out of mourning for him, and I couldn't bear the thought of going through it all again. One could only survive that sort of anguish once in her life.

"It's your choice, Queen Esther. Will you protect your precious morality . . . or him?"

God, what would you have me do?

An old verse swept over my mind, clearing away all other thoughts: *Greater love hath no man than this, that a man lay down his life for his friends.*

How about just one very precious friend?

I swallowed hard, Prendergast's words plunging into my heart and lighting every spark of loyalty that was so easily fanned into flame. It was as if he knew my every weakness, for I would rather give up a tiny corner of my overactive conscience than be the perfectly moral woman who refused to help those dear to me. In that dark moment, my endless view of possibilities and choices narrowed to exactly one.

He whispered near my face. "Let's keep this between us, shall we, Countess? If he finds out about our little arrangement, I'm afraid I'll have to end it."

His calm words sliced like a knife.

"I know you'll come around to seeing my way of things. A few of the servants in this house already have."

The air left my lungs as he winked.

That night I lay upon the finest imported sheets I'd ever seen, but all I could do was stare at the window and wonder how long Sully would wait at the end of the lane before giving up on me — and what he'd do when he did.

I did not pray before climbing into bed that night, and I avoided the Holy Bible lying on a side table. I knew I was likely not making a righteous decision, but I couldn't make any other. I rose at one point and scratched out several more missives directed toward the perpetrators of wrongs I'd seen and left them in a folded stack on the desk. Another page was filled with the poetic musings of a would-be countess as I forced myself into the façade that had now become necessary, but it was not a comfortable fit. When my hand was cramped, I blew out the candle, once again bypassing the Bible on the little table, and attempted sleep.

I tossed about until my troubled mind admitted there was only one way out of this mess: I had to find out the truth about the countess and bring her back. Sully had to be patient with me until I could — he just had to.

Please, was my whispered thought toward both Sully and God. *Please understand.*

8

Those we love know exactly what we are in spite of everything — and that is both a benefit and a dilemma.

~ Diary of a Substitute Countess

What a relief that the woman now lifting adoring brown eyes to him was already married. "You are *him*. I know it."

Sully gave the stable master's wife a brief bow. "Sullivan McKenna, ma'am. At your service."

"Mercy, it is you! My William has been looking for you. Come in, come in."

She threw the door to their little cottage wide and bid him entry into their neat but humble home beside the stables. The man in question approached with his hand extended and a warm smile lighting his features. "You disappeared on us. We thought you were returning straightaway when you dashed off from the barn, but not

115

a sight of you."

"I had to speak to someone. I suppose it carried on a bit longer than I expected."

At a warning glance from her husband, the bright-eyed woman neatly avoided the topic of his letters for a space of nearly five minutes. By the sixth minute, her husband ducked behind a curtain and she burst out with the thought that had been glowing on her face since he entered. "Come on then, tell us about the girl."

"She's all the usual things a girl ought to be, in my book — intelligent, spirited, pretty." Sully schooled his features. Silence reigned while images and memories flitted through his mind, each one striking a chord both painful and sweet. Then he leaned back in his chair and nodded at the fireplace that glowed from behind a screen. "The way that fire's hidden behind that screen there, it reminds me of her. Guarded, perhaps, but nothing can fully hide the light of those flames."

"She was a passionate lass, then?" The woman's eyes sparkled with delight.

"In the best sort of way." He stared at the orange glow behind the screen, thinking of the snap of her eyes when she was lured into a challenge, or when her loyalty was tested. That loyalty — it warmed the people around her, but it burned up what lay in her path too. "Always full of adventure and purpose. She spent her life on those who needed her, and there were always plenty of them. Some scrap of a little orphan boy, a deaf beggar woman on the street — she fought for them as if they were kin. She made me want to burst with joy and anger in the space of a single day sometimes, but I never tired of being near her."

He stopped short of describing the time she'd nearly drowned in the Thames. She'd tried to stow away on a barge to rescue her soused father who had run away after he'd lost yet another position, and Sully had to drag her back to the docks. She'd not given up on the poor man, on the hope of him being restored to life, until the day he'd died in a sorry puddle of rum and broken glass. No one else would have given a second thought to the old man, or the many other castoffs whose gaze she'd lifted to the stars.

"Perhaps she's off fighting those battles right now."

Sully stared down at his hands framing the teacup. "Perhaps."

"You miss her?"

"I miss the sweetness of her welcome after I'd been gone a spell. I miss my partner in adventure. Everything about the way things

117

were, I miss it." He ran one finger over the worn knee of his trousers, wondering if he'd have her back. One short hour until he found out where he stood. He had to talk with her the minute they left — had to. No more uncertainty, no guessing and hoping. It was time he knew how she felt.

"Why'd you go off to sea, then?"

He looked up at William, who'd returned to join the conversation. "She always made me think of grander things and hope for more than life in the East End." He paused, nipping his gaze down. "I taught her the Bible and she gave me eyes of eternity. Me, the son of a vicar."

"Were you betrothed, then?" The besotted woman leaned her cheek against her hands.

Sully bowed his head. "We hadn't gotten as far as that, ma'am." He exhaled. "It's my biggest regret now, looking back on it. I hadn't the courage to ask her."

The stable master seated himself beside his wife. "Perhaps it's prepared you for a new adventure. I've seen many a fine lass about these parts, and perhaps one of them —"

A sharp jab from his wife ended his suggestion with an *oof.* "He's not meant to be with any of *them,* William. Do you not know anything?" She grumbled and shook her

118

head, rising from the table.

When she turned to the fire to tend to her other food, William folded his arms on the table and leaned in. "I'm sorry about your troubles with the countess, McKenna. I heard she didn't take to you. That Lady Enderly doesn't warm to anyone right away, it seems, so it'll likely pass. There's plenty you can do to endear yourself to her, intimidating as she is."

Sully tensed, recalling the image of Raina looking down her little nose at him with that delicate frown. The hurt surfaced again, quick and sharp. "I've never gone out of me way to endear myself to any lady."

He sliced another piece of bread for himself and offered one to Sully. "She's a bit different than your Raina, I imagine."

He considered this, fingering the edge of his dented metal cup. "Aye, a sight different." Sully ate the bread in a few bites and chased the remaining crumbs down with a swig of tea.

"The countess has had a hard go of it, you know. Try to look at it that way."

"That so?" He frowned, thoughts pivoting to the real woman behind the name. "What sort of hardship could a lady like that ever have?"

The man gripped his cup and stared down

into the remaining liquid. "You'll understand when you meet the earl. It cannot be easy to live under the weight of such a man, and I've heard her father was even worse. They say the steel from his mill seeped into his blood."

Sully frowned, unsure of what to say. "Has she a great many enemies, then?"

He shrugged. "What titled person doesn't?"

Sully stared down at the wood plank table, eternally grateful that, within an hour, he and Raina would turn their backs on this place and all the danger involved. Poverty never looked so wonderful.

9

When you set out to change someone's opinion of you, you must first start with your own.

~ Diary of a Substitute Countess

"Let me see you walk." Prendergast beckoned me across the study awash in pink and orange sunrise. "Imagine you are the queen herself."

I'd been cornered into this tedious training session after I'd been caught running about the grounds that morning. Why must the man arise at the crack of dawn, anyway? It gave one precious little time to accomplish any covert tasks, such as searching out Sully and attempting an explanation — if he remained. I'd left a message for him in an Austen novel, and I waited for the moment to point him toward it, praying I'd see his familiar face come luncheon-time.

"Show me you are in queenly command

of the room by the way you walk through it, just as the countess would."

Summoning the poise of a royal, I walked across the room, stiff and overly self-conscious. Oh, how I hated all of this. Every bit.

He watched with a frown, his fingers supporting his chin, then waved me to a stop. "You're far too rigid. Stop trying to be someone you're not, and boldly be who you are. Be sure of yourself."

I raised my eyebrows, not bothering to voice the obvious.

"What I mean is this. I can supply you with every gown and bit of finery, but there's nothing you can wear that'll be more convincing of your role than self-assurance. Of which you seem to have none."

"Then perhaps you should find someone else for this position. I do not have that sort of charm. It isn't who I am."

"My dear lady, carrying yourself with poise doesn't mean you believe yourself to be perfect. It simply means you aren't bothered by the parts that aren't. Start by telling yourself you are confident and you're halfway there. Believe it, and that'll take care of the rest."

"Nothing to it, then." Tiredness sharpened my sarcasm.

"Lady Enderly has this incredible ability of persuasion. Why, she once persuaded a duke to sign an amendment that stood to lose him half his own fortune, simply by being so utterly charming that he hadn't any idea that he had not made up his own mind on the matter. That's all you need to do — charm people into believing you are the countess."

"I am a *rag woman,* in case you have forgotten."

Eyeing me, Prendergast stepped over to the door and pulled the little bell. Sarah, the parlor maid, stepped in.

"Sarah, have you seen a rag woman about the place of late?"

She looked between Prendergast and me, her pockmarked face wrinkling with confusion. "No sir, I haven't seen one for some months now."

"Not a single trace of anyone resembling one?"

She frowned and shook her head.

"Thank you. That is all."

The girl gave a swift curtsy and departed, and Prendergast spun on me with a sparkling smile. "There, you see? There is no rag woman here."

"You know who I truly am."

"My dear, it's like I told you before. 'Rag

woman' was never your real identity. Nothing based on circumstances can be. The rags are gone, yet here you are. So the question remains — who are you, truly?"

I stared at him, for I had no answer. As much as I'd loathed being buried in them, my rags had always been the sum total of my existence. Without them, what was left?

"Now, let us continue to change your mind. We've done away with the old, and we shall endeavor to replace it with something better." He approached, studying me. "Have you ever been to a bathing hole?"

I blushed at the question. "Not outside of a metal tub, sir. Although I was pushed off the dock once into the Thames, and I dove in another time to rescue my brother. Nothing graceful about that, though." I remembered the panicked swim toward his flailing white limbs.

"Quite all right, we'll imagine it. Close your eyes and pretend you're standing in placid warm water and you're gliding through it." He slid his hand under my fingertips and guided me toward him with a gentle pressure. I moved forward obediently and imagined treading through water, relaxed and weighted with grace.

This was new. Delightful. The feel of those movements solidified in my mind, becoming more natural with each step until I'd formed a rhythm. Yet I felt certain I'd lose it the moment I left the room. "You still cannot make me what I am not."

"In the words of a great reformer of English society, 'It's never too late to become what you might have been.' That's George Eliot, former editor of *Westminster Review*, writer of six famously received novels and counting, and despite the name, a *woman.* You have the gusto of that brave soul and ten more besides. Look how far you've come in a few days. Look at where you are. You are courageous."

I blinked. I'd never been called that. Foolish, sometimes a bit scandalous when I raced through graveyards or befriended beggars, but never courageous. I turned the word over in my mind, letting it absorb into my spirit.

"Yet you are more beautiful than ever a rag woman has need of being, and there must be a reason for it." He rested his hands on my shoulders and turned me toward a gilded mirror, forcing me to study my reflection. "You, dear one, were meant for exactly this sort of life, and you can no longer deny it. We could not uncover beauty that was never there to begin with. This, my dear, is who you are."

"But this is a temporary identity, isn't it?"

"With lasting effects."

He pulled my shoulders back in a way that felt unnatural at first, but as I relaxed, the new position lifted my chest and straightened my back in a way that felt quite suitable, as if it was how God had designed a person to stand.

So this was how poise felt. This was what it meant to be a lady.

Prendergast pointed toward the mirror, but this time the woman reflected there watched with a calm face and fresh dignity I had never known I possessed. My rosy lips bloomed against pale skin, complementing my darkly lashed eyes that arrested even me. "Look what difference a little confidence makes. Add a little polish to your speech and weight to your voice to even it out, and you would fit into any drawing room around London.

"Now, I want you to start acting on what you see there. Behave as a countess, speak and move like her. Throw out commands and watch them be followed to the letter."

"And then what?"

"Then, my dear, you dance like a countess."

"I have to *dance*?" I'd only now mastered walking.

"Just at a small reception to honor your visit to the area. Come, I'll show you." He arranged my arms, positioning me before him, and explaining how I must hold myself, then swept into large, smooth circles about the wide open room. A melody emanated from his chest in a fine baritone. I stared down at his feet with rapt attention, memorizing the patterns, stumbling through them with my own.

"Chin up, love." His knuckle tipped the edge of my chin to match his words, and my gaze flew up to his smiling face so near to mine, his confidence beaming down on me.

I instinctively broke away, stumbling over the rug, but he frowned and moved near, taking hold of my shoulders and bringing his face down beside mine, far too close once again. My heart rebelled, but I forced myself to permit his familiarity.

"Don't forget how important this is for you. One look at that man tells me just what you mean to each other. The way he watches you, those stolen glances . . . He's so deeply in love with you I fear he may drown in his feelings." He breathed the words in sweet bursts of minty tea–scented air across my face.

This brought an instant ache to my heart,

and I couldn't help but picture Sully, imagine him holding me this close. My heart raced. Sully, my loyal rescuer with the brilliant smile, the last and first thought of so many hopeless days. I thought of his eyes most of all when I pictured him, dark and laughing, exuding the powerful music of his soul even when he was not playing. The very notion of those eyes cast toward me with such devotion . . . it was too much. My cheeks burned. Longing flamed through me.

A knock sounded on the door and the man released me instantly. My hands flew to my overheated face, and I kept my back to the door while trying to regain control of my emotions. If only I could stop thinking of Sully, I had a chance at maintaining the poise I needed.

"Breakfast, my lady."

I closed my eyes, still unable to face the butler. "Yes, thank you, Bradford. That will be fine." His footsteps retreated and a cart squeaked into the room.

"This is your chance. Command your servants, my lady." Prendergast whispered the words so only I could hear.

I turned, and my gaze snapped onto the very face that had me so unsettled. Stormy and passionate with eyes that sparked with unspoken opinions, Sully watched me with heart-pounding silence as he arranged the plates on the cart he'd wheeled in and poured tea. My blush deepened, reaching warm fingers up into my scalp. My breath caught in my throat.

It had been many years since I'd seen him without even a trace of a smile.

"You can't be serious," I breathed in Prendergast's direction.

He merely raised an eyebrow in challenge.

I forced myself to look at Sully as he laid out our food. "I have something I'd like you to do, if you please."

After what felt like a painfully long silence, Sully straightened and looked to me with an expression devoid of his usual merriment. His direct gaze pierced all my new confidence, and I could be nothing but Ragna in the face of it. "I'll do whatever you need, m'lady."

I lifted my chin. "I'd like you to fetch me a different teacup. I prefer the gold-rimmed one with the inlaid flowers."

His jaw twitched. "Of course."

Prendergast smiled at me until I wanted to slap the grin from his face. "I'm certain you'll do splendid here. You are a most suitable mistress of Rothburne." His smiling face glowed with hidden meaning.

Sully's darkened with very different

thoughts.

My beloved friend slipped out the service entrance to fetch the teacup. When he did, he'd find a small scrap of paper directing him to a message in Jane Austen's *Sense and Sensibility* that I'd left him last night: "I do hope you're not vexed with me. Nothing shall be right in my world if you are."

Farther down the page I marked a line spoken about the hero: "If I could but know his heart, everything would become easy."

There were not words enough in the novels we shared to explain what had occurred since last night, so these would have to suffice.

I laid one hand on the smooth bodice of my day dress, hoping to calm my tumultuous insides. I tried to summon the ardent words of love in Sully's letters, but they had begun to fade into indistinct memories. Did he regret writing those things now? Perhaps in his long absence he'd forgotten all my faults — my impetuousness, my quick-flaring temper, my constant tangles with trouble . . . Surely the man wouldn't change his mind about me so suddenly, after all he'd written.

But his face. The angry shadows looming over his countenance tainted my assurance with powerful doubts.

When Prendergast left me, it was as if a fire had been lit. That terrible look on Sully's face knotted my stomach and drove me forward. I had to learn the truth about the real Lady Enderly, for it was the only thing that would untangle me from this mess. I reached the large desk in three strides and glanced about. Finally, a chance to investigate the story that had led to her need of a replacement, maybe even discover where she was hiding.

Or being hidden.

Skimming a book of accounts, I found nothing of what I'd expected. There were a host of charges for milliners and dressmakers, washerwomen and greengrocers, but not a scrap of paper that pointed to the many travels Prendergast had claimed she'd made. There were lavish amounts of money spent on season tickets to the opera, art exhibits, even the derby — all inside London and none of it charitably spent. This countess was not the world-traveling queen of benevolence he had painted, and I suppose I should not have been surprised to discover this.

Yet it left me intensely curious — who was this woman, and what else had my new employer lied about concerning her?

10

No matter what else I lose, no one is capable of separating me from my dignity — except on occasion myself.

~ Diary of a Substitute Countess

"I suppose you'll want to host your evening here. Your grand reception, that is." Philip strode across the grand salon when I arrived for my meeting with the staff at ten the following morning. "Far be it from the lovely Lady Enderly to enter a town without the proper fanfare and trumpet blasts."

A grand reception. Nothing sounded more intimidating, but if it was what Lady Enderly would do, it must be done. I inhaled and imagined gowns and flowers, smiling faces and warm cider, delectable food to fill my belly. Perhaps it could be made enjoyable if I could convince myself to relax.

"Will it be a musical performance or dancing?"

I looked around at the vast emptiness of the gilded room and the blue brocade chairs lining the walls. "Oh, music. Always music." What a change it would bring to this empty space. Perhaps the beauty of it would even seep into poor Philip's heart as well. I studied the bitter face of the man far too young to be hardened so. He needed a taste of music even more than I did. Oh, to take that dried-up, cracked old heart of his and saturate it with loveliness and life. There was true spirit and heart in him, I was certain, for that passionate bitterness had come from somewhere.

"Music." He frowned. "You know of a performer who remains out here during the season? So be it, if that is what you desire. You are queen of Rothburne."

My brain stuttered, grasping for an answer as heat washed over my skin. I shot a glance toward the door — where was Prendergast? Before I had to speak, the double doors burst open and a blessed little woman scurried in, saving me from having to fumble a response.

"Hello, hello. Mr. Scatchard sent for me. We're to plan the event of the season, my lady, and what a night it'll be." She bustled across the long room, her skirt swirling against her stocky frame as she stopped before me. Cheery little eyes stood out on a rounded face framed by curls, underscoring her glowing enthusiasm as she bobbed two curtsies. "It's wonderful to meet you at last, Lady Enderly, after all I've heard." She bobbed another curtsy and smiled up at me. "We don't take one minute of your presence in this place for granted. We'll make a sensation of your holiday to the country, and everyone will adore you."

I caught sight of Cousin Philip's eye roll in my peripheral vision and straightened, smiling with delight at the little round woman before me. "Thank you, Mrs. . . ."

"Shirley Shackley. Oh, my apologies, my lady, I thought you'd know me. Faces don't appear in letters now, do they?" Her contagious giggle drew forth a smile from me. "I am the one Mr. Scatchard has hired to coordinate social matters during your stay. It's quite an honor to finally set about organizing the social calendar of a true lady."

"We call her Curly Shirley around here, and a fine job she does of entertaining guests for all the gentry from here to Bristol." Cousin Philip laid a hand on her shoulder, earning a scrunch-nosed smile from the energetic little woman.

"I knew you wouldn't want to be bothered with the details after a long journey, so I've taken the liberty of preparing the menu and arranging the schedule. The entertainment will, of course, be left to your discretion."

"She's already chosen, Shirl. She wishes for a musical night."

"Oh, wonderful." Her face nearly burst with sunshine. "How ever did you manage to find a performer to — ? Oh, but of course you can, and without any trouble. You are Lady Enderly."

Another eye roll from poor Cousin Philip, who must be drowning in this sea of my praise.

"I'll have the menu sent up for your approval the moment it's finalized, but I'm certain you'll love it." Shirley fluttered her hands, adding even more energy to her words. "What a night it'll be. I'd love to see you make a wonderful success of this evening, and I'm certain you will. Do send word if I can do anything to facilitate that in any way."

As she hurried out the door, Cousin Philip crossed his arms and scowled at the empty fireplace. "And I'd love to see you fall flat on your sorry face at that reception, but I'm sure you know that. Do ring if I can facilitate *that* in any way." With a mock bow, he backed toward the door.

I straightened, pushing my shoulders

back. "I hope you'll attend." I *would* change his mind about me. Or rather, her.

He snorted. "Not if you paid me a king's ransom. Stuffy musical nights don't suit me."

"Maybe this one won't be stuffy."

He lingered in the doorway, eyes dancing at the suggestion. "Well then, why not invite a peasant or two? Maybe have fiddle music instead of —"

"That's perfect." I tensed with sudden inspiration. "Yes, fiddle music. I believe I'll do that. Why don't you see if that new footman will play for us? I saw him carrying a fiddle about the yard. Would that entice you to come?"

He studied me, eyebrows raised. "With pleasure."

With another look, he exited, leaving me standing alone in the ballroom-style salon, staring at my own silhouette in the window across the room, awash with panic at what I'd just done. The lure of a challenge had tempted me into something foolish . . . or perhaps utterly brilliant. I walked out into the hall. What a mess I'd taken on, and it grew stickier by the minute. Even the house itself felt cold and unwelcoming, and I didn't wish to stay. If only —

I jerked at a cold hand on my arm. I spun

into the crisp-suited chest of Victor Prendergast and looked up into his smiling, overconfident face. "Well? How did it go with your dear cousin?"

I cringed at the question and backed the two available inches into a window. "One can never be certain."

"He still believes your ruse, does he not?"

"He does, but he hates me fiercely." I omitted all the things I couldn't bear to cast before his piercing gaze.

"As well he should, for he despises the real Lady Enderly. They've never seen eye to eye, especially on matters of the estate. If he liked you, I would think you an utter failure in the role."

I ran my fingertip along the window's pane behind me. "Is she that terrible of a person? Does she deserve all this hatred?"

He smiled, his eyes glittering. "Every bit of it. She's accomplished, well-liked, wealthy, and titled. Everything poor Scatchard wishes he could be. He'd especially set his sights on this estate, the most profitable piece of land bestowed by a mutual uncle, so you can imagine his feelings about being made manager instead of owner. Rather a slap in the face, don't you think? The man would kill to have the deed in his name."

"If looks could do a person in, he'd have

already done it to me. That's what I think."

My glum voice drew a rumble of laughter from the man who stood so near. "Being hated is far from the worst thing a person can be. Why, it's practically a requirement for anyone who's anyone. My dear father had a saying: ' 'Tis a success to be hated or adored. The only failure is one who's ignored.' "

Being ignored seemed a luxury just then, as I inched away from my captor, but I closed my mouth over the thought.

He moved close, lowering his voice. "Remember, you are not here to convince people to like you — only that you are Lady Enderly. You must become her in every way."

I leaned into the window and closed my eyes as fiddle music drifted up to my ears, muffled by the distance between us.

"Ah, it's your fiddle player." He watched me with shining eyes and a wicked smile. "Lucky for him, no inspector or constable would ever think to look for him way out here in Havard. Not unless they were alerted, of course." He winked.

I shuddered.

"Chin up, Countess. His safety is in very capable hands."

Thunk. I cringed as the swinging service

door struck something, someone, on the other side. My nerves were rattled. Two days in this place had not instilled in me the necessary grace required for this role, and I was ever afraid of the next misstep. I moved back, heart pounding, and pushed the door again to catch a glimpse of my victim rubbing his forehead.

My other hand flew to my mouth. "Oh Bradford, I'm terribly sorry." I slipped through the door into the main hall.

"Quite all right, your ladyship. I've just posted those letters you gave me." He looked past me to the servants' hall I was exiting and raised his eyebrows. "Is there anything else I can fetch for you?"

A distinct out-of-place feeling made me want to flee. What mistress hung about, or even set foot in, her servants' hall?

"I was only looking" — but I stopped short of voicing Sully's name — "for bread. I was looking for bread. I suddenly feel quite famished."

"Why did you not ring for it, then? Any one of us would have brought it."

I tensed, fingering the fabric of my day gown. "I am quite capable of doing some things myself." Which was the last thing any real countess would do. I ducked my head. "I'm afraid I'm not always the picture of convention and formality."

An easy smile warmed his face. "And that is to your great credit, my lady. Conventional countesses are plentiful in this world."

I gave a weak smile.

He hesitated, his brow knit, as if wishing to say more. "I hope there's nothing amiss, my lady. The staff has worked tirelessly to make the place acceptable to you, and you'd honor their efforts by remaining, at least for a time."

"I'm not certain it'll be a long stay." If I could help it, it would be over before another week was.

He cleared his throat, the sound echoing through the quiet of the hall. "If there's anything wrong, anything we've done to displease —"

"Oh, no. It's just . . ." I sighed and my shoulders drooped forward. His face melted into a gentle smile, drawing me to open my hurting heart and release to him a small piece of what was caged there. "I'm simply not certain I fit here." The whispered half truth escaped with an utter sense of helplessness.

"Well then," he said with a sparkle to his eyes, "you must change 'here' to fit you, my lady."

I folded my arms over my chest with a

frown, but as I glanced around the somber gray space, ideas and possibilities bloomed in my mind. How easy it would be to add a few small touches and make it warmer — more like a home. Perhaps it would become more bearable, at least. Prendergast had demanded that I begin to act as Lady Enderly, and what mistress would not be free to change the house to suit her?

I turned back to the butler, ready to call him brilliant, and he smiled at what he saw in my expression.

"Simply point and command, and it shall be done," Bradford said. "May I bring to your attention the unfinished rooms in the center of the abbey? They'll need the most, as they are yet untouched by the renovations. They will soon become a hazard if left untended."

I glanced down the dark passageway that led deep into the heart of the abbey and stiffened at the thought of working on them, or entering them at all. Something repelled me from that murky tomb-like space. If any part of Rothburne was haunted, it would be those grand old rooms.

"Setting out to change the place, are you?" A ruddy-haired parlor maid slowed near us. "If I might be so bold, your ladyship, it might be wise to begin with the rooms where the guests will be for the reception. No one will see those decrepit interior rooms."

I eyed them both. "All right then, we'll save them for later. Bradford, perhaps you can see what is needed to repair the inner rooms and at least keep them from ruin. Let me have a look around the front rooms." I strode forward, but the old servant remained rooted to his place. I turned back and he was blinking, his lashes darkened by moisture. "Why, Bradford, what is it?"

"Forgive me, mistress. It's just been so long since anyone's seen the value in this old place."

I smiled at him, aching with questions about the abbey — and the countess. *Every house is a reflection of its mistress.* The place was grand and beautiful, stately and charming, yet at the core a terrible chaos lay secreted from outside observers. How I wished to know what inner chaos existed in the countess's life, what had led to her sudden need of a replacement, but how did one ask questions about herself?

"We were afraid that you did not care much for Rothburne."

I stepped carefully through the exchange. "What gave such an impression?"

"It was your instructions, my lady." He

fidgeted, looking down as he prepared to discuss something that was obviously uncomfortable for him. "That we were to be . . . prudent with the abbey expenses. Frugal. Above all else." He lifted his head and hurried on. "There's much wisdom in such commands, and we were happy to carry them out, mind you."

It seemed there was no money to spend on the place. Was that the secret at the heart of this woman — that she was actually poor?

I glanced about the place with a keen eye and imagined what it would take to brighten up the dim rooms without expense. Light was the first thought that came to me. "I happened to spot some delightful candelabras in those abandoned rooms. Do you suppose they could be freshened and put to use? The great hall could do with a fair bit more candlelight." I pointed toward the dark corners of the room.

He brightened. "If those please you, there are a wealth of them in the attic. They could be brought down and polished."

"The attic." I smiled, ideas unfurling. "Yes, let's explore the attic and see what we can make use of."

The topmost part of the house turned out to be a veritable treasure trove of mismatched furniture, rolled-up rugs, and dusty drapes. I looked about with hope swelling and imagination brimming. I might not be able to host a sensational dinner party, but I knew how to make something useful out of castoffs.

Sully's answer to my silent question came Tuesday evening on a scrap of paper tucked strategically into my empty teacup when I took afternoon tea alone, and it contained two references. The first was from Anne Brontë's haunting tale, *The Tenant of Wildfell Hall:* "I would rather have your friendship than the love of any other woman in the world."

I caught my breath, squeezing my eyes shut for a moment to let the pure love in that message wash over me. My trembling fingers flipped through the pages of the second book, Thomas Hardy's *Far from the Madding Crowd,* to find the underlined message on page 163: "And at home by the fire, whenever you look up there I shall be — and whenever I look up, there will be you."

Tears seeped out and I blinked my clumped lashes. I read the words over and over, letting the promise in them warm me. The response was so very Sully, and his assurances were precious to my heart.

If only it would last until I found the

countess. *Oh please, Lord, let it last.* If ever I saw the hand of God in my life, it was in him sending Sully with his Bible and fiddle into my path. Yet I now hung on to that blessing by a single thread. If Sully's patience wore thin, he might leave. And if I failed at this ruse . . .

I could barely breathe at the thought.

"Can you hold a pen?" Prendergast extended the writing utensil to me when I'd been at the abbey a full week. He shoved blank paper across the desk.

I lifted flashing eyes to him. "What do you take me for? I've got fingers, haven't I?"

"You'll need to practice her signature. Simply lay this paper on top of it and trace the lines, see if you can learn it. Then if you are asked to sign something, you shall know how."

I did as requested, the fine pen making slow swoops across the page to create her very elegant, very feminine signature. Again my conscience jarred the peace of my new life. This was *her* name, and it carried all the flavor of her life and personality. Not a bit of mine. Yet I dared not stop, for I felt that unyielding gaze upon the back of my neck. When I finished, I sat back and waited for his response.

145

"It'll do. Take it up with you and practice at night."

When he left, I pulled the oversized Bible from a shelf and leafed through the pages Sully and I had pored over together. Hadn't God changed several names in the Bible? Every time something significant occurred, he'd given the person a new name to match it. Even Esther, according to Prendergast. I flipped to Esther and found my employer's words to be true — her name *had* changed.

I glanced at my reflection in a wide gilded mirror across the room. Perhaps it was time mine changed to match everything else that was shifting in me, for I was no longer the same woman. Prendergast was right — the change had been permanent even if the position was not.

I skimmed the passages I could find where God changed the names of Abraham and Sarah and my conscience abated. *God, is this your way of changing my name, of lifting the burden of my wretched old identity and giving me a new one?* I seemed to remember similar words in Scripture — God would give us a new identity. I stared down at the page that contained Lady Enderly's signature created by my hand. Was this mine?

I cast my mind and strength into working

on the abbey in the following days, readying it for the reception — especially since Cousin Philip had departed on business and the freedom was palpable. Beautiful old pieces were pulled from storage and arranged to great advantage throughout the place. My heart delighted in overseeing the transformation taking place and watching my ideas unfold. When I was able to push aside thoughts of impending danger, it was like a dream.

Polished brass candle stands appeared at becoming angles in the darkest corners, and I could imagine the light from their candles warming the walls with a soft glow. Rugs and drapes were taken outside, and the dust and neglect beaten from them. The dark, foreboding rooms brightened with light and color as my small touches softened the edges of the place, bringing life to its solemn chambers.

I turned to Bradford, who had become my partner in the renovations. "Where did all these things come from? Surely the monks did not have such trappings."

"I believe they came from the former master's London house. He intended to use them in the rooms once renovations were complete, but then he passed the estate along and here it sits."

The servants proved to be another treasure trove. Just as the attic had contained a vast store of forgotten beauty, the servants possessed surprising talents that worked together to create a marvelous display throughout the house. Stained drapes were creatively embroidered and cleaned, flowers arranged as if by a professional hand, and candles dipped and made fresh so there was no need to purchase new ones. A quiet vigor returned to the abbey as we all threw our skill into the place and brought out the grandeur that had been lying dormant.

On the fourth day, work moved outside to the pond, and the staff began cleaning around it, revealing a healthy groundcover that spread around its sloping borders. Taller men yanked dead vines down from a forgotten white-pillared structure with intricate ironwork spanning in a dome overtop.

I stepped back into the abbey at dusk, marveling at the elegant, inviting nature of the place that was changing under my hand, blossoming in beauty. It drew a person in now, with old walls softened by the glow of candles and rugs warming the floors, as if it were glad a person had come. I imagined bright flowers on tables and gowns twirling across the floor, and it made my heart glad.

Livening up the dreary house had livened something in me, as well.

In the hushed emptiness of the gleaming hall, footsteps echoed from the shadows. Bradford approached, holding out a salver. "These came for you today, your ladyship."

"Thank you, Bradford." I took the envelopes and slipped into the privacy of the abbey library to read them.

It is with deep regret that I acknowledge your displeasure with my operations, and I wish to assure you of its immediate remedy . . .

My jaw went slack. I flipped it back to the address lines and saw it had come from the owner of Mum's factory. I devoured his abject apology full of groveling and sincere promises for change. I read it again to be sure it was real, and excitement bubbled up in my chest. This was truly happening. It had worked — better than I'd ever imagined. Another similar letter lay beneath it.

When I'd read them both, I lifted my eyes from the pages and stared into the candlelit room. Queen Esther had stepped up into her exalted position and begun her reign. My pen was a scepter, ready to dole out words whose effect would send ripples far and wide. I was giddy with this newfound influence.

Finally, my life was about to count for something.

So it was that my heart was made ready for the intimidating reception even before my appearance. It was not until the morning of the event that I remembered offering to make Sully the musician for the night. I hadn't even spoken to him of it, and perhaps nothing would come of my wild idea. With any hope, Cousin Philip had forgotten to ask him, or Sully had refused.

Although I couldn't imagine either of those things happening.

11

Our truest selves are sometimes buried below the debris of circumstances, but to unbury such a thing, we must first be able to recognize it.

~ Diary of a Substitute Countess

I hardly recognized myself. Simone and the chambermaid arrayed me in the lawn undergarments and muslin stays by late in the afternoon. Even before the corset had been tightened over my churning belly, my form held a new poise and quiet assurance that was visible in the mirror. I was changing, becoming less Ragna and more a lady, like a flower unfolding its petals, and finery was becoming a part of me — or it was shaping me into something new. Simone drew out a small jar and opened a lightly tinted cosmetic.

When she had completed her artistry, I stood poised on a tiny platform in the middle of the dressing room and gazed at the garment being carried toward me in her arms. It was a full skirt of deep crimson and gold.

"I hope it meets your approval." Simone held the rich garment aloft and I couldn't stop staring. It exceeded my dreams, which were plenty elaborate.

"I don't know what to say."

The woman blinked. "You do not like it?"

"I've never seen anything like it." The words spilled out of my overwrought heart that had fallen in love at first sight. "It's beautiful."

"It's Parisian, my lady."

French, like me. I felt an instant connection to the gown, as if my own Huguenot ancestors had spun the silk. She hefted the gown overhead with the help of two chambermaids and tugged it down until it slipped into perfect position about my torso and hips, flaring out atop the layers of framing. They wrapped the long, sleek bodice of modern fashion around me. The waistline dropped to a handsome point at the center and rested atop the wealth of material that billowed into a stunning skirt.

"Don't she look like a painting, framed in the mirror that way." It was the little chambermaid who breathed into words the same thoughts I'd had, her stage whisper reaching my ears from the main room. I did look like a painting — a very specific one, though. From the deep red gown to the upswept hair and pure face, I looked exactly like her. More, in fact, than I looked like Ragna of Spitalfields. The time spent in this place had transformed me until I hardly knew anymore what was me and what was merely the dust of circumstances settling on me.

I turned again, trying to take in the entire effect, but in my distracted wonder I stepped on the edge of the platform, tipped to the side, and after a flailing of arms, fell into a heap against the wall. With little cries, the women rushed in to help me up and smooth my skirts, my hair. I closed my eyes and focused on my smarting hip that was now imprinted with the delicate edge of whalebone frame holding out my skirts. Despite all the work, parts of Raina remained. This night could be enchanted, or it could be a nightmare. One little mistake was all it would take to bring about the latter.

Below me, Victor Prendergast stepped out from a side room and paused to clear his throat as he shut the door. He lifted his gaze and stiffened at the sight of me, the usual easy confidence drained from his face. In its place was a sort of helpless astonishment.

"My dear, you're stunning." The words were a hoarse whisper as he stepped toward me, taking my hands. "I daresay that Simone is an artist and you are the finest canvas she's ever had. Congratulations, my lady. You're a fabulous success."

"I'm glad you approve." How I wished to yank my fingers from those hands that had once pinned me against the wall.

"Approve?" He gave a breathy laugh. "Heaven above, I can hardly take my eyes off you. Your guests will feel the same." He lifted my fingertips, spinning me to have a look at the entire costume. Then he faced me toward a gilded mirror set against gold floral paper. "You will enchant anyone who comes within three yards of you. It will be as if you're casting a spell, and you won't know what to do with yourself."

"A shame that mirrors only show us the outside." I murmured the words as I stretched my sore hip. How long before my true self surfaced in public and people saw through the façade?

"Then you shall have to change the inside, change your mind." His confident smile did little to untangle my nerves. "It's time you get your largest hurdle out of the way. It's not poverty, because I took that away, not a physical deformity or lack of beauty. The only thing limiting you . . . is you."

"That leaves me in an awkward position."

"Not at all. You have only to convince yourself of who you are. Recite every word that describes Lady Enderly, everything you wish to be, while looking in this mirror at your enchanting face. Memorize what you see along with those words, and see what effect it has on your little heart. Go on, try it."

I lifted my gaze to the mirror, staring at my eyes bright with fear, and mentally repeated all the words Prendergast had used to describe Lady Enderly. *Quiet grace. Poised. Elegant.* The sound of the gathering guests down the hall further unbalanced my fledgling composure, and I dipped my gaze toward the red rug at my feet. My throat felt tight.

"Try again." Prendergast nudged my chin up and smiled at the reflection of my hesitant face in the mirror. "Dear one, confidence is simply a muscle like any other. The more you use it, the stronger it grows."

I inhaled and looked back up to the mirror. This was for Sully.

Refined. Immune to criticism. Accomplished. Well-respected and charming.

Prendergast smiled at me. "There now, don't you feel —"

The sound of footsteps made us both turn, Prendergast dropping his hands from me, and there down the hall came Curly Shirley, brown hair arranged atop her head and a flattering taupe-colored gown adorning her curvy frame. Her hands fluttered about her chest. "Oh, what a sight. What history you'll make in that gown, your ladyship. I can hardly believe such a beauty has come to roost at Rothburne Abbey."

Just like that, my assurance buoyed even more.

"I do hope you'll stay the winter, and I'll be sure to make it —"

"Thank you, Mrs. Shackley." Prendergast cut her off with silvery elegance, always in control. "I believe the hour is growing late. Are the guests ready to be presented to our hostess?"

"More than ready, Mr. Prendergast, and oh what a treat they will have." She slipped her gloved hand under my elbow and escorted me toward the salon as Prendergast gave a brief nod to wish me luck.

Down a long hallway we moved, toward the low hum of polite voices. I could feel Prendergast's prying gaze on my back as I walked away.

"I am delighted to see you get on well with Mr. Prendergast. He's done so much good for the earl. Why, I believe he's the man's one and only friend on this earth."

"His only —"

"Not everyone can stand close to the fire without being burned and — Oh, forgive me for speaking so about the earl." Her poor little face paled. "He is a great man with a lot of power in the House of Lords, but anything in great quantities can be overwhelming to common folk. That's why Victor Prendergast is so good for him, being halfway between nobility and working class. I'd heard rumors you wished to dismiss Mr. Prendergast, but I can't imagine what would become of the earl if that happened. I'm relieved to see you have kept him on."

So the countess had tried to rid the household of Victor Prendergast.

I watched the animated face of the woman escorting me, blessing her silently for her uncontrolled tongue. She could not stop herself from talking, it seemed, and for that I was grateful.

"Come now, the musician is present already as well."

Sully. How had I forgotten all about that mess? This could be disastrous in so many ways. I knew Sully well enough to realize I could never guess what to expect tonight.

When Shirley slipped through the doors to ready the room, I peeked in at the clusters of people, richly colored gowns paired with dark suits and liveried servants bobbing between them with silver trays. I clung to the doorknob. *Father God, give me strength. I need —*

I exhaled, the prayer disintegrating. Calling on God now, in the midst of this, felt a bit like accepting this position in the first place — undeserved, uncomfortable, and too large a favor. How could I ask God to give me the strength to deceive? If only I could talk to Sully, filling his ear with my many questions about God and the nuances of the Bible. He'd have an answer that made sense. I had none.

As Shirley Shackley spouted a fantastical introduction, I focused my mind on the painting I'd seen of Lady Enderly in that old library and attempted to re-create the becoming smile she'd worn. I trembled.

Sully. This is for Sully.

Then the doors were flung open, the chatter hushed, and I glided into the midst of them, my heart pounding loud enough to be heard by them all. *Breathe. Keep breathing.* I straightened my back, lacing my gloved fingertips in front of me. *Walking through water.* Was Prendergast watching? The click of my gold evening slippers echoed in the massive room, and with each graceful stride, a calm strength settled over me. When I forced myself to look around, I caught a glimpse of my appearance reflected in the faces before me that glowed with awe and admiration, and it shocked me. Emboldened me. Had I truly changed that much? Weeks ago I never would have been allowed near this room, and now the same woman parted the crowds with her very presence, everyone watching the entrance. The sudden power was heady.

The introductions swirled around me as each guest was presented, and my jaw hurt from clenching and smiling. It only relaxed when the introductions were complete and I was free to wander among my guests. What had Prendergast said about this part? I was to ensure each guest was paired with another for conversation and that everyone had what was needed.

What I needed was a moment of quiet. Accepting a small delicacy from a tray, I stepped behind a pillar near the wall and exhaled, feeling the tension release.

"Do you suppose she's kept the rings?" A low female voice sounded nearby.

"I certainly wouldn't. It's hardly good taste, if you reject the man who gave it to you."

"*Men,* Cecelia. I heard there were four, and plenty more who wished to ask it but hadn't the courage."

"Was it that many? My, what a sensation her debut must have been."

"She even tamed the Duke of Charlot, you know, and caught the attention of Prince Edward."

"Who hasn't?" The woman humphed. "That Lady Enderly isn't much to look at, for all the sensation she's caused. She's becoming, I'll admit, but no more than my Maryanne."

"It's more than comeliness, Cecelia. Why, I heard she can bring a man to his knees with a mere look. She had that awful Lord Stainbridge groveling after her, didn't she? That takes something far deeper than a lovely face."

"Where on earth did you hear all this? You're not hobnobbing around with titled lords."

"The *Telegraph* had a piece on her in the society pages. Ran for weeks before her return to the area. One look at her and I believe every word of it."

"She does have a presence about her, a

sort of controlled grace that looks as though it would part the waters. Do you know if she . . ."

As the women moved away, their voices fading into the hum of the crowd, I forced my posture straighter and harnessed the look of benign politeness, clamping it firmly in place over my crumbling nerves as I sailed back out to the room. After another smile toward a passing guest, I eyed the brown item I'd taken from the tray and wondered if it would settle my stomach. The very moment I bit into the surprisingly bitter morsel, Sully's voice cut through my thoughts. I spun and there he was, a few yards away.

I'd recognize that boyish grin anywhere, that tall and agile frame. I caught my breath at the stunning sight of him clothed in black from head to shiny shoe, the twinkle in his eyes setting him apart. Even if he said not a word, I'd still be a puddle every time I looked his direction. How on earth would I survive this? I had to keep away from him or he'd unsettle the delicate balance of my façade.

Yet somehow I couldn't wait for him to catch a glimpse of me, the little girl he'd loved in rags who'd grown up into something far better.

12

Pride makes a terrible living companion,
for it takes up a great deal of room.
~ Diary of a Substitute Countess

"What's the story to that Prendergast fellow?" Sully hovered in the service alcove,
watching the vibrant swirl of activity in the
main room. The man in question looked
over the guests with veiled glances from
under heavy lids, noticing everything that
occurred even while holding a conversation.
Sully's blood ran hot when he recalled the
man casting his piercing gaze toward Raina
at dinner and letting it linger, seeming to
see everything meant to be shielded from
decent folk.

The first footman sighed with pursed lips
and buffed water marks off a silver tray with
a rag. "He is the family solicitor and helps
manage the earl's estates. He's been to the
abbey a handful of times, and he always

makes quite an impression. But that's what he does, you know. No matter where he is."

"Aye, I can see that." Sully's gaze followed the man across the room where he entered a small circle of women standing around a tiny hors d'oeuvres table covered in white linen. The group opened to receive him, every female face glowing with welcome.

"He's a slick one, and a mighty fine deceiver," the footman said. "I'd never want to cross him. Wouldn't imagine he'd put on a fair fight."

"What do they keep him on for, if he isn't honest? He sounds like one who should be sacked."

"He's paid for his effectiveness, not his honesty. Based on the rumors flying about below stairs, I'd guess he wins many cases that shouldn't be won for clients who shouldn't go free."

Sully frowned. Did Raina know this about her employer?

"That's how he's made his success, you know. Makes people believe that acting against him is somehow acting against their own interests. It's uncanny, really, the ability he has to sway one's will."

"Well, he'll never sway mine."

The footman arranged empty glasses on his now-clean tray. "I hear he's managed to convince you to perform tonight. I don't suppose he's offered to pay you more for it."

"Aye, Mr. Scatchard arranged it, but it didn't take much convincing, truth be told. I can play the fiddle with me eyes closed, on one leg in a rocking ship. Gets my heart a-pumping and makes me feel alive."

The man's eyes sparkled like the crystal he was arranging. "It shows in your playing. Quite a bit of life you've brought to the tired old servants' hall after a day's labor. We're glad to have you."

"Well, thank you kindly. Say, do I hear a bit of the brogue in you too?"

The man's lips pursed. "If you did, it was merely a slip. I've worked hard to smooth it away and sound every bit the accomplished Brit my recommendations say I am."

Sully cracked a smile. "Nothing wrong with being Irish, says I."

"Out here, the Irish are lower-class people, tolerated only a bit more than mangy dogs and feral cats. Too many of us came here after the blight, and mostly farmers, who they find dirty and common."

"I suppose I am both at times, but I can't say I'm ashamed. They both point to hard work, which is something a man can be proud of."

"Hard work is the opposite of gentility, which is what they respect most." The footman poured a little trickle of liquid into each glass. "One cannot be both. Take your man Prendergast, for example. You see him enjoying himself, pattering about? This is the hardest he works all day, and he's held in higher regard than anyone else around here who takes a wage. Ah, there's the lady herself. I'd best be out serving her guests." The man balanced the tray of glasses on his gloved fingertips and moved out into the crowds.

Tucking himself into the shadows of the service alcove, Sully peered out with a thudding pulse, eyes scanning the room for the face that had been carved upon his memory for years. Many pretty women moved through this room tonight, but none compared to the cameo-like profile, the face glowing with life and willful strength, that he sought.

Suddenly a striking figure in deep red turned to receive the introduction of a guest, and it was *her.* He stopped breathing for a moment, blinking to be sure. He forced his chest out to gulp in air and watched the lovely creature moving about, a light feathering of curls framing that familiar face now free of all traces of poverty. A nervous energy lighted her eyes and colored her cheeks, making her even more becoming.

Something about the way her gown fit her so perfectly struck him. It was more than the way it embraced her slender frame — it suited her in every possible way, from the rich red color to the very flow of it. The effect was stunning. It was as if she belonged in this place, in those clothes, among these people.

He gulped hard. His aim in being here was, he realized, solely to take her away from all this and return her to Spitalfields.

God, this isn't what you have for her, is it? The words became almost a plea as he faced the reality that she might eventually be lost to him, absorbed into the world of opulence she seemed to fit so well. *Help me convince her, Lord. Help me take her away from here before she's too attached to leave. Help me reach the bottom of what is keeping her here.*

He'd already failed once, and even when she had not come to the end of the lane, he couldn't bring himself to leave her alone in this place. Something was not right. Another man might have been offended into leaving, but Sully knew her. It hadn't been a rejection but a sign of trouble. Danger.

He watched her glide away, and it felt like

gripping a silky material as it slipped through his fingers. He'd always known she was unusually beautiful — inside and out — and it delighted his soul to see her this way, with her true beauty revealed. Except that now everyone else could see it too.

"Here's the sensation of the night."

A slap on his shoulder sent him stumbling forward. Sully turned to see the clean-shaven solicitor behind him, grinning as if they were old chums.

"You're a fine fiddler, and I'm delighted to give you this opportunity. Of course, you'll focus on the more conventional songs, rather than the tunes you'd sing by the docks. You've brought your instrument, I hope."

"That I have. Hasn't left me sight the whole evening."

The man's eyelid twitched, but his grin remained. "Good, good. By the by, perhaps we'll have you avoid speaking. You'll be introduced, then you can play. We'll keep it a little secret between us gents that you're Irish, shall we? People in rural areas are so tied to the way things are that they don't appreciate new and fresh people the way we do in London."

Sully said nothing, unwilling to agree with the man's preposterous explanation. How anyone was fooled by this snakeskin was beyond him, but it was certainly not to his advantage to anger the man. At least, not yet. He needed to find out first what Prendergast was up to.

"So we're agreed then, yes? No speaking, just performing."

Sully raised his eyebrows. "I suppose I can abide by that." There were many possibilities within those parameters, after all.

Prendergast's long lips curved up at the ends. "Good lad. Now, listen for the introduction and be ready to perform."

Sully ducked his head to hide the irrepressible grin taking over his face. Ah yes, he'd be ready, and he'd definitely perform.

13

There's beauty in what's real, but we miss it as long as we strive to be something else.

~ Diary of a Substitute Countess

I avoided Sully. The mere sight of him punctured my poise and deflated me to reality, especially if his hazel gaze bore into mine with that knowing look.

Summoning the dramatic-poetry reading voice, I stood before the gathered guests and met their gazes with a smile. Prendergast had disappeared for the moment, which made this the perfect time to launch my musician's performance. "I'm honored to have you all in my — at Rothburne. It's been a true pleasure to be among you tonight." The words came forth with surprising ease, which strengthened my courage. I took another breath. "I look forward to a happy time at the abbey, however long my stay may be. I hope you will enjoy the music prepared for you tonight and find amusement in its uniqueness."

I hadn't any notion of what he would play, but I knew only one thing — *unique* would describe it.

I spun toward the rows of chairs to find my seat, but my traitorous peripheral vision caught sight of Sully's perfectly cut form striding toward the front, fiddle tucked under his arm as if it were a part of him. A shiny strip of satin traveled down the side of his trousers, making him look taller and leaner and even more perfect. The fiddle had been polished to a high sheen I'd never seen before, but just like its owner, underneath the glow of polish resided the same well-worn, ever-faithful, slightly dented piece from Spitalfields.

I darted my gaze about the room and away from him, but I was trembling by the time I reached my seat in the first row and perched there. The underlayers absorbed the slight quiver of my legs, but I had to clasp my hands in the folds of my skirt to keep them still. I forced poise into my body and breathed in and out, returning to the calm I was learning to don like a gossamer cloak. I recalled the words of the woman from earlier — a presence, a sort of controlled grace that might part the waters.

An expectant hush fell over the crowd as the impossibly handsome man I loved stood before us, fitted his instrument snug against his collarbone, and inclined his head toward it, cradling the beloved fiddle with his face. If it had been lodged against his shoulder, it would mean we'd hear a litany of lively Irish folk songs, but when he tucked it this way against the curve of his solid jaw, I knew he was about to let his heart speak. I looked away out of sheer necessity.

Voices softened and faded away until there was silence. Then the lone voice of the fiddle like smooth velvet, achingly familiar, spilled over the room with more power than even Victor Prendergast and all his charm, moving us all to hushed awe.

My chest tightened. The first low, melodic notes pulled my gaze involuntarily to him and I could not look away. Clutching the edge of my chair, I soaked in the sight of him. How different he looked framed by the sleek black clothing, his dark hair neatly trimmed and combed away from his face. Yet all those alterations couldn't disguise the unquenchable soul of the man that radiated through his face as he spoke so vividly through his instrument.

Not a soul moved, no chair creaked

against the floor. Every head was inclined to soak up the music that had for years been as much a part of my life as air. Hearing it in close range again reminded me of the great lack it had left in my life when I'd been without it — and without the man creating it. My eyes fluttered closed to absorb the impact of his song.

As the performance swept on, I sank back against the layers of bustle, hoping I was not crushing them beyond repair, and allowed the sound of his fiddle to wrap itself around me as his arms could not. I clutched my gloved hands in my lap and reveled in the music as it swelled to a finale and faded. When the silence lingered, I looked up and found his purposeful hazel eyes on me, closing the distance between us and caressing me in that glance. Drawing a single red flower from a nearby stand, he strode to me, his footsteps the only sound in the room. He paused before me with a bow and extended the flower. "For the lady of the house."

I forced a gulp, unable to even utter my thanks, and then he lifted his fiddle and began playing for me, a mere two feet from the hem of my skirt. Little gasps of surprise lifted from the people around me as he wove words into the music. The soulful tone carried only a hint of his Irish lilt, but the lovely words smoothed the song into a thing of beauty.

"The fair lass Adora always gazed at the
   sky,
For she was a girl full of dreams.
The lad tried to wake her, but he couldn't
   make her
end her magnificent schemes.
She then made him try to reach his hand
   high
And catch at the starry gleam.
While he tried to ground her, she taught
   him to fly,
And she woke him up to a dream.
Aye, she woke him up to a dream."

I looked away, unable to bear his nearness along with the heartfelt words of our love story, but his ballad continued with verses and my gaze edged up toward him again.

"Unable to give more to this spirit so free,
With youthful bravado he set out to sea;
He'd gain the rich bounty to lay at her
   feet,
But fate the hard mistress is not always
   sweet.

"He shared not his feelings before he
    depart,
How the lively young spirit had stolen his
    heart;
The soul can behold that which words
    can't describe,
And his saw more clearly what resided
    inside.

"So anxious was he to return to his lass,
That he dare not let another day pass
with them torn asunder, and him left to
    wonder
if she returned his affection at last."

I ripped my gaze away as the fiddle took
over, and I looked to Victor Prendergast
who had just come back in the side door
like a thundercloud about to torrent onto
someone. Sully, from the looks of it. I
turned back to the man who sang to me
with a gaze both tender and intense. His
bow swept over the strings of his fiddle, the
music catching my heart up like a gentle
whirlwind and spinning it around, and he
sang the finale to me as if we were alone
before the fire in my flat.

"But her uplifted spirit drew fate's friendly
    smile,

It dressed her in beauty and wealth all
   the while;
When again he beheld her, her beauty
   set free,
He thought, I have nothing to offer but
   me.
Aye, I've nothing to offer but me."

He held the final note in a long, tender glide of his bow over the strings, letting the song ripple out over the audience and shudder through my being. Then in the awed silence, he took my hand, closing his familiar fingers over mine with the warmth I knew and loved, and bowed over them. I closed my eyes. My heart pounded in my ears, making everything else seem far away.

Applause shattered the moment, and when he released my hand, I forced myself back into the present and clapped. Sully straightened. A steady look passed between Sully and Prendergast, who watched from the fringes with a dangerous light in his face. Still, the words of his song echoed through my heart, striking chords of tenderness along with the fear of loss. The final line of that powerful song lodged itself in my mind.

Prendergast closed the distance between himself and the musician in a few long strides amid the applause and grabbed Sully's hand, pumping it as he guided him away. They vanished together through the service door beside my chair.

"You've forgotten our agreement, Mr. Mc-Kenna." Prendergast's terse whisper carried over to my waiting ears from the other room as the guests rose and the low hum of voices began.

"I did not." Sully's candid words rang a tad louder than Prendergast's. "I abided by every letter of me word. I never spoke more than the proper introduction."

"What do you call what you just did?"

"Singing."

I coughed into my gloved hand and rose to cover my giggles. When I stood, my black-garbed lady's maid appeared from nowhere and fluffed the compressed layers of fabric on which I'd sat, smoothing them to perfection. Then she stepped close and spoke into my ear. "The earl's cousin is asking after you."

"Mr. Scatchard?" A moment of weakness softened my knees, but I forced myself to recover. "Thank you, Simone. I'll find him."

I looked about the room for him and instead saw a tall, slender woman moving toward me who must have once been given the same advice about gliding through

176

water, for she did so masterfully. This was who they should have chosen to be the countess. I might resemble Lady Enderly in features and coloring, but this woman possessed her exact radiance and composure. An invisible force pulled her entire body, giving it the control and poise I only dreamed of achieving. *Please, don't come this way.* Her beauty unsettled me as effectively as it must draw others, much like Lady Enderly's was said to do. How could I hope to maintain a shred of dignity in this woman's presence?

But approach she did, with a stunning smile that made mine seem weak. "What a surprise you had for us this evening, Lady Enderly." She moved like a feline, and I wondered if she also possessed the animal's cunning and slyness. To my surprise, her face opened into a becoming expression of welcome as she spoke, yet I couldn't decide if I liked her or not. "A wonderful hidden gem that turned out to be far more original than any other lady dared present to her guests. You are as impressive as they've said."

A genuine grin spread over my face. "You flatter me. How wonderful to hear that you enjoyed the performance." But her words had been far more than kind — they had been validating. Her final sentence gave me a distinct hope that I'd succeeded this night, that I'd stepped into my role and played it well. "I'm so glad you could come, Lady . . ." I struggled to remember her name in the jumble of titles that had swarmed my brain over the last few hours.

Her eyes sparkled. "Don't concern yourself with remembering every name you hear tonight." She extended one gloved hand, and I took it, my anxiety melting away like frost in the presence of glorious sunshine. "Lady Luvenia Remington, living quite against her will in Littenden Manor just along the way to the west, past your walled garden and over the fields."

I raised my eyebrows, amused at her words. "Against your will?"

"I was wooed away from my moors twenty-one years ago by a dashing young man who promised me a world of flowers if I married him, and the closest thing I've found is your lovely estate with the wildflower gardens. The Rothburne grounds have always been a haven for my blossom-starved heart, but the changes you've wrought here left me breathless as we rode up the lane. They were a wonderful introduction to the woman who arranged them so beautifully, and I've found the inside of the abbey has impressed me even more."

"I am delighted you enjoy the gardens so."
I felt my aching shoulders ease down.

"Your cousin has been wonderfully accommodating in sharing some of Rothburne's bounty with my gardener, and I've taken advantage of the offer every chance I can."

I laughed, a little bubble of freedom as my insecurities loosened their grip on me. "You've met the earl's cousin? And you do not hate me?"

The woman laughed, a pure and delightful sound that firmly connected us. "I never give up an opportunity to pass judgment, and I'll not let that Philip Scatchard do it for me. It's one of the few pleasures left to me in life."

Oh, how I enjoyed this woman. Her presence drew me, making me wish for more of her. I would learn from her, studying the way she moved and spoke and even laughed. Everything about her declared her highborn and accomplished, yet her nature was warm and inviting too. The very combination of everything I'd ever wanted to be in life was embodied in this woman who was, thankfully, my neighbor.

"How can you stand to be away from such a stunning estate? Surely your London home does not hold this much appeal."

"It's travel that excites my heart." The answer slipped out as readily as if it were true and shocked me. It was, in fact, the first time I had answered as the countess rather than myself. I pressed on despite the gnawing pangs of deceit. "I have such a yearning for adventure and no one place holds my interest for long."

"Were you planning to introduce me as well, lovey, or just leave me in the corner?" A jovial man with silvered temples appeared beside Lady Remington, drawing a special grin from her as if they possessed a shared secret.

She turned to him. "Ah, here you are. And now, Lady Enderly, you'll see what made me leave my moors."

He stepped forward with a nod, his animated features saying much even before he spoke. "Felix Remington, my lady. A pleasure to welcome you to our little corner of the world for the season. We hope to see much more of you."

I couldn't help but fall under the charm of this pair — as individuals and even more so as a duo. "I'm fortunate to have such fine neighbors."

Soon we were laughing together, and the natural camaraderie made me feel so normal. Connected.

"Where have you been lately? I heard you've been to India."

The names of all countries flew from my mind. "Umm . . . Abington." I'd seen it listed at the train station when we boarded.

The man's eyebrows rose. "South of Oxford? How exotic."

I shrugged, heat pouring up my neck and tickling my scalp. "Certainly a whole other world from my usual."

"Of course." He murmured the reply, studying me. "I'm surprised your little reception has not drawn old Wells into attending. I assume he was invited."

I smiled to cover the spike of panic his words elicited in me. Who was old Wells? I should know this and so many other things. "Perhaps he was. I would have to check my guest list to be sure." This conversation was edging toward thin ice, and it seemed inevitable that I'd eventually fall through.

"I much preferred the days old Wells owned this place. He came around a lot more than the earl. It's a shame Wells didn't simply keep it himself."

Wells. Prendergast had mentioned something about an uncle who had gifted the estate to the earl, and that must be him. I slid that knowledge into my mind. Wells, the great former owner of the abbey. Old Wells. This must also be the man Bradford mentioned who had loved the gardens. I smiled as the pieces came together and I cemented them in place in my mind.

"Darling, you mustn't speak so of the earl, especially in front of Lady Enderly. You've enjoyed his company on many occasions too."

"He isn't the jolly sort old Wells was, though. I'm certain Lady Enderly is well aware of how surly a man the earl is. His reputation in the House of Lords is widespread. No amendment that works itself into that man's head is ignored in the House. He wields his words like a sword until they find their mark."

"He would show more kindness to Lady Enderly than he would to a room of government men, of course."

Guardian. The earl must be her guardian. I shivered at the thought, for he sounded very far from a gentle protector.

"Either way, I'm honored to make your acquaintance, Lady Enderly. I had hoped to find a reputable lady living in this abbey, but I've found one better — a possible friend." She touched my arm before moving on, and I smiled, sinking deeper into the role. I had a foothold on this task, it seemed.

But as I turned with a gratified sigh, I felt a pair of knowing eyes on me. I turned this way and that to find them until I locked gazes with a man whose heavy-lidded countenance struck me as only slightly familiar — and not from my current life at Rothburne. I should know him. His gaze narrowed at me now across the salon, as if trying to place me but not quite able. I turned my head to hide my face and felt him studying the back of my exposed shoulders, the curls tickling the back of my neck.

I looked back and he shifted, as if intending to come and speak with me, and I moved with purpose toward Cousin Philip, trading one lion's den for another.

14

Making a stunning impression is often as simple as not caring if you do.
~ Diary of a Substitute Countess

"Sociable as ever, I see." I approached Philip, who was brooding near the far wall and swirling liquid in a cup. Drinks were a regular extension of his hand, it seemed, for I seldom saw him without one.

"Why be sociable with people I dislike?"

"Yet you requested *my* presence just now. I find you hard to take seriously."

"Shall I tell you what I find you?"

"I am sure you will, with or without my permission." Especially with a tongue loosened by drink.

"All right, then." He frowned. "I find you ridiculously extravagant. That's the matter I wished to discuss with you. Vulgar as it is to discuss money at a time like this, I find it my duty as your estate manager to warn you of such a misstep before your lavish expenditures harm the entire estate and the people living here."

"There's nothing lavish about my spending habits, of that I assure you."

"You are foolish to lie to me, Countess. The one privilege of being on par with the servants in this house is that they talk to me, and when I returned for this" — he waved his glass around the room — "this monstrosity of flattery, which I was promised would be nothing of the sort, they've told me of the extensive renovations you've been undertaking in my absence. I call that grossly extravagant, which is what you are. I can see with my own eyes all the new furniture and draperies about the place tonight. And don't forget, as the abbey's manager I'll also see the notes for everything concerning this place when I settle the accounts."

"Actually, you will not." I glared at him. "The only cost for all my renovations is time and effort, including my own. We have pulled furniture and drapes from the attic, and I had them refreshed by the staff for use in the main rooms. Did the wonderfully informative servants also tell you that?"

His frown deepened. "Surely you do not mean that you have spent *nothing*."

"You may verify my claims with the lack of notes you'll find in the study. Extravagant I am not."

His rare silence, the look of shock on his face, lightened my heart. In this moment, at least, I had won.

I smiled. "A word of wisdom for you, Cousin, from Wilkie Collins. 'No sensible man engages, unprepared, in a fencing match of words with a woman.' I suggest you come armed next time with the facts and leave off with the assumptions. They only weigh you down in battle."

He narrowed his eyes. "Self-important. That's my second word for you. You flit about with your nose in the air, swishing your gowns as if you were a royal, speaking only to high-class guests like the Remingtons. Far be it from you to socialize with common people like your musician or even thank him for his performance. Lavish or thrifty, you are full of yourself and deserve to be taken down a notch . . . or ten." He spat out the final words as if they left a bitter taste and glared at me for a response.

But I had none. Not this time. I'd have to reveal far more than I should to convey the absolute absurdity of his claim against me. Self-important — me? The woman who was tasting extravagance for the first time and barely holding together her thin shreds of poise? I had a great many flaws and weaknesses, more than he even knew, but self-important was the furthest thing from what I was. With my heart fluttering like butterfly wings to match the feeling in my stomach, I merely lowered my voice and said, "If only you knew how wrong you were."

Lifting my skirt, I pivoted and swept away from his dark presence before it suffocated me. I tried to move about among the guests with the same lighthearted grace I'd had moments before, but every smile and laugh was false. I felt Cousin Philip's glare upon my back no matter where I turned. Why did I let him unsettle me so?

A light touch on my arm made me turn, smile ready to bestow on the guest. When I glimpsed the overdressed woman grinning at me, I froze. Recognition came too late to retreat.

"How kind of you to invite me, Lady Enderly. What a happy surprise to find you alone at last." She fumbled two quick curtsies, which I answered with a nod, watching her. Mr. John Reese Stockton — that was the name of the man who had observed me with such interest from across the room, and this charming confection was his wife.

"I hope you are enjoying the evening." I lowered my voice, hoping she would not recognize it.

"Oh, but of course! How could a body do less, with such a sumptuous spread?"

As we passed light conversation back and forth, I looked over this plump face for the second time in my life, clearly remembering the first. It had been just outside her grand townhouse in Chelsea, and I had been called a thief. Her housekeeper had screeched at me as I'd made off with a sack of what I believed to be castoffs laid out for the rag and bone man. The sound had startled me into running, and her servants gave chase until they caught me. She'd run after me with a broom as if I were a rat, and her underhousemaid called the constable to have me arrested.

It had been my one and only night in jail, ended abruptly when an anonymous donor, whom I'd always known to be Sully, had paid my fee and had me released. I'd left the prison, but its stench had marred me. It had chiseled another mark into the shape of my young identity and made me realize exactly what I was — and what I was not.

". . . So I told Lord Wellington to call on the lady and settle the whole matter without delay. Such a foolish thing it was."

My mind surfaced to the woman's endless rambling, bringing me back to the present. How could she not know me? Had she not given chase, then faced me in court with pointed finger? Was I truly that unmemorable, or . . . When she paused, I looked up, my head still swimming in foggy thoughts.

She frowned. "Lady Enderly?"

"Hmm?" At my instinctive reply, an odd sensation swept over me. I answered to her name more naturally than my own. Somehow it both delighted and bothered me.

"Perhaps I should fetch you a drink. Am I tiring you?"

I looked at this woman who had known Ragna yet sat here and conversed with me freely, seeing no trace of that girl in me.

She prompted me by repeating her question. "Am I tiring you, my lady?"

I smiled, forcing my mind to remain in the present moment. "No, of course not. I always grow tired in the evening. A product of all my traveling. My mind never knows whether it is in India, France, or England." Misery swept over me at the blatant untruth, and my instinctual urge to turn in silent prayer to God was stopped short by guilt. There was no question now, I was fully dishonest and sinking further into it. I had no business approaching God.

189

The woman laughed more than necessary. "You've no idea how pleased I am to become acquainted with you. A lady such as yourself seldom has time for the likes of me. I know we shall become friends, though. I'm certain we have a great deal in common. We both have such a taste for fine things." She ran one chubby finger along the oiled wood of a settee back.

She was groveling. Flattering me. This woman who had treated me as less than a human would now kiss my fingertips and sing my praises in the same breath if I asked it of her.

"We're only on holiday here for a brief time to see my sister in Chaffcombe, but I'd be honored to renew our acquaintance a time or two before we return to town."

I offered a benign smile. "I shall have to see what my schedule will allow."

The feel of my gown as I moved away solidified it — nothing of Ragna remained. I had succeeded in removing my old identity, thoroughly becoming someone else. And the victory left me feeling odd. Guilty. Nervous.

Her husband's eyes narrowed at me now from across the salon, as if trying to place me but not quite able. I turned my head to hide my face.

I'd entered into an enchanting easy conversation with Lady Butte, when a familiar voice spoke behind me. "Something sweet for your evening, my lady?" I spun to find Sully offering a solemn bow, extending a tray of truffles. The sight of him both rattled and comforted me, my troubled thoughts calming for the moment.

I turned to the footman. "Sully." Speaking his name aloud brought a rush of tender memories. I turned my gaze away, hoping my guest had not caught my mistake. "Thank you, Mr. McKenna. You should not be serving tonight. You are the musician."

"I'm the footman, and I'll act like it. Nothing shameful about being who you are."

I looked helplessly up at him. "That depends on who you are." Never again did I want to be thrown out into the alley and struggling to salvage the castoffs of other women. What a dismal life I'd had then! Looking into Sully's frank, open face, I wanted to toss aside this façade that haunted my conscience, yet I saw no way to do it and still hold on to this version of myself I was coming to enjoy a great deal. "Your song —"

"I must congratulate you on a fine performance tonight, young man. You have a splendid musical talent." The gray-haired woman beside me inserted herself into our conversation, which she could not possibly understand.

"Thank you." He nodded at Lady Butte, then looked back at me. "I hope my musical performance also pleased you, my lady." His dark eyes asked a question beyond his spoken words.

"It was magnificent." I said each word with marked feeling, low and careful.

His eyes softened. "I'm glad you liked it."

Prendergast appeared behind him, eager to separate us. "Ah, here's our rogue performer. You're a fine musician, and I'm certain Lady Enderly appreciates your contribution to her reception tonight. Now if you'll kindly excuse —"

"I was just telling him as much." My voice came out quiet yet strong. "In fact, the only fault I can find with it is that it ends too abruptly. Surely there were more verses to your song. One might wonder if he ever gave up on the girl in the story, or if he still loved her."

Sully lifted a crooked grin to me. "One might, eh? I suppose Mr. Prendergast here should have let me finish then." He gave a brief bow. "It was my pleasure to play for you, my lady."

I turned, and that terrible Mr. Stockton hovered like a shadow by the door, cradling a glass in his large hand. His stare was fixed and sure, yet he said not a word to me, even when he departed. Not a word of thanks or parting pleasantries.

When the last of the guests swept toward the door, the tall clock in the hall bonged a single time to mark the half hour. Only then was I overcome with the foolishness of my missed opportunity. I hadn't discovered a single thing about Lady Enderly that night. So consumed had I been with the guests and gowns that I had not given a single thought to learning more about the secrets this woman held. I had been distracted from my purpose — no, charmed away from it. I'd experienced an intoxicating, addictive sense of admiration among these guests, in these garments, and it came so near to touching the ache in me that all else had been forgotten as I'd striven to grasp the remedy. Now that the salon had emptied and weariness overcame me, regret settled firmly inside.

I moved out into the hall, ready to quit the night, and nearly collided with a dark-suited gent. I stumbled back and his solid arms caught me and pulled me upright again. Victor Prendergast looked down at me with eyes that sparkled in the shadows. "Like Cinderella, your grace ends at the stroke of midnight, it seems."

I straightened, but he remained close in the dark. "You cannot expect me to see you in this dim hall, sir."

He leaned near enough for me to smell brandy on his breath. It was a fresher, cleaner scent than the sticky alcohol consumed in Spitalfields, with a hint of mintiness, but I knew it all the same. I leaned away, but his hold tightened, his look intensifying. "You must learn to see yourself as everyone's superior if you expect everyone else to. Call me Victor."

"Very well then, Victor." My voice, low and smooth, held no trace of the fear that reverberated through my head. The words *Get away from him* screamed through my mind, followed by the quieter *Get away from here.* Yet every Spitalfields girl knew not to run when pursued. I'd have to bide my time, wait for the right moment to escape. If only I'd managed to leave with Sully that first night. Slowly, with remarkable composure, I pulled my gloved hand out of Victor's grasp, but he caught it again and pulled it close, inspecting my fingers with eerie fascination.

It's the drink, I reminded myself. Yet that

knowledge didn't ease the tremor that coursed through me at his forceful nearness. Watching my face, he turned my hand and kissed my open palm. Despite the glove separating my skin from his lips, I felt as if I'd been touched by a snake.

He swept back a step to look at the whole of me, and I smiled with relief at the cool air between us.

"You approve of the gown, I hope," he said. "I knew it would suit you. It made quite an impression on your guests tonight. One in particular." His gaze lingered on my face. "Remember when I told you of the spell you'd cast over men, the power you could wield? I'm afraid I'm one of your victims." His gaze lingered on my exposed shoulder, then swept back up. "Who would have guessed that a scrawny rag woman could wield such power?"

I felt my face heat, which made him grin further. Thankfully he said nothing more, and after another lingering moment he took himself away. When he had shifted out of my vision, I saw another dark-clad figure much farther down the hall, blatantly watching the entire display from a distance.

Sully?

The shadowed man continued to stare, and it was only when he turned and candlelight flicked over his scowl that I recognized Cousin Philip. I suppose it wasn't customary for a countess to have a liaison with a mere solicitor, which is what that moment must have appeared to be.

If only he knew. Seeing Mr. Stockton and his wife that night had threatened my façade, but it had also been a mirror reflecting reality — I was Ragna the rag woman playing at being a lady, dressing up in her clothing. The secret I kept was nothing close to what Philip believed.

The way he stalked out, however, made me feel as if I'd found that thin ice and fallen through.

15

I'm not sure which I fear more — failing to fit into this new role or losing myself in it completely.

~ Diary of a Substitute Countess

I slipped the papers back into Philip's desk drawer and slid it closed. Last night's festivities had left Victor indisposed this morning and me with the freedom to poke about. Now I wished I hadn't. I'd only been trying to distract myself from Sully, purging the lines of his song from my mind, but this discovery had not brought me relief from my growing worry. Letter after letter to Philip Scatchard mentioned the countess's benevolent trips abroad and vast generosity to those in need. Yet the private accounts brought over from the London house showed only lavish spending in town during that time and plenty of gambling at the derby. Expensive gowns and hats, gloves and shoes comprised the rest of the notes. The woman was not a victim but a liar — an utter fraud.

Spread out over the top of the desk were Bradford's findings on the repairs needed for those inner rooms, and the large numbers summed up on the right side of the sheets made me cringe. This would be no easy task.

I slipped back out to the abandoned monastic library to see for myself the rotting window joists and splintering rafter beams but instead found myself standing before that gold-framed painting, wondering at the carefree tilt to the real Lady Enderly's head, the enchanting laughter in her face. How could one so beautiful also be so self-serving, so false? Glimpsing those secret inner parts of her life chilled me as much as these abandoned rooms at the core of her house. How could she bear to carry on such a false existence?

The cold fingers of my conscience tightened around me, turning my condemnation back upon myself, the mirror image of this woman in many ways. Yet my situation was different, I argued. I had been hemmed into this.

And I have not? her laughing eyes seemed to ask.

Slipping back out of these rooms that demanded money not mine to spend and immediate decisions I could not rightfully make, I tied a straw hat on my head and stepped through the front doors to walk in the gardens and clear my head.

"Those rooms should be repaired," I had told Prendergast before the soiree. "I've no idea where to begin. You must tell me what I'm allowed to do."

"Must you begin at all?" He had folded his arms after placing the dewy glass on a little table, and his words admittedly brought me relief. "Forcing yourself into tasks at which you aren't comfortable will be a waste, for you'll produce nothing but mediocrity and the world has far too much of that. Fly like a lightning bug to whatever light draws you and linger there. That, my dear, is how you find your truest self."

Rothburne was beautiful on the outside and even in the front entertaining rooms, charming visitors from the first glance, but something very different resided deeper inside. Close it up and keep it from view, Victor had said, but anything left to neglect would eventually fall to ruin. Perhaps he had given Lady Enderly the same advice. Close up the uncomfortable parts of your life, hide them from view. Go on to the things that make you happy.

What ruin had she now come to?

I shivered and turned in time to see movement that jolted me from my thoughts. The edge of a dark skirt fluttered around the corner of a hedge, beckoning to my curious spirit.

Countess?

I hurried along the path framed by tall box bushes toward the sound of trickling water, slowing to turn this way and that whenever I glimpsed the frock ahead.

Finally the path broadened and spilled down over a set of stone steps, opening out into a vast expanse of wildflowers and a sparkling pond. At the far end stood a magnificent willow, bending down to dip its finger-leaves into the water. There among the natural beauty stood a lone woman in a fluttering dress of deep purple which contrasted with the grass that it seemed she'd been placed there on purpose to enhance the exquisite mix of colors before me.

I strode toward her, and when I drew near, she spun.

Shock paled her features at the sight of me, long eyelashes fluttering over lightly aged cheeks. "Oh, my lady. We meet again." Lady Remington smiled and met my gaze with sparkling blue sapphire eyes.

Her self-assured poise spoke of her station in life almost as clearly as the lush day gown she carried on her elegant frame, and the streaks of lightness in her honey-colored hair did nothing to diminish her timeless beauty.

"I should offer you my sincerest apologies for trespassing, but instead I believe I'll throw myself upon your mercy and claim a kinship of the heart." Her words were like the waters of a cool stream, sparkling and poetic, yet carried forward with an unstoppable strength until they reached their conclusion. "I've developed the terrible habit of wandering in your gardens at will when we visit our Havard estate, and I find it a practice impossible to end, even now that its mistress has returned. Mr. Scatchard has always been gracious in indulging me with this forwardness."

"Has he, now?"

Her voice softened. "Be merciful toward Philip Scatchard, my lady. He loves Rothburne so. We all do, but none so much as he. You've no idea the attachment he has to this place."

I sighed, releasing my tension. "It is a delightful little piece of Eden, is it not? You're welcome anytime."

"I suppose it's audacious of me to have

expected that from you, isn't it?" She smiled, and her lightness of spirit lightened mine as well. "Everything I've heard of you makes me feel we could be sisters. I cannot wait to hear your opinions on Parliament's new property act and everything else blossoming out for us these days."

I blanched, tongue frozen to the roof of my mouth. My life before Rothburne had been absorbed by the immediate needs of the day. Survival. I had not indulged in a newspaper, and I knew nothing of political movements. Though now with a relative in the House of Lords, I should.

Victor Prendergast should have realized this too. With all the parts of me he'd perfected for this role, he'd utterly neglected my brain.

"Oh, I know it isn't becoming of ladies to discuss such things, but I've heard rumors of your opinions on different matters and I know you pay attention to these things as much as I do. We mustn't be afraid to share our minds with one another at least. We can sharpen and improve ourselves together so we're even more well-spoken than the men."

I cleared my throat. "Speaking of improvements, would you like to see the rest of the abbey? I'm making changes and I'd love your keen eye on the place."

My little pivot had been forced and awkward, but she brightened, those lovely eyes widening for a brief moment. "A tour of Rothburne? It would be the delight of my day."

She strode with me across the yard, then lifted her skirts to climb the steps off the patio and enter the great drawing room. A hushed awe fell over her as soon as we stepped into the first space that had received my touch, and it gratified me. Little white cherub statues greeted us from recessed shelves, and the floor gleamed with polish, the faint lemon scent still pleasantly noticeable. "I hardly recognized the abbey. Who knew this old place could look so splendid, and that the staff had such immense hidden talents. I assume you did not hire out any of this work."

"The staff have been very gracious in helping me." Through another passageway we entered the abbot's wing, which had seen most of my work. Empty rooms had been graced with newly restored furniture and décor, breaking up their emptiness. A long refractory table ran down the center of one grand room, prepared to host a large gathering of men discussing business matters.

I told her what I knew of each room's history as we went, glad I'd listened to the servants as we'd worked on these spaces. "When the estate was an abbey, this was the abbot's hall where they took meals. I haven't yet decided what I'll do with it, so for now we've left it sparse and practical."

"It's magnificent." She paused inside the doors and spun to take it in, her comely cheeks flushed with the impact of it all. "What about a few small walnut tables with light-colored vases on them and perhaps a few tapestries draped between the windows to give a person something to look at? It needs a gold chandelier centered over the table too." She walked to the giant fireplace and ran her hand along the carvings up the side. "You mustn't touch any of this. It adds such charm. My, you have such a fine home. It's as elegant as its mistress."

I watched her graceful movements wistfully. "I do hope you'll lend me your touch and help me improve even more."

She spun, her boot squeaking on the shiny floor, and beamed a playful smile toward me. "Do you refer to the house or yourself?"

I blinked in shock, for she'd voiced what I hadn't the courage to ask. I wanted nothing more than to study this woman and attempt to emulate the charm and grace she naturally exuded. "Both?" I offered a hopeful little smile.

She released a mirthful laugh, throwing out her gloved hands and striding toward me to take me by the shoulders. "Neither one needs more than a bit of gentle polish to shine, and I'd be delighted to help." She smiled and I exhaled, relaxing in her presence. "The first step with this house is to simply enhance what is already there, learning its tone and nature and adding only what fits it." She paused and smiled at me, clasping her hands in front of her skirt. "And the same is true of you. The first secret about beauty is unearthing more of who you already are and enhancing it."

I cringed inside.

We moved into the study, a great square space with a new, ornately designed floor that had been the abbot's lodging quarters. Lady Remington paused to admire an ivory statuette on a stand and a tall vase. "This room needs a masculine touch with all this exposed wood and heavy designs. Maybe red drapes and a few dark wood pieces."

"That would suit it perfectly."

She strode farther, glancing around. "Will you host a harvest soiree? Oh, please tell me you will. And do let me help you plan it. I know everyone about the area and what they'll expect." She sidled across the room to me with a cunning grin. "That way you can create something that is completely the opposite of that."

I smiled, already intrigued by the concept. She spun in the open room like a delighted girl, her arms spread wide. It made me smile.

That's when I saw it, and my heart slammed in my chest. A hasty notation was scrawled on the stationery lying on my little writing desk in the hand I knew so well.

CD:MHC 16

Earlier this morning, unable to bear the torment any longer, I had left Jane Austen's *Pride and Prejudice* open on my desk when I happened upon a line spoken by Elizabeth Bennet near the end that resonated so perfectly with my angst. "I am half agony, half hope. Tell me not that I am too late, that such precious feelings are gone for ever." I left a pen on the book pointing at the line and rang the service bell. When I saw Sully coming to answer my summons from down the hall, I left a small flower on the open pages as well, so he'd be sure to know my intentions and slipped from the room. His song at the reception had lodged in my heart.

I had tried to recall his earlier message, but I remembered nothing in it of his feelings — only assurances that he would remain. Fear had crept in that perhaps, even if we escaped this place, the experience had dried up the well of his love for me. So I had taken my question one step further this time and addressed the unspoken feelings we had not mentioned since his return. I'd begun to believe I'd imagined the ardent phrases in his letters.

At last it was here — the answer I craved like food after a fast. My cheeks burned with the awareness of those ink marks embedded on paper and soon on my mind, for I could not stop staring at them.

"Ah, look at this." I strode to the desk and snatched up the dinner menu left beside the message. "Cook wished to have me review the menu for tonight and I've neglected it." With a forced smile, I waved her on. "You wander ahead and continue your assessment. I'll find you presently."

Her eyes sparkled. "I won't promise to keep out of trouble. I've so longed to explore this abbey and I cannot contain my curiosity."

As soon as she swept out of the room, I stared at the bookshelves, looking through the alphabet until I reached Charles Dickens, for the "CD" portion of the note, and looked for the correct title. What was MHC?

I studied each title, but nothing matched. I scanned the room desperately, heart pounding, until my gaze landed on a messy stack of *Master Humphrey's Clock,* Dickens's weekly periodical, fanned out on a little side table. I snatched up the skinny volume on top and thumbed to page 16 to find the underlined message. "To conceal anything from those to whom I am attached, is not in my nature. I can never close my lips where I have opened my heart."

A second reference scrawled on a torn corner of paper lay like a bookmark between the pages, and it read *CD:GE 258. Great Expectations.* I hurried over, reached for it, and flipped to the page on the little note. My eyes drank in the underlined words as soon as my trembling finger turned to the right ones. "Once for all; I knew to my sorrow, often and often, if not always, that I loved her against reason, against promise, against peace, against hope, against happiness, against all discouragement that could be."

I drank in those words with a meek little sob, reading them over and over and hearing them in Sully's voice. I bowed my head over that book and allowed waves of relief and longing to pour over me. If only we could be together now, walk through this with one another. Yet to leave with him now meant to risk losing him forever.

Abandoning my find, I bolted through the hall into the depths of the house in search of my guest. At the center, elegant Lady Remington stood framed in the double doors of the old decrepit chapel that smelled of trapped moisture and decay, a backdrop of chaos just beyond her. Of all the places for her to be — I'd never intended these rooms as part of the tour. I hastened over and tried to guide her away, but she strode farther into the room as if drawn as thoroughly as I was repelled. "What is this? It seems not every part of the abbey is glorious after all."

"We've not begun to work on these rooms yet, and —"

"Evidently not." She moved like an unstoppable current into the space, debris crunching under her feet and dust swishing around her skirts as she walked. "You'd never believe this existed in the same house as those lavish front rooms and the becoming garden outside. So many hidden secrets no one would guess from a first glance."

I followed, determined to draw her away before she saw the painting in the old library, but she stood in the center of the room as a sliver of daylight pierced the dimness where a curtain sagged away from its rod. I took her arm as if we were old chums, but she glided forward toward the library doors, pondering the great rooms. "A house pretending to be what it is not. How very human."

My neck heated, the warmth stretching narrow fingers up to my cheeks. I swallowed hard as we crossed into the library and lifted my reluctant gaze to the now-uncovered portrait of Lady Enderly looming over us from her perch on the wall. There she was, posed on a stone portico in that vivid red dress, shielded by a parasol with red flowers tucked in her hair. Her head was tipped back playfully as if she was amused by her portraitist and about to laugh. Her face drew me, somewhat against my will, and I stared at it.

Sully's words echoed through the chambers of my heart, settling like lead inside. *Rest? There's something more to this cockamamy scheme and I think you know it.* "I should ring for tea. It must be —"

She gasped when she spotted the portrait and stared at it for endless moments. Thousands of possible reactions spun through my head as I waited for what she'd say. I could explain it away. Yes, I would. Whatever she said, I'd combat it with a few carefully chosen —

"How different you looked then. So untroubled and beautifully innocent."

I gulped, a muscle twitching along my collarbone.

She turned her bright gaze on me, probing deeper than I wished to allow her. "What has he done to you?" She grasped my elbow and pulled me closer, as an elder sister might.

I blinked in that surreal moment, trying to grasp her meaning. It struck me in pieces — she had seen the portrait of the real countess and believed me to be her.

"The minute I met that earl I began to worry about you, before I'd even known you. I saw no one could be happy anywhere near him. He's just . . . oh, you know how he is." She looked at me expectantly as if she'd asked a question. But of course, I *didn't* know.

"I suppose."

"Come, you can tell me all of it."

I only wished I could. I heaved a sigh and relayed the little information I had on the mysterious evil-sounding earl. "He isn't always pleasant, but he only has a small role in my life."

Her gaze snapped of strong opinions she did not speak. "Indeed." She broke the stare and fingered the hem of my sleeve. "Promise me you'll be careful."

Flutters of worry swept through my chest as it occurred to me that in adopting this woman's glorious life, I'd also taken on her problems, the dark parts no one saw.

When I had shown Lady Remington out, I moved toward the stairs and found Victor Prendergast in the hall outside the morning room.

"Well, how did the evening go?" he said. "I've been anxiously awaiting the news."

"Everyone seemed to have a nice time."

"Was there anyone there you . . . recognized?" He gave a jaunty wink.

I backed up to glare at him, realization washing over me. "You arranged that? You arranged for them to come here?"

"I had to prove something to you. I made the acquaintance of Mr. and Mrs. John Reese Stockton through a few business contacts and added their names to the invitation. You can imagine her enthusiasm to make such a connection."

"How did you even find her? All I'd ever told you was —"

"I am quite good at finding out what I wish to know. Your arrest and imprisonment was a matter of public record, as was the name of your accuser." He smiled again, his hands clasped behind his back. "You are welcome."

"For what, parading me before the pains of my past?"

"For proving to you that it has no hold over you anymore. You see? You lay down as Ragna and then rose from her pile of rags to become the magnificent Countess of Enderly. So much so that you are not recognized, even by those who once knew you."

I looked down at the plush carpet, battling the odd sensation that stole over me and warmed my clammy skin. "But I cannot *be* Lady Enderly. No one is her but *her.*" My voice hurried like water skipping over stones, directed more toward myself than Victor as I scrambled to grasp at reality that was becoming elusive. "And one day she'll return to her life and I'll go back to being . . ." my voice trailed away, for I had no idea what I *would* be when this ended.

He took my arms in the dark, holding them in a firm grasp. "You *are* the countess. You have changed entirely into her. What difference exists between you? You wear the same gowns with the same measurements, have identical features, and you even share the same tastes. You walk and talk and even reason like the countess. What part of you is not her?"

My head swam as my sensible logic tilted and spun, leaving me certain of nothing. Beliefs and thoughts swirled along with Victor's words that attempted to define truth to me. How naturally I had responded to the countess's name when I spoke to that woman from my past. My heart pounded with all manner of internal battles — both victory and utter guilt at accomplishing my goal. How could it be a victory to become something I was not, to so thoroughly succeed in deceit? How could it be an improved version of me if it was not *me*?

"You're a lucky girl, Raina. More than you even know. You've been released from a worthless identity and given one that most people could only dream of possessing."

"You almost sound like it'll be permanent." Suppose the countess decided she didn't want her life back? That her troubles were better off on someone else's shoulders?

This question dimmed the intensity in his eyes, replacing the sparks with a dull darkness. "No, it will not. That I can promise you. The change is thorough, but it is not permanent."

16

People are often afraid to truly look into the heart of who they are, because those inner rooms echo so loudly with one lonely question: Am I enough?

~ Diary of a Substitute Countess

She followed me about like a vapor as I strode through her home that evening, attempting not to think about the woman whose life I had so thoroughly stolen — or borrowed, or kindly accepted as a gracious favor. When I paced through the house to shut up the abandoned rooms again, I heard movement within and paused to be sure it was not simply my skittish imagination. Hardly anyone ventured into them.

When a thunk sounded inside, curiosity drew me, and I pushed through the double doors. Only bluish moon glow lit the space. A lone figure stood with his back to me across the old library, hands in his pockets.

My toe kicked loose debris and the intruder spun. It was Sully, and he studied me with flecks of intensity lighting his shadowed eyes. I remained still in the hushed room and allowed his steady gaze to pass over me. "What are you doing in here?"

"Bradford is worried about a collapse. He didn't want the whole house to go with it, so I said I'd see if anything could be done."

"Repairs will be made."

"The matter is becoming urgent. You'd best not put it off much longer." He folded his arms over his chest and stared at me for several silent moments. "How long will you put off reality, Raina? You are not her. This is not your life, and it's time you face it."

"What would you have me do, go back to Spitalfields? Give up on everything?" *Give up on you?* I looked at the floor as the truth gathered and clogged in my throat. "I'm in a position to help people, Sully."

"This isn't about helping people anymore, is it? Maybe it started that way, but now it's something else. It's about you, and what you think you want to be. You've lost sight of everything else — including who you truly are."

I remembered Philip's bold accusation. *Self-important. That's my second word for you.* I nearly poured out the truth, everything

216

about Victor's threats, but that was like starting a fire in the woods and hoping it didn't spread. One word from me would create a giant blaze I'd never be able to contain. "Believe me when I tell you that self-importance is the furthest thing from my list of flaws. In fact, it's quite the opposite. Insecurity is one of the greatest hurdles I face, and it always has been."

"One feeds the other. A person can find a whole lot of flaws when she spends lots of time staring at herself."

"How could you —"

"Do you ever think about her? Wonder what truly happened to her?" His words, quiet and sure, cut across my angry bursts. "In all of this splendor, have you stopped to ask yourself what you were helping to cover up? You might have risen into a finer life with all the respect and admiration you desire, but what happens to her while you're doing it?"

I stiffened. "She'll rest and strengthen her health so she can resume her life." I gulped and the image of her portrait rose in my mind. Suddenly it struck me why I couldn't bear to look at it. Questions about her troubled life poked at me all the time, assaulting me like little pebbles, but I had deflected them however I could because I didn't want to face them, didn't want to know the truth concerning the Countess of Enderly.

In truth, I'd avoided thinking about the details of the entire charade — of my deceit, of the danger, of the uncertain future. My mission was to keep beside me the man I had thought I lost, to save his life. The fate of a wealthy socialite who might or might not be in danger simply did not compare in my mind.

And in some buried corner of my heart, I did not want to pause to face the reality of who I truly was outside of this ruse. Of all the people who lacked respect for Ragna the rag seller, I topped them all.

"You are many things, Raina Bretton, but daft isn't one of them. You can see as well as I do that there's more to this story."

"So what if there is?" My breath came hard and strong. "I know as much as you do on the matter. I am utterly in the dark and cannot do a thing about it. That isn't self-importance, just ignorance. Perhaps she truly did need a rest from life. It isn't easy, you know, living this way. Victor's story might well be true."

He glared at me, and my eyes flicked up to that portrait against my will, and I looked into her mesmerizing eyes so soft with great depth and heart. They seemed to be challenging me now, demanding that I understand her and untangle her secrets. Save her life. *A house is merely a reflection of its mistress.* I could no longer ignore what these rooms conveyed about the secrets in her life.

Sully's voice cut through my thoughts. "The truth is, this woman is missing, and as long as you pretend to be her, enjoying her clothes and her house and her servants, no one knows to look for her. She could go on being missing forever and no one would know as long as you're standing in her stead."

I slanted my gaze at the floor, my arms trembling even though I tensed them. That was the odd feeling that surfaced in these rooms — it was guilt. Despite the worry and danger, I had enjoyed living a different life, having fine clothing and esteem I'd never experienced before.

Sully strode forward and brushed a stray tendril from my forehead. My tension melted at his longed-for nearness. "What's so bad about the girl you used to be? Tell me that. Why do you despise her so?"

"Because everyone else did." The answer snapped out before even a breath of thought. I covered my mouth with my

219

hands, wishing I could take back the foolish-sounding words.

"People are not mirrors, Raina. Just because some like you better as the countess in your fine clothes and fancy house doesn't mean you *are* better." He paused, looking into my eyes. "Your dreams used to be bigger than impressing people and dressing fancy. You had such passion, fighting for people, chasing down adventures, and wrestling an income from castoffs. What happened to that girl?"

Hot tears squeezed out and trickled down my cheeks. "I am still those things, but I'm learning how to be more too."

"I'll tell you a secret, Raina. The weakest version of the real you is stronger than the best imitation of someone else."

I wished I could agree. If only I could have been a normal girl, wearing normal clothes and working at a normal trade, perhaps I'd have been content to be who I was. Yet I wasn't — I was the seller of castoffs. The wearer of castoffs. The ultimate castoff. Panic tightened my chest as if I were even now facing the scorn that was like the musty air I'd breathed. Was I doomed to such an identity?

I couldn't go back. Just couldn't. "I don't want to be what I was. No more Ragna."

This countess had handed over her life, asked for a replacement. She'd wanted this. And I definitely hadn't gone out seeking this lot. I'd been requested, nearly begged, to take it. All I'd done was agree — and then become enraptured with the taste of it.

"There's far more to it than that." He gripped my arms, and I became overly aware of him, this wonderful, lively man who had loomed large in my life and his memory even larger when he left. Now he was here, before me. Delightfully, achingly near. Alone with me. His breath fanned over my face. "You don't merely sell rags. You find value in what is cast aside and bring it back to life, make it valuable again. Give it a piece of your own beauty. That's powerful, Raina, and just one of the many things that makes you so . . ." He searched my eyes, his passion for me glowing from every plane and helplessly melting the end off his sentence.

His breath grew shaky as he became aware as I was of our nearness. So long we'd craved one another, separately counting the days until we could be together again, and now we stood mere inches apart yet still separated. I felt the certainty of his feelings in his very posture, in the gentle yet firm grip on my arms. "Do you love me, Raina?

Do you? How desperately I wished you could respond to my letters, tell me how you felt. It was like tossing my heart into a black hole and hoping someone would catch it. I want to hear it from you, in your own words, your voice."

As I sank into the dizzying moment, scrambling for words eloquent enough to carry the weight of years' worth of feelings for this man, he touched my lips with his thumb, stopping the flow of my thoughts in a sacred moment suspended in the chaos around us. His caress slid to my cheek with the barest brush of his finger, as if afraid I'd run away. I gulped and looked up into his eyes. "Sully, I want —"

He moved close until his forehead touched mine. His eager eyes watched me with an inviting sparkle. "Kiss me."

"Now? Here?"

"Or I'll tell everyone your secret."

I slid my hands up to his arms, delighting in the nearness. "That's bribery."

His mouth twitched up in a gentle grin. "So?"

I closed my eyes and imagined in a thousand fleeting sensations what it would feel like to kiss this man I'd adored for years. His nose brushed my cheek, then a door slammed and I jerked back, heart thumping clear up to my throat. Footsteps sounded nearby, coming closer.

"We can't. Not now."

He stepped back, the playful twinkle dulled. "I'm not an actor, Raina. You may be able to pretend what isn't true, but I cannot promise to keep this up. Not anymore."

"It's just for a time, and then we can walk away from this and into our own life, together and . . . alive." I wavered at the edge of my secrecy, wondering if I should take the plunge and tell him the truth. I drank in the sight of his face, the wonderful knowledge that he was alive and here, and I couldn't do it. He was my rescuer, and for once, I was rescuing him. I owed him that, and so much more. "For now, everyone must believe I'm the countess. Including me."

He lifted his bright gaze to mine. "I'll know. I'll always know you're not her. No amount of looking alike or wishful thinking will make you her."

I pivoted away as crushing defeat consumed me. "Stop it. Just . . . stop." I had to find her. This had to end.

"Why must you stay here? What is it that ties you to this place? Help me understand, Raina. Explain it."

Tension curled in me. The answer burned

the tip of my tongue. Sentences formed and disintegrated.

"Tell me." He took hold of my shoulders. "I cannot bear to pretend anymore that I feel nothing for you."

My stress exploded in a dagger of words. "It's what you've done for years!"

I pinched my lips after the terrible outburst. His face paled. I closed my eyes, hands over my face. When I opened them, he was gone.

I glanced over at Victor in the study as he shuffled through papers, and I looked out over the gardens. The weight of my interlude with Sully still lay heavily on me, demanding that I end this by finding the real countess. I'd never felt more ready to leave this place, but I had to tread carefully.

I ambled toward Victor, lifted a casual frown. "I'm bound to make a mistake, you know. I nearly did, when Lady Remington tried to open a debate with me. Lady Enderly was well versed in politics, and I know next to nothing on the matter."

"Hardly. Lady Enderly has a much finer skill than political expertise — keen wit. It provides her with the right words for any question, and she is always a huge success at gatherings."

"She must have more than wit."

He looked away with a shrug, but I glimpsed a strange energy in his eyes. "There's something about her, about the way she speaks, that makes a person excited about anything simply because she is. She can make anyone believe something as firmly as she does after a single conversation with them. It's like magic."

"That *is* a valuable talent." I fingered the top rail of a little chair before me. "I was thinking. Might it be a wise idea to have Lady Enderly herself teach me that?"

He froze, then turned back to me. "Why ever would you do that?"

"Who better to teach me to be the countess than her? I've been thinking about how much I could learn from her about many things, from dress to —"

"No. We've no need to bring her into it."

"But if —"

"I said no." He turned a powerful look on me that stilled my speech. "She deserves a break from this, and I'll not have you intruding upon her. You're not to ask again. Is that clear?"

He sank back into the desk chair, and I watched his suddenly stoic face. A tiny chill curled around my belly. Half of me had believed his story of the countess needing rest until that exact moment. Then I knew in every part of my being that there was evil hidden somewhere in this mess. Somehow I found myself in the position of being one of the only people who could stop it.

Excusing myself, I exited and made my way to my bedchamber. Dinner would be soon, and I needed to be ready.

I tensed as Simone brushed out my hair, pulling it this way and that to ensure her brush attacked every strand. This exercise had left my scalp aching when I'd first arrived, but now I hardly flinched. They'd begun to oil my hair as well, and the healthy sheen was only improved by the silver brush wielded by my lady's maid.

I inhaled the aroma of all the powders and potions lining my table and exhaled the worries still plaguing my mind about dinner. I craved privacy, which seemed a rarity in this place. "You needn't bother with an elaborate toilette tonight, Simone. I've no one to impress." I wished desperately to be free of her fingers.

"Will you be dining alone tonight, mistress?"

"No, but there is no one at the dinner table who will pay any mind to my appearance."

Her burnished black eyes met mine in the

mirror. "And the second footman?"

Tension collected along my spine, stiffening my muscles. "What of him?"

"He notices."

I met her steady gaze with more courage than I felt. Was it a warning or a taunt? I stared at her placid face in the mirror, but it revealed as much as a murky pond.

When I descended the stairs, my hand gliding along the well-oiled bannister, the front door slammed below with the power of thunder that rattled my tender nerves, and boot stomps echoed up from the front entry. I slowed my steps and watched from my perch halfway up the grand staircase, and an odd sense of worry assailed me.

Then he strode into the candlelight of the front hall, a stranger tall and dashing in a long coat. He whipped off his coat and practically threw it toward the poor butler, who seemed unmoved by the display. His angry gaze whipped about the room as a low, beastly growl emanated from his chest. Three words tore from down deep in his being. "Where is she?"

I shuddered as I realized who this was — at last I'd come face-to-face with the great and terrible earl. I huddled back into the shadows, clinging to the wooden embellishment on the railing and wondering if I should flee.

"She'll be along for dinner, my lord."

The man growled again and pulled a pocket watch from his jacket, inspecting it with a deep frown freezing over his features. It was a handsome face, severe as it was, and younger than I'd imagined. He couldn't have been older than thirty, but a world of bitterness had etched itself deep into the lines of his countenance, aging him considerably. Long sideburns that extended to his jawline only made him look more severe, like a wolf.

Lady Remington's warnings about the earl flooded my mind with the force of the ocean and swayed me on my feet. The earl's gaze was now fixed to the floor, his face like one of the stone lions flanking the entryway. He bent and picked something up from the floor with a frown, studying it in his open palm. It looked so familiar.

Suddenly my hand flew to my sash where Sully's stone had been. It must have fallen before I'd dressed for dinner.

He straightened as he jammed the rock into his pocket and looked up, pausing as his deeply intense gaze rested on me. The sight of me ignited a flame of emotion behind his face, from shock to pure horror that glowed in his eyes.

I shifted and became aware of the moisture that had gathered along the boning of my stays, cooling my skin and making me desperate for fresh air. He was here, alone with me in this quiet hall, as the light of many candles bounced over his terrible face. I didn't move, but I clung so hard to that railing that my nails dug into the hard wood. My pulse thudded in my ears.

The man stared like an animal preparing to devour. His eyes narrowed, two slits of angry light flashing up at me. The weight of animosity meant for another woman bore down on me and held me in place. I forced myself to breathe and stared back. I didn't dare speak and say the wrong thing before this man. He'd be less than charitable toward any missteps.

Finally when I felt I'd drown in anxiety, footsteps clicked along the shiny entryway floor and Cousin Philip's pale face appeared below. Scanning the situation as he removed his hat, he raised his eyebrows and smiled back and forth at us both. "I see I've interrupted the reunion."

The earl's gaze jerked toward Cousin Philip, and the array of emotions continued, horror melting into confusion, then anger.

"What a lovely moment I've happened upon." He smiled. "Just lovely."

No one else spoke and the silence was thick with unvoiced secrets.

Cousin Philip's foolish grin only widened. "Time to dress for dinner, I suppose. I'll leave you alone." The surprisingly jovial cousin carried himself up the stairs with jaunty springs, but he slowed as he neared me and leaned near to whisper. "Yes, it was me who wrote him to come. Pardon my intrusion, but after what I witnessed in the hall the other day, I believe it healthy for a lady to be reminded, once in a great while, that she does have a husband."

I spun on him, shock flaring through me, but he was gone, coattails flapping as he took the steps two at a time and disappeared down the hall at the top.

Husband. *Husband.* I glanced back at the raw anger on the beastly face below, trying to wrap that word around the man I saw.

17

Even when you have everything you want, there will be days you wish desperately for what you once cast aside.

~ Diary of a Substitute Countess

He must know. That notion rang through my head as the earl fixed his steely gaze on me from across the table over his trout. Distant relations and strangers could be fooled, but surely a man knew the details of his wife's face enough to realize I wasn't her. With each forkful lifted to his mouth, his sharp glare stayed on me. I was grateful for the great length of that table separating us, but I knew it would not be between us forever.

Anxiousness buzzed inside me that contrasted with the smooth movements of my arms as I cut my food with fork and knife and took a bite. Outwardly, at least, I maintained control. What did an earl and his wife discuss over dinner?

I cleared my throat and sipped my drink. "I hope your travels were uneventful." Should I call him earl? My lord? If only Prendergast had not disappeared.

He slowed his chewing and stared at me harder but said nothing. The insufferable Cousin Philip sat between us, looking from one to the other with a smile as if seated in a theater for a performance.

I tried again. "Everything has been well at Rothburne in your absence. I hope you are pleased with the changes I've made."

The earl narrowed his gaze at me. "All but one."

I shrank back into my seat. Was he talking about my presence here? He must know the truth, yet he wouldn't say anything before the servants. For once, a person's deep concern for appearances was in my favor.

I breathed deeply and mentally repeated the words that described the countess. *Poised. Elegant. Controlled. Graceful.* If ever I needed to believe I was those things, it was now.

And then there was Sully, standing at my elbow, holding out a tray with creamer and sugar. Eager for the sweetness, I dumped several spoonfuls of sugar into my tea and stirred rapidly. "Thank you."

I swallowed the tea and my mouth was seized with the briny taste. I spit it into the cup and coughed, drawing the attention of everyone at the table. "Heavens, there is salt in my tea." I coughed again and sat upright, my neck warming.

Sully gave a solemn bow and bent to blot at the table surface that had received a splash of my rejected tea. "My humble apologies, my lady, but someone must have mistaken the salt for sugar. They do look exactly alike."

"They are quite different."

He moved back and caught my gaze with a meaningful look. "I'll be sure to fetch the sugar." He disappeared through the service door, and I exhaled, rubbing my throbbing temples.

"Lady Enderly, you seem piqued today." Cousin Philip was the only one at the table eating with abandon. "There's nothing troubling you, I hope."

"Of course not." I forced a trembling smile, my gaze going to each of the diners separated by the table.

The earl grumbled at the other end. "There very well ought to be."

I coughed. Moments passed, marked by the thunk of the clock. The tension pressurized to an unbearable level until I rose, napkin falling to the floor. "I'll leave you to talk to Mr. Scatchard. I'm sure there is plenty about the estate you have to discuss, and I'll merely be in the way."

"Nonsense, my lady." Cousin Philip grinned at me, his eyes sparkling in the soft light of the chandelier. It was the silly grin of a man in his cups. "I insist you stay so we may enjoy your company. No estate matters are as urgent as renewing one's connection with one's wife. I'm sure the earl agrees."

The man in question glowered at the both of us and stabbed another piece of meat.

Sully slipped back into the room and poured me another cup of tea, spooning generous amounts of what I hoped was sugar into my cup.

Cousin Philip began again. "I insist you not allow my presence to hurry you out, my lady. You must remain and enjoy the rare company of the earl."

I sighed. "Perhaps I can tarry with you for a moment in the parlor before you adjourn to the smoking room."

"I won't hear of it. McKenna, where's that superb fiddle of yours? I've a taste for some music this evening to settle my food."

"Of course, sir." Sully bowed and backed out of the room.

My stomach clenched. Everything would be fine — I merely had to close my ears to the music. As we waited for him to fetch his instrument, my heart hammered with dread. I could manage, as long as there were no words. *Please, God. Let there be no words.* Moisture clung to every surface of my skin, chilling me as I sat at the ancient table.

When Sully strode back into the room, I concentrated on my fingernails in my lap. A hush fell over us as eating paused and attention moved to the man fitting his beloved instrument under his jaw. I could hear my own breath.

Then a familiar melody rolled over my senses like a great tidal wave, my mind filling in the words even though he did not sing them, and I was powerless to escape them.

"I know the shape of her, no matter how
    long we're apart.
The curve of her cheek and the swell of
    her heart;
The height of her adventures, and the
    breadth of her art.
Looking at her smiling eyes, those sweet
    crescents of joy,
I know that this girl, this lovely pearl,
This bold and daring upstart
has changed the shape of my heart."

The unsung words hovered about my mind in aching clarity, made fresh by everything that had occurred since he'd written it. Ten years ago he'd first sung it to me on a snowy day in February when he'd rescued me from one of my many adventures. What had I even done to find trouble that time? Who could remember. The strongest memory I had of that day was Sully carrying me, wet and trembling, up to my flat where he lit a blazing fire and set me on the worn rug before it.

In that quiet moment of deep and wide friendship, I'd confessed to him my supreme unhappiness, that I felt buried beneath my many layers of rags. I hadn't explained the deeper meaning of my statement, but he'd understood. He pulled out his fiddle where it had hung across his body by a frayed rope and wrote that song for me in the moment. *I know the shape of her.*

I had used the words of that song as practice when I learned to write, and I'd kept the page pinned to the cracked mirror in my flat. I knew those words like I knew my own face. He'd meant the song as a lively melody of lighthearted fun to lift my mood and make me laugh, and they had succeeded on that blustery winter day.

But this time there was nothing lighthearted about the way he played it.

Now the song hit me with the full force of the love behind it. He'd always seen beyond the surface of my words, just like the day he'd written this song, yet for years I'd missed the depth of his. Had he loved me even then? When I lifted my gaze, his eyes met mine briefly with a look that only emphasized the unsung words and their true meaning. *I see the real you. And I love what I see.*

With a slow exhale, I looked away and remembered that Connemara stone now languishing in the earl's pocket, the meaning behind it overwhelming me yet again. How would I ever be able to see this ruse through with Sully hovering near? I had to do this — for so many reasons, I had to. Victor's cunning face came to mind, making me shiver. If only Sully's life did not depend on such a man — or on me. *Father God, protect me. Help me.*

Again, my conscience smarted at the idea of approaching God.

"Ah, look at the hour. I have correspondence to attend to yet, so I will excuse myself from dessert and allow the reunited couple to reacquaint themselves in private."

I grabbed the arms of my chair. "Perhaps I should —"

"I wouldn't hear of it, Countess." Philip watched me with glowing eyes. "Cook has prepared a lemon tart especially for you. I mentioned it was your favorite, and she's spent the afternoon preparing it. I'd hate to see her disappointed."

The doors opened as if on cue, and a delectable tart dusted with powdered sugar entered the room. I sank back into my seat. My mouth watered at the mere thought of the zesty treat, but my stomach was far too unsettled to receive something so rich. Looking at Cook's bright eyes glowing in the candlelight as she brought it to me herself, I knew I'd have to attempt a few bites and pray it remained where I put it.

"Your ladyship, in honor of your gracious visit here, and the earl's return."

"Thank you kindly."

She scurried back through the service door, and before anyone could speak further, that rat of a cousin sprang up and was gone, closing the earl and myself into this dimly lit chamber alone together like a tomb being sealed. Moments ticked by on the mantel clock. The silence seemed tangible. I cringed as another door banged somewhere in the house, the sound echoing through the vastness.

The presence of servants kept us from

speaking freely, but even if we could, what would I say? I cut a dainty portion of the tart with my fork and set it against my lips.

"Where is Prendergast?" He growled the question like a bear hovering across the dining hall.

"I believe he was called away for the day. He'll return presently." I lifted apologetic eyes to him.

He glared back with unrelenting anger. Finally, he stood, shoving his chair back and tossing down his napkin as he towered over his untouched dessert. "I never liked lemon tart."

He left the room, and I began to breathe again.

It was not until much later that night, while I sat curled into a rose-colored armchair in my bedchamber with a book, that I heard footsteps and remembered one very important fact — the earl's suite adjoined my own. I slammed shut the novel on which I could not focus and curled my knees to my chest as his distinctive boot clomps grew louder with his approach. I drew the blanket up to my chin over my nightdress and prayed. I held my breath. My knees trembled against each other, rocking my body in the little seat.

His footsteps thumped into his room and boots were kicked off, thudding against solid wood somewhere. I shivered underneath my blanket. I could hear him grumbling like a bear on the other side of the wall, then the quick pops of different footsteps sounded in the hall and stepped into the earl's chamber.

"So sorry for the delay." It was Victor Prendergast. "If you'd only sent word you were coming, I —"

"What, would've hidden her before I arrived?"

I cringed at the sound of his voice, even through the wall.

"I would have been here to greet you." His tone was indefatigably buoyant. "How was your journey? I know how you loathe train travel."

"Enough with this nonsense. What are you doing?"

Prendergast's voice lowered. "I told you I'd handle it, didn't I?"

"This? *This* is how you're handling it?"

"You know the alternative."

"I blame you for this entirely. All of it."

"I suppose you also blame me for you sitting here in your fine house, carrying on your important life, instead of paying for your misdeeds. Perhaps you'd prefer I remedy that?"

A low growl was his only answer.

"So we have a guest for a time. How bad is that, truly?"

"I don't want some stranger having access to everything here, my bank papers, my deeds and titles, all my personal correspondences . . ."

"Relax. This is no educated woman I've brought us. She's a rag rat from the East End. The girl can't even read."

I lifted one eyebrow and glanced down at the novel in my lap, my thumb holding my place.

"If it'll help you sleep at night, we'll go now to the study and lock up anything you would not wish her to see. Come, I'll tell you the whole of it in the study, and you can commend my brilliance."

Another grumble from the earl and the two departed his room, closing the door behind them. I waited long minutes, listening to the fire crack in my hearth, before casting aside my blanket and crossing the room to my desk and drawing out the countess's stationery. The earl was a villain in the countess's story, along with his more villainous but charming solicitor, but how? What was the rest of the tale?

Dipping the pen into the ink, I breathed

deeply and imagined what the countess might write about him. He had done me some wrong, of that I was certain, but what? Angry, controlling, and taciturn, the man had earned my fear and my distance. I felt in danger whenever he was near and knew not what he was capable of doing. I feared he might be after my money — did I have money before marrying him? — or at least anxious for my demise. I filled a page with random thoughts that brought me no clarity and increased my anxiousness.

I lay awake for many hours that night, startling at every boot clomp, every shuffle in the hall. Worry haunted me, swirling about my tired brain and keeping me from sleep. When he finally did return, I listened to the noises in his suite, picturing where he was in the room, how close he was to the door between our suites. Then when the noises ceased and the light under the door dimmed, I relaxed back onto my pillow and slept.

When I stirred from a deep slumber the next morning, cracking one tired eyelid open, the hazy figure of the earl was in the doorway between our rooms, staring at me with a look of torture contorting his face. I forced aside the remaining traces of sleep and sat straight up, but he vanished in an instant, leaving me huddled in the covers, wondering if I'd imagined him.

I remained there until I felt chilled by the fresh morning air that seeped through the back of my nightdress. I rose and tiptoed to the door, leaning my ear against it, but the silence beyond signaled a vacant room. With a sigh I returned to my chamber and pulled the little bell that would summon Simone.

I straightened on the little stool, imagining the stays were already bracing my spine as she entered. "I'm ready to dress, Simone. Has the earl risen already?"

Her dark eyes bore into my reflection in the mirror as she unplaited my hair and smoothed a brush through it. "You are eager to see more of him, no? I've heard it has been weeks since you've been together. Months, perhaps."

I had been at the abbey for weeks now, so the true couple had been separated at least that long, but when had she actually disappeared? I couldn't help but wonder if theirs had been an arranged marriage, for I could not imagine any woman welcoming the advances of such a bear-man.

"He is in the study, my lady, going over the accounts."

When my long curls lay in smoothed waves down my back, Simone moved toward my dressing room to select a gown, and I stood to retrieve the tea she'd brought. How quickly I'd grown accustomed to warming my insides both day and night with it. When I'd lifted the cup to my lips, Simone called from the opened wardrobe. "I've also brought the book you had requested. It's there beside the tea."

I frowned. When had I requested a book? It was Thomas Hardy's *Far from the Madding Crowd.* Lifting the volume, I saw a slip of paper marking a page, and I knew immediately who had told her I'd requested it. As soon as Simone had dressed me and taken her leave, I turned to the marked section. "When a strong woman recklessly throws away her strength, she is worse than a weak woman who has never had any strength to throw away."

I clenched my jaw and flipped to the next bookmark, almost dreading what I would find.

"The perfect woman, you see, is a working-woman; not an idler; not a fine lady; but one who uses her hands and her head and her heart for the good of others."

A swift rebuttal rose in my mind, but as I thought back over my time here, reality cooled my anger. I looked down at my slender white hands grasping the edges of the book. What had they done since coming here? They had touched fine imported silk and faille, shaken the hand of many a gentleman and lady, and lifted silver forks laden with the tenderest meat. My poised reflection stared back at me, unrecognizable. I hated to admit it, even to myself, but Sully was right. Perfecting my appearance had consumed me, and even though it had noble reasons, important ones, I had lost sight of my bigger role in this house — that of Queen Esther.

After flipping through the Hardy novel some more, I placed it on the tea tray with one new notation, a single scrap of paper marking the passage, and rang for the second footman to fetch the tray. The underlined passage read, "Don't suppose, because I'm a woman, I don't know the difference between bad goings-on and good. I shall be up before you're awake. I shall be a-field before you are up. It is my intention to astonish you all."

And I would.

18

All beauty fades, unless it has seeped into the core of your nature and changed something there as well.

~ Diary of a Substitute Countess

Within the hour I hoisted the hem of my skirt above the grass as I trod out toward the lane that would, I supposed, lead me to the tenants' homes. As the steady spring breeze whipped my skirt about my legs, I saw a figure moving toward me from the other side of the house, and he broke into a light jog to meet me.

"Cousin Philip." I didn't even bother to force a smile.

"What on earth are you doing?"

I gripped the cloak of my confidence with a firm hand, straightening beside him. "Paying a call to my tenants. It's time I see for myself that they're well cared for."

He jammed his hands into his pockets and

frowned, his stride slowing. "You do not trust me."

"What do you mean?"

"It is I, your estate manager, who is tasked with seeing to your tenants. Besides, you can never make such a journey by foot. Have you any idea how spread out these homes are? Come, we'll ride together if you insist on going. I can make my rounds now, I suppose."

I followed him with hesitation toward the stable, wondering if riding lessons would ever be part of my training. I'd simply have to make do — how hard could it be? Yet when we entered the musty-smelling place and the gigantic animals snorted and huffed in greeting, I grimaced, staying back and staring at the beasts. How did one ever control such a large animal? And what happened if one sat astride it who did not possess that secret?

Cousin Philip turned back and started as he glimpsed my face. "You've not ridden before, have you?" His frown deepened as his gaze stayed upon me. "What sort of lady has never been astride a horse?"

I straightened. "One who has been afraid of them since a childhood accident." That much was true, at least, for I'd been nearly trampled by a man on his horse as he'd charged after a pack of young thieves running through my alley.

"Come, I'll help you. Normally you'd wear a riding habit, but I haven't time for the rigors of womanhood and fashion. If you'll select a horse, I shall guide you through the details of riding." He still eyed me with suspicion.

Soon I found myself propped sidesaddle on a brown horse trotting down a path and to the east, where the sun was still burning in its ascent, and found the horse did more controlling than I did, for he seemed to know he was meant to follow Cousin Philip's mount.

Little houses lay scattered about the open fields beyond the estate and rows of crops filled the landscape. When the horses slowed to a walk, my companion breathed in deeply and exhaled the fresh air. "Rothburne is quite a special place, you know. I hope you care for it well."

"I intend to. I've already begun inside the house, and I won't stop there."

He watched me with a critical stare, not smiling or frowning, as if he wouldn't believe my words until he saw proof of them.

I was reminded of what Lady Remington had said concerning Cousin Philip's deep love of this place and saw for myself the truth of it. "You care about Rothburne a great deal, don't you?"

There was a long silence as he shifted with his horse, eyes to the horizon. Finally he said, "It's home to me."

"I didn't know you'd ever lived here."

He hesitated. "I haven't. Not outside of my dreams, that is. I've only ever been a guest. But what do you know of home? You've never desired one." And with those words he jerked his heels into his horse's sides and galloped across the golden field.

With an exasperated sigh, I leaned forward into my horse's neck, and he lurched forward, easily catching Cousin Philip's horse as I clung to him.

There were about twenty houses on the sprawling acres of property, and we visited each one. I asked Cousin Philip for a page from his ledger and a pencil so I could record the needs of each household. The awe and excitement on their faces at the sight of their mistress at their door warmed right through that hard ball of guilt, making it feel lighter and easier to bear. At least I was doing some good in all my deception. *I hope it pleases you, God.* I did not bother to phrase this as a question, for I could not alter my course now. I would not risk Sully's life for my mistakes.

At the third house, we met an elderly widow who housed two neighbor girls after the death of their parents and was now prepared to send them to a foundling home. "I cannot care for them anymore. Much as my heart wishes it, my coin jar is empty." The pair hid behind her, and she reached back as she spoke to lay one hand on each of their blonde heads, idly fingering the girls' long braids. They were neat and clean even in their patched clothing, and the two pairs of large blue eyes watched me with solemn fear that was far too adult for their little faces.

Philip explained that the widow had been granted lifelong tenancy of her cottage upon the death of her husband, per his contract with Rothburne's former owner, and a very meager pittance of income by her son.

" 'Tain't enough to keep 'em, though." Her aged hands rested on the girls beside her.

"How much would it take?" I asked.

She blinked at me. "Take?"

"How much would it take to keep them with you?"

She named a sum that was even less than I'd earned selling rags in London.

"Done. A sovereign will be brought to you posthaste, and you will be given a weekly stipend from here on out. I wish to reward your generosity toward these orphans whom I consider wards of Rothburne."

"You'll pay me to keep them?"

I gave one nod.

She stared at me endlessly — just stared — her lined face brimming with surprise. Her mouth contorted in all shapes with emotion as she worked through what she wished to say. Finally she stepped forward and took my hand in both of hers. I could feel every knobby knuckle as her hand grasped mine with the strength of much work. Her hands were solid and sure despite her age.

"Bless you, my lady. Bless your heart." And then she bowed her head and wept onto our clasped hands.

I'd never seen such happiness expressed at something I was able to do, and the sight forever imprinted itself on my heart. I returned her spontaneous embrace, patting her curved back and feeling the weight of my own sins lift. Beyond her, Cousin Philip watched with many thoughts darkening his features.

As we journeyed to more houses, I found this part of my new role to be wholly satisfying and I could not convince myself to stop. I was throwing about money and promises like a queen bestowing gifts, and it felt even finer than the compliments I'd received at the reception.

That morning I cast aside another layer of Ragna's rags and became even more like the countess, sure and decisive in another way, enjoying life and not thinking of the cost until the bill was presented. I would have to explain the expenses to Prendergast, and likely to the earl, but hadn't he told me to go and be Lady Enderly? Well, I was doing exactly that. More so every day.

New seeds were promised to one farmer who had lost half his crops to some risky yet ill-advised planting decisions, and books to a surprisingly intelligent young girl who wished to study herbal medicine. I even arranged to transfer a whole host of flowers from my own new gardens to the wrung-out mother of five who had lost the pitiful rows of daffodils before her house.

"What exactly are you doing?" Philip spoke the words as we paused on the trail toward home that dipped toward a creek. An odd expression distorted his features. The sun was now firmly overhead, warming my face and lighting my little corner of the world.

"Caring for my tenants."

"By giving them seeds and books?"

"The seeds cost very little and will mean a great deal to the man and his family. If they have no crop, they cannot pay us, now can they? And the books will only improve their little community. An herbalist will be a valuable asset to Rothburne's tenants in the future, if she continues her study, and anything that helps the tenants and their health is profitable for the abbey."

He glanced toward Rothburne in the distance, frowning into the sun. "And the flowers?"

I licked my lips. "Those cost me nothing." In my eagerness to be an Esther to these people, I would betray myself, wouldn't I? Yet I couldn't resist doing such things. If I was going to be in this position, I would make use of it. He'd been the first to call me self-important, and now he would be the first to witness the changes in me.

After a long frown, he swung his leg around, jumped down from his mount, and took hold of the bridle as the horse jerked his head. He helped me dismount, then he placed the reins of my horse into my gloved hands, returning to his own steed. As we walked, I looked ahead toward the abbey lit up in its full glory by the sun, the flowers dotting the landscape with color, and caught my breath in wonder. I'd seen it up close and in small pieces, but I hadn't yet seen it from a distance as a stunning whole, since I'd had the staff working on the gardens. Yes, Rothburne truly was magnificent. And its new mistress was beginning to reflect a little of that beauty.

Cousin Philip watched the abbey as well, and I detected the pride of ownership in his bearing. Watching my companion's face heavy with emotion, I braved a question. "Why is it that you feel such an attachment to this estate, Philip? Why is a place you've never lived home to you?"

He kept his gaze on the distant house. "I'm a part of Rothburne and it's a part of me. Uncle Wells brought me here when he owned it and taught me to run it in the off-season."

"Then perhaps you should have inherited it."

He fell silent for a moment, staring at the abbey. A muscle jerked in his shallow cheeks. I began to regret my words, but then he spoke. "I used to be dear old Uncle Wells's favorite. Then I grew up, life became hard, and I made foolish mistakes like my father. Uncle Wells found out, and suddenly I was like this . . . this old broken-down chair. It's useless to everyone, but you cannot be rid of it, so there it sits, in the middle of the hall to be tripped over."

I gulped, unable to look at the man as he said such things about himself.

"Uncle rarely came here, so this empty old place was my refuge when Mother died, and then again when Father was killed beneath a trolley just a year later. So many things in my life changed, but Rothburne didn't. It couldn't. For hundreds of years it's been here, and it'll be here well after I'm dead and gone."

I squinted at the great tower, picturing the monks that had lived here so many years ago contrasted with the wealthy owners who had come after them. The great fortress was the backdrop for hundreds of lives and all their stories. Interesting how the costumes and the characters all changed, but the setting always remained the same. "I can see why you're attached."

This drew an even darker frown from Cousin Philip, yet he continued in silence into the stables where we handed our horses over to stable boys. I followed him unconsciously around a corner into an unoccupied portion of the stables, and suddenly he turned on me, his face dark and angry as he strode closer. "Who are you? What are you doing here?"

I backed into the wall, breath coming in

panicked gasps. It felt as though he was about to name me a fraud and call out my deception. What could I say to that? "Wh-what do you mean?"

"You're no lady, prancing about and throwing out favors like a fairy waving her wand. What lady cannot ride? What lady would ever venture into the noonday sun without guarding her precious complexion with a parasol or at the very least, a ridiculous-looking hat?"

I tensed, suddenly aware of the tightness of my sun-warmed face that would soon be showing freckles and perhaps a little color.

"You fooled my cousin into marrying you, but I always suspected it was a farce of a marriage. I've not been blind to the way you carry on with Prendergast, how you cast aside your husband to travel the world on the coin of this estate."

I tried to force strength into my voice. "Your understanding is far from the truth." But was it? I hadn't any idea what the truth was.

"You think you can fool me with your grand promises to these people and your charming manner, but I know you." He snarled these last words. "I know the real you. How many times did you tell me to cut back expenses, to let people find their own way rather than helping them? I know who you are under that façade, and I refuse to bow to your charm as everyone else has. I'll continue hating you with great delight for what you've done and who you've been all this time, no matter what I see before me."

"You're being irrational." I tried in vain to stand tall, but his menacing posture made me shrink away as he moved closer.

A commanding voice nearby cut the mounting tension. "Hello there!"

Philip growled and moved back and I heaved a great sigh of relief. I stiffened my back against my stays and clammy chemise and breathed deeply to restore my poise.

Victor Prendergast strode into our section of the stables, looking back and forth between us. "Ah, here she is. I was hoping to have a private word with you, Lady Enderly, if Mr. Scatchard would excuse us."

I stepped back, away from these two men watching me so intently, and indecision gnawed at me. I had so many questions to put to Victor just now, almost as a challenge: Why was Philip not given the estate? And why hadn't Prendergast bothered to tell me that the great and mysterious earl, of whom everyone seemed afraid, was my husband?

Yet Philip's words concerning this very

man, the impropriety he'd insinuated between us, rang in my ears, and I shook my head. "We needn't be alone, Mr. Prendergast. Cousin Philip is as much a part of this estate as I am, for it is his hands that have shaped it all these years. I insist that any discussions we have include him."

The flash of anger on Prendergast's face told me I'd made the wrong choice, but Cousin Philip's look of shock assured me I hadn't.

"Very well, then. I'm afraid I must steal your husband away for a time. It's a matter of the crown and we must see to it immediately. I hope you will not be too lonesome without us." He raised his eyebrows, his look heavy with silent questions: Would I manage alone at the abbey? Could he trust me?

Philip's eyes blazed in the shadows, no doubt at what Prendergast's must have insinuated concerning us.

I stiffened and kept my eyes on Prendergast. "I'll look forward to Lord Enderly's speedy return."

So it was that the earl and his solicitor departed in Rothburne's carriage, leaving me in blessed peace, and soon after, Philip left to post orders for needed materials. I entered the silent abbey where all the life and noise had been sucked down to the kitchen to attend dinner preparations and slipped into the study for a moment of peace. Somehow the house seemed even grander when it was quiet, and I loved it.

It was the opportunity I'd been waiting for to poke about unobserved, explore hidden parts of the abbey. It struck me then that my busy schedule had kept me from several nights of praying in the window bay, and this would be the perfect time to remedy that, but my utter exhaustion had me clamoring for an escape from my life, not an analysis of it.

Curling into a large settee by the window with a Nathaniel Hawthorne novel in my lap, I sank into the imaginary world he'd created for me. Soon tiredness pulled at my poor mind. I laid my head on my arm and rested, the sun coming through the window, warming my face into utter relaxation. Drowsiness rose like the tide, and I happily gave in to it. My sleep had been so troubled since arriving, and my body craved rest. I was vaguely aware of footsteps drawing near, but I ignored them. It would only be a servant, for everyone else was gone. How delicious to simply drift off to sleep for a while.

19

True beauty is not the absence of flaws, merely the parts of us that can outshine them.

~ Diary of a Substitute Countess

Sully spotted her across the study the moment he entered the hushed space, and he paused to consider what to do. He'd sought her out the moment the carriage had departed, eager for the chance to speak with her alone, yet now he couldn't bring himself to wake her, to have her watching and listening as he said what needed to be said.

In the silence he studied her sleeping form draped over the plush red settee as if she were a part of it. How well she fit into this place of great beauty and fine things, with her golden curls and delicate features, her long, willowy frame. Yet she was his Raina, his plucky and loyal childhood chum.

The kitchen was busy and he should

return, but as he looked upon the silent face of the girl who'd become a permanent fixture in his mind and heart, with no one to disturb them, he couldn't resist drawing near. The girl always slept like a rock, which emboldened him further. He strode over and knelt beside her, gazing down at her pure face, so peaceful amidst the chaos of the situation.

"I suppose it's easier to offer my apologies when you can't answer back." He exhaled. How could he say it? He had let his hurt make him childish and he shouldn't have. "You didn't deserve all those things I said. You always do have a reason for the scrapes you get into, and they're kind and loving ones even when they're foolish. And I . . . I truly love you for it."

He drew a shuddering breath as the all-important words hung in the air and studied her long eyelashes resting on pink cheeks. They seemed even rosier than when he'd first entered the room — perhaps her sleep had deepened. "I know I make things harder on you by being here, Raina, but I cannot stay away. I made that mistake once and I'll not risk it again. Even if you'll never have me, I'll be nearby from now on. Forgive your foolish friend his weaknesses, but I cannot stand to be away from you again."

This was his fault. All his. If only he'd continued to remain in Spitalfields as her protector, perhaps he could have kept her from this trap.

He knelt closer and breathed in the fresh scent of her hair, the sweet aroma of her flushed skin. He'd once had this lass in his own arms, leaned her against him before a well-lit hearth. He'd loved her then, but through his absence his feelings had swelled to an unbearable intensity both sweet and painful.

"It's funny how, even in the midst of finery, you come to appreciate the ordinary, everyday things, like being around your favorite person. I miss that." He sat forward and pulled the tip of one loose curl that rested against her shoulder, stretching out its golden length and releasing it. "And being that favorite person's favorite person too. I think I miss that most of all." She'd always had a unique way about her — one of utter adoration and optimism combined. With one upturned look of her face, eyes bright and kind, a man believed he could do anything. It always made his heart jolt in his chest when she looked up at him that way, as if she saw some strength in him that even he did not.

Unable to resist, he reached up and trailed

his fingertips over her long hair with hesitant movements as he never dared do while she was awake. How soft it was. It filled him with an aching desire to bury his hand in the mass of curls and pull her close. If only he could have those moments in Spitalfields back. The ones where she needed him as her rescuer, where they had adventures together, where she looked upon him with blatant admiration and affection shining up from her girlish face. Even after the row with his father, how could he have found Spitalfields so terrible with her in it?

A long sigh escaped him. "Oh, Raina. You were right. What you said in the other room . . . I'm a coward of a man, running away on that ship without telling you the way I felt. If only you knew how hard it was to say such things to your face — your beautiful face." He curled the end of one strand around his finger. "I'm an ordinary man, and I couldn't bear to lose your friendship if you wouldn't have me, for it lit up me sorry days."

He shifted and traced her hand, her long fingers that lay cast over the arm of the settee. These hands had grasped his countless times and pulled him into her adventures and clung to him for comfort. "I love you so thoroughly, Raina, my Raina. Forgive me, but I can't help it. I only wish I weren't too late."

With a gentle kiss to her forehead, he let his lips linger on her warm skin and then stood, stretching stiff muscles and looking down at the girl who had always been beside him. That face, always so alive with love and mischief, was the same, even if cleansed of the smudges of Spitalfields and adorned with finer things. Hearing below stairs what she'd done for the tenants that day, breathing life into the forgotten and giving them a chance, had given him a renewed surge of love for her, and of hope. Buried beneath the gowns of another woman lay his Raina, fighting and working for those who couldn't do for themselves. Nothing had changed — not truly.

How wonderful her troublesome adventures of long ago now seemed, how precious those moments huddled before her hearth with a book between them as she learned to read, brightening with each new understanding. And he ached anew for those everyday moments he'd lost. "I should have stayed and made a go of it. Spitalfields was better than any ship, just because you were in it. Aye, there's a real charm to the ordinary, everyday parts of life."

He shifted, but he wasn't ready to tear

himself away. "I should have told you this when you were awake, but I'll say it now, while I have the courage. No matter what you think of me, no matter what you do, I love you. Deeply, wholly, passionately." He dug the recovered Connemara stone from his pocket and tucked it into her palm. "And there's nothing you can do to change it."

Sully hurried down the hall with deep breaths, clearing his head and preparing himself to face the kitchen staff again.

"Might I have a word with you, Mc-Kenna?" Philip Scatchard intercepted his course and waved him toward a sunny hallway with tall windows overlooking the front of the house. "I suppose you have practice holding your tongue."

"I've kept a fair number of secrets in me day."

"I thought you might. You have all the skills of a servant, but you're more than that, aren't you, Sullivan McKenna?"

"Everyone is."

His eyes shone. "Smart as a whip you are, lad. I like that. What would you say to a special task?" He pulled Sully's hand close and dropped coin after coin into it. "Just between us. No one else needs to hear of this, and I must count on you for the utmost discretion." More coins hit his palm.

"I'll do my best, sir. I never tell another man's secrets. It isn't my place." He held out the coins. "And I don't need money to do what I ought."

"Superb answer, but keep it anyway." He shoved Sully's hand away and led him deeper into the little parlor, looking back at the open doors behind them. "It's about the countess. There's something about her that isn't right. You sense it too, I can tell. The way you watch her, the way you first spoke to her when you came to Rothburne . . . I know you feel as I do."

Sully straightened, clasping his hands behind him and looking at the floor.

"I want you to keep a close watch on that woman. As much as possible, at least. I'm not certain yet what it is I'm looking for, but there's bound to be something. She isn't what she seems, and I need to know why. Is that clear?"

"You're asking me to spy on her, sir?"

"You want to see her taken down a peg, do you not? This is how you can do it. Together we'll make sure she's found out and everything set to right."

The words *You're mistaken about her* perched on the edge of Sully's tongue, but he swallowed them. If he didn't agree to this task, someone else would. "I'll keep my eyes open, Mr. Scatchard, but can I ask one thing?"

"Of course."

"What is it about her that's made you so suspicious? What's she done?"

His face hardened. "She's cheap and selfish in the way she runs this estate, and she doesn't appreciate it. Besides, every lady with inherited wealth can stand to see a little trouble in her life. The countess has gotten more than her share of riches — in fact, she's gotten mine."

Sully frowned. "How's that?"

"She inherited what should have come to me, a family estate she cares nothing about and did not grow up loving. She's not even a relation except by marriage, and she's a woman, no less. A *woman.* She has no business owning and running Rothburne Abbey, and Uncle Wells never should have given it to her."

"I believe that's up to the giver."

His eyes blazed. "See here, will you do it or not?"

Sully pocketed the coins, telling himself over and over that it wasn't thirty pieces of silver. This was done to protect, not betray. Either way, it felt traitorous.

He recalled her sleeping face flushed with such vulnerable, pure beauty. For her, anything. "You can count on me."

20

Not even the most poetic compliment from strangers touched me as deeply as one loving word spoken from a true friend.

~ Diary of a Substitute Countess

When his footsteps retreated, I lifted my warm face and stared at the door Sully had just closed, his quietly spoken words pulsing through my heart. I should have told him I was awake, for his voice had slipped into my dreams and interrupted my sleep, but I couldn't bear to bring a stop to it. Not when every word was like sweet pearls.

I sat upright and looked down at the book he'd placed on my lap before leaving. It was Jane Austen's *Emma,* a long white flower petal across a paragraph in the middle of the page. With a deep sigh, I lifted the petal and read the words underneath. "If I loved you less, I might be able to talk about it more. But you know what I am. You hear nothing but truth from me. I have blamed you, and lectured you, and you have borne it as no other woman in England would have borne it."

I blinked back tears and reread the words spoken by my favorite Austen hero — the older, wiser, longtime friend of the heroine who had a habit of speaking honestly with his heroine when needed.

Now I understood why I'd always favored that particular Austen man.

I exhaled and hugged the open book to my chest, letting Hawthorne's tome slip to the floor with a gentle thud. Had I truly been as foolish as young Emma Woodhouse, needing harsh truth from my practical hero? I rose, determined of two things. One, that I would find the countess and get us home as soon as I could, and two, that I would never, even under the worst of circumstances, lose my very own fiddle-playing Mr. Knightley. No matter what it cost me.

When a door banged somewhere in the house, I jumped, closing the book. How skittish I'd become these days, and I could feel the tension tightening my muscles and straining my head. Determined to unearth more about this missing woman, I ascended to my bedchamber and shivered when I glanced at the door between my suite and

270

the earl's. I could still picture him standing there.

Narrowing my eyes, I studied the ornate wood panels that separated our rooms. What would such a man's bedchamber be like? Full of dark secrets, of that I felt certain. I opened the door and slipped in with a hushed sense of awe. Perhaps his secrets would explain hers.

I stepped into the dark, drape-shrouded room where no unnecessary thing filled the large open space, glancing around with bated breath and ears perked for the sound of footsteps. Sparsely furnished with heavy wooden pieces and a few thick books, the room seemed as austere as its master. Apparently when a person dwelled in a room long enough, it absorbed the essence of his personality.

Daylight sliced through the dimness where the heavy curtains had parted, and it was barely enough light to see as my eyes adjusted to the dark. I spun, looking for a figure lurking in the shadows, for I was certain someone was watching me. No one appeared. With trembling fingers, I dug through the pockets of the jacket he'd been wearing upon arrival, which still hung over the back of a chair, but not even a shred of lint remained in them. His bedtable held nothing but a candle, and its drawer was empty.

I turned, eager to leave this chilling place, but I stopped before a leather-topped writing desk with four drawers. This was my one and only chance to search this place, for I would not be setting foot in it again. I likely wouldn't have the opportunity, either. Anything they wouldn't wish me to find would be gone soon enough too, and I had to find it — had to find something that would lead me to the truth.

With a resigned sigh, I searched all its drawers except for the long slender top one, which was tightly locked. Grumbling, I yanked on the thing again, but it held firm. Taking a letter opener from a cup on top, I worked the lock with it, and eventually slid it into the crack of the drawer. I pushed against the resistance deep within until the lock shifted and the drawer sprang open a crack. With a pounding heart, I pulled the drawer toward me and squinted to see the mess of papers inside.

Letters. So many letters. A feminine scrawl covered every page. Barely daring to breathe, straining to hear the slightest footstep in the hall, I lifted a page to the slender beam of light and forced my eyes to read the words.

My beloved Mitchell,

You have been exceedingly kind, more than I deserve, but I cannot accept any more gifts from you. Take this scarf and speak no more of such things. She will find out soon, I'm certain of it, and then what will become of me?

E. E. L.

"Do you wish for a candle?"

I shrieked and spun around. A statuesque figure in black stood framed in the doorway between the suites, the eerily pale face of Simone watching me as if she'd been there the whole time.

"I thought you might be ready to dress for dinner, my lady." Her warm, liquid voice sent chills up my spine. "But if you have matters to attend to in the earl's chamber, perhaps I can bring you a candle."

I straightened, shoving the letter into the drawer and jamming it closed. "Is it time to dress already? The day has gotten away from me." I forced cheeriness into my voice and swept through the sparse room to fling open the highboy doors and pretend to make note of everything. "I was merely checking to see if the earl had what he needed. He's so very particular, you know, and the servants don't always know how to do it right."

"Of course, my lady. It's a shame the earl hides all his keys, which would let you check the contents of his desk more easily." She stepped farther into the room, a dangerous glitter in her countenance. "Now where does he keep them? You would know, of course."

Her lips curled into an odd smile, half amused and half cunning, like a cat playing with its mouse, preparing for the fatal pounce. For one fearful moment, I thought, *She knows. She knows and is toying with me. Mocking me.*

"All is well, it seems. Shall we return to my suite and dress for dinner?"

"Yes, of course." She moved through the adjoining doors behind me.

She held my gaze in the mirror as she began taking my hair down and smoothing it with the brush. "Lord Enderly asked me this morning to inform you that you'll be hosting guests for dinner tonight. Lord and Lady Remington."

This pleased me immensely, and I breathed more easily, even as Simone twisted my hair until it pulled my scalp. Being among friends eased the burden of sharing a table with the bear of a man who was supposed to be my husband.

■ ■ ■ ■

I swept down the wide steps in a crisp plum-colored gown trimmed with little feathers and paused at the landing to listen for the men. They should have returned by now.

"There's the lady of the house." I spun at the sound of a low voice at the bottom.

"Mr. Prendergast."

"Splendid, as always."

I frowned and strode over to him, uttering a harsh whisper. "You could have told me, you know." I waved toward the closed drawing room doors. "Apparently I have a husband. That would have been helpful to know *before* he marched through the front door."

His amused grin stoked the flames of my irritation. "I assumed you already did. For every queen there is a king, for every countess . . . I *did* mention the earl, I'm quite certain."

"As a sort of guardian. A protector." My voice faltered at my foolishness.

"A splendid definition of what every husband should be. My apologies if you misunderstood, but frankly, I never thought you could."

"What do you intend for me to do now that he's here, and . . ." My throat swelled at the memory of his boot clomps in the next room, only a door separating us, his ghostly form staring at me the next morning. "Surely you don't intend for me to truly be his wife." The very idea made me squirm, my skin heating, and Prendergast laughed outright.

"You mustn't worry. That isn't what I've hired you to do."

Just then the drawing room door opened, and Bradford stepped out. "Mr. Prendergast, I thought I heard you."

Prendergast moved close for a parting word, his voice barely above a whisper. "Simply avoid being alone with the man and all will be well. He may be intimidating, but he cannot hurt you in my presence."

Bradford threw wide the doors and we entered for dinner. Sully watched from inside the dining room, where he and the other dark-haired footman leaned over the long table to place crystal and flatware at each place. I strode into the drawing room and found a chair as we awaited the dinner summons.

In a moment the earl's deep voice just behind me pierced my thoughts. "I take it you are to blame for the recent deficit to my pocketbook."

I turned and looked up at his stoic expression that was neither bitter nor pleased.

"It was you who made the changes, was it not?"

"I've taken the liberty of adding a mistress's touch to the house and grounds, but only because it was so dreary. And I did not spend a farthing."

His mouth twitched. "I'm referring to the recent favors granted to my tenants, including a stipend allowed one Mrs. Lawry of Turret Cottage for the care and keeping of two orphaned children."

"Wards of the estate." I straightened and attempted to regain my façade. "She is doing you a service, my lord, and she has been compensated a mere pittance for it."

I held my breath after releasing these daring words. He stared but said nothing. I shifted my face away, afraid his gaze might scorch it, and caught sight of Cousin Philip standing near the couch to my right, eavesdropping. He watched me, hands clasped behind his back, a queer light of admiration masked behind his incredulous face.

When the butler admitted our guests into the drawing room, the earl strode away to greet them and Cousin Philip restrained me with a gentle touch to my arm. "I suppose you think I should be impressed by your little display."

"It was not for your benefit, Cousin Philip. You already heard me make the promise to the tenants themselves."

"I'm never impressed by a promise until it's kept."

"I was merely doing what any mistress would."

He frowned, his eyes unpacking whatever they found in my countenance as he watched me. It was not the stare of judgment he had so often turned my way, but one of a riddle-solver who has been stumped by a dead end. Somehow, turning this corner with the man made me glad. With a nod I turned to greet Lady Remington on a cloud of hope. Things were looking up and I was accomplishing my goals on many fronts.

I approached the Remingtons with a smile. With a distant, ladylike embrace and kiss on the cheek, we reestablished our acquaintanceship and spoke as old friends. Once again I was warmed by this couple's unspoken affection for each other, hands brushing even as they spoke to separate people. The sight renewed my gladness that they'd come.

Soon the earl extended his arm to escort me into the dining room, and I held my breath as I always did when in close proximity with the man. Yet slipping my hand into the crook of his arm, I was surprised at the warmth my fingertips found there. What had I expected, granite?

As we marched into the long room and down the table to our seats, my nerves eased. Things were going well — I was being absorbed into this world, I'd gained a friend, I had begun helping the local tenants in real ways, and I'd soon rescue Sully.

Seated across the long table from the earl, I noticed his face had settled into stony smoothness — cold and hard, yet free of the harsh lines from before. At least he did not lash out over my bold decisions. Silence reigned as the servers brought platters of food and began to serve the meal.

As Sully placed a plate before me, his nearness overwhelmed me with memories of everything said to one another, the near-kiss that I now desperately wished I had tasted. I tried to will away the warmth climbing into my face as Sully walked away, but it only seemed to increase. I glanced up to see Lady Remington's intelligent gaze on me. "You look well. Quite happy too." Her eyes searched my face as if to verify her words, and I offered a smile.

"I am well. Rothburne has been a wonderful change for me these last weeks."

But I did wonder how the coming days would unfold. I glanced up at the man on the opposite end of the table whose features had a permanent weight to them, as if the air was heavier and thicker around him than it was for anyone else. We couldn't linger in this dance forever, avoiding one another and that odious topic that hovered over us, yet I dreaded the moment of truth. I didn't even know for sure what he knew, or what he'd done.

"So I see. Perhaps I was mistaken in worrying over you." Lady Remington's soft voice drew me back. "You must forgive my tongue. I seem to gather opinions with each passing year, and as I'm rather advanced in age, I have quite a lot of them. Unfortunately not all of them are worth listening to." She threw a glittering, friendly smile toward me and lifted her knife and fork.

"Your concern has solidified our friendship, for which I'm grateful. I've not met many people here yet."

"As well you shouldn't," she quipped as she finished her delicate bite. "Most of them are vultures when anyone from the peerage waltzes into their social circles. It's so rare out here."

I accepted a slice of bread. "I'll bear that in mind."

As Sully slipped into the room, my attention shifted. I couldn't help but glance up at him as he bent toward Cousin Philip to offer stewed potatoes.

When our gazes met, a tiny smile flickered over his lips, and the sight of it washed my soul in gladness. I felt with powerful truth the words I'd skimmed over in the Hardy book while choosing my message to Sully a few days ago: "They spoke very little of their mutual feelings: pretty phrases and warm attentions being probably unnecessary between such tried friends." No matter my worries and doubts, his looks and tenderness, his very presence in this house, drove the truth of his affection directly into my heart when I set aside my apprehensions long enough to see it.

When I broke the gaze and turned back to my neglected guest, it seemed she too had been distracted. Lord Remington winked at his wife, and she fluttered her lashes in an amusing attempt to remain poised, but then she caught me looking at her. A coy smile turned her lips. "I suppose you've seen a great deal of romance in your travels. None so silly as an old married couple."

"Far from silly."

Sully approached then, and the power of

his nearness, this man I'd adored since childhood, cut off anything else I'd meant to say. He leaned toward me, stopping much too far away with the bowl of potatoes.

I nodded my assent and forced my attention once more toward my guest as he began serving them. "What I mean to say is, it's actually quite lovely to witness."

She laughed. "Ah, how you flatter me."

"Not at all. Those dramatic serial novel romances are exciting, but one never knows how they'll fare on the rocks of everyday life. There's something rare and intensely beautiful in a person who knows you well and loves you anyway. Ordinary men and everyday romances are the sweetest and deepest." I took a breath, stealing a glance at Sully, who still hovered, spooning potatoes onto my plate. "There's a wonderful charm to ordinary, everyday moments, and the people who remain through them."

The spoon paused as his own words settled over him, revealing just how asleep I'd been when he'd spoken to me in the study.

"Ah, finally. A lady who understands a true hero." Lord Remington looked my way with an appreciative sparkle to his countenance. "You must have experienced such a love yourself, to have those sentiments."

Oh yes, I had. Lord Remington winked at the earl, while I forced myself not to look at Sully. I thought of that study full of books, each spine representing a world that had been opened to me by the man standing near. "I've learned that a true hero is not an extraordinary man. He may not impress the world, but he so greatly changes hers. That makes him utterly heroic indeed."

For a moment my heart-drenched words hung in the air. Lady Remington sat up in her chair with a smile. "What intelligence you have for such a young woman. Your governess must have been the finest sort."

I did not answer but turned back to my plate of food, which I found to be heaped with a tumbling mountain of potatoes. I smiled as Sully left, hoping no one would guess our secret.

As I pondered the guarded expressions of each diner, I wondered what other secrets lay beneath the surface. I had the feeling there was an abundance of them, and they would change the entire household if the fog of pretense were to lift and reveal them.

"Did you have a great many governesses or just one very smart one?"

I turned back to Lady Remington, summoning a proper reply with a smile. "Everything I learned about men and marriage I learned from observing the missteps and mistakes of real people. Especially myself."

Her smile glittered. "My, but I'm glad I've discovered you, Lady Enderly. There's something about you and your enchanting house that draws me in and awakens my mind. You have more poise than you'd believe, for you are a woman who knows exactly who you are, and you live that well."

I stared at the damask tablecloth, uncomfortable with the direction of this conversation.

"I cannot wait to show you off to all of Somerset society. Which reminds me, perhaps we should discuss the upcoming soiree after dinner. There are so many pl—"

"No." The earl's voice sliced through hers. "I wish to speak to her alone. In my suite."

I tensed and looked to Prendergast, who cast his anxious gaze toward me, his shoulders stiff under his jacket. He should say something, prevent me from being alone with this man, be the buffer he'd promised to be, but how could he? How could he demand, before all these guests, that a man — his employer, no less — not be alone with his wife? I swallowed and clutched the arms of my chair. In the corner, Sully's eyes blazed like hot coals on the white ash of his face. Oh how dearly I needed him to rescue me — and *not* to.

I inhaled and felt dizzy, the fresh air seeming too heady for my senses.

21

Even without meeting a person, we can determine a lot about her by looking at the people she allows into her life.
    ~ Diary of a Substitute Countess

I perched in the wingback chair in his over-warm sitting room, the great shadows of the fire leaping garishly. Shut into this private chamber with nothing but the fire to light the space, fear made my skin clammy and my fingers restless in my lap.

"You look so much like her." Haunted by some terrible beast of the past, the man hunched against the fireplace, his dark hair flopping in contrast over his pale forehead. His voice was gravelly. "How is it possible that you look so much like her? Are you a relation?"

"Not that I know of. I've never even met her."

"When I saw you on the stairs, I . . . I

286

could barely breathe." He broke into pacing before the fire like a lion, head down and hand shoved back into his mussed hair. He grumbled something I couldn't decipher. I gripped the upholstered arms of the chair and waited, unable to even cast up a silent prayer. I felt the weight of this mess, as well as my own responsibility involved, and could not bear to invite God into it.

He stopped and stared at me, his look piercing. "You must know how this torments me. Is that what Prendergast secretly aims to do — punish me?"

I pressed my lips together to consider my reply as my pulse ticked with painful intensity in the quiet room. I didn't wish to know more, but I needed to. "Do you believe you should be?"

"Of course I do. I had my part in it." He exhaled, pacing again. "That scoundrel told you it was my idea, though, didn't he? Well, it wasn't. Not that you'd believe me over the man who could charm dirt."

I studied this broken shell of a man so different than the veneered evil of Prendergast, and my fear and dislike melted into pity tinged with compassion. "In fact, I do believe you." There was something authentic in his brokenness, something worth restoring. I found myself wanting to help, but the idea overwhelmed me too. There was nothing simple about this man or the chaos raging within him.

He paused before the fire, his face haggard and drawn, his dark hair an erratic mess where his fingers had mussed it over and over. Firelight highlighted the gaunt hollows of his face. He crossed to me in two long strides and lowered himself into the matching armchair beside mine. "Of course you do. You're just like her. She always believed in me too."

Those simple words tightened the embrace of fear on my insides. He spoke of her in the past tense, as if her belief in him had died — or she herself had. I gulped, sick with anticipation as I stood on the edge of learning what I had wanted to know but wishing I didn't have to hear it. "Perhaps you should tell me your side of the story, then."

He turned large, haunted eyes on me for endless moments, and I wondered if perhaps I hadn't voiced my suggestion out loud. Finally, he answered. "This has gone so much further than I ever meant it to. The money appealed to me initially, but not like it did to Prendergast. Never that much."

He turned away. "It was he who set the fool thing in motion, then he approached me with what he'd done afterward. He made it sound easy. Seamless. No one would ever know — but how could they not? *How could they not?*" He bowed his head into his hands and his broad shoulders trembled in the jumping shadows. "And now everything is a disaster, and I haven't any idea what to do."

I cringed as he admitted feelings that so mirrored my own recently. "Could you do some good to those you've wronged?"

He gave a flat laugh. "I've wronged a lot of people."

"Then I suggest you begin repaying." I thought of the freedom from my own guilt I'd tasted as I helped the tenants, like Queen Esther saving her people. "If anything's ill-gained, it should be given away."

He leaned forward to rest his elbows on his knees and pondered my suggestion. "But then I would have nothing."

I studied the little bags under his eyes, the fear stretching his features, and didn't know whether to pity his own self-entrapment or despise him for what he'd taken from others. "Then think of one person. One who is very deserving of your help and start there."

More silence. When he finally lifted his dark, hollow gaze to mine, the wild intensity in his expression frightened me. It seemed unstable, unpredictable. "It's you."

"Me?" I was breathless.

"The only one who deserves anything in this is you. I wronged you first, and that's what started this mess. I know it now, and I even knew it then, but I was too arrogant to admit it. You were always right, and I hated that." He took my hand in his giant one, and my Spitalfields instincts took over, forcing me to remain still, to let it play out. Don't run and no one will chase you. Yet my insides trembled as this powerful man looked past me and spoke in a distant, troubled voice, smoothing his thumb over my hand. "Surely you know I would do anything for you, Lyn. Anything."

I shuddered at his use of her given name toward me in such an intimate tone. The heat of the fire became suffocating. I shifted. "Lord Enderly."

He blinked and dropped my hand. "Her. I mean her." He jerked away with a growl, and I flinched. "I cannot stand to look at you any longer. It's as if I'm speaking to her and I cannot bear it. Mostly because I know you are not her. *Could* not be her."

A quiet ache rolled around inside me as my hands lay helplessly in my lap. The question screamed through my mind — *Where is she?* I dared not voice it, though. Oh, how badly I wanted to. Yet another part of me realized I might not want to know the answer.

A knock sounded on his door, causing us both to jump. The butler's voice came through, muffled by the wooden barrier. "My lord, you are wanted downstairs by Philip Scatchard."

The next morning my chambermaid was quiet as she helped me dress. She eyed the pages of stationery still sprawled over my desk as she left, and I shuffled them together and hurried with them to the abandoned rooms, where I could write freely.

In the old library, I sat in the deep windowsill, staring at the name embossed across the top. I had wanted people to think I was the countess, but when that brute had looked at me and seen her . . . I shivered. In one smooth swoop I drew a line through her elegant name and penned mine just below. How much sweeter was that name upon the lips of the man I loved than her name upon the lips of her husband.

With my nerves knotted and my head throbbing, I knew it was time to leave. I could not share a house — a false marriage — with this earl who was more wolf than man, who was unstable and unpredictable.

291

"Victor," I said to my reflection in the glass. "Victor, it has to end. I'm no liar and you have made me into one. It's too much for me and I will not continue it. No, I absolutely will not. I don't care what you say . . ."

The words came easily when I told them to myself, when his gaze was not scorching clear down to my thoughts.

Setting aside the notepaper, I stared up at Lady Enderly. Her vitality emanated even through this painting, as if inviting everyone around her to share in her enthusiasm for every little thing.

A knock startled me, but it was only the downstairs maid summoning me to meet a visitor in the study. "Very well, I'll be along." Stashing the pages in a derelict shelf when she'd ducked out, I made my way toward the east end of the house. An eerie silence pervaded the main floor, and I wondered at the quiet.

Pausing before the windows to look for a carriage, a terse whisper nearby startled me. Senses alert, I glanced around. I paced toward where I'd heard the sound and saw the doors to the monks' dormitory wing open. With a frown, I strode closer to investigate. When I neared, I saw the source of the whisper — Prendergast waved to me from the shadows.

I slipped into the hall, and he grabbed my arm, pulling me into an empty room and shutting the door. Before he spoke a word, I could feel the tension exuding from him. "It's time to pull out every trick we have. You must behave perfectly, speak impeccably. Do you understand? I thought we had a little more time, but it seems dear old Uncle Wells is impatient."

"He's here?" Perhaps this charade would soon come to an end on its own.

"His solicitor. He sent his man down to handle some paperwork for the estate. Have you been practicing that signature I gave you?" I nodded, and he thrust a paper and pencil at me. "Show me."

Steadying my hand, I drew out the signature I'd placed at the end of every diary entry written upon the countess's stationery.

"Good, good. It'll do. All you need to do is sign where he tells you and say little. Silence is even better. It'll be an easy task as long as you stay focused and remember who you are. Can you do that?"

I shuddered to remember the earl calling me "Lyn" the night before in that deep, impassioned voice of a soul slightly unbalanced. That moment had brought the reality of this mess crashing down around me. I couldn't bring myself to agree anymore —

I merely lifted helpless eyes to Prendergast, pleading for release.

Anger lit his face in a flash. "You *will* do this."

"It's the earl. I'm afraid of him. I don't want —"

He grabbed my arms and shoved me back against the door. "I don't care what you want. You *must* do this. You are Lady Enderly and you'll do exactly as I say. Is that clear?"

I stuck out my chin, bracing to keep it from trembling. "What if I don't?"

His long fingers sank harder into my upper arms until I felt my pulse against them. He drew closer and his mint-tea breath fanned over my face. "I've killed before without a second thought. I choose people who are like wildflowers, plentiful and untended. Your type grows without being planted and dies without being missed."

"Kill me and you'll have no one to play countess."

His eyes narrowed. "I never said it was you I'd kill."

I turned away. *Sully.*

"I have a great many powerful connections, and he has nothing but a charge of mutiny hanging over his poor, doomed head. I do hope these facts have sufficed to change your mind."

"He didn't kill anyone on that ship."

"That matters little to a judge. All that matters is what I will say about him, and I haven't yet decided that." His features hardened. "You *will* play this part for the solicitor. You *will* be the countess in every single way."

Helpless anger burned through my body, my stiff limbs trapped against the door. I stared back at him with the force of it, then he released my arms, blood flowing back into them with painful pulses. With that, he slipped out into the hall, with whispered instructions for me to follow after a safe amount of time had passed. I steadied myself against the wall, breathing hard and touching my fingertips to my warm cheeks. What a sight I must look. After a moment of collecting myself, I exited to check my flushed appearance.

Before I could pass the gilded mirror in the hall, a familiar voice arrested my movements. "The truth, Raina." Sully's terse words made me tense. "For once in this whole charade, speak plainly with me. Are you staying because of him? Are you in love with him?"

With an ache inside, I turned to look up into his impassioned face, eyes raging like a storm over the ocean. "How could you ever think that?"

"I didn't until now." He jerked his head toward the room where I'd just been alone with Prendergast and come out crimson as a rose.

My hands flew again to my cheeks. "Sully, you must believe me. I hate that man with every hair on my head."

"I know you, Raina." His nostrils flared. "You'd only do something this daring for love. So who is it? Who could you possibly be so smitten with that you've remained here through all this?"

"I told you, it's a rescue mission."

"Someone you love."

My eyes flicked over his face, lips trembling, my helpless expression revealing everything. I dropped my gaze and took his hand, running my thumb over his knuckles. "Yes."

The truth hit him, paling his features and shuddering through him. He dropped my hand and backed away, horrified. *Me?* his look asked with disbelief.

I looked at him with heart-aching adoration. "Yes." I reached up and touched his cheek, allowing myself that small show of my mighty affection, then I turned and tore myself away. Leaving him frozen like a statue in the long white hall, I turned and fled into the grand hall.

Please. Please understand.

Regret pounded through me with each step I took away from him, for I'd turned a corner. Sully was not the sort to lie down and let someone rescue him. What would come now? Would he attempt to take Prendergast down? Would everything fall to pieces?

With a slow, steady breath in the hall outside the room to which I'd been summoned, I forced myself back into the role I'd been hired to play. Sure and controlled, I entered the study and released a smile that was as false as my entire life here. Prendergast watched with calculated analysis as I carried out one of my most important performances yet.

The man seated before the desk had a long white mustache neatly trimmed and a set of wire spectacles propped into the folds of his thick face. His pleasant, deeply settled countenance spoke of true gentility and kindness. He stood as I entered and bowed with deep sincerity. "Lady Enderly, it's my honor to finally meet you. I'm Lawrence Fitzgerald, solicitor of Lord Darlington, your husband's uncle."

"Just the formal name for dear Uncle

Wells." Prendergast's interjection went mostly unnoticed.

"I'm glad to make your acquaintance." I said those words with full sincerity. His mere presence smoothed the edges of my tension, despite what this meeting meant to us. "I look forward to Uncle Wells visiting himself one day."

"He mentioned his intentions of an early spring visit, if the weather is kinder and his health remains improved."

"Of course." As I moved to sit behind the desk, Prendergast followed me like a noxious odor, and I cringed. Did he have to watch over my shoulder?

Then I realized that no, he did not. His explicit instructions returned to me now, emboldening where they'd drained strength before. *You will be the countess in every way.*

I turned to my shadow with a charming smile. "That will be all, Mr. Prendergast. Thank you."

He blinked, his smile still in place. "I beg your pardon?"

"I'll manage without you for the moment, but I thank you for your concern."

A muscle in his cheek twitched. "I assumed you'd want my counsel as you looked over documents that will be utterly confusing to you."

I smiled patronizingly. "How good of you to care, but as these documents only concern the Countess of Enderly, I believe I'll handle them myself."

He made several stiff, jerky movements, then took himself away with barely concealed frustration ripping across his face. When the door slid shut behind him, I released a light chuckle and seated myself at the desk across from my visitor.

Mr. Fitzgerald showed a flicker of a smile. "A bit less crowded in the room."

I grinned. "More than you know. Now, what is it you'd like to discuss, Mr. Fitzgerald?"

He seated himself and lifted a stack of papers from a file beside his chair, thumbing through the pages with a frown. "My client has asked me to go over several matters with you in the transfer of the estate and its income that occurred recently." He splayed them across the desk, moving them about to look for the ones requiring a signature. "He had previously withheld full ownership of the estate, but as you know, he's now granting you everything. Not only will you receive the income from the land, but you will be the full and rightful owner of the estate."

My gaze flew over a few of the papers, trying to gather an understanding of the contents. "Forgive my lack of information on the matter, but can you tell me why it is my signature and not the earl's that is required on all these documents?"

"Why, your ladyship, the estate is a gift specifically to you, not the earl."

I blinked. "How can something be mine and not his?"

He smiled. "Because you are making history, my lady. Parliament recently passed an amendment that gives property rights to married women, and my client, the earl's uncle, was a prime supporter of the movement. He wishes to make an example of this law by granting this very profitable and sizable estate to a woman — you — to encourage the rest of England to follow suit. Congratulations on being on the edge of a revolution, Lady Enderly."

Stunned, I forced myself to scan the documents before me, trying to pick out words I recognized in the mess of formal writing. Truly, a married woman with her own property!

"You not only have the right to inherit property, but to earn money from its profits and sell parcels of land at will."

No wonder they needed someone to replace the countess while she was indisposed.

What a great deal of money the woman had in her power. It made one dizzy to consider the amount. Perhaps she was not indisposed at all, but uncooperative. A chill convulsed me as I remembered the forceful intent of Prendergast, like a train charging through whatever stood in its path. It should not be Prendergast running this estate, but her. No . . . Philip Scatchard.

I lifted my gaze. "What other rights do I have?"

He explained everything the countess had the legal ability to do concerning the estate, and I soaked it up hungrily. "What if I wish to change one of these documents? Could I do that?"

He blinked. "I'm afraid not. These documents have already been signed by my client. The only option you have is to sign them or not."

I had promised Prendergast I would, but how greatly I wished not to sign them. I toyed with the pen, twirling it in my fingers.

"If I may, what exactly displeases you about these arrangements, my lady?"

I explained, in as vague terms as possible, how I felt that the property rightly belonged to someone else.

He brightened with understanding. "Well, then. I can suggest one thing you can do, if you wish it. I can even help you from the legal perspective."

He explained his solution to me, and my smile grew, mind alive with possibilities. "I believe I'll do that. Thank you, Mr. Fitzgerald. You've been most helpful." My heart hammered. It was within my reach to set things right, and finally crush this hard ball of guilt and anxiousness that had grown to a nearly unbearable weight inside. I would be Esther to one more person, in a magnificent manner.

So, Victor Prendergast. You wish me to be Lady Enderly in every way. I smiled down at the papers before me. *I will heartily consent to your demand.*

Mr. Fitzgerald held out a beautiful, gold-tipped pen to me like the king's scepter extended to Queen Esther. With a pounding heart I accepted it, smooth and cold in my fingers and, after dipping it in ink, went to work righting the great wrong of which I'd been a part. Philip Scatchard's name looked so handsome and bold on those papers, and I stared at it proudly. The best part was that Prendergast would never figure out what I'd done until I was gone. For a brief moment, the Spitalfields fighter returned, armed with cunning and determination to battle those who had pitted themselves against her.

I straightened and looked over my paperwork when I was finished, brimming with satisfaction. I had set in motion a course of events which would one day have huge consequences — and of which I was exceedingly proud.

22

On occasion you may charm people by convincing them of your worth, but you will never fail to do so when you assure them of their own.

~ Diary of a Substitute Countess

Sully turned for one last glimpse of the great hall, his bag slung over one shoulder. This was the only way to handle this mess. He was the rescuer, and this time the only way to save Raina was by removing himself from the equation. She'd never leave otherwise, if she believed she could help him, but it wasn't her problem to untangle.

He stepped toward the door, but footsteps on the staircase made him stop. Leaping into the shadows, he watched as the object of his affection glided out of the study and shut the doors behind her. Flattening himself against the walls, he prayed the shadows would hide him.

But they failed. She turned and froze, her eyes locking on his face, then on the bag slung over his arm and the fiddle hanging at his side. Something bobbed in her throat and her lovely wide eyes watched him. She took two steps closer, her face pleading with him not to follow through on his obvious intentions.

He took in the sight of her, the slender white figure so tiny in that great hall. His breathing quickened. Did he have the strength to leave her here?

He'd beg her to go with him, right this minute. They could escape together, go into hiding. He took a step toward her, but Victor Prendergast's dark form appeared from another doorway, and he paused before them with a frown. He eyed the bag now hanging at his side, and then his face. "I see you have your things packed. Do you not enjoy your new mistress, Mr. McKenna? Is she too strict for your tastes? Too demanding?"

He was overly aware of Raina hovering on the fringes of his vision, but he did not look at her. "I'm afraid it's me, sir. I am the problem. I no longer fit the role I was meant to have." He was her rescuer. It defined his part in their relationship, and if he was no longer that . . .

305

Pain streaked across Raina's face as she grasped his meaning.

"Lady Enderly, a word with you, please." The aged guest stepped from the study. "There's just one more concern."

"You'd best go, my lady." Victor did not smile. "I will deal with this situation."

She stared at Sully, her pleading eyes the only spots of color in her pale face. She stepped backward toward the study, then finally tore herself away.

Victor ushered him into the servants' hall just behind them and narrowed his eyes. "She's such a delicate little thing, isn't she? Most London women are. So easily broken."

"You don't know her well if you think so."

"Like fine china." He lifted a nearly empty teacup from the counter, turning it in his fingertips. "Solid and long-lasting, pure and ever so smooth." He ran the tip of his thumb over its white surface, and a chill passed over Sully. "Yet all it takes is a fumble —"

He released the cup, and Sully lunged to catch it, lukewarm liquid splashing onto his sleeve.

"Well done, Sullivan. How fortunate you were here to catch it." With a wry smile, he turned on his heel, but Sully grabbed his shoulder and spun him around.

"Why don't you let her alone? She met with the man, didn't she?"

"She's not going anywhere until the final papers are signed in a month. Uncle Wells will want to meet with her himself. Then we'll discuss her . . . exit."

With another satisfied smile of triumph, Victor turned and moved back into the hall.

Clenching his jaw, Sully marched to the bucket of water and sloshed his arm through it, cleansing it of the spilled tea. What could he do now? What could he possibly do to rescue her? Victor was now aware that he knew of his schemes. He'd be watching them, and being alone together would be impossible. So would escape. His only options were to remain and continue to let her rescue him, which turned his stomach, or leave her here with that man — which made him want to punch a wall.

Or . . .

Truth. The truth will set you free. An age-old verse that his father had bellowed many times from his pulpit, followed by a fist-pounding against the battered wood. Those words rang through his head now, but with the comfort of another Father. With the hope of a promise assured. Yes, truth. It was the finest — and only — weapon left to him.

Yet this must be done strategically. Carefully. With a grim set to his shoulders, Sully marched to his tiny sleeping quarters and fumbled about for a paper, smoothing it out against his chest. Perhaps there was a way to remain *and* be her rescuer. Only by defeating Victor would escape ever be possible for either of them.

Returning to the study with his letter, Sully cast a curious glance over the documents spread over the desk, trying to assess what had occurred here behind closed doors. It was a draft of a will — for the Countess of Enderly. To his utter surprise, Raina had left the estate to Philip Scatchard upon the death of the countess. The move was so brilliant Sully could hardly stand it. If the worst was true concerning the real countess — and Sully believed it was — the estate would soon pass out of the hands of those scheming men and into those of the earl's cousin. His weren't the most fit to possess such an estate, and the gloomy cousin so oft found with a drink was far from deserving of such a reward, but they were a fair bit better than Prendergast's evil claws. Admiration for his quick-witted childhood friend swelled in his chest.

Sully slipped a long envelope from his jacket and tucked it into the visitor's satchel with a deep breath. *God, do what you will with this. Keep it hidden from those who shouldn't see it, and make it clearly visible to whoever should.*

Slipping out of the room, he nearly collided with Philip Scatchard.

"Hello there, old man. No news for me, I assume?"

The spying. Yes, he was supposed to be doing that. Sully's shoulders stiffened under his uniform. "No sir, nothing of note to report."

He grimaced, toying with a half-empty glass in his hand. "I suppose she's tidied up any little indiscretions that might be found. I've half a mind to slip into her bedchamber and dig through that little desk —"

"Do not count on my assistance for that, sir." Sully spoke through clenched teeth as he thought of the papers sitting on the desk just past these doors. What a wretched little brute.

"Come off it, old man. I mean no harm. I only want to know what she's about and protect this estate." He ran a hand through his hair and threw back the remainder of his drink, plunking the little glass on a side table. "I don't suppose we have any more of that delightful stuff, do we?"

Sully stared at the mildly besotted man,

those red-rimmed eyes and the greasy hair on his forehead. Meeting his gaze, Sully clasped his hands behind his back. "I believe there's a touch more. I'll bring it to you in the study."

His expression hardened. "I'm afraid there are private papers in there that her highness and that solicitor wouldn't wish me to see. Estate business, you know."

"And are you not the estate's manager? They've a great deal to do with you, sir, and I believe you should take a peek at them." Sully lifted a meaningful glance to the man.

"Right on, good work." With a salute, Philip disappeared into the study.

Sully remained stationed before the door, on guard in case the solicitor should return and find Philip snooping.

He stared at the elegant hall clock as it ticked the endless seconds, studied the gentle curves of the pure-white angel statue on a stand by a doorway.

When the door opened again some minutes later, Philip stepped out, ashen and shaken, the drink Sully was to fetch forgotten. His searching eyes openly stared at Sully, as if seeking answers in his face. He looked away and shoved his fingers through his dark hair again. "That woman." He lifted his gaze to Sully. "Such a mystery."

"Most are, sir."

"Right you are." His voice was dry. Scratchy. "Yet none more so than her."

"Shall I bring you tea for that throat, sir?"

He cleared it. "I suppose that would be nice. Thank you, McKenna."

Head down, Sully strode toward the servants' wing with a sigh. He had accomplished something helpful, at least, and that had settled his mind to a small degree. Yet the knowledge of that shift between him and Raina jarred his peace. Not only was he taken from the position of rescuer, but he was now the one being rescued, and he did not like it.

In the kitchen, he poured tea from the ever-present pot on the stove and turned to find a saucer. Yet there on the edge of the sideboard lay a book, *Jane Eyre* — her favorite. Discarding the tea, he snapped up the book and flipped to the page marked with string. She'd left him a message.

"No — no — Jane; you must not go. No — I have touched you, heard you, felt the comfort of your presence — the sweetness of your consolation: I cannot give up these joys. I have little left in myself — I must have you."

He held the little volume to his chest and

exhaled. Never before had he felt so help-less.

23

Mirrors reflect our appearance, but what we create reflects the beauty within us.

~ Diary of a Substitute Countess

"Do you think it will be chilly by then?" I leaned over the calendar in the morning room and held my finger on the 26th. That would be the evening for the harvest soiree Lady Remington had insisted we host. "We could have a fire and spiced cider."

"It's likely, with the way the winds are turning, but we'll do our best to make the inside plenty festive either way, my lady." Shirley Shackley tugged long sashes and table runners from their crates and shook them out.

"Will there be time enough to have everything cleaned and pressed?"

"You have a brigade of servants at your command, my lady, and they can accomplish a great deal." She smiled. "You should be proud of your staff. They are capable and willing, all prepared to trim the house with such spirit and joy." She heaved a deep sigh of happiness at this last comment, as if the very idea of this festive soiree was to her like a fresh cup of tea in the morning beside a warm fireplace.

"What does the earl typically do for his soirees?"

She paused her unpacking and looked at me with an odd mix of pity and surprise.

Of course, a wife would know this. I ducked my face and hurried to repair the mistake. "I meant before our marriage. What did he do in the past? He rarely speaks of his life before."

She continued her work but watched me. "I wouldn't know much about that, my lady, but I do know Rothburne used to be so full of grand parties in years past, and he came to them often. The earl's aunt and uncle loved the people here, and they held parties with a great deal of fanfare. Why, I believe they even used to open the house up to the public for an evening and greet their neighbors. It was quite a splendid event."

"What a lovely idea." I could imagine the decorated hall filled with people and gaiety. "We shall do exactly that and bring the tradition back to Rothburne. We'll serve spiced cider and crepes, maybe a little plum pudding in tiny cups. Then afterward we'll turn it into a ball of the finest sort and have dancing."

Shirley stood with a rosy smile and shifted an armload of ribbon. "It's good to have you at Rothburne, my lady. This old house had need of you, but so did that earl. Perhaps you can find that long-buried piece of him that used to enjoy these things and bring it to the surface again. Every man needs a good woman to draw out neglected parts of himself and shine them up a bit." She winked.

Again my heart melted into pity at the broken man. Had he always been this way? "Did you know him when he was younger?"

"I did, when he visited his aunt and uncle at Rothburne."

"And he was different? Happy?"

She smiled warmly. "He was bold and courageous, full of passion and ambition. All that's left is the boldness, I'm afraid. Over time every hardship in his young life, from his father's death to his brother's enlistment, hardened that boldness into anger." Her face took on a wistful cast as she glanced with a half smile toward the distant windows. "There's a charming gentleman inside that stony government man somewhere, I just know it. And nothing will bring it out like the lady he loves."

She smiled kindly at me, but I shrank from her encouragement. I was actually keeping him from his love. The missing woman seemed to float about the house, present but not truly, as if she were a specter. Yet to be a ghost, one had to be . . .

Simone watched me in the mirror without a smile as she brushed my hair that evening. "The earl must be so happy to be home with you, my lady."

I offered a wan smile.

"He is very different from Mr. Prendergast, is he not?" Her eyes blazed with silent intent, two glowing black orbs in a white face.

I focused my gaze on her. "What is it you mean to say?"

"Only that we see much of him, unlike the earl. Your estate must be one of his only clients, for he is here quite often, no?"

Clenching my jaw against the words the old Spitalfields Ragna would have spat out, I spun on my stool, yanking my hair from the tug of the brush. "That's more than enough strokes for one head of hair, thank you."

Simone stepped back and busied herself

with cleaning up the pins and combs scattered across the table's surface.

"I believe I'll retire early. Perhaps we should turn down the bed."

When she did not respond, I turned. She stood like a statue, eyebrows arched as she stared at something behind me. There on the mirror beside my bed was the familiar scrawl of Sully's handwriting, a message left with some black substance upon the glass. *SOS:2.* The sight of it in the presence of this woman unsettled me.

I strode before her and flipped my loose hair. "Won't you help me prepare for bed? The day has worn on me." My voice sounded high and pinched.

"Of course." But even as she plaited my hair and unfastened my gown, her gaze traveled often to that mirror. "Are you unwell, my lady?"

"I'm perfectly well."

"Shall I bring you a tincture? Perhaps a little tea."

"I assure you, I'm in excellent health."

Her gaze went pointedly to the mirror as she finished unlacing my stays and strode to the drawers for my nightclothes. "It's as if you were summoning help."

"A simple notation."

"On a mirror." She set garments on the

end of my bed and smoothed imaginary wrinkles with slow movements. "Often writing on walls is a sign of . . ." Voice drifting, she strode toward me and helped me out of my garments and into my nightclothes. "You may ring for me if you require anything else, my lady."

When she left the room, I hurried to the mirror and scrubbed the letters away with a square of linen, then closed the door. Then with a sigh I sank onto the bed and pondered what they meant. *SOS*. Was he in danger? But from whom — and why? He'd written them there some time ago, and he remained well. Then I remembered the bag slung over his shoulder and wondered if he'd meant this as a farewell message.

It was only after I'd slipped into my dressing gown and paced around the room that I spotted the intended reference — there on the table below the mirror, the little oil lamp had been pushed aside to make room for a leather-bound Bible with Sully's stone on top. I ran to it and grasped the stone, sinking onto the bed and running my fingertips over the stone's smooth surface. My other hand rested on the Bible below it. SOS would be the Song of Solomon. Drawing the large book onto my lap, I leafed through it in chunks.

When I found the spot, I carried the book over to the window seat to read in the glow of silvery moonlight. One candle burned on the shelf nearby, and I curled toward it, tucking my feet under me. I leafed through each page and found several underlined passages, and I drank them in.

Set me as a seal upon thine heart, as a
    seal upon thine arm: for love is strong
    as death . . .
Many waters cannot quench love, neither
    can the floods drown it . . .

On and on they carried. I read them all many times over, soaking in these beautiful words, then I let the open Bible fall onto my lap and laid my head back against the window frame. I remained this way for several peaceful moments as I recalled the lovely words. We'd have a future together, I was sure of it. If only he'd remain long enough for me to safely finish my task and get us out of danger.

I'd fallen into a drowsy near-slumber when I suddenly sensed a presence in the room. My eyes flew open, and there stood the earl in the doorway again, hanging about like a shadow of one who used to exist. I bolted upright in a second and looked at him.

"I saw your lady's maid bring a tea service to the room, and I thought perhaps . . . if you wouldn't mind the company . . . perhaps we could have tea together."

My gaze flew to the tray now lying on the table inside my door — I hadn't even heard her enter. I looked at him hesitantly, but I thought of no excuse to turn him away. And the longer I stared, the more this bear of a man simply looked wrung out and hurting. The sight softened me. "I suppose there's nothing improper in our being alone together, is there?"

"Forgive my intrusion. I won't stay long. I wanted to apologize for my behavior the night before. I'm sure I frightened you."

I offered a small smile, and he returned it, stepping farther into the room. "You're forgiven." Striding over to the tea service, I poured the single cup of tea and carried it to him.

He lowered himself into the seat, and his tension seemed to sink into the chair as his body did. He released a long sigh and closed his eyes for a moment before accepting the steaming liquid. I curled into my window seat again and waited. We remained silent, and the passing moments seemed to calm him.

"I feel better being here with you. Perhaps because I can fool myself, for a moment, into thinking you're her. I have not felt that well in some time."

His words toyed with the edges of my fear and dislike, threatening to unravel it. Pity and sorrow colored my vision as I looked at the tortured soul before me. "Do you feel ill often, sir?"

He fingered the edge of the chair arm. "Old. I feel old. I'm only one and thirty, but you'd never know it to look at my face, would you?"

"You couldn't pass for a young man."

He gave a humph, then rested again in silence as he pondered. "It is not so much my skin that has been wrinkled by life, but my soul. And it isn't the sun that's to blame but the darkness — that is, darkness that's in me. Every tiny erosion of my integrity is like a fine line, and one by one the wrinkles gather across the surface until I'm suddenly old and ugly — inside and out, for what's inside eventually wears through to the outside." He turned to study me then, his gaze caressing my face. "You're so pure and lovely still. So young. Here you sit, your hair down like a girl's, a Bible open beside you."

I swallowed past the lump in my throat, for even that image was deceiving. I had not, in fact, peered into the pages of a Bible in quite some time, except to read Sully's message.

What had become of me? All these changes wrought in me — were they improvements or perhaps a growing evil? My stomach tightened.

"You never think a single wrinkle's of any importance until you have a face full of them — and then they cannot be erased."

My breath thinned as I took in his words. How many small nicks had I allowed in my integrity since coming here? How often had I brushed aside my conscience?

"Keep your innocence. Take yourself away from here." His face pleaded. "I'll find another way out of this mess. It's all of my own making. It's my trouble to untangle, and I cannot drag —"

I held up a hand to stop him. "It's Victor who pulled me into it, and I cannot leave yet."

"Why not? You should." He sat back into the chair again, watching me.

I thought for a moment. Why not? Why didn't I simply leave? I looked around the room and tried to remember the reason, until I put my hand on the bench and felt

322

the stone.

Sully. It was for Sully.

Yet it was something else too. Sully had been right. I thought about that notepaper that held my handwriting but Lady Enderly's identity imprinted across the top, and again I felt that odd surge I'd experienced when Mrs. Stockton had appeared in the abbey. I was not Ragna anymore. Whatever had made me that girl was gone, and I was living out a borrowed identity — one I'd eventually have to return. Then what? Who would I be? I inhaled deeply, catching the scent of a sputtering candle stub and I gave the truest answer I knew. "I stay because I have nowhere else to go."

He considered me then, seeing only me for the first time instead of her. "You must have had a difficult life. This is not a terrible imposition for you then, is it?"

"Mr. Prendergast called me little Cinderella when we met. I suppose that's how it feels. Mostly." I did not say more, for wasn't this the man who claimed guilt for the countess's disappearance? Who knew what he'd done? I couldn't trust him with the details concerning Sully.

He gave a single nod.

I took a breath. "It hasn't been as pleasant for you, it seems, to have me here."

"Pleasant, no. But it has been helpful. Confession is cleansing to the soul, and I thank you wholeheartedly for hearing it."

"Think nothing of it."

"You mean it?" He sat forward with eagerness that made me regret my casual response. "I need to tell someone everything. Everything."

My heart pounded. "Maybe I —"

"It started when I met *her.*"

I gulped.

"She looked just as you do, so charming of face and bearing, but she had something more too. Something that glowed from deep within. It was a spirit of pure beauty that changed the air in the room the moment she entered." He closed his eyes. "I can still smell her soft curls piled on her head that came right to my chin. I've never found another woman like her, not even you who looks —"

His words had begun to strangle me with the reality of my failure. "Please, I don't need to know. It is not me you've wronged."

"Maybe you're right. Some secrets are better taken to the grave."

When he took a deep inhale, a knock sounded on the door and Prendergast's voice shattered the tension. "A word with you, old chap?"

My companion looked at me, his face grim, and rose. With a look of apology, he crossed the room and exited, leaving me alone with a flickering candle, an unfinished story, and my wild imagination.

24

It's allowable to judge a lady by her dress, for it is how she chose to express herself to strangers before she speaks a word to them.

~ Diary of a Substitute Countess

"You seem unwell." On the day of the soiree, I looked at Simone's stoic face in the mirror beside mine. She had the same inner chaos I imagined the countess might, only hers had leaked through to the surface, hardening her features and shadowing her eyes. How did so dark a person create a display of such beauty and light out of the rag woman?

"I'm well enough, my lady."

"Have you anything festive to wear? You must dress and come down as well, as my guest." It was the day we would open the doors to the local public, welcoming them to enjoy the abbey with us. Somehow I did not fear this night as I had the reception, but Simone seemed agitated.

She hesitated, her fingers pausing in my hair. "I did not bring any suitable gowns with me to this position. I was given to understand it would be temporary and limited in scope."

I tried to imagine her arrayed in a light-colored gown with her hair loosened in a romantic upsweep with stray tendrils framing her severe face. If gowns could transform Ragna into a countess, what might they do to my austere shadow of a lady's maid? With her slender figure and strikingly lovely face, perfect complexion and jet-black hair, she could be the most dramatic beauty in the room.

"You must wear one of my gowns. I insist." I was growing accustomed to having my desires granted.

She finally allowed herself to be arrayed by the chambermaid in a stunning garnet-colored frock with a velvet sash. When she swept back into the main room, I gasped at the transformation from a stony maid to an uncertain yet delicately feminine woman. I beckoned her over to the mirrors and had her face them to see how she looked from every angle. All at once the shadows melted away from her face in unabashed surprise at her appearance. She stared with longing and tenderness, as if remembering. After the chambermaid arranged her hair in a looser sweep, I placed a jeweled band on her head to accent its rich darkness, and the overall look was magnificent.

"You'll attend me in my grand entrance on the stairs, of course. I cannot wait to see everyone's reaction to you."

Her lashes fluttered over those rose-colored cheeks as her head dipped, and I realized that she, too, couldn't wait to see the reaction of everyone.

"Who will be there? Everyone in the household?"

I studied her anxious face. There seemed to be a specific someone she wished to know about. "They will all be waiting to witness our descent."

Her eyes glittered with something passionate — fear or excitement, I couldn't tell which. We glided arm in arm to the head of the stairs and looked down over the small gathering. Servants and members of the household spoke to one another in hushed groups. For the moment she clung to me, seeming to forget her hatred. It was as if she were a nervous debutante coming out into society.

I tugged at her arm to follow me and

glided down the steps, watching my slippers peeping out from the frothy layers of skirt that glittered in the light of countless candelabra. The collective gasp of the watchers below made me smile for Simone.

At the landing halfway, I released Simone as the earl extended his arm to accompany me for the remainder of the descent, but he hardly looked at me. Immediately I noticed the pinch of his lips and the tremble of his chin. "Are you well?"

He shook his head. "Not unless you, by some miracle, become her."

His words jarred me with negative emotions I couldn't decipher until I remembered his earlier comparison of me to the countess. A spirit of beauty, he'd said. One that changed the air as she entered the room. Summoning every ounce of courage and spirit I could muster, I straightened my shoulders and walked myself through her attributes. *Grace, poise, beauty.*

We reached the bottom and I greeted each member of the household with anxiousness hidden beneath well-practiced poise. A glint of appreciation sparked in Cousin Philip's face as I bade him good evening, and Lady Remington wore her approval plainly on her face, but the utter fascination in Victor Prendergast's eyes shocked me. Usually reserved for those moments alone before escorting me into an event, that look was now out in the open for anyone to see, but no one seemed to notice the man or his expression except me. He breathed his words into my ear. "Is that truly little Cinderella? You are absolutely astonishing." His eyes followed me as I walked past him.

When I turned to greet the two lines of staff my gaze snapped to the second footman who stood tall and still, watching me with no change to his expression. Every time I saw him, my relief was immense, but fear of his leaving always simmered near the surface.

The other servants bowed or curtsied and murmured polite responses, but Sully remained stiff, watching me with eyes that did not smile or turn toward my face. Had it been any other man I would assume indifference had settled in, but not so with Sully. His stance indicated a supreme effort to school his emotions. His very presence here, despite everything, said so much.

Forcing myself to pivot away from him, I turned to smile at the butler.

"If I may say so, my lady, you look sensational tonight." Bradford uttered the words with a respectful hush to his voice.

"They've all come to stare at me tonight.

I thought I'd make it worth their while. Would you do the honor of opening the doors for our guests? I believe it's time to open this house to the public."

With a deep bow, he strode to the door to comply, and soon a crowd of locals in their Sunday best surged into the well-lit hall and exclaimed over the fine things, reaching out to touch the long gold tassels and the handsome pewter on stands.

For the first time since I'd found him in the shadows with a bag in tow, Sully and I had a moment of near-privacy. "Thank you." I whispered these words over my shoulder with a tilt of my head. "Thank you for staying."

"I couldn't bear to leave you alone with him. We'll figure a way out of this together."

As his words melted my insides, I turned to glimpse my lady's maid on her evening of freedom and merriment, but I was surprised to see her even more stoic and closed off than ever before. Her fathomless dark eyes had narrowed into feline-like slits, and her face looked even paler than it did against her black service dresses. I recognized immediately the look that had seldom been cast my direction — pure female jealousy. Who was it? Whose attention did she seek that I had stolen? I glanced at each of the men from the household in turn and wondered — Philip Scatchard, Victor Prendergast, Bradford, the earl . . . None fit.

Surely it wasn't Sully. No, it couldn't be. She couldn't have even known we'd been talking.

Within an hour the guests had consumed all the fresh pudding in the large silver compotes on stands. Liveried servants worked quickly to dole out more spiced cider as the guests swarmed through the rooms open to them. Among the hum of conversation around me, a presence near my elbow made me spin to face a guest in a long dark gown. "Lady Enderly, I had the honor of making your acquaintance at the charming reception you hosted some weeks ago. Perhaps you recall — Mrs. Harrison of Landham?"

I didn't. "Mrs. Harrison, how kind of you to join us tonight." My lips lifted in a smile I did not feel. "I hope you are enjoying the festivities."

"Once I settled in and decided to enjoy myself, I had a fine time." She smiled and patted my arm. "I merely had to overcome my surprise at the . . . wide variety of guests you included tonight. I was given to understand it was a formal affair."

I pinched my lips into a smile. "It is quite

formal. Did the invitations not specify that?"

"Oh they did, and that is what confused me. It's just . . . I've never attended a party with so many people. So many *different* people." She held her glass of cider aloft to indicate the whole room and flashed a smile even more fraudulent than mine.

I blinked and glanced around the room again. Surely she couldn't mean mixing the peasants with the society guests. Odd as it was, Rothburne's former owners had done it for years with wild success. I returned her smile. "You must not have had the pleasure of attending Rothburne's open houses in the past. Gatherings such as this were a tradition."

"I most assuredly have attended. They would not have considered omitting me from their guest list. They were just as festive, but without your unique blend of guests. The event I attended was held the day *after* the house was opened to locals, but I imagine that's a great deal of work — two gatherings instead of one large, happy soiree such as this." Her forced smile nearly broke her mouth.

I struggled to find words, but the façade of Lady Enderly was lost in the presence of this high-bred woman and her sticky-sweet words of condemnation.

"Congratulations to you on the most unique guest list of the season. It's a mixture no other lady would dare attempt." With that she sailed away, leaving me with my delicate spirit crumbled and scattered miserably around my jeweled slippers. The earl was right — we may look similar, but there was something innate in her that I simply did not possess.

"And look at all the life and color in our midst because of it, my lady." Dear Bradford slipped up beside me, a tray tucked under his arm as he watched our guests. "As I said before, conventional countesses are plentiful. We're thankful to have an original."

"Thank you, Bradford." I blinked away the sting of tears. This would be the worst time to give in to them.

"Did you happen to notice the fine silver in use tonight?"

I glanced about at the glittering trays and flatware spread out on tables and among the guests. "It's stunning."

"It was brought out by the request of someone who truly wanted to see you succeed this night and find favor with the locals."

I raised my eyebrows. "Who?"

He jerked his head to the side, indicating a well-dressed gent with dark hair who conversed graciously with several guests. He turned his face for a moment, and I caught my breath at the sight of his profile. "Cousin Philip." Yes, it was. The hateful cousin was neatly shaven and pressed, his stance natural and — oddly enough — somewhat friendly.

"Perhaps you've not been watching him the last few days, but he's become quite a new man. He's worked diligently on the estate books every day, and he's asked for nothing but tea to drink."

I gawked at the young man who had emerged from beneath layers of bitterness and despair. Dark hair waved away from his face that now had a freshly cleaned and oiled look to it. "I hardly know what to say. I hadn't noticed."

"Yet another part of this house that our unconventional countess has touched with her special brand of color." He winked.

The change was undeniable, yet how could I have had any hand in it? The kind butler simply saw me in too generous a light.

He stepped closer and lowered his voice. "Never be ashamed of who you are, your ladyship, for you have something powerful in you."

A wobbly smile hid the turmoil his words stirred up inside. How could I bear it? How could I stand here and continue to lie to these people? There was nothing powerful in the real me. Not at all.

"There is only one Lady Enderly, and we are grateful to have her at our abbey."

"You are too kind, Bradford." Truly. "If you'll excuse me . . ." I fled from the room, unable to take any more. He was right, there was only one Lady Enderly — but she wasn't at the abbey. I was here in her stead.

Escaping the crowds, I tucked myself into the cloister walk to soak up the beauty there, needing every last morsel of it I could come by. Perhaps a moment of solitude would restore me. I had to carry out the evening well.

Once alone, I leaned against the windows, shut my eyes, and allowed myself to acknowledge the painful truth — deep inside, I wished I was her. I wished all the things said of this magnificent woman were true of me, and I wished this was really my life to spend in whatever way I chose.

After three long, cleansing breaths, a deep, rumbling voice jarred me from my thoughts. "Pardon me, but do you happen to know what this one is called?"

Shoving aside my worries, I spun to face an older local man towering over the plants. Brown-and-gray wavy hair framed his face from his dark, frowning eyebrows to his jawline, leaving the top of his shiny head without adornment, yet his gaze was not unkind.

I mustered a pleasant smile. "I've no idea, but I call it the purple mist."

He lifted that probing gaze to me. He was a giant of a man, but not just in his stature — his very nature seemed large and imposing. "I'd heard the countess was partial to flowers." His words held an edge of accusation.

I forced the smile to remain in place, nerves raw. "One can appreciate flowers without knowing everything about them. A name means little, really."

He stepped closer, large hands shoved deep into his trouser pockets. "A name is a plant's identity and it is far from random. Like this hydrangea. *Hydra* means water, because it needs a lot of it. Knowing that is important."

I could not match this farmer's knowledge of plants, so I forced another smile. "Fortunately I have gardeners who care for the plants. I merely enjoy them."

But he was persistent. "Then take you, for example. Your name tells me everything about you that's important to know."

My fingers trembled as they brushed the leaves of the "water" plant whose name I'd already forgotten. "How can you know anything about me from a name?" How I hated names. My original one declared me the rag woman, the castoff, and the other sat like a target on my forehead, placing me in danger while also turning the knife of my conscience.

"Well, I don't know them all, but the fact that there are four of them tells me you are a woman of rank. The last tells me who your husband is, and your title makes it clear that you have a position in politics."

"It is the earl who sits in the House of Lords. I merely sit in *his* house."

"Where you hold great influence over him, I suspect. Which he in turn carries into the House."

"I listen more than I speak where it comes to the earl." Truer words I'd never spoken.

He studied me for a moment, as if judging what he should say. "I heard you were renovating the abbey. Is it true?"

I nodded. "A bit slowly, but yes. Renovating."

"I'd like to offer my help. I noticed you have truss weakness in the inner rooms. Water damage has rotted the wood and weakened the masonry too."

I stiffened. "Those rooms are closed to guests." They were embarrassingly disastrous, holding not only the unrenovated ruin but much of the debris from work in the other rooms as well. It had been a catch-all for wreckage of all kinds with the understanding that no one would see it. His comment on them felt as invasive as if he'd stepped into my soul and seen the chaos churning my insides beneath the exquisite gown I wore.

He raised one massive eyebrow. "Overlooked and underestimated, I see. But they won't be for long. It's the inner rooms of a house that hold it all up. I suggest you let me help before they crash in around you. I'm the cheapest worker you'll find, and quite willing. Plenty of experience too."

"I'll bear the offer in mind." So the nosey man was trying to sell me his services. Wavering on the edge of my patience, overflowing with the thousands of worries pulling me in different directions, I excused myself from this most opinionated guest.

His voice rumbled behind me. "Tomorrow is for maybes, today is for what's truly important."

No, today was for the *urgent.* For me, at least. The only thing in that category was convincing a roomful of people who had already seen my flaws that I was truly the countess. It was vital. I would untangle everything else later, all those nagging pokes to my conscience, when Sully and I had escaped this place alive.

"If you'll excuse me, I am neglecting my other guests."

Hurrying back through the cloister walk and toward the grand hall, I glided past the little gatherings of guests in the passageways, smiling with a gracious, detached air, willing my heart to be calm.

I caught a glimpse of my reflection in a long window and was struck with the elegant beauty Simone had made of me this night. *It's the inner rooms that hold it all up.* Those inner rooms, the ugliest, debris-laden, neglected part that no one was ever allowed to see. Hand to my silk-wrapped waist, I glanced into a distant mirror. Beautiful.

But crumbling inside.

I glanced at the tall clock standing against the far wall and lifted a cup of cider. How much longer? Was it too early to slip away from the guests? It was not quite midnight, and no hostess would leave this early. I slipped into the entry hall away from the crowds for air. In the hush of blue-black moonlight, I sighed and brushed stray hairs off my forehead. The air was cooler out here, and I inhaled it into my warm chest.

It was time to admit it — I was in too deep. This role was more than I could handle. Victor Prendergast could attempt to convince me I wasn't made to be a rag woman, but neither did I have the makings of a lady. Even if I desperately wished it.

"Haven't you had enough?"

I spun around to face Sully in the quiet hall. "You shouldn't be here. If Prendergast sees —"

"You'll never be her." His face was shadowed, his voice low. "You've tried and failed. There, I've said it. You will never successfully be anyone but yourself. Now can we leave?"

I shuddered at the blunt statement of my failure, even more so because it came from *him*. "I have to do this, Sully. It's —"

"No, you don't. We can run away this minute and go into hiding. If rescuing me is truly your only reason for staying, let us rescue one another right now. He'll never find us."

"He can. He will." I shuddered at the memory of his intensity that had left marks on my arm. And if he didn't find us, the law eventually would. "If I stay, we are safe for now, and we can go free when this is all over."

He stepped close, his stormy eyes inches

from mine. "I've half a mind to throw you over my shoulder and carry you out of here."

"I wouldn't let you."

He shoved his fingers through his hair, then grabbed my shoulders. "Don't do this to me, Raina. I am your rescuer. It's all I know how to be to you."

I searched his tormented face. It was an agony I understood. Then I spoke — lovingly, firmly. "This time, I must do the rescuing."

"You'll not rescue anyone by staying. He wants you to believe you will, but when has he ever —"

Slow footsteps echoed on the tile. I spun to face whoever approached, and in that breath of time, Sully vanished.

Simone stepped into the circle of light from the candelabra in the corner. "He's right."

"Simone. I hope you're enjoying the night."

"Your presence here won't save anyone."

She knows. *She knows.* My heart hammered that thought painfully against my chest.

"You'll do nothing but cause harm to yourself and others the longer you remain."

But with all that was at stake, what could I do? What could I do? The question tortured my battered heart as thoughts of Sully weakened me.

"If you wish to do any good at all, you'll leave now and never look back." Her voice cracked. What had occurred tonight? I remembered clearly her look of angst after our grand descent, but what could it mean? What man had driven her to such fierce jealousy?

"It's much more complicated than you believe."

"No, actually it's much simpler than *you* believe." She moved forward, her dress brushing mine as we stood together in the same dim circle of candle glow. "You wish to know the great secret of our missing countess you're trying so hard to rescue?"

I held my breath to know the truth of the woman I'd envied, emulated, and admired in turns, the woman whose essence escaped me like a dissolving fog. Here at last I would discover the inner secret of the countess's abandoned rooms, the great mystery of her soul. I felt sick with anticipation for what was about to be revealed about the woman to whom I could never measure up.

"She doesn't exist." She took a deep breath, her eyes never leaving my face. "That's right — there is no Countess of Enderly."

25

Comparison is always an unfair battle because it pits your own reality against another woman's façade. Always assume there is more to someone than what they show the world.

~ Diary of a Substitute Countess

Impossible. Impossible. The word echoed through my dreams. I skimmed the shallow end of the sleep pond all night and woke in a tangle of bed linens. Terrible dreams had leaked out of my imagination and troubled my sleep. Implications of Simone's revelation rained down on me from every angle and poked my overtired mind. Exhaustion clouded my logic, and I kept repeating one thing — *there is no countess.*

As I perched at the vanity, a scrawled note caught my eye on the tea tray just delivered —

I have it on good authority that the abbey's previous owner is arriving sooner than expected, most likely today. He loved this estate and will want to see everything. I thought you should be prepared.

~ Bradford

I groaned, and all I could think of was those closed-up disastrous rooms. After arraying myself in a simple front-closing frock, I found myself before the closed doors of the abandoned space. I'd granted the entire staff the morning off after the hard work of the soiree, and it was just as well. Quiet was the best cure for the noise of my thoughts.

Yet now I was left with a large project by myself, for the neglected inner rooms must be attended to. I couldn't let Uncle Wells see the disrepair there.

Inserting the key and rattling the doors, I pushed them open with the usual *swoof* of dust and stepped into the silent space. A powerful chill hung on the air that matched the cold fear inside me. Sunlight pierced the dusty dimness from somewhere above, and I walked through the ancient chapel room and took in the muted colors and faded woodwork. A distant echoing drip signified that the farmer had been right — a leak had begun. Soon the place would crumble, and hopefully I would be long gone before it did.

I paused before a lumpy glass window that seemed to melt into the bottom sill with the weight of years, and I stared at the reflection of the girl I'd become. Without the aid of cosmetics and upswept hair, I saw the evidence of the ruin inside me that had leaked through to my pale face after many nights of fitful sleep, and it shocked me. It was true what Bradford had hinted at — one can only ignore rotting insides for so long before the ruin seeps out. If only I could have this place torn down and rebuilt.

And do the same with myself.

An anxious energy poured through me and into my limbs, but what could I do now to fix what was fractured in so many ways? The only way I knew to cope with such frustration was to dig in and begin to work on something. On anything.

With the sudden determination of Spital-fields Ragna, I turned to face the chaos, more than ready to accomplish something huge, to move forward, to do something productive. Shoving up the sleeves of the simple day gown, I marched up the aisle to the front of the great chapel and dragged a large caldron that had been carelessly stored there into the center. I scooped armfuls of musty paper debris that lay around the pews and front steps and tossed it into that caldron with a *thwump* that echoed in the emptiness.

After gathering two more armloads and dumping them in, I looked back over the whole chapel and wanted to weep at the hundreds of armloads it would take me, and the tiny fragments of ancient paper that floated through the air from the disturbance. Would this place ever come clean?

I had to try. I was the only one here to work on it. The only one who could rescue Sully. The only one who could pull off the charade. I knelt to lift an overturned kneeling bench as my thoughts spiraled, and the bench's weight surprised me, discouraged me. As I struggled to right the thing, hot tears sprouted from my eyes that were dry with dust. I strained against its weight, and all the weight on my spirit that had piled up in the weeks here. How had it become so heavy?

God, I can't. I cannot do this. Have mercy on me. I struggled to keep my tears from pouring out and put my shoulder into the hunk of wood. Suddenly its immense weight lightened with blessed relief, and I opened my eyes to see a tall, massive man at the other end, lifting along with me. I staggered under the shift in weight and blinked in the dimness. *God?* The man's face, obscured by floating dust and sunlight, melted into a gentle smile. "Are you ready for my help yet?"

I blinked, my vision cleared. It was the local farmer from the cloister walk. Together we righted the bench and stood to dust off our hands. "It's you."

He bowed and stepped closer, his boots scuffing along the grime and debris on the floor. "All the day long, my lady."

"What are you doing here?" I wasn't sure whether to be affronted or simply shocked, but I couldn't force an edge of authority into my voice for anything that morning.

"I was right about the damage. It seems the rooms here are ready to cave in on themselves."

"How did you get in here?"

"I am an invited guest. I spent the night in your Danube room."

I squinted at this man who seemed to have appeared from nowhere. "Who are you, exactly?"

"Ah! Now you've asked the right question — my name. In this house I'm known as Uncle Wells."

I gasped, my cold fingertips covering my lips, which were void of meaningful words.

"Never judge a man's identity by the outside. That can all be changed in an instant. One wrong step around a muddy puddle, and —" He made a swooping motion with his hand. "When you're tall as I am, it's a long way to fall and a lot of wet to wear on a man's frame. Wouldn't you know, the only suit here in my giant size happened to be an old worn-out one, which worked in my favor." He stepped forward and looked about the ruins and straight up to the leak somewhere above, where the great dome had begun to crumble. "I've come as somewhat of a surprise to see firsthand what use you've made of my gift."

I squirmed as if God himself had entered into the chaos of my soul that resembled this room. "You were not meant to arrive until spring. I assure you, I planned to have these rooms much more presentable by then."

"Which is one reason I came unannounced. I don't want impressive, I want truth."

"There's far too much work to be done. I simply haven't had the time . . ." My voice faltered.

But his smile was gracious. Warm. "Perhaps we can do it together."

I cringed at the thought of him working

on such a disaster.

"Besides, they won't survive the neglect much longer."

"It seems impossible to fully restore them, and I've no idea what use these rooms would be, anyway. I've toyed with the notion of removing them altogether, but . . ."

"I lunched with a man once who knew the history of the place, and he told me the monks had called these rooms the *Kardinia,* from *kardiá,* the Greek word for 'heart,' the essence of one's inner being — mind, soul, emotion, everything. It was the piece around which all else centered, and that's precisely what these rooms were to those men — their center of worship in the chapel and center of knowledge in the library. I foolishly neglected them during my renovations, because the repair work seemed overwhelming, and the other rooms kept me sufficiently distracted." He walked over to one of the grimy stone walls and laid a hand on it with reverence. "Yet this is the actual abbey, the point of life here." He breathed in deeply of the dusty air. "So you see, it's important to keep them up, for around that, everything else is built. The house would begin to crumble without them."

As if triggered by his dire words, pieces of old rotted wood and slate roofing crumbled down from above and shattered on the floor between us. I leaped back and looked up at the spot with panic, wondering what would come next. Wasn't this uncle recovering from illness? I couldn't let him remain in this room and possibly be injured.

"Why don't we break our fast in the morning room?" I hurried the man out of the crumbling chapel, looking over my shoulder as we went.

Over small plates of food, I tried to force myself to relax. Perhaps I could win him over despite the rooms. We talked of Rothburne's past, of the soirees and guests and lively music that had filled it. The man spoke of his long-deceased wife with the tenderness of a jeweler handling rubies, which made me want to weep.

"She is the reason I passed this estate on the way I did. It was to honor her memory."

"Was she very beautiful?"

"Golden as the sunshine, inside and out. I adored that woman until the day she died. It was she who opened my eyes to how worthy of my respect women are, for she had more heart, more intelligence, than I ever did, and it often lay quietly behind those smiling eyes of hers." He paused to close his eyes and inhale the sweetness of her memory.

"It troubled her that women had no say in government, or even their own home, and then it began to trouble me too. When she died I was compelled to give a voice to others like her, and to make other men do the same. I advocated for amendments to the law that allowed women legal rights over property and such, and when it seemed like it might come to pass several years ago, I decided I must act upon it. I had two unmarried and highly arrogant nephews, both of whom could benefit greatly from the refining influence of marriage. I put it to them that the first to marry would receive the benefits of my estate, starting with this abbey and its profits."

I blinked as the pieces to the entire conspiracy came together into a whole, ugly picture.

"The earl was, of course, the one to achieve this, so I allowed him to take over the abbey and reap the rewards of this estate with one small detail — I would retain legal ownership of the estate until the amendment passed. Then I planned that it would be fully gifted under this new law — to his *wife.*"

"I see." My reply came out in one low breath as the enormity of my position sank in. My heart teetered on the edge of revealing everything, but that would be like throwing Sully before an oncoming train.

"Now Rothburne has a new mistress, as lovely and bewitching as the place itself." He smiled. "You've changed him, you know. Begun to lighten his burdens. That's as I intended when I urged him to marry. Yet you are not at all what you are said to be."

I clasped the wooden arms of the chair. "What do you mean?"

"You've become such a mystery to me, Lady Enderly, and I find that fascinating. All reports of you call you poised and accomplished, yet here you are convincing yourself in private to be self-assured." He flipped out my little stack of stationery, waving it, then dropping it on the glass table before me. There were my ramblings under her name, my attempts at persuading myself I was her.

"You read that?"

"With utmost fascination."

I groaned and dropped my head into my hands.

"Forgive me, but I didn't know what it was when I found it hidden here. I had no idea it contained private thoughts until I read them, and then I could not stop." He sat back and sipped his tea. "Why do you call yourself Ragna in it?"

I swallowed, my throat thick with the tension of near-discovery. "It was a nickname. I'm afraid I didn't come from very noble circumstances."

"It seems to me you suffered from a poverty of spirit more than of the pocketbook."

"How is that?"

"Ragna." He grunted his disapproval. "Never let anyone else name you, child. No one has that right."

"But the name had a bit of truth, sir. My family was . . . we were in the textile industry." My face heated. "We sold rags."

"*Sold* them, not 'were' them."

I slowed my chewing to think on this.

"It's important to remember who you are. Names have great significance, and we cannot let the world twist them."

When he departed, I hurried back to peer into those abandoned rooms. Who I am — he wouldn't have suggested I hold onto that if he knew who I was. I looked down at the lumpy floor stones, my thoughts spinning. I was Raina the rag woman, the fake, the castoff playing at being countess. But there was more now too — all the pieces of the countess had become part of me. Perhaps that would form my new identity, for there was no other countess but me.

It was only when I walked into the old library that a pair of jewel-green eyes sliced through my moment of hope as they stared down at me from their perch on the wall. My gaze shot up to hers in an instant, and my world shifted yet again as I was met with a painful reality.

I do exist. I do. And you are not me.

26

Our identity is one of the few things in life that truly belongs to us, whether or not we accept what it is.
~ Diary of a Substitute Countess

Boots pounded the bed of the dray, and work-roughened hands clapped to the beat of Sully's music, their voices belting out raucous folk tunes as his heart pounded and his fingers flew. The lively songs kept blood pumping through his veins. It made him feel alive to be out in the crisp autumn air, drawing spirited singing from this band of good folk. He swept the bow up after the last note, and the applause followed, cheering the worry out of his heart and making him want to play forever.

Soon the dray stopped before the service entrance, and the boisterous group hurried inside to gather around the long table to chatter before the big open fire. Rothburne's cook had stayed behind, promising to have spiced cider ready for everyone's return.

"Never did a hot drink smell so good, Mrs. Williams." He lifted his mug to her in thanks and sipped the liquid, even though it burned his tongue a little. A trickle of heat warmed his insides.

The stout cook thunked mugs down in front of the footman and stable master who were lost in noisy conversation and easy laughter. "The only good that comes from those outlandish affairs — leftover treats for all of us."

"You should have come with us."

The woman grunted and turned back to the stove.

The trek to Havard had been good for the overworked staff, allowing them fresh air and leisure time. Yet back in this house, his mind was heavy with worry. Sully stared down into the amber liquid with specks of cinnamon floating on top. The words he'd overheard from that woman in red refused to leave his mind — *The countess does not exist.* But she had to. What could she mean? Knowing the answer to that could be the key to their freedom.

He eyed the hardworking cook who seemed as much a part of this old kitchen as the cast iron skillets or the jars of colorful preserves. "I suppose you've seen a great many gatherings at the abbey, have you?"

"More than I can count." She carried mugs to the two chambermaids farther down the long table, then returned to her pot on the stove for more. "It's the only excitement at a dreary place like this. Before the countess came, it was mostly guests on a short holiday, and most were duller than sticks."

"The countess has brought a great deal of life to this place, then. Is this her first visit to the abbey?"

"Aye, that it is." She ladled more cider into mugs and plunked them onto the sideboard.

"So you've not met the woman before this trip?"

She frowned at him and smeared her apron across the gathering moisture on her face. "Are yer ears broken, laddie? Didn't I say it was her first time here?"

She moved down the long table with more steaming cups, leaving Sully to his thoughts. When the first footman left his seat, Sully slid closer to the stable master. "I suppose you're quite used to these events, are you?"

"Not so much, since the property transferred hands. The earl was never one for big goings-on, and his wife makes a home out of the whole world, it seems, traveling to this land and that. Some have trouble holding still for their governesses in the classroom. She never outgrew that, I suppose."

"But you've met her before this visit, haven't you?"

"I've not." The older man ran his hand along the stubble on the side of his face and looked toward the window. "The earl met his wife abroad and married her quite suddenly. She's been nothing short of a legend around here since we had word of the elopement, and we were all anxious to meet her."

But the cousin — Philip Scatchard's hatred of the woman had gone back much further than the few weeks Raina had been here. There was some other object for his disdain. And then there was the painting . . .

In the moments it took Sully to down the rest of his drink and cough on the broken bits of cinnamon stick from the bottom of the cup, he knew his next course of action. Rising from the bench and thanking the cook for the cider, he took himself out of the hearty gathering of servants and went in search of Philip Scatchard.

He found the man entering the main doors, stamping mud from his boots.

Sully hurried to remove his greatcoat and

accept his hat and gloves. "A fine day for a drive, sir."

"If fine is an Irish word for cold, then yes. Quite. We've gotten a brash taste of fall all of a sudden, it seems."

Sully smiled. "I'll bring tea service to the study and that'll take the chill right out of your bones. Or perhaps you would prefer a little cider?"

"Thank you, McKenna, but I believe I'll just rub my hands together before the fire." He paused long enough to meet Sully's gaze. "It's kind of you to think of me on your day off, though. Much appreciated."

"Shall I freshen the fire for you in the study? I'm afraid it's been neglected the whole day, seeing as no one's using the room."

He smiled and gave one nod of approval. "I would be in your debt."

Sully hurried in to poke at the fire and throw fresh wood onto the flames until it snapped smartly and heat emanated from the hearth. When Scatchard entered and came to pace before the fire, Sully cleared his throat. "It's convenient we have this moment of privacy, sir. I've wanted to speak to you about that mission you gave me."

The pacing stopped then, and the man turned his attention fully on Sully. "Go on.

Have you found something?"

"Perhaps, but I was hoping you could give me a little direction. I've only lately come to Rothburne and met these people for the first time, so I cannot tell what it is about this woman I'm supposed to be searching for. What can you tell me about the way she was before? Has she changed a great deal?"

His brows lowered. "Certainly she's changed. From stingy to generous, and from arrogant and lofty to, well, downright normal, she's an entirely new person."

"Perhaps it's merely been a long time since you've been around her."

"We've mostly corresponded by letter regarding matters of the estate. She gave directions, and I carried them out. She had very set ideas about the way things should run, and I forced myself to carry out her wishes."

Sully turned from the fire to watch the man's face as he asked the all-important question, even though he could already guess what the answer would be. "But does she seem different to you, sir? Has she changed in appearance or manner?"

The frown deepened as Scatchard huddled in toward the fire, arms over his chest. "I couldn't tell you. Before this trip I'd never actually met the woman in person."

27

Many people who go out looking for themselves will become lost, for they look outside themselves or inward, rather than up to the God we reflect.

~ Diary of a Substitute Countess

I felt like hiding. Not just because of the ridiculous gown laced with little feathers that now graced my frame, but because I felt trapped. Being the countess had lost all appeal, and I wished I could shed it the way I wanted to shed this awful gown. Whether she was real or imagined, I wanted to hand her back her life and all the chaos that went with it. I closed my eyes and pretended I was home. What would it be like to return there? Who would I be after all this?

When I was young, I had once fallen asleep reading late at night, and the candle stub had melted onto the book. Peeling apart all those pages the next morning had been impossible, and the effort destroyed them entirely. That's exactly how it felt now, attempting to separate my identity from Lady Enderly's, but I had been enticed to search out my own. Certainly there was more to me than rags and a dirty flat in Spitalfields.

Don't let anyone else name you, child. No one has that right.

Ragna. Oh, how I loathed that name. I pondered my real name, the one thoughtfully chosen by my mother with hopes that I'd one day grow into it — Raina meant *queen,* or one who reigns.

I nearly laughed at the irony. The girl who had pretended and schemed to live up to the title of countess was actually, in reality, a queen.

Sort of.

Why this name, God? Did you truly mean for me to grow into it?

Thoughts of Queen Esther rose and were discarded. I hadn't saved anyone. In fact, I'd only endangered the best man I'd ever known — over and over again, on my hundreds of adventures. Including this one. *Especially* this one. The weight of guilt bore down on me.

I slipped back into the house from the gardens in time for dinner that night, questions still circling through my mind. A door opened to my right and Sully hurried through, silver tray tucked under his arm. He glanced up at me for a fleeting moment, trouble clouding that usually joyful face, and I could hear his painfully uttered words: *I am your rescuer. It's all I know how to be.* In other words, what am I worth to you outside of that role?

If only he knew.

But how would he? Pangs of remorse racked me. Even in our brief moment of privacy, the near-kiss, I'd said next to nothing to him about my own feelings. I'd been so busy looking deep within that I'd neglected to look around me and see the needs of people I loved. Despite the lateness of the hour, I hurried to the study to retrieve some books, leafing through their familiar pages to underline the passages I sought in each. If there was one truth I could convey even within this life of secrecy, it was my deep love for this man who wanted to flee rather than put me in danger, and who stayed only to protect me. He had to know, in this moment, exactly what he meant to me even when our roles were reversed.

In the study, I started with the book he'd already underlined for me, Hardy's *Far from the Madding Crowd,* searching out and underlining another passage. "Sometimes I shrink from your knowing what I have felt for you, and sometimes I am distressed that all of it you will never know."

Underneath I tucked Brontë's *Jane Eyre*, which always managed to wrap words around the love and longing I felt, and marked a longer section: "I have for the first time found what I can truly love — I have found you. You are my sympathy — my better self — my good angel — I am bound to you with a strong attachment. I think you good, gifted, lovely: a fervent, a solemn passion is conceived in my heart; it leans to you, draws you to my centre and spring of life, wraps my existence about you — and, kindling in pure, powerful flame, fuses you and me in one."

I closed my eyes and imagined him reading those passages that laid bare the feelings that had warmed my heart for years, the pure delight on his eager face. Why hadn't I done this before? I had hungrily accepted his declarations of affection from abroad and in the messages he'd left about at the abbey, but when had I assured him of mine? Sully had been right — my problems had made me self-consumed. I had lost sight of so much.

Please, God. Help these messages to sink

into his heart and convince him of my affection. And that he must stay.

The door creaked open and I dropped the book with a start. I jerked myself out of my thoughts and into my role as I turned with a smile to see who had entered.

Cousin Philip strode in. "Ah, there you are. I've something to discuss . . ." He slowed and eyed my gown with a small grimace. "How many birds have you killed to achieve such a look?"

I self-consciously fingered the little feathers trimming the gown around the shoulders and top of the bodice, feeling even more foolish than when I'd put it on. Why had I not insisted on a different gown? Simone had assured me it was one that "Lady Enderly" had ordered months ago. She'd dared me with a cunning smile to deny it was true. With the other maids present, all I could do was allow her to clothe me in that dress.

The feathers tickled my collarbone. "Let's leave off with the pleasantries and discuss the matter at hand."

His cocky smile broadened. "Very well, then." Crossing to the desk, he unrolled several papers and laid them flat, anchoring them with paperweights on either end.

I came around to stand beside him. He

366

smelled like lemon and shaving soap.

"I've come up with several plans for renovating the interior of the abbey. They shouldn't cost a great deal, and we're largely utilizing local labor. It'll keep the inside from collapsing, and in time perhaps we can shift focus to making the rooms usable again. If you'll take a look at this sketch, you'll see weight-bearing trusses that should do the trick. And in this sketch, I've fashioned a set of pillars to add later that may be more in keeping with the style of the rest of the abbey."

I blinked. "Where is all this coming from?" Cousin Philip had never been excited about anything like this since I'd arrived.

"There's been talk of renovating the place before it collapses. Isn't that what you wish?"

"Certainly. I've just never seen you so . . . That is, you're . . ."

He crossed his arms and leaned on the edge of the desk, watching me. The dinner bell summoned us for the evening meal.

"You seem quite different. That's all."

He shrugged. "Perhaps I want to be something more than an old chair everyone trips over."

My heart squeezed. "You already were."

His steady gaze centered on me as we

faced one another, sobriety sharpening his eyes. "Only to you, it seems."

I frowned. "What do you mean?"

"Oh come off it, I know what you've done. What you gave me. You are the only one on this whole estate who dares to truly see a person — from the tenants to the sorry drunk who now stands to gain the estate."

I exhaled, turning away. "I didn't exactly *give* it to you."

"Bequeathed it, then. However you wish to say it. Not that I'd live long enough to inherit it, of course. That is, unless you accidentally choke to death on all those unsightly feathers."

I couldn't hide my smile.

He sobered. "Your confidence in me means everything. I won't let you down."

In silent camaraderie we moved into the drawing room. I felt doused in the sunny warmth of Cousin Philip's approval, which was, to my surprise, just as intense as his disdain.

"Ah, there you are, old man." Our dinner guest Lord Remington crossed the room to us, hand extended. His wife followed him, then Prendergast appeared in the doorway and greetings were exchanged.

As Bradford beckoned us all in to dinner, Cousin Philip moved up beside me. "So why did you do it?"

I hesitated, meeting his intense blue eyes. "Because there's more to an old chair than what's broken."

A muscle jerked in his jaw. His shoulders shifted and something bobbed in his throat.

"That is, unless you have no desire to own Rothburne. It's quite a challenge."

He stepped forward and took my hand, raising it to his lips for the gentlest kiss. "I suppose I could bear up under the weight of it, my lady."

I offered him a smile. "Friends?"

His lips twitched. "I promise not to hate you."

I pinched my lips into a smile. "Be careful, Cousin. You nearly paid me a compliment."

His smile widened. "Because I finally understand who you are."

Who I was. Somewhere in the midst of elegant gowns and opulent dinner parties, I had lost sight of that. I so desperately wanted to announce my secret, yet revealing the truth would nullify the will that had so impacted Cousin Philip for the better. I swallowed hard, staring at the back of Uncle Wells ahead of me. Perhaps if I talked to him, explained everything I'd learned of Cousin Philip, something could be done.

Every glance he'd cast my way since we met had been inviting and watchful, as if he was prompting me with a look to open up to him with the truth. There was something so fundamentally trustworthy and steady about the man that made me wish to open the doors of every secret room inside me, and invite his unusual wisdom to right everything that had gone awry.

Uncle Wells was seated beside me as the guest of honor, and this was a stroke of great fortune. I lowered my voice as I passed him on my way toward the head of the table. "There's something on my mind that I'd like to discuss with you, sir." Perhaps Prendergast would not notice us talking in so casual a setting, out in the open. I tasted the hope of freedom on my tongue.

"Of course, any time."

"Good evening, Lady Enderly." Prendergast's voice cut through my thoughts as he seated himself on the other side of me. Our eyes met, the secret between us always evident there, and my uncertainty solidified into dread. He seemed to read my intentions in a single glance, and his eyes lit with warning. Yet I'd said nothing — how could he know?

My heart pounded as the ordinary evening ticked on, waiting for the right moment.

This could be it — the end of the charade. The ruse would be out in the open, and I would have no more part to play. The thought was terrifying, yet liberating. I looked about the red and gilded room and could not remember a single reason I had wished to remain.

But then, when we'd been seated, the service door cracked open and through that entrance walked my *reason*. Sully lifted his face to look at me from the shadows as he slipped in, and the full glory of his smile beamed out in rays so powerful I felt my heart would burst. I turned so I would not be swept away by it. The messages. He must have read them. My heart fluttered as I attempted to swallow, but the lump wouldn't move from my throat. For several moments I could only pretend to eat.

When the second course was carried in by footmen, I arranged the words I'd say in my head. I sent Sully on a petty errand to take him from the room. He'd stand a chance of escape this way, even if I did not. I cleared my throat and Uncle Wells's gaze shifted to mine, waiting and watching with interest.

Before I could speak, Victor Prendergast raised his glass and smiled upon the gathered diners. "I wish to give you all notice that I may be departing from your presence in the coming weeks, but just for a time. I've taken it into my heart to defend a pack of mutinous sailors who have aroused my charitable interest."

Cousin Philip paused, his knife and fork aloft, and frowned at the solicitor. "Someone with whom we're acquainted?"

My heart pounded. I stared at the swinging door Sully had just exited.

Prendergast smiled in his dismissive way and shrugged. "Doubtful, unless you rub shoulders with poor wretches on the docks. They say the leader is still missing, but they will deal fiercely with him when he is found."

I sucked in air as if I could not get enough and stared at the herbed lamb on my plate.

"Have they much hope, Mr. Prendergast?" This from Uncle Wells.

The man's knife slid across the rim of his plate as he allowed a moment to pass. "Perhaps. My representing them will make all the difference, though, of that you can be sure."

I turned away as my brave declaration sank back into the depths of my soul and settled there.

28

If a lady's beauty comes from what is within, no one can threaten or change it because it is out of reach.

~ Diary of a Substitute Countess

"He's a fine musician." Uncle Wells approached me after the meal and nodded toward Sully. Cousin Philip had asked him to play, as he often did, while we settled into the drawing room with tea. Of all people Victor wished me to convince of my false identity, this uncle was the most important. He'd made that clear of late.

"That he is." The happy lilt of Sully's music filled my heart with bittersweet feelings, even as I avoided looking at him directly. He would be staring at me, I could tell, but I couldn't meet his gaze just now.

"I'd like to think we've become sound acquaintances, my lady." He paused for a sip of tea. "Enough so that you can speak plainly with me, at least, and tell me what's on your mind. For example, what you might have been trying to say at dinner tonight?"

My throat clenched as I tried to swallow. "I'm afraid the timing was poor. I've changed my mind."

Uncle Wells studied me with a frown, running one hand along the muttonchops framing his jaw. "I see." His gaze flicked past me. "Ah, it seems someone is listening to our conversation."

My gaze instinctively jumped over to Victor, who stood at the opposite end of the drawing room laughing with Lord Remington — but most assuredly not listening.

"Then again, perhaps I was mistaken." Uncle Wells smiled knowingly, and I realized I'd been duped. "It's Mr. Prendergast who has a hold on you, is it?"

I glanced away, shoulders tensing.

"As I suspected." The man took a final sip of tea and placed the cup and saucer on a nearby table. "Keep in mind that when it comes to enemies, they only threaten those they believe are a threat to them. There's something in you that frightens him."

Muscles tightened across my back.

"Come now, tell me what it is you meant to say. I've a sense it was important."

I was nearly overcome with the desire to

pour out everything I knew about this conspiracy, but the sound of Sully's lovely fiddle stiffened my throat and stilled my temptation. I couldn't bring myself to do it.

Victor parted from Lord Remington with polite smiles and nods, making his way toward us. He soon stood behind me, beaming his charming smile over us. "What a remarkable evening. I wanted to thank you personally for your kind attentions and your hospitality toward your solicitor, Lady Enderly. Now, if I might steal a moment of your time in the study, there are a few matters I must go over with you."

He strode away, expecting me to follow, but Uncle Wells laid a hand on my shoulder. "There's great significance in a name, and yours carries much weight. Remember that."

I tore myself away on the heels of those words, hurrying after Victor toward the study. His voice echoed around the chamber of my chaotic mind: *Great significance in a name.* In my real name? In hers? What did that mean if she didn't even exist?

An idea settled on me as I passed the closed-up rooms. Slowing before the abandoned monastic library, I let myself in and glanced around. With a breath I approached the painting that would forever remain imprinted upon my mind and inspected every brushstroke. *A name. A name.* Didn't every artist leave his signature somewhere on his work? It was a stretch, but if I found the artist who had painted this supposedly nonexistent woman, I would have a direction. Finally my flitting gaze found an angled signature in the bottom right corner — *E. M. Lockharte, London.*

I slipped out and saw no sign of Prendergast. Turning my steps toward the study, I was startled to a stop by a soft whisper. I slowed. "Sully?"

"I need to speak with you." He stepped from the shadows but stood at a distance in case anyone happened upon us.

"There's no place in this —"

"The warming room. The calefactory out in the center courtyard. It's the only spot of privacy in this place."

"Prendergast is waiting for me."

"Soon, then. Will you go there? I'll leave a message."

"When I can." I hurried away, but that name — E. M. Lockharte — still eclipsed my thoughts.

In the empty study, I listened for Victor's footsteps and hurriedly flipped through papers in the desk until I found what I needed — the earl's book of contacts. Leafing with trembling fingers, I finally located the name Lockharte and followed the line across to an address in London: 33 Bury Place. What an unfortunate street name. Even in Spitalfields, the street names were not as fantastically dismal as this one, and it struck me with incurable curiosity. If names had such significance, what was this name meant to convey? Perhaps only that searching out this artist would come to no account in the end.

I spun away when the door opened and Victor strode in with a frown. "Where were you? I thought I asked you to follow me."

"I was distracted by something in another room." If I had any delusions of slipping off to London to speak with this artist, they were crushed by the weight of Prendergast's anger. Even if he did go to London as he threatened, he had the means to know my whereabouts, even from a distance.

After a long frown, he began prodding me for details on every inch of my conversation with Uncle Wells and offering instructions for continuing the ruse. It seemed Prendergast's summons was nothing more than an excuse to separate me from Uncle Wells before I did something that crumbled our delicate tower of deceit.

"We'll need to host another soiree in his

honor, of course."

"Another one? Have we not done enough?"

"That is one of your purposes here — to be seen by people and convince them the countess is here and well. She was known for her dinner parties in town, you know. Everything was a reason for celebration and gathering of one's friends."

"But I do not even know these people. Neither does she, if we can fool them into —"

"Wise choice, by the by, on keeping quiet at dinner." He walked to me and squeezed my arm. I did not pull back, but I deeply wished to. "We get on famously, as I knew we would. First-rate partners, and fine actors, the both of us. I couldn't have done this without you."

His compliment unsettled me as I walked back to my chamber that night and tried to speak with God. The heaviness would not release me. What now? I couldn't face Sully in that calefactory — not tonight, with that evil comparison ringing in my ears. How on earth would this ever end? Where was the way out?

When I sat in the window alcove of my bedchamber, an idea struck. It was so brilliant I jumped up to carry it out immediately. I drew the guest list from the drawer and added one name to the bottom: *E. M. Lockharte, 33 Bury Place, London.*

If I could not go to him, I would bring him to me.

29

I'm beginning to understand that the power never lies in the gown, but in the heart of the lady who dons it.

~ Diary of a Substitute Countess

It was not until the morning of the soiree for Uncle Wells that my courage failed, my fear of Prendergast rising to the surface like driftwood in the ocean. I couldn't let him find out who I'd invited. I'd informed Shirley Shackley just before the invitations were sent that it was to be a costume ball, yet I couldn't help but wonder if that was enough. The masks, in reality, did little to hide one's true identity. Would Victor recognize this artist, even behind a mask, and guess what I was doing?

I found Bradford, the man who had often acted as my accomplice, in the front parlor toward luncheon time, and waited to ask him for yet another favor. I kept out of sight as he directed the maids, who were placing cut flowers in vases, and waved him over when he looked my way.

He approached with a ready smile on his long face that drew up his muttonchop sideburns. "What can I do for you, my lady?"

"I need you to waylay a certain guest for me when he arrives. His invitation will bear the name Lockharte. I want you to escort this guest to a private space and alert me as soon as you can. And tell no one else I've asked it of you."

"Happy to do it. I assume the front parlor will be sufficient for such a meeting. Shall I offer an explanation for the delay when I show him there?"

I fidgeted, pulling at the fingers of my gloves. "I've no idea. Will he need one?"

"He'd be pleased to hear that the countess herself wished a brief audience with him in private."

"Perfect. Oh and, Bradford, be certain no one else knows the guest has arrived until I've had a chance to speak with him."

He gave a brief bow. "Very good, my lady. Mr. Prendergast will be kept conveniently distracted."

I shot him a smile of camaraderie, and he winked.

■ ■ ■ ■

I gripped the rail and looked down over the great salon from my balcony above, the dizzying splendor of high white walls and gilded trim, with polished chandeliers lowered into the festive room full of people. Candlelight winked off silver platters and gems on white necks as the guests murmured against a backdrop of luscious red drapes and velvety music. Uncle Wells, the guest of honor, stood out among the others, his fine black cutaway coat sitting well on his tall frame. I ran my fingertips over my glittering blue gown, whose brilliance rivaled a starry night sky, and forced myself to breathe. Below, the guests were mingling, numerous bell-shaped skirts weaving through the crowds.

I clung harder as the room tilted and my heart raced. Growing worries had invaded my sleep every night, leaving me weary and trembling more often than not. Especially in heady moments like this.

"It's time, your ladyship." Shirley Shackley approached me in the little overlook, motioning toward the wide staircase.

I glanced past her toward the waiting Bradford with a question in my expression, and he shook his head — no, there had been no Lockharte.

It was early yet. He still had time.

"Come, my lady. Your gentleman is coming to escort you." Shirley Shackley's quiet voice prodded me forward.

I looked down the red-carpeted steps into the blinding sparkle of chandeliers and saw a tall figure springing up the steps, black mask covering the top half of his face. I nearly fainted from enchantment until my eyes adjusted and saw it was the earl. Of course, it would be my husband coming to escort me. Delicately lifting my skirt hem, I descended to meet him, then he took my arm, pausing to study me. "You look more like her than ever." He breathed the words out in a tortured whisper. "Magnificent."

I swallowed and slipped my gloved hand into the crook of his arm. "That's quite a compliment."

"You're quite a lady, Countess." He gave a sad smile as we descended into the crowds of our glittering guests.

I adjusted my sparkling blue mask over my eyes, fitting it to my face, and scanned the room. Finally my gaze locked onto one familiar man, which it always did, as he moved through the crowds with a tray aloft. His jaunty smile quickened my heart, making me wish he'd direct that look toward me.

I moved closer, but a silver-haired woman intervened, fascination clear on her full white face as she approached Sully. "There you are, young man. I must say, we've hardly ceased speaking of you since that fine performance at the reception."

"Well, thank you kindly, ma'am."

A younger woman they called Kitty stepped in. "There must be more to that story, we've decided. No man sings with that sort of passion about a girl who isn't real."

His eyebrows moved up and down as if he had no notion of how to answer.

"Well then?" she prodded. "Is there a girl?"

He cleared his throat. "I've never met one named Adora, if that's what you mean."

The older woman's disapproving gaze demanded more.

"I suppose she may be inspired by a real girl." His voice was hesitant. "T'weren't no happy ending, I'm afraid."

"I suspected as much. A shame to see such a handsome young man all alone." She set her cup on a little round table and stood closer. "I've a mind to see that changed. Mark my words, I'll have you singing about

384

your own girl soon enough, Sullivan Mc-Kenna, even if I have to give up one of my own maids to do it. What do you say, will you allow me to arrange a meeting?"

A whisper-thin young serving girl with wide violet eyes intruded. "Perhaps he has a mind to find his own. There are plenty of girls right in front of him that would be enchanted to make his acquaintance." Her upturned eyes only clarified her none-too-subtle hint.

He raised his eyebrows and peeked at me over her shoulder with a playful sparkle to his eyes.

I forced myself to unclench my teeth.

A tall, middle-aged woman with peacock feathers broke into the group. "I couldn't help but overhear, and I'm glad I did. Will you be performing again tonight, young man? You must finish your lovely story."

Another one joined from a nearby circle. "What a fabulous idea. You must tell us the rest. Did the girl come back to him?"

He shifted his tray under his arm and shot a beguiling smile at me. "You'll have to take that up with her."

I choked on my cider and nearly spit it back into my cup. Another sip enabled me to speak again. "I beg your pardon?"

"The performance. This is your event, my

385

lady. I merely do as I'm told."

"Lady Enderly, you must have him perform again tonight." Another pretty young girl barely out in society joined the ring around my footman. "Won't you let him finish his song?"

This drew the attention of yet another woman in a nearby conversation. "He will be performing again? I'd certainly love to hear it."

I looked at all the ladies gathering around Sully, begging me to let him douse them again with his powerful music. Knots formed along the back of my bare shoulders. With at least twenty pairs of hopeful eyes turned my way, what could I do but assent? I inhaled and nodded. "The musicians must have a break, so I suppose Mr. McKenna may perform one song, if he would be so inclined."

"As you wish, mistress." He bowed, dark hair falling over his eyes but failing to hide the sparkle there. Chittering laughter and gossip filled the air as Sully departed to find his fiddle. Word spread about the coming performance, and the guests came to stand in a clump at the east end of the room, awaiting their promised song.

Sully soon returned and walked to the head of the room with echoing clicks of shoes on tile and cradled his instrument in its usual place, tucked beneath his jaw.

I closed my eyes as he drew his bow across the strings. Color and light and beauty filled the room on the strings of his instrument, hushing the crowd and enlivening it with a special power that belonged only to this man. I could hardly focus on the words he sang about the lad and his endless love for the missing lass.

"They'd grown up together, that lad and
    his lass,
Filling him up to the brim
With love for the girl of a higher class
Who followed her every whim.
And she took him along, because he was
    strong,
ready to risk life and limb.

"How to describe her, the girl of your
    dreams,
For not even heaven is grander, and it
    seems
Words fail to be there to tell what you
    know,
Of the lovely young lass that has so
    touched your soul."

He closed his eyes as he brought the ballad to a close with lines that would forever bring an ache to my heart.

"How do you capture a spirit so free,
So loving and beautiful, how can it be?
You try, and you fly on the wings of her
    joy
Watching stars she taught you to see.
Then like a song, one day she is gone,
to return to the stars that she showed 'im.
Aye, she returned to the stars that she
    showed 'im."

There was silence for a moment, awed and enthralled, then the applause pelted my senses like tiny pebbles.

"Do you suppose he kens the way he affects the ladies about this place?" The whispered words came from a kitchen maid holding an empty tray to her chest.

"Not a bit, and that's what makes it so," the first footman replied as he stood straight and ready beside her.

"What I wouldn't give to be a fair bonny lass of two and twenty right now." She sighed.

Heart aching, I turned away and came face to chest with the earl. I looked up and he extended his hand. "Dance with me?" Handsome, debonair, and here he was offering to whisk me into a few moments of forgetfulness. He lowered his voice. "The guests might wonder if the host does not dance with his wife. Simply lean on me and I'll lead."

I assented. I barely remembered the dance steps Victor had drilled into me, but a man like this would know how to lead. I stepped into the frame of his arms as the music began and allowed him to sweep me into the dizzying circles of the waltz. Around and around we went, mercifully blurring the background. With each slow beat, a different face came into focus. Victor, Sully, smiling Lady Remington, gentle Bradford. My heart pounded faster than the three-quarters beat, making me breathless. How dizzying, how endless.

I wanted to break away, and not just from the dance.

The earl closed his eyes as if dancing by feel, carried on the melody filling this room. Was he imagining I was her? Finally the music rose to a finale and our whirling slowed.

"Who is she?" I whispered these words in the chaos of applause as his hold on my arms tightened. Curiosity plagued me, especially as I watched his troubled face. How greatly I wished to know the whole story, and to replace that constant pain settled just behind his eyes with peace.

He stiffened.

"The woman in the picture. The one always in your mind. The one who *should* be here with you." I looked up at him, that pitiable face I'd once feared. "Lord Enderly, what has become of her?"

"I'm not certain I wish to find out." Finally his eyes met mine through the masks and he sighed. "Yet some days I'd give my fortune to know." He tipped his head and brushed his fingers across my cheek. "You've made it bearable somehow, and I thank you. You've no idea what a blessing you've been to my life."

I smiled up at him as I remembered no one would think anything of this display. How much we resembled a young married couple settled into the comforts of wedded bliss.

He dropped his hands and turned away, moving with long strides into the crowd. I knew so little of the earl's mysterious love, yet I understood their plight far too well. I caught sight of Sully in the distance, silver tray aloft and gaze focused on me. His somber brown eyes, now bright and anxious, watched me steadily, and my chest ached with each breath at the knowledge of what he'd just seen. He couldn't possibly believe that the earl and I —

Oh how desperately I wished to leap this minute into Sully's arms and a happy ending with him, yet so much filled the few feet between us.

Victor stepped into my line of vision, cutting off my view of Sully's precious face and blinding me with a bold smile and the scent of his strong drink. "Ah, there you are." His black mask glittered in the glow from chandeliers overhead.

I did not return the smile. Did he have any idea what a mess he'd made of my life? Of my head? "I'd like to be alone."

"Splendid idea. Perhaps we need to escape for a moment." I cringed as Victor's low voice snaked through my senses. "Clear your head, convince you of your . . . astounding loveliness."

A full shiver streaked up my back. I looked up at him and the light of hunger in his eyes multiplied my unrest. He always seemed more unstable, unpredictable, when in his cups. "I believe I can handle myself, Victor."

"Victor now, is it? Even before your guests." His glittering smile turned my stomach.

How had I ever been tempted to trust this man in the alley, to step into this giant mess that was the grandest of all my mistakes?

"You've grown so beautiful. These gowns have changed something in you, woken it up."

I caught sight of Uncle Wells watching from across the room, his fingers toying with a cup as he frowned in our direction.

"The guests should not see you speaking so intimately with me, Mr. Prendergast."

"Is that not why you made this a masked ball? So no one would know which man spoke to which lady? Which man ventured to . . ." He reached out to touch my bare arm. With a pointed warning glare, I turned away, leaving him standing alone. I glided through the room, attempting polite greetings and warm smiles. They were a thin veneer for the wretched turmoil burning inside. Two personas, and now three men. A hundred guests with a hundred sets of differing expectations to match. Sully stared at us from across the room, his face a mask of disappointment, then strode out the service door.

My gut clenched, the panic of impending loss tightening my insides. He had to know that I meant what I'd said concerning my affections, but it wouldn't make displays like these easier for him to bear. How long before it became too much? I hurried toward the door to find him.

"Where are you going?" Victor was soon at my elbow, as always.

"I need to clear my head." I faced him, my finger in his face. "And *don't* follow me."

But his eyes did. I could tell.

In the hall I glanced about for Sully's dark form. "Sully?" I whispered the name into the emptiness, turning in a slow circle at the sound of evening shoes on tile. Even Bradford had abandoned the hall at this hour, his task of admitting guests completed.

The slap of cheap boots sounded behind me and I spun toward the arched doorway. "Hello? Who's there?"

A shabbily cloaked woman without a mask turned in the depths of the barely lit gallery, moving into the candle glow of the hall. Foreboding snaked through me as I watched. She glided toward me and cast back her hood.

My gasp echoed in the hall as I looked upon the face of the missing countess.

30

Beauty can bring one a certain self-assured poise, but most often it is the other way around.

~ Diary of a Substitute Countess

"You are the new wife?" She stared at me with those green eyes, two oceans of lovely sadness. She reached out as if to touch me but drew back.

"Who are you?" I croaked out the words in awe, watching her face that looked so much like my own.

Without a word, she lifted a ragged envelope from the folds of her cloak. It bore the name *E. M. Lockharte.*

"You! You are the one who painted that portrait . . . of yourself."

"It was my brother. Mitchell begged me to pose for it when he heard my brother was a portraitist." Her voice was light and flowery to match her delicate features, but weighted with such elegance, despite her clothing.

Mitchell. That was the earl's name, I now recalled.

"I suppose it was he you intended to invite tonight, but I have come instead." Her steady eyes watched me, as if waiting for me to send her away.

Questions clawed their way out of my brain. "You are not Lady Enderly?"

Her face shuttered and she turned toward the door. "I shouldn't have come here. It was a terrible mistake."

I caught her arm beneath the cloak and urged her back. "Please. Nothing is as it seems, I promise you that." I inhaled a long breath, then lifted my mask. Her jaw went slack, the pretty little rosebud lips slightly opened, and her fingertips danced at her throat.

I poured out the story as I knew it — the earl's plight, the plot to fake a marriage for an inheritance. "So you see, I am not his wife. No one is, in fact."

She pulled back, blinking her dark lashes. "A hoax. All that for an inheritance."

"A tangled web we weave, you know. I don't think they had any idea it would become this complicated."

"But why on earth did he not simply

marry someone else? Surely some fine lady would have had him. And to find one who looks —"

"He's still heartbroken over you." I said the words plainly and simply. "I don't understand the whole mess of it, but I know that much as well as I know my own name. He pines for you."

She covered her mouth as a small sob slipped out. Her lashes fluttered on her pale cheek.

"What has become of you all this time? Why did you disappear? And who are you, exactly?"

She waved off my question. "It hardly matters. I only meant to slip in and speak with Mitchell tonight. To clear up the past." She looked down at her cloak, running a gloved hand over its length. "I see now that I do not belong here. Perhaps it's best I go."

She turned, but I stepped up beside her. "I have an idea." I lifted a steady gaze to her. "Will you speak with him if I give you the chance to fit in?" As those words left my lips, visions danced in my head — the romantic, fanciful happily-ever-after between the broken man in the salon and the woman of worn-down elegance standing before me. "Give him one dance. Please, just one."

She unpinned her cloak and parted it to reveal a high-necked plain green gown with the creases of travel running down its skirt. "In this?"

I grinned, lifting a fistful of my sparkling blue gown. "No, in *this*."

Her face blossomed with understanding at my idea, yet she hesitated. "This gown is exquisite, but no one will be fooled."

I grinned at her over my shoulder. "Oh yes they will." I held out one gloved hand and she took it. "Raina Bretton of Spitalfields, seller of rags." I snuck her up the stairs to my bedchamber and turned my back to her. "Come, help me undo these fastenings. We must hurry."

Together we dressed her in a crinolette to fit the gown and clean stockings. Then I slipped out of my frock with her help and donned a plainer blue dinner gown.

Soon I had completed her dress and pinned her hair into a comely arrangement on her head. Strapping my mask to her face completed the costume, and we had fully switched places. "There, you'll do nicely." I looked at her flushed face beneath the sparkling mask that did not cover the gleam of her eyes, her rising and falling chest perfectly filling the bodice of my gown. "While you're dancing, you'll have the freedom to say what needs to be said between you. No one will hear if you keep your voice down." I led her back down the stairs, careful to keep in the shadows and watch for servants passing through. "Make certain you speak to no one but the earl."

She clamped her hands into fists. "If he does not toss me out on my ear when he finds out who it is."

"He *will* speak with you, that I promise. Whatever passed between you is the biggest regret in his life."

She nodded, her slender back straight. With a deep breath, she turned toward the salon's open doors, sweeping like the true Cinderella toward the ball that should have been hers all along. I could almost feel her pounding heart as she approached the double doors. Head straight, shoulders pressed back, she stepped inside and glanced around.

Draping myself in the woman's cloak, I slipped through the shadowed hall to the unused east doors that were blocked on the inside by a great display of flowers and vines. I nudged the doors open a crack and watched.

The woman in the sparkling blue dress stopped just before the rows of swirling dancers and stared across the room at the earl, who stood alone in the back of the room, turning when he spotted her. Would he know immediately? Did he know even now? They remained this way for the rest of the song, these two watching each other through the crowds. When the music ended and the dancers broke apart, she moved forward and approached him with measured tread, her gait steady and sure while he waited, gaze fixed on her.

I could barely breathe as their love story unfolded before me. Then she was standing before him, looking up into his face. The next song swelled and the dancers again took their positions. Without a word, the earl lifted her arms into position, placing one on his shoulder, and swept his lady into the waltz around them. They soared around the room, gazes locked as if no one else existed. He embraced her frame with one arm as he danced, as if shielding her from the rest of the world, keeping her selfishly to himself.

Then another thought struck me. Those letters in the desk — if her brother was E. M. Lockharte, then she was E. E. L., with *L* for Lockharte. It all made sense, watching them together. With every spin, his movements were more alive, more vigorous, than I'd ever seen in him. It was as if he were a music box and she the key that wound its spring and made it play. Around the room they flew, so wrapped up in the vision of each other and whatever they must be whispering back and forth.

I still love you, I imagined him saying. *I love you so much it hurts.*

Oh, I'm glad, Mitchell! I was so afraid our story was over.

As the song ended, they slowed their spins. He lifted her gloved arm and led her in one final twirl, then wrapped his arm around her waist possessively and drew her away from the crowds, through the curtains, and onto the balcony.

I turned away from the doors, leaning my back against them, and lived out the rest in my dreamy imagination. My heart thudded as if it were me being drawn onto that balcony with the man I loved, finally within reach of a happily-ever-after to an epic love story.

He would speak in that low, solemn tone the minute they were separated from the view of the crowd. *I cannot bear to be parted from you again.*

But it's far too complicated. Everyone believes you are married.

Yes, to a girl who looks remarkably like you.

I closed my eyes as the images swirled,

eclipsing all the questions from my practical side that wondered what might become of me, the extra countess.

I must go home before someone stumbles on both her and me together and realizes the truth.

No, my love. What you must do is stay. Stay, and be the woman those papers claim I married. Be my wife, beautiful E. E. Lockharte, and live in this abbey with me forever. It can all be yours, and all the lovely gowns besides. It's as if they were made for you anyway. It's perfect, and you must say yes. I will not let you slip out into the night and disappear again — I must have you for my own.

But what of the other girl? She'll never want to leave this life.

Oh, I believe she will. You see, she's in love with someone else, and she wants nothing but to flee from this place. The position is yours for the taking. Please, be my wife. Stay by my side and —

A door slammed. My eyes flew open and dainty slippers echoed on the tile floor. I spun and put my eye to the crack again. The earl leaned against a large pillar, his head down, and the blue gown had disappeared.

No!

I hurried back out into the hall to watch a

glittering figure slip through the dimness toward the stairs, then the front door. I ran to her, blocking her exit.

"I'll return your gown by post." She was breathless, harried.

"Where are you going?"

"Home. It's where I belong." She wove around me as I tugged off her cloak.

I stepped before her again, handing her the cloak with hesitation. "What about the earl?"

"I'll launder them thoroughly and have them sent straightaway." She threw her cloak around herself and turned.

I laid a hand on her arm as my heart crumpled in my chest. "Did you speak with him?"

She paused, arm stiff under my hand, and looked up. Tears blurred her bright eyes. "We spoke."

"It did not go well?"

"Everything is set to right. I'm glad I came. Thank you. Thank you so much for allowing me — no, convincing me — to do this."

"But you will not stay and be the countess?"

She removed my costume mask from her eyes, revealing the smile so full of that splendid spirit that the earl had spoken of, that natural elegance I'd so desired, and placed the jeweled thing in my hands. "I will never be the countess. The position is forever yours, and may you enjoy your good fortune."

"But I don't want it. I —"

She silenced me with a gloved fingertip to her lips, then lowered her hand to pull off the gloves, finger by silken finger. "This house needs a lady of the manor. So does Mitchell. You are the rightful countess now. Make the most of it and live well." Her eyes glowed just as they did in the portrait as she handed me the gloves. "Enjoy everything for the both of us."

I opened my mouth to tell her of Sully, of my utter hatred for living a charade, but like a wraith she turned in a whish of grand skirts and slipped out of the abbey forever.

Strength left my body in a whoosh, and I sank back onto a narrow bench in the hall. How could it have come to this? Had I not succeeded more than I'd ever imagined? I'd found her, that mysterious woman in the portrait, and I'd brought her to the abbey. I'd put her together with the earl . . . yet she had left alone. I looked down at the gloves and mask, realizing one thing more terrible than being suddenly displaced — I was now forever stuck in this position, for there was no one left to claim it.

I jumped at the sound of laughter nearby and hurried into the little front parlor set aside for my meeting with the woman who had just left, closing the door behind me. I still had a night of guests to survive. I had only to carry the charade through tonight, then in the morning I would decide what must be done. Perhaps there was nothing for it but to escape with Sully — but how? How could we possibly evade Prendergast? Fumbling with the gloves, I put them on and stood before the long window. I had lost my glittering gown, but perhaps no one would notice. I fixed the mask back onto my face. Or I could say I spilled —

No. No more deception. This was all too much.

I stared at the reflection of who I had become. The plainer dinner gown hugged my frame, my curls swept into an elaborate arrangement, creating a most becoming picture, but my face — oh, my face! The pale contours revealed the trouble within and the sleepless nights I had spent in this abbey. My stomach twisted into knots. Deep within the abbey, the rotting, splintering timbers in the old chapel creaked and groaned against the force of strong gusts. The woman had been right — I truly was the rightful Lady Enderly. This house with its neglected, derelict center so greatly resembled its mistress, and I was the only one it had. This house . . . this house was me.

"Raina!" Sully's terse whisper came from somewhere near the service entrance. He was searching after me.

I hurried to a side door. Did I dare show myself to him?

Then another voice. "Lady Enderly?" It was Prendergast. "Countess!"

I put a shaking hand to my forehead. Many conflicting names circled my brain like a flock of dizzy birds, each fighting for the right to lay claim to me. *Ragna. Lovelyn Shaunghess. Queen Esther. Raina Bretton. Lady Enderly. Cinderella.* Each had so many responsibilities tied to it, and I couldn't stand up under the weight of them all. But the truth was, I was trapped forever as *this*. As *her*.

Then Victor Prendergast was flinging the door wide, marching across the tiny room in two strides, and throwing his powerful arms around me. "There you are." His gaze devoured me, as if I sated some hunger in him he was desperate to fulfill, then he was smothering me with rum-scented kisses upon my jaw, my neck, my cheek.

I struggled against his grasp, shoving back against his chest even as he pushed in more forcefully. The stench of alcohol burned my nose. I wanted to yell for Sully but didn't dare. In a flash I grabbed the first hard object I could reach and smashed it against the side of his face with a dull thud. He cried out and I fell back, clutching my weapon. It was a book.

Prendergast pressed his hand to the gash in his lip and drew it away to see blood on his fingers. I stiffened as he growled, then he spun and stalked out of the room. I closed my eyes and tried to convince myself that everything was all right, the disaster had been averted, yet I didn't believe it any more than I believed I was Lady Enderly.

My heart cried out for God, twisting with the knowledge that I had no right to do so.

I leaned against the wall as my trembling legs threatened to give way and took several dizzying deep breaths. I had to go back out there, carry on for at least a little longer. I forced myself to move out into the hall, still shaking and overwhelmed, and Simone was the first one I saw. Standing alone and perfectly still like one of the pillars around her, she watched me, silently condemning me for the private moment with the solicitor. "Your guests wish to bid you good

406

night, but they cannot find you."

Good. The night would soon be over.

Somehow I managed to smile as I wished my guests a good evening and watched them take their leave, escorted toward waiting carriages lined up down the drive. No one breathed a word about the plainer gown. I waved with a steady hand and my smile held, even as the chaos within my soul clamored against its polished exterior. Soon it would leak out.

Where was Sully? I searched the crowds for his face, his handsomely liveried figure, but he was nowhere. Perhaps when everyone had gone I would be able to find him. We desperately needed to talk. Even if I closed us into a closet in the hall, we had to speak of escape before panic strangled me.

I stood alone momentarily in the hushed front hall, my heart thudding with dread. It was in that moment of fear and wondering that Anna the scullery maid hurried up to me and lowered her voice. "My lady, there's a man in the abandoned chapel who says he knows you. He's hurt badly and he'll speak to none but you."

"Who is he?"

"Some vagabond from Spitalfields in London's East End. Won't come out of the chapel room, either."

The familiar name rang through my head like a painful echo of the past. It had to be one of my brothers. But how had they found me?

"Did he give a name?"

"No, my lady. Won't say anything but to ask for you."

"Thank you, Anna. Keep everyone else away from there so they're not alarmed. Just until I see what he wants."

"Yes, ma'am." She bobbed a curtsy and hurried back into the salon where the cleanup had begun with the rest of the servants.

Heart pounding, I ran to find Bradford coming out of the servants' hall. "Bradford, the key. I need the key to the locked rooms."

He fished it out of his breast pocket and handed it over with a frown. "Everything is all right, my lady?"

"Perfectly fine." I met his gaze. "I must ask you to trust me. I'll explain everything later."

His hesitation both warmed and worried me, as if he was concerned for my safety, but he remained behind as I flew down the dim hall, grabbing a candle as I went. The groaning of the timbers in the chapel grew louder as I approached, and a snap inside startled me, but I pressed on. Who would I find on the other side of those doors? It couldn't be Paul, for they would have mentioned his uniform. Samuel wouldn't know where to find me, and Peter —

More pops and groans, then a crash. I flung open the doors and a wave of heat rolled over my skin from a blaze already engulfing the room. Panicked, I darted into the leaping shadows, calling out for whoever had summoned me.

The doors slammed shut behind me, and panicked realization flooded my being. A trap! I cried out as fire billowed up around a pillar. It groaned against the assault and buckled, bringing pieces of the chapel roof down as it folded and fell. I scrambled away as more of the roof collapsed into the room. Flames crawled up the ancient drapes around the windows and covered the doorway.

I wasn't ready to die. That thought of coming face-to-face with God, standing before him with nothing but my heart full of chaos, drove me into a frantic sprint across the room, desperate for escape.

Then I saw her, a still, dark figure like a shadow standing outside the window just beyond. Simone's eyes blazed like the fire from where she stood in the courtyard, then she vanished. I turned and ran toward that window, but my shoe caught on a loose rug, sending me sprawling. My head struck hard wood and the room narrowed and blurred. A heavy, liquid sleep forced its way over me.

In the dimming consciousness, I heard voices calling from different directions. *Lady Enderly. Countess. Raina.* The circling birds whipped into a frenzy, cawing and pecking at my heart, demanding and scolding. *Lovelyn Shaunghess. Ragna. Queen Esther. Countess. Cinderella.* Splintering and crashing around me seemed like only background noise.

The voices blended, and the room faded to black.

31

I never needed a new identity — just a better understanding of the one who gave it to me.

~ Diary of a Substitute Countess

The coolness of night air washed over my tired body, mercifully refreshing it. What had I been worried about? I couldn't even remember. Everything felt wonderful. I felt wonderful. Lolling in peace, I rolled over and opened my eyes, and there was Sully, propped on one elbow and smiling down at me. I took a deep breath of moist Spitalfields air and exhaled with a smile. How wonderful it was simply to be in his presence.

"Serendipity. The name for that star over there."

I smiled. "A fitting name."

We reclined together on the terraced roof of my building, naming stars as if we were king and queen of the skies.

I pointed to an especially bright star. Those were always the ones that drew my attention. "That one is too dazzling to be simply an Alice. It needs a sensational name like Allesoria or Sophronia or . . ."

"Or Raina?" He grinned playfully at me.

I batted his arm and rolled onto my back again, lifting my eyes to the faraway lights muffled by the city. Still, it was such a grand view of something so enormous in the midst of our small lives. It gave me a notion that heaven, that place to which we looked forward, would possess all the immensity and beauty I lacked in this cramped place. "It doesn't sound like much, just two boring syllables, but Mum says it means 'queen.' "

He jumped up and curtsied, pinching the sides of his tattered vest and dipping low. "My lady."

"Oh, stop." I laughed and lay back on the slate again, adjusting my head until the roof didn't hurt my scalp.

He joined me, hands behind his head. "It doesn't suit."

"What, the star's name?"

"Yours." He stared at the sky. "Queen is just too . . . I don't know, too high horse. I'd never be able to lie on a roof and name stars with a royal lass."

I shrugged. "Maybe I'd be a different sort of queen."

After a brief silence, my mind drifted to the stars and I closed my eyes. When he continued, his voice was little more than pleasant background noise for this perfect moment. "You know, the first time you told me your name, I thought for all the world I heard you say a word from me own Irish hills. 'Renaugh,' it was, and I says to meself, why would a girl be called 'renew'? But it fits you."

I sighed with my eyes closed, letting his pleasant Irish lilt waft over me. "Does it, now?"

"I think it's more fitting than 'queen' in any case, don't you? Now that I know you, I like to think of you that way. *Renaugh.*"

The word swam through my hazy subconscious as that faraway evening dimmed.

Renaugh.

Renaugh.

Raina.

A popping noise drew my brain out of its hazy slumber and into a dimmer space with a crackling fire somewhere nearby. I forced my gritty eyes open, and the enchanted rooftop moment with Sully slid back to the pages of my memories where it had come from.

I lay huddled in a cramped, dim little space, garbed in my old rags. The clock had struck the final hour of the night, and like Cinderella I had lost the magic of the lovely ball gown and once again become the rag woman. I glanced around my dirty little flat in Spitalfields and deflated my aching chest with an exhale. All those gowns, those elegant people . . . it had all been a dream. I was still Ragna of Spitalfields and Sully was dead.

I blinked and looked around with a frown, turning my head. There was no cracked mirror or corner cot for the widow. The walls looked different. No, this wasn't my flat. Had the abbey and everything in it been a dream? Or had Spitalfields?

My vision swam. So did my conscious thought, and I waded through thick cotton in an effort to find answers. All my names made a lazy circle around my mind, but I cast them all aside as my brain righted itself.

Raina. I was Raina. That thought oriented me, even when I hadn't any idea where I was or how I'd arrived there. The scent of ash and fire still burned in my nose. With each breath of fresh air through tinged nostrils, my hazy mind drew clarity and a small measure of strength returned to my body. I struggled to sit and look around, despite my chest feeling weighted with some inexplicable thing. What had happened to me? Why did everything smell of —

The fire. There had been a fire at the abbey, a trap set by Simone, and I had lain dying. Yet here I was, rescued. But by whom? I turned my stiff neck for a look about the dim space that seemed to be a farmer's cabin, lit only by a fire in the shallow hearth. I shoved back the covers and saw my dress had been stripped and replaced with a tattered and many-times-patched garment I didn't recognize. I lifted my head, and there by the fire hunched my rescuer, a cloaked figure stirring a caldron of steaming food. She unclasped her cloak and let it sag about her shoulders, and when she shook out her long dark hair, the face I saw made me gasp.

Simone.

My temples began to throb with those few moments of sitting upright, and when pain stabbed through my skull, I collapsed back onto the bed with a groan. Simone saw I was awake, and she leaped up and launched herself toward me, covering my mouth with both of her hands. "You will not scream?" Her wild eyes searched mine.

I nodded my pounding head, the friction against the straw mattress making the ache worse.

She slid her cold hands up to my head and poked at a tender place on my scalp. She seemed shaken. Jittery. "I suppose you'll heal. That wasn't part of the plan, you know — you tripping and knocking yourself senseless like a fool."

"Was my death?" The words escaped as a harsh croak, then I was consumed by coughing.

A flicker of a smile turned up her lips for the first time I could remember. "In a manner of speaking. You see, now the Countess of Enderly is dead. And you are not."

I stared at her. "You nearly killed me."

"I saved you." Her eyes glowed. "Don't you see? When you refused to leave the abbey on your own, the only way to keep you alive was to arrange your death myself so Victor wouldn't. You would not have survived the death he'd have planned."

Thoughts flew like lively tadpoles through my brain, but I could scarcely find my voice.

"I couldn't let him kill you. You're just a poor girl from the East End. At least the others were crooks and swindlers."

"Others?"

"The other people Victor's killed. Certainly that is no surprise to you."

"He was going to kill me?" I struggled to keep up.

"Eventually." She thrust a tin cup of water at me. "It was the only way out of the stage he'd set, for you couldn't play at being countess forever."

I cleared my throat, making it sting worse. I frowned at her, trying to make my dry throat form a question, but she shushed me. Rising, she towered over me in the little hovel. "I must return to Rothburne and keep up appearances, especially with Victor. He cannot know what we've done."

We?

"Sleep now, and I'll be back."

I grabbed her hand. "Simone, who is she? The real countess, I mean? Someone gave all those orders, spent all that money."

Her unchanging eyes searched mine. "You truly wish to know?"

I nodded.

"Victor."

I blinked.

"Lady Enderly was his creation, a figment of his imagination — nothing more than a pile of false papers and wild stories."

"All so the earl could have that fortune."

"It began as a simple scheme — a romantic story of a couple meeting abroad and marrying in haste, then the woman traveling extensively while her husband sat in the House of Lords. It was common enough, and everyone would believe it, especially with a man as private as the earl. They had only to convince a dying old uncle that the earl had married, receive the inheritance, then later pretend she was lost at sea or some other calamity."

I struggled to grasp it all. "But why would he do all this? Victor wasn't inheriting the fortune."

"Not directly, but what belongs to the earl is accessible to Victor. He takes what he wants."

"That's terrible. The poor earl."

"I wouldn't waste pity on the man." She shrugged. "When the earl was poor, he stole. There were funds, and he — what's the word — embezzled them. Victor was the one who helped him cover it up, and he has had one hand in the man's pocket ever since."

"When was the earl ever poor?"

"Rich men fall hard when money is tight. A poor man, he is used to going without. He has nothing to sustain. When a man has great houses and many servants requiring money, he cannot be poor. He made some bad investments and hit a low. He struggled through until this farce of a marriage and his uncle's gift of Rothburne and all its wealth. Victor promised him it would be an easy way to get what he needed, and it was — until the uncle ruined their plans by recovering."

"How wretched of him."

"He even went to visit the earl in London once, so they had to continue to convince him that everything was as they said. They showed him some painting of a woman and told him she was the new bride, and the uncle believed it all.

"The earl was wrapped up in his work, so Victor took the helm, drafting letters from her and running the estate in her name, creating an entire writing style and signature for her, making it seem as if she truly existed. The 'simple' scheme grew more and more complicated with each turn of events. When it was clear the uncle was in no danger of dying, and that he wished to have his solicitor meet with the new wife, they needed a better plan — a real woman. Only, she had to look like the one in that picture they'd showed the uncle. That's when Victor found you."

"And the woman in the painting?" I held my breath.

"She is the lost love of the earl. He has

been pining for her for years, and he refuses to marry anyone else. This ruse is the most he would agree to do."

If he'd refused all others in the hope of marrying that elusive woman, why hadn't he snatched up his chance last night at the masquerade? My heart broke all over again at the memory of her slipping away into the night. I sighed. "What happens now?"

"The countess will be declared dead, the estate will fall to the earl, and Victor will continue to take what he can from everyone."

I stiffened. There was one small problem. Should I tell her? I closed my eyes with a small sigh and pictured that will with Philip Scatchard's name at the top and my signature at the bottom.

"Victor will go free, but so will you."

Free. I opened my eyes again. "I will return to Spitalfields?"

"Only if you wish to be dead. No, I am giving you a new life, a new name, and a new home." She dug in a little bag hanging on a door hook and brought me a train ticket. "You are going into hiding, where you will find life very affordable and many people in need of well-pieced rags such as you can provide."

My heart sank to my stomach. Was I

420

destined to be a rag woman forever? Was that all I was worth? Renaugh, the girl who renewed rags — that was my identity and my lifelong work, it seemed. "I don't want it." I held out the ticket.

Her eyes snapped. "I don't recall giving you the choice."

I looked at the slip again and panic clutched my throat. "Wait — there is only one ticket here. Where is —"

Sully.

"You cannot mean to separate us."

Simone watched me, unflinching. "Everyone at Rothburne is dead to you now, as you are to them."

"Sully!" I grabbed the rough bedpost and scrambled out from the tangled covers.

Simone pinned me to the bed, her grip like shackles. "It's too late."

"No!" I was dizzy with panic and horror. Pain shot through my chest. Thrashing and beating the air with my feet, I screamed with all the agony that burst in my soul until Simone's strength won out over my damaged body. "Sully!" He'd come to find me. He always did.

"There's nothing you can do. You are dead, remember?" Her eyes were wide and dark, her breathing labored as she looked down at me pinned on the bed. "You'll put everything at risk if you go back now. Do you want to lose your life and his? Mine too, now. Don't forget I risked myself for you."

"I have to tell him. He has to know where I am."

"It's too great a risk. He already thinks you dead."

I curled away from her on the bed around the great hole in my heart. How could a hole cause so much pain? I couldn't even cry — I'd emptied the great basin of my tears onto the windowsill of Spitalfields months ago when I thought him drowned.

My rigid soul, twisted up with tension and pain, grabbed at the sliver of hope this memory brought me and I began breathing again. He'd come back to me once — he could do it again.

"This is the only way. He cannot simply disappear from the abbey, or Victor will suspect. He'll come looking for you and it'll all be for naught."

"Maybe that is best." I mumbled this facedown into the clammy blanket.

Her steady voice slipped out into the dark room. "You'll begin a new life. You can be anyone you wish, and it will be a fresh start. Stop fretting over what you leave behind and think instead on what you will have, on the possibilities before you."

How like Victor's little speech in the alley. *What do you have to lose?* That had been his question to me, and it was only now that I had an answer for him.

"You would truly have all those people think me dead? Bradford, Philip, the earl. Will you allow Lord Enderly to believe he was partly to blame for my death? He's already drowning in sorrow for what happened with his lost love."

"Don't waste your pity on that man. He's no different than any other who takes a fancy to some poor girl. It isn't love that weighs him down, but guilt. She was but a common girl that he left with child before refusing to marry her. He awoke to the atrocity of his actions one day, and now he cannot live with himself, knowing he's left her penniless and alone with his child." Simone rose and the pallet shifted. "You have no idea what a turn of fate this is for you. Perhaps you thought living as the countess was the finest stroke of luck, but this is. Your freedom, a new start, that is the true blessing. Use it wisely."

Bitterness welled. I didn't wish to start over away from Sully, leaving this great mess behind me. Who was she to decide who and what I would become?

Yet her words echoed in the darkness as she left the little cottage and locked it from the outside. I rose and felt my way to the door, testing it with my feeble strength, but it was secured. The stone walls offered no other way out. I felt along the walls for a window, growing agitated until I clawed at the rocks in desperation. There was no exit from these four tight walls. I climbed back onto the bed, defeated, and shook. What would become of Sully, after all this effort to save him? With me gone, would Victor turn him in anyway?

And my new life — what would become of me there?

I laid my head on the mattress, but my brain spun thoughts like silken webs, this way and that until I had a mess of them weaving through my weary mind and the chaos inside multiplied once again.

I opened my eyes toward the dark ceiling. Here I was, without excuses or distractions, facing nothing but those empty rooms in the core of me that I'd neglected for so long. Yet it was too much — too much for my small hands to unclutter and repair. How had it gotten so heavy?

Guilt warred with desperation in my soul. I wanted God — *needed* him — but my chaotic mess inside wasn't fit for a holy

God's presence. I'd worked and pushed and strove, stopping before God for the briefest of prayers to ask his help as I tumbled forward on my own. How arrogant and foolish. How bold of me it was to even cry out to him at all in this state.

Yet I had nothing else.

God, I can't! Please help. I've come to the end of my abilities, and they are not nearly enough. I need to untangle the mess I've become.

I waited. Awareness of God's greatness beside my brokenness made me want to weep, to give up. Then came an echo of the beautiful, merciful words spoken by Uncle Wells: *Why don't we do it together?*

At the blessed invitation, my tired soul sank into God's presence, and like the weight of the bench suddenly lifting, the release was sudden and immense. It was more than I deserved, but I grabbed on.

Then I began to pray, in that long and thorough way of one who has all the time in the world. His grace rolled in like pleasant, welcome waves on my tired body, bathing it in peace I had never felt before. It left me with a sense of clean emptiness, a blank slate waiting to be filled.

But with what? Heavens, what did God expect to do with a woman who was somewhere between a rag vendor and a countess, but with several good-sized mistakes marring her character? Everything was upside down, and I hadn't any idea who I was from this point forward. I'd asked so many other people this question lately, seeking answers in their expressions, their reactions, their praise or rejection of me. And there was God, waiting for me to try everything else before I finally landed at the feet of the only One who knew the true answer. *Who am I, God? What on earth did you have in mind for me?*

Again I waited, but he'd already given the answer, spoken on the lips of the one who had drawn me to him in the first place. *Renaugh.* The whisper came like an unexpected breeze through my thoughts, settling into the cracks of my heart and solidifying there. Renew. It was who I'd always known I was.

Yet in quiet reflection, I could almost hear the voices from the past few weeks, brought unexpectedly to memory.

Perhaps you've not been watching him the last few days, but Cousin Philip has become quite a new man.

You've changed the earl, you know. Begun to lighten his burdens.

I hardly recognized the abbey. Who knew

this old place could look so splendid, and that the staff had such immense hidden talents?

It had been that way in Spitalfields too. I was a rag woman. A restorer of castoffs. Rejected clothing, forgotten people — I was drawn to them all.

So was I drawn to you.

Awareness sank through my spirit, along with enough gratitude to make me want to weep. The one everyone — including myself — considered a castoff had been swept up by God and taught to go and do the same. By his grace, before I was even ready for it, I had been made a reflection of God, the ultimate restorer.

That's what we all were, wasn't it? Created beings who bore traces of their Creator, each with a different piece of his nature augmented in order to show the world who he was. *You have something powerful in you,* Bradford had told me, and for once I believed him — because when I dug deep inside myself, I found evidence of God. His mercy healing my heart, traces of his nature reflected in mine, and an emptiness waiting for him to fill. I felt for the first time that I was more than a rag woman, because there was more to me than *me* — and more to life than what happened on this earth.

Yet I was trapped now, and alone. Tears

pooled in my eyes and I blinked. What good was such knowledge when I was not free to live it out? If only I'd realized it sooner, rather than worrying so much about impressing and accomplishing. I might have had a chance.

God, what do I do with this?

32

That's just what God does — he takes the identity the world has tarnished, polishes it up, and hands back the name he gave us in the beginning.
~ Diary of a Substitute Countess

A door closed. It was morning. I lifted my head from the pillow and blinked away the heavy slumber that had finally come to rest on me last night. I was refreshed from the inside out, and the feeling was immense. I stretched, remembering the long and gloriously cleansing conversation I'd had with God last night. I'd put off talking with him for so long — what had I been waiting for?

Simone was unpacking a basket of food onto the table, and she turned to me with a dark look. My uncluttered mind glimpsed something different in her face — a thousand painful stories were walled up behind that impenetrable mask, her own ruined inner chamber. The darkness that had so intimidated me was not evil, but fear. Anxiousness. And it nearly consumed her. How had I missed this before?

It was amazing what one noticed when mirrors became windows.

"I trust you slept well." She said the words as a statement while she set out bread and cheese.

My bitterness melted into curiosity. "Did you?"

She looked at me, chin lifted as if in constant defiance, questions in her eyes, but continued setting out the food. "Victor is suspicious already, so we must be cautious. He's smart, so we must work to get you away from England as soon as possible."

Panic swirled up around my chest, tightened on my throat, but I held on to the peace I'd found as I used to hold Sully's stone. No matter what happened, I would always be Raina, the one who renews, the one God chose to renew, and I would be that in any circumstance.

"He is still about the abbey, which means he does not yet consider this scheme successfully completed."

I sat at the table, studying this woman who had seen more of me than any other person in recent weeks, the woman who was my captor and also, oddly enough, my rescuer.

"What is Victor to you?"

She set her jaw and ignored the question.

Then suddenly I caught sight of a plain gold band flashing on the hand that was slicing bread. Another thing I'd missed all this time.

"Oh Simone, you are his *wife.*"

She did not look up. "Unfortunately."

My heart ached at that single word. "And all the times he stared at me, with you nearby . . ."

She shifted on the chair, her hand stilling over the cheese.

"Do you still care for him?"

"No." Her reply was quick and sure, as if she'd spent a great deal of time working out the state of her heart on the matter. "The man charmed the heart right out of my chest, then proceeded to shatter it over and over. Any love we had is long past."

"You seemed so upset by his attention toward me." It was a quiet statement, and it stilled her hands again.

"You cannot understand what it is to have that gaze meant only for you turned on another woman." Her lashes fluttered. She straightened a little.

"You needn't defend yourself to me,

Simone. You rescued me from your husband."

"Only to keep my own hands clean. I spotted a blue vial among his things before he brought you here, and I knew what it meant, knew what his ultimate plan for you would be. And this time, since he'd placed me in the position of your lady's maid, it would be me administering it. He does such things with alarming ease, but I . . . I could not."

"Thank you." The two words seemed inadequate.

"I tried to convince you to leave long ago. I wanted it for me, and for you." She lifted her gaze to mine. "You are who I used to be. Loyal and good. Beautiful. *Free.*"

Her pale face reflected the deep angst, the painful longing, I had worn so often while gazing up at the portrait in the abandoned rooms, wishing to be someone else. With a weak smile, I spoke the first thought that came to mind. "It's a terrible shame you are trapped in this position, but I'm grateful there is someone so very noble working beside Victor to defuse his evil with good."

Shock lit her features for a brief moment, then receded into the shadowed planes of her face. "I was at one time, but I have become nothing more than a partner to his crimes."

"If that was true, I'd be dead."

She humphed, eyes downcast as she worked.

"Were there others? Other people you saved from Victor?"

"Yes." The single word carried great weight.

"You see? You are no more evil for being married to Victor than I am a countess simply because of my gowns."

Pale and silent, she rose and left, slamming and locking the door behind her. I watched the doorway in silence for a long time. Fighting against fear, I remained at the table sipping the lukewarm tea and munching bread, but she did not return.

It was not until much later that I heard the metal key scraping, and the door creaked open. Simone stood in its shadows, cradling another basket of food. She considered me for a moment without a word, then strode in, securing the door behind her, and brought me the food. Her fingers worked rapidly over the bits of meat pie and the cooked potatoes. Bread came out too.

"I hope you are well, Simone."

"I will be soon." Bright lights in her eyes told me she'd wrestled with my words — maybe she still was. They had unsettled something. She hustled more than necessary to prepare the food, and I stood to help. Finally her hands slowed, and she stared down at what she'd laid out on the tin plate for me. "I've set a plan in motion with a single letter that may just bring Victor the final blow. He'll be in prison before the week's out if the constable has any sense."

"This means I can go back."

"Absolutely not. Everything will be ruined if you are ever seen again." She rose and shoved the dishes back into the basket, lips pinched. "You walked into this mess, you know. I'm merely helping you out of it the only way I can. Don't forget I'm saving your life."

"What life will it be if I cannot make things right? I need to go back."

"This is best. Everyone will believe the countess dead, you'll be out of Victor's grasp, and life will move on."

Everyone. Everyone would believe me dead, including the poor earl, dear Bradford, and Sully. *Sully.* They would all be made miserable by the conclusion of this awful scheme that I had helped carry out, and nothing would be right.

"Why not be done with all of this deception? What hold does he have over you, Simone?"

She lifted a tarnished locket from inside her dress and opened it up to reveal a miniature of a young girl. "Our daughter. Her name is Priscilla and she's only ten. Victor has the legal right to take her away from me forever. He cannot know I've done anything against him."

"Where is she now?"

"Miss Hutchins's School for Girls in Northampton. She's not with me, but at least I can still visit her."

I watched her rapid movements, her pale face. "Doesn't your daughter deserve some good in her life? Someone to set an honorable example? She won't find it in Victor."

She reared up, flinging the tin plate against the far wall with a clatter and a growl. "Don't you dare speak to me of her. She's none of your concern. You've no idea about anything." Abandoning the basket and dishes, she bolted out the door, banging it behind her.

After a deep breath, I rested my folded hands on the table and stared into the flame encased in cloudy glass. My heartbeat thudded in my ears as I waited.

When nothing but the lamp's oil level had changed in the house, I put out the flame and climbed into bed.

33

Dreams are lovely little diversions for tired minds, but we must at some point wake up and live in the splendid real world, pursuing things that are eternal and lasting, significant and very uniquely us.

~ Diary of a Substitute Countess

Nobody ever asks the footman what he knows, but they should. Sullivan McKenna ushered the somber-looking men through the front doors with a bow and accepted their hats and calling cards. They'd introduced themselves as investigators and asked to speak with the earl, but they'd learn far more by standing right there and talking to Sully. He was the one who had plunged into the flames after his beloved and seen that there was no one there. A murder meant a death, and although there was indeed wrong done here, there had been no death.

He'd let them investigate the murder.

That's what Victor intended when he had arranged the fire, Sully was certain. And as long as Victor had his way, Raina might be safe. His heart thudded as he forced himself to remain calm, fighting the urge to run out the front door and find her. He had to bide his time and watch the man.

He escorted them past the crumbling ruins of the old chapel, which left the main wing of the abbey wide open to the chilly outside, and into the unscathed abbot's wing. Here the earl and Victor had arranged a makeshift study in the abbot's great hall and taken up residence in his sparse but functional bedchambers and sitting room. Much of the rest of the main house was useless and exposed.

"My lord, these men are here from London concerning the inquisition."

The earl and his solicitor rose together and welcomed the men in with somber voices. Sully cast a sideways glance at Prendergast, the refined gent, aware of every movement the man made. He'd be watching him, and the second he left the abbey, Sully would be on his heels. Wherever he'd hidden Raina, Sully would find her.

"Bring us some tea, would you, McKenna?" Victor tossed the order out with barely a glance at Sully, but then something caught his attention and he turned back to study Sully's face, his gaze lingering there with a frown.

Sully held Prendergast's stare without blinking, letting him read what he would from his expression. Yes, he was watching and he would continue to do so. The man couldn't keep Raina hidden forever. Sully turned and left but hovered outside the door, pulse thrumming. He had to know what Prendergast told them.

One of the visitors began. "We've heard from a witness who was present the night of the fire, and we'd like to ask you both a few questions."

Sully held his breath as he waited.

"Of course, by all means, ask anything you'd like." Hatred for Prendergast curled through Sully's gut.

"Where were both of you when the fire broke out?"

"I was with my guests, in the ballroom." The earl's low voice came first. "I was speaking with the Marquis De LaFond and his brother, and both will attest to this fact."

"And you, Mr. Prendergast? Were you present?"

A brief hesitation. "I was somewhere about, I'm sure. Ask any of the guests."

"Did either of you have cause to be angry

with Lady Enderly? It's been said that some were on strained terms with her."

Prendergast growled his response. "See here, what is this about? You cannot possibly believe that either of us started that fire on purpose. The whole thing was a terrible accident."

The man turned to Prendergast. "Sir, someone has informed against you, claiming the fire was no accident and that you in particular held malice against Lady Enderly. If you don't mind, we'd like to speak with you about your association with her."

"You cannot truly believe I did this. The countess and I were very close."

"We've already spoken to a few other guests, and several have vouched for the earl's presence at the end of the night. No one, however, has been able to attest to your whereabouts when the fire broke out."

"Very well then, if you must know, I was in my room."

"By yourself?"

"I was attending to a rather nasty gash on my lip."

"How did you get the gash, Mr. Prendergast?"

A moment of silence ensued, leaving Sully immensely curious for his answer.

"I doubt he was responsible for the fire."

The earl's deep voice slid through the tension.

After this, Sully doubted it too. The man couldn't have set the fire after all, could he? Sully had been on the upper landing as the slightly besotted man charged up the stairs with a handkerchief to his bloody lip, his face red with anger. He truly hadn't been there. And most convincing of all, someone was pointing the finger at him, which meant this whole fire was *not* Victor's scheme.

Which meant he did not have Raina.

Discarding the empty tray on a side table, Sully bolted for the service door. He had to find her, rescue her. But who had her now? Where could she be?

As he raced toward his little room, he shoved aside the notion that she had planned this and escaped without him, without even a word. Surely she couldn't have — no, she had gone through with this whole scheme to help *him* in the first place. She wouldn't have left him behind. He gulped down the constant lump of guilt at the mess she'd tangled herself in for his sake and threw his few belongings into a bag. When he reached for his fiddle on the crooked shelf above his cot, a shadow darkened the doorway behind him. He spun to face the prevailing form of Victor Prendergast.

"Well, hello there, Mr. Prendergast, sir. A little out of your normal route in the servants' quarters, aren't you?"

"I'm nothing more than a servant myself, when it comes down to it. Paid to do someone else's bidding, always the master of another. But that is changing. Thanks to a fortune that is nearly within my grasp." He stepped into the tiny room, his face hard. "Where is she, Sullivan? Where's your girl?"

Sully's fingers clasped the neck of his fiddle and pulled it close. "Wouldn't you like to know."

"I suggest you tell me, or I'll have to wire a very eager inspector in London about your whereabouts."

The hairs on Sully's neck stood up, anger tightening in his gut. "Leave off with your threats, Prendergast. You've done more than enough damage."

"Then tell me —"

"Not on your life."

With a snarl, Victor lunged for the fiddle and smashed it against the wall with the force of his ire. "Tell me now!"

Sully stared at the pile of splintered wood and curled strings, heat surging through his chest. Everything precious to him, destroyed by this man's hand.

"I'll find her and utterly *ruin* —"

Sully sprang on the man with a growl, but Victor shoved him with arms like iron, strengthened by anger. He stumbled onto the cot and it buckled under him. Victor pinned him with one sharp-soled boot to his heaving chest. "One more chance, McKenna, that's all I've the patience for."

Sully glared with eyes of fire. No word passed his lips, and neither would it if he knew where she was. Not in a million years would he turn the pearl over to a swine.

Eyes bulging with anger, Victor grabbed Sully's collar and yanked him up with a sharp snap felt in the back of his neck. A grunt escaped Sully's lips and he coughed.

"I'm overdue to visit the magistrate in London anyway. Perhaps we'll pay him a call together." He yanked Sully's collar, making him scramble to keep on his feet. "They've been looking for you, and the execution will be very public. We'll see if that doesn't draw our little countess out of hiding."

"She's been captured, I'm sure of it. She cannot save me, even if she gets word of this."

Victor slowed in the hall, staring into

442

Sully's face with dull eyes. "Then I suppose no one will care to stop the execution." A wicked smile curled the man's lips. "Did you honestly think I'd care if you lived or died?"

34

How beautiful that when I dug into the deepest parts of myself, I did not find that hidden source of confidence I wanted or a better self, but God.

~ Diary of a Substitute Countess

A thud startled me awake the next morning, and there was Simone, pale and steadfast, her slender form blocking the sunlight in the doorway. I sat up and looked at her, scrunching the blanket to my chest.

"Here, take this." She tossed a heavy cloak to me, and I fingered the garment with a smile at the irony. This cloak was the one that had hidden me so I could enter Rothburne for the first time, and now here it was again, covering me as I embarked on the close of this adventure that was just as unknown. Yet this time, I was armed and ready.

"Where are we going?"

Her only answer was a hard stare. "Are you ready?"

It truly was a ruin now, that glorious chapel that had inspired such awe in centuries of the abbey's inhabitants — including myself. The top had collapsed, allowing sunlight to stream into the darkness. I stepped over the rubble, looking with wonder over the disaster of fallen stone and glass that still somehow embodied the same hushed reverence in me I'd discovered on that first night. God was present even in a collapsed ruin, and perhaps even more powerfully felt without the dilution of man-made grandeur.

I closed my eyes and breathed deeply of the age-old room whose stale air now mingled with the fresh breeze from outdoors. How great was the God whose presence was felt here, even in ruin. Gratitude filled me for the chance to be here, to make things right.

"I will not be a part of this, you understand." Those were Simone's parting words to me as she'd handed me off in the lane. "I'll not feel any responsibility for what becomes of you, for I've done my best by you." She watched me with unchecked fear.

"What will become of you?" I asked.

"I haven't decided yet."

But at least she'd given me a chance, and I would take it. I'd set things right as much as I could. *Father God, I'm turning this adventure over to you now. Help me rebuild from the inside out. Walk with me through this mess.*

Now that I was here, I had no idea how to go about declaring the truth.

I ask that you help me to happen upon exactly the right person just now and know what to say.

Unexplainable tranquility spread through the inner parts of me where chaos had once been. I stepped through the rubble to what used to be the old monastic library. Perhaps that painting had survived. Charred remains of books and papers littered the floor among fallen stones and beams. The painting, what was left of it, had been splintered and torn, that crimson gown sliced into pieces that curled up toward the sunlight dulled by clouds. I bent to touch the image, to see that familiar face once again.

The smell of smoke burned my nose and tickled my throat, seizing it with dryness. Burying my face into my sleeve, I coughed until my lashes were clumped with tears and my face clammy. A door slammed nearby, with footsteps following — someone had heard me.

The warming room. It's the only private spot about this place. Sully's words swooped back to save me even when he couldn't. I ran toward the tiny calefactory, a little alcove in the now-exposed center cloister, and shut the door as I curled into the tiny room. Used as a respite for the monks when they worked in the outdoor cloister in winter, the little space boasted nothing but a long-dead coal fireplace, a Bible shelf, and a stool.

I shifted in the cramped compartment, banging my head on the shelf, and the Bible struck my shoulder and thunked onto the dirt floor. "Ow!" I lifted the offending book and dusted it off. Then my hand slowed on the cloth cover of a book that was smaller than the Bible, lying next to it.

The warming room. Go there when you can. I'll leave a message. In all the turmoil, I'd forgotten. With a cry, I held the book up to the window in the door. It was a fresh green-cloth-bound copy of *Jane Eyre.* It was perfect.

Blinking back tears that clogged my lashes, I opened the front cover and ran my fingers over the inscription written in a painfully familiar hand: *To my splendid adventurer.* Emotion welled. Several pages had been marked with frayed twine, just as he'd done years ago when our message passing system

447

began. I opened the book with wonder, excitement, and unrelenting hope. Flipping to the first marked section, I read what he'd underlined.

"He was the first to recognize me, and to love what he saw." I ran my fingertip over the precious words and flipped to the next. They brought a sob to my throat, as it brought back the memory of telling him with marked frustration that I resembled Brontë's heroine, Jane the lowly governess.

"You — poor and obscure, and small and plain as you are — I entreat to accept me as a husband."

I gasped at the final word, blinking and reading it over again. A proposal? I looked hungrily for the next underline.

"I offer you my hand, my heart, and a share of all my possessions. I ask you to pass through life at my side — to be my second self, and best earthly companion."

With a sob, I traced the crooked pencil lines. No wonder he'd been so distant in the days before the party. He'd offered up his heart to me and I had said nothing.

To think of what had been awaiting me while I'd been so busy planning a useless soiree with a façade that had all been lost in the end. I turned with trembling fingers to the last one and read with a pounding heart.

"I have for the first time found what I can truly love — I have found you." I shut the book and hugged it, wrapping my arms around the slender volume that could offer little comfort in return.

Why did I feel as though it was too late? It was an odd sense of foreboding hanging about the smoke-tinged air, but it must be my nerves. Sully would not give up so easily, after all he'd weathered with me. He'd be happy I was ready to speak the truth now, and there would be nothing between us. I patted my sash absently. Where was that Connemara stone when I needed to feel its solidness most?

Sitting in that little room, I leafed tenderly through the pages of his gift until I reached the back cover, where I found another inscription.

I always wanted a life of peace, but I'm afraid I've attached myself to the wrong girl for that. So I'm asking you to let us join our futures into one glorious adventure lived out together. A girl so full of escapades needs her rescuer, after all, no? In the words of Dickens, "There is a man who would give his life to keep a life you love beside you." I aim to be that man, if you'll have me.

Yes. Yes, I would have him — with joyful eagerness. I was about to throw off the last of my fetters and run to him with a free heart and conscience. He would open his arms and I would fly to them. After all these years, the two best friends could become one — and we would be inseparable.

The sudden need to find him, to see his precious face, burned in my chest. Before anything prevented me, I must find Sully. I lifted the cloak's hood over me and took a deep breath, sneaking back out into the rubble and across the debris, but my plans only got as far as the door. When I slipped out, there was Victor.

He spun and grabbed my arm with a vice grip. "I knew it. I knew you were here somewhere. You are responsible for this mess, and it ends *now.*" He yanked me forward and I stumbled with a cry. "I warned you what it would mean to double-cross me."

I coughed again. "What are you doing?" My voice was scratchy. Scared.

"Proving to everyone that I did not kill you, you little wretch."

35

No human has the power to take away the inherent dignity given by God, or change the identity he has granted you of belonging to him.

~ Diary of a Substitute Countess

As we hurried through the hallway, his grip on my arm tightened until I half expected to hear my bones snap. There was no Uncle Wells in sight to protect me, no Sully to swoop in to my rescue.

"A very clever trick you played, faking your own death, even being kind enough to frame me for the mishap. Did you know I've had men from the Yard breathing down my neck, peering into my personal affairs, finding ways to prove I murdered you?" He jerked me forward and I stumbled, nearly losing one shoe in the hall. "Did you truly think an insignificant little rag girl could outwit me?" A clock bonged in the hall, echoing through the empty rooms.

The words *insignificant little rag girl* rang through my overwhelmed brain and my heart dropped. *What now, God? Have my mistakes taken me too far from righteousness to even have a chance?*

Victor banged open the study doors and thrust me in, where I stumbled and fell onto the rug. I stared at the carpet fibers beneath my hands, taking in dizzying breaths, pulsing with shame.

"Here is your proof, gentlemen. Sergeant Brackenly, Inspector Rhys, gentlemen, I give you our murder victim, alive and well. Stand up and show yourself."

My pulse quickened, heart pounding at the heady awareness of what he was asking me to do yet again.

"You claim this woman is the countess?" A gruff voice spoke out for the well-dressed men in the room. "This woman you are handling so, and who is dressed . . ."

"She's been through a great deal," offered another of the men. "She wouldn't have taken pains with her appearance after that fire."

"I assure you, this is her, and no other." As Victor towered over me, his silence demanding my assent, I waged an internal battle against this enemy of my soul, the one who had attempted to reshape my identity. The one who made me forget who I was and Whose I was.

There is great significance in a name. Even in his absence, Uncle Wells's voice carried into me like a sweet breeze, calming and comforting me. Bringing strength. What God had bestowed on me could not be taken away by anyone — even Victor Prendergast.

So this is what confidence feels like.

It did not make me proud or poised or beautiful, but deeply awed.

I rose, my cloak falling away like a rose unfurling its petals and stood tall before those gentlemen and the man of charm who seemed so small compared to the One who had named me. "Sir, I am Raina." My name felt both sweet and powerful on my lips. "My name is Raina Bretton and I am no countess."

My pulse skittered at the mounting tension as I stepped back. I had done it. I'd told the truth — and I was still alive. Despite the heavy silence in the room, there was a breathy lightness to my heart that made me wonder once again why I hadn't done this sooner.

I steadied myself and stood tall and poised before the earl, Prendergast, several strangers, and a very shocked Philip Scatchard. The men from Scotland Yard exchanged looks, one grimacing. "What is the meaning of this display? You would pass this woman off as the countess?"

"I tell you, she *is* the countess! She's attempting to frame me for her own murder. Do not let that horrid garment fool you, for it is her underneath." Victor's tight voice thrust over theirs. "Ask anyone from Rothburne. They will all testify that this is she."

Scatchard stared at me openly, as if glimpsing me for the first time, wonder and understanding dawning over his features. All his doubts and suspicions were finally coming together to form the truth, like a completed puzzle that shows the entire picture. "Amazing." He breathed the word quietly, but all the men turned to look at him.

"What's that, Scatchard?"

He stepped closer, arms crossed over his narrow chest as he looked me over with a brilliant glow to his features. Approval, or victory over his former enemy? "Well, gentlemen, I've worked closely with Lady Enderly in running this estate for quite a while now, and I can attest to the fact that this woman . . . she is *not* Lady Enderly."

"He's not to be trusted." Prendergast spat

the words, growing tense. "Did we not just read a newly made will leaving this man everything in the estate? His word means nothing."

"And mine?" The earl stepped closer with a resolute face, offering a glimpse of the powerful man who made such waves in the House of Lords. "I've nothing to gain by telling you that this woman is who she claims to be, and that she most certainly is *not* my wife."

"It's true." Stepping away from Prendergast, I faced the gentlemen. "I was hired by Mr. Prendergast to take a position here. It turned out he wished me to stand in for the countess as her lookalike." When I had the courage, I lifted my gaze to Victor's face. "But I am not her."

His gaze locked onto mine, his eyes narrow and bright as he spoke in a low, private voice. "You." His clean-shaven chin trembled, nostrils flared. "You worthless little rat. Do you know why I picked you for this? I could have chosen any number of women for the position, made her look like the countess, but there was one thing that made you perfect for this task — you are disposable. Just like the castoffs you sell, no one misses people like you."

You are who God made you and nothing can

change that. Not even you.

As the long-ago words of my sweet mother rose up before me, deflecting the arrows from going deep into the core of my being, I looked into this man's angry, hardened face with immense sorrow. It was *he* who had the disposable life, for he had no one. Not even his wife valued him.

Before I could speak again, Scatchard cut in. "It seems you'll need to arrest this man on murder charges after all."

Prendergast backed away from them. "Horsefeathers! I'll not suffer an indictment for a murder I haven't committed. I've killed no one."

"Well, then." Philip Scatchard spoke with a barely contained smile and glittering eyes as one very much amused by what was occurring. "I hope you are prepared to prove your innocence when you're brought before the magistrate for the disappearance of the real countess."

"The real —"

"It is said you were overheard threatening her life." Uncle Wells strode in from the other doorway, arms folded across his chest. "More than one servant can attest to such threats, and with such proof, I'd personally name you the primary suspect."

I caught my breath at the sight of this formidable man towering over the others.

"Mr. Prendergast, can you tell us where Lady Enderly is now?" The gentlemen callers turned to him.

Victor turned a dreadful shade of pea-soup green and something bobbed in his throat. The only defense he had now was the truth — the glaring, painful, condemning truth of the entire conspiracy. It was the only way to prove he did not murder or kidnap the countess. His eyes rounded and his jaw slacked. For once he was the one afraid, the one under threat — by his own devices.

The words of Brontë's novel *Shirley* rang through my mind. It was something to the effect of "Give a man enough rope, and he will hang himself," and the wickedly grinning Philip Scatchard had handed him a ship's length of it.

"Go on, then, Prendergast." The earl spoke from the shadows. "Tell us the whole of it."

Prendergast spun on the man. "Don't be so haughty, my lord. It would be your undoing too, for you were in this scheme as much as I."

"So be it." Lord Enderly moved toward his solicitor and lowered his voice. "And just because you aren't guilty of murdering the countess, do not forget there are others."

"You've no proof of anything, Mitchell. Not a single thing." Prendergast stepped back, speaking to the entire room at large. "None of you has a shred of proof for any of these wild stories, and you'll not touch me without it." He turned and stalked toward the door, calling back over his shoulder. "We'll speak again if you manage to find proof of anything, and not before."

"Perhaps I can help with that." We all spun at the low, sultry voice of a woman standing just inside the doorway. Simone glided in from the shadows and looked over her husband with a solemn smile. "Hello, Victor. Going somewhere?"

Prendergast froze, his eye twitching as he looked upon his wife with mortal fear.

"Perhaps we'd best sit down for this." Simone gestured with a gracious sweep of her arm toward the far table and chairs, as if she were hostess of this event. And in a way, I suppose she was. She lifted those dark, solemn eyes to me one last time, and a flicker of kinship, of silent understanding, passed between us as she crossed the room.

I moved to join them, but a hand on my shoulder stopped me. Uncle Wells looked down at me with a gentle smile. "What a relief to see you safe and alive." He squeezed my hands affectionately.

With an ache, I pulled away and looked up into his face with great regret. "I owe you so much more than an apology." My throat clogged on the words. "I never should have let you believe —"

"Come, come, now. I never believed. Why do you think I appeared at your door so suddenly?"

"You knew?"

"My solicitor received a very informative anonymous letter when he was here that revealed a great deal. Then when he informed me of the will this supposed countess had created, leaving everything to Philip Scatchard, of all people, I knew there must be something to it and came to see for myself who this rather interesting lady truly was."

I blinked. "So all along you knew, as you worked with me on these rooms, offering to help, giving advice, and speaking of your wife . . ."

"Even then."

I gulped.

"Please tell me, though, that you did not set fire to my beloved abbey and plan this whole escape to save yourself."

I shook my head. "It was my lady's maid,

Simone Bouvier." I inclined my head toward the woman now in private conversation with the visitors. "Simone *Prendergast.*"

His brow furrowed. "Well, well, that is a surprise. It seems there's a great deal of significance to her name too. Who knew there was another snake in our midst?"

"You must think on her with mercy, sir, for she did it to save my life. She may be married to Victor, but there is so much good in her. I know it."

His cheeks folded up in a wide smile as he turned to join the group huddled over the table in conversation. "I was right to like you from the beginning."

Regret washed over me anew. If only I had been honest with this man, and with everyone, despite Victor's threats. I turned my warm face away from his painfully kind countenance and caught sight of Bradford in the distance, his long face troubled, worry folding the aged skin of his forehead into his hairline. Dear Bradford! My heart lurched as our gazes met. I turned, eager to heap my gratitude on him for what he'd been to me during my stay. "Bradford, I —"

But his shuttered face didn't melt into its usual smile. Without a word, he bowed his head as one bearing the weight of betrayal and turned to slip out the exit. My heart fell to the floor. The full burden of my deception settled on me again, and I fought its hold. I dared not move from my spot, my worn boots planted directly on the spiraling flower in the rug's corner.

When the little group rose from the table and moved toward me, I held my breath. Uncle Wells returned to me with a solemn expression hardening his features. "They will have to take you with them, I'm afraid, but do not lose heart. I have decided to take you under my wing, and I shall personally see to it that you receive what I think is a fair consequence for your part in this and no more."

I released a shuddering sigh as I recalled the utter betrayal on Bradford's face. "I do not deserve your mercy any more than Prendergast does."

"Fortunately for you, I disagree. You have one thing that man does not — pure, authentic remorse. And therefore, me." He withdrew a small white card from his vest and handed it to me. "If you ever run into trouble, reach out and find me."

"Thank you, sir. I —" My mumbled words halted as I turned it over and glimpsed his name printed in clear letters across the front. "Edwin Wells Darlington III?"

"That would be my full name."

My throat tightened as I looked up at him. "You . . . you are . . ."

"The owner of far too fancy a name?"

"The *prime minister.*" I looked up at the man I'd worked beside, casually befriended, and with whom I'd stumbled through the details of my insignificant little heart.

"There is great significance in a name. Use mine whenever you have need, and it'll help you navigate whatever comes next. I cannot keep you entirely from the consequences, for you officially entered into the fraud by creating that will and signing Lady Enderly's name. The law will deal with you, but know that you always have an ally in me."

"I had no idea you were . . ." I glanced up at him, then over at Prendergast, now surrounded by men in dark suits, all his charm drained like a tub that had been uncorked.

"I always had the ability to help you, you know. I was merely waiting for you to ask. It is as I said — your enemy has power, *but I have more.*"

I trembled and looked down at the hem of my limp dress. It was something akin to God, the great God of the world, stretching out his hand to me and drawing me near, even in the midst of my confusion. It was more than I deserved.

"Is something the matter?"

"It's just . . . you doing all this for me, after what I did, it makes no sense."

His face creased into a pleasant smile. "The greatest things in life never do. Go and make good use of the grace given to you."

"That I will. Whatever comes, I will."

"Now, perhaps you'll deem me worthy to know exactly what hold he had over you, and why you agreed to this scheme in the first place."

I cleared my throat, then unfurled to him the entire story of meeting in the alley, and of my beloved Sully, who had risen up against abuse and been called mutinous when violence ensued by the men he'd rallied. "He isn't a criminal. Prendergast only threatened to have him imprisoned to —"

He grabbed my hand. "To imprison you." With a groan, he dropped my hand and covered his face. "You wouldn't be talking about the former second footman, would you? Is that your Sully?"

Fear clutched me. "Former?"

He pressed thick fingertips to his forehead. "I'm afraid Victor had him arrested when he found out he was wanted in London. Charges of mutiny."

The room tilted forcefully. With a cry, I

grabbed the back of a chair, digging my nails into its wood frame. "How long ago? Can we catch them?" But even if we could, what could we do now?

"It was yesterday. He left in the morning."

I forced back a strangled cry as the men approached. Victor was being led out the doors toward the great hall.

"You'll need to come with us now, miss."

I nodded, my throat tight, and looked back helplessly at Uncle Wells, my face one big, wide question to which I didn't truly want an answer.

He watched me go. "The sentence for mutiny is always the same, especially for the leaders."

Execution.

"I'm so sorry."

In a breath my legs failed and I crumpled. The two men pulled me up by the arms, pain shooting through my shoulders. White edged my vision.

Somehow I tumbled into the carriage and landed beside the earl. I righted myself, moved to the other seat, and leaned against the window, my oily cheek leaving an unattractive mark on the glass. I didn't care. The vibration of the carriage echoed through my body, shaking everything loose, until despair and then sleep overtook me.

Chaotic thoughts whipped through my tired mind in my haze of slumber until my head banged against a hard surface, jerking me awake. I groaned and touched my temple where it had struck the carriage wall when the vehicle jolted. I curled my knees to my chest, no more the proper lady, and locked gazes with the earl, who was seated across from me.

"Don't be discouraged over Uncle Wells. He's upset over everything now, but he'll come around eventually." He reclined on the rear-facing seat, arms folded and ankles crossed. "You've truly upended our little country estate, you know, and Uncle doesn't take well to changes in it that are not limited to construction."

I sat up a little, mind numb from the pain of everything that had happened — because of me. "I'm sorry." For so much.

"Don't be." He held out a hand, offering a sad smile. "It needed to happen. I've been a coward for so long, and you gave me a reason to be better."

I closed my eyes and took a deep breath. His words settled into my heart. The lines of sorrow across his face, particularly around his eyes, reminded me of the love he himself had lost yet again. "You're no stranger to heartache."

"It was as painful as having a bullet pried out of my arm in my days as a soldier. But do you know, I nearly proposed to the nurse who removed it because it brought relief. And it was only after her painful work that I began to heal."

Heal. That word sounded magical, like cool water on a dry throat. I wished for it myself. "So you did speak with her, then? It was . . . helpful?"

He shrugged. "As much as a bullet being pried from my arm." He looked down. "Necessary, healing, but . . ."

"Painful." My voice was so weak. "Tell me about her."

"Victor did not tell you our story?"

I shook my head.

With a great sigh, he began a tragic tale of two matched souls who were not allowed to marry. "She was a milliner's daughter with a shop in Belgravia, and we were one of the clients she served. I saw nothing but a plain little shopgirl until one day I caught her unawares in the park, feeding pigeons and tucking little flowers in her hair. Something about Evelyn Lockharte enchanted me, and when she began to speak . . . I was hopelessly lost."

When the earl's father had found out about the little dalliances, as he called their passionate relationship, he nearly put the girl's father out of business and severed their connection. The girl's mother, a poor but wise woman, had never approved of the match between her daughter and the haughty, spoiled earl. She had forbidden their acquaintance, and they'd had to sneak around behind her.

"I was foolish and headstrong, and I should have turned my back on her enchantment or simply married the girl. Unfortunately I did neither, and soon I learned she was with child. The world is never kind to girls in that situation, and for weeks I could do nothing but picture her, waking or sleeping, huddled in some sorry alley, starving and sick."

"Didn't you —"

"She disappeared. I had no idea what became of her and none of them would tell me."

"So that's why you refused to marry — because you wanted to be available for her if you ever found her again. How noble of you."

"Well, there was quite a bit of selfishness involved as well. I did truly love her. In fact, I named the countess after her — Lovely Lyn is what I called her, so my pretend wife became —"

"Lovelyn." I pondered this. "So then why did you not seize upon the opportunity when she was here? You are not married — not really."

He heaved a great sigh. "No, but . . . she is."

I gasped.

"There was a better man than I among her acquaintances who married her to give the child a name."

I gripped the edge of the leather seat, speechless.

He shrugged. "She says they are quite happy together. They've had six more children too. Who would have thought it?" He gave a hollow laugh. "She's made a wonderful life for herself despite the past, and now . . . well, now, I suppose I should too."

Despite his feigned nonchalance, anguish tightened the muscles of his neck and shadowed his eyes.

I reached across the vehicle and laid my hand over his. "This cannot be easy for you."

A single sob was wrenched from his throat, then he sat back, closing his eyes. "Knowing her sweetness has been preserved, her life spared . . . that is enough. It'll have to be, anyway." He opened his red-rimmed eyes.

"I'm glad I sent that invitation, then, and glad it found its way to her after all."

"I'll admit I thought none too kindly of you at first. Seeing her again, dancing with her, then watching her float away . . ."

"Now you know what became of her."

"Yes." He frowned and patted at the wetness around his eyes with a monogrammed handkerchief. "That I do. It nearly ripped my heart from my chest, but I suppose it's the only way I can move forward. Who knew a shopgirl could so change my life?" He took my hand. "There is one other woman who has managed to make a rather considerable impact, you know. That is, the one sitting in front of me."

"I've made a fine mess of it, that's what."

"I hope you will continue to do so."

My hand stiffened in my lap. "What do you mean?"

"I've no idea what will become of us as this all unfolds, but perhaps . . . if there is any living yet to be done for me, maybe you'd care to live it out with me."

"Oh no, I can't —"

"I know the timing of my suggestion is terrible, but you've been left in wretched straits, and it occurs to me that you might not have anywhere to go. I've no qualms about where you came from or who your family is. The truth is, I simply like who you are, and I enjoy your presence in my home." He offered a weak smile that melted my defenses. "My titled status prevents me from enduring much besides a hefty fine, and if we marry, the courts will look much more favorably upon you. Unless you find me less agreeable than the inside of a prison."

"It isn't that."

"What is it, then? Have you a man already?"

I trembled at the echo of Victor's words from months earlier, for the agonizing answer was nearly the same. And then, facing this noble gent in the dark carriage, I wept. He slid over to my seat and his arm came around me, holding me up and pulling me to his chest where I poured out my tears. I forced out a few sentences of explanation, that the man I loved was in trouble, and I had no idea if I'd ever see him again. I couldn't bear to utter the terrible word that pervaded my mind.

Once the truth was out, he heaved a sigh and let the silence rest on us for a moment before speaking again. "Maybe one day we could make a new life together. Just know you've reason to hope. You'll not be alone."

I pushed back to look into his face and

accepted his clean white handkerchief to wipe my tears. "I'm not certain I could forget about the man I love."

"You needn't ever forget." His eyes were filled with great tenderness. "They both deserve to be treasured as memories, those early loves of ours, but perhaps together we can build something from the ashes." He wiped a trace of remaining moisture from my warm cheek, his solemn, steadfast gaze burrowing into mine.

"I'll never be the poised and graceful woman you need."

"Is that so? Well, I'll tell you, what I truly need is someone who can tolerate my company, and there aren't many women who fit that description."

I giggled through my tears and sniffled.

"You've made my life better, and I'd like a chance to return the favor. Unless you have another situation you hope to pursue."

I sank back into the shadows, looking down at my hands twisting his limp handkerchief. It broke my loyal heart to picture myself beside anyone other than the man I'd loved for so long.

It seemed my search to understand who I was would last forever, for even after discovering the core of my created being, I now had to determine all over again who I was without Sully.

36

Living out your true identity may repel plenty of people, but the ones it attracts are yours forever.

~ Diary of a Substitute Countess

My second stay in prison bothered me far less than the first, even though it was longer. I languished alone in the damp cell that echoed with bangs and shuffles. The little square window set high into the wall let through the noises outside, carts and horse clops and voices ringing against the bars that separated us. I had asked about Sully at first, speaking of him to every guard who approached my cell until his name stuck in my throat, but I heard no news of him.

When I lay upon the clammy cot at night, the earl's forlorn face came to mind, pulling at me with the overwhelming desire to go to him and draw out the flicker of light I'd seen inside. I asked myself a hundred times a day if I should have reconsidered his offer, but the question hit my brain with dull acceptance. It was over now, and the prison walls separated us.

When several days had passed in painful, mind-numbing isolation, the gruel they fed me sitting like mud in my belly, a guard banged his bobby stick against the rough wood door, startling me back to life. "Visit with the clergy."

It was one of the few connections with other humans allowed to us. The only solution to reforming criminals was, they were convinced, total isolation. I stood, planting one palm on the moist brick of the wall to steady myself, and shuffled toward the door then creaking open. Clergy — did that mean I was being given final rites?

The grizzly face of the keeper with the shiny forehead met my blinking gaze, then behind him the somber face of Bradford, clutching a Bible. My jaw went slack, but I said nothing. My brain had forgotten how to form words, it seemed. He removed his hat to stoop into the doorway and enter my cell, which was promptly locked behind his giant form the minute he'd stepped in. I blinked at the man, waiting for him to state his purpose.

He shuffled farther in and leaned against

the wall. "I'm not certain what to call you anymore." He spoke without looking at me.

"My name is Raina. You could call me that."

He hesitated, as if searching for the perfect scone to offer his mistress on her tea tray, angst wrinkling his brow. "I knew you weren't a countess in the usual manner. I told you that from the start."

The pain in his eyes intensified mine. "Back when you were the only friend I had in that place, whether or not I deserved one."

He looked down at the book in his hand, his thumbs running along its spine. "Most of the staff is scandalized by what has happened, all except the stable master. We had a long talk, and it occurred to me that I gained nothing by resenting you, and that our friendship was not entirely unfounded."

Hope fluttered in my chest. "Is that so?"

"Well, you see, everything I liked about who you are is still true. It was only the name I had wrong."

Blinking back tears, I stepped forward and laid a hand on his arm. "Thank you, Bradford. You are a man among men."

He shrugged. "The great Uncle Wells has found you blameless in this matter, my lady. I suppose we can do no less." A gentle smile lit his face as he looked down at me. "What you have done there will not be forgotten. You've made an impact on Rothburne Abbey."

He'd meant it as a compliment, I knew, but I bowed my head and pictured the crumbled ruins. If not for me, they might still be standing — for a while, at least.

"I don't know what's to become of us now. I suppose the abbey will be sold at a loss."

"You'll find new positions."

He shook his head. "That is not likely. You see, that entire abbey is nothing but a collection of discarded things. From the old, decrepit cast-off furniture sent from London houses to all the servants who are useless to the rest of the world."

"What do you mean?"

"Every one of us that was brought here had nowhere else to go. I am in my seventieth year, and Cook is lame in her left arm. She has to delegate most tasks. I once was a minister in the great Church of England, but whispers of scandal ended my ministry in my advanced age. All the servants are ruined women with no references, grown-up waifs pulled from the workhouses in London . . ."

I blinked, studying his wise, old face.

"How can that be?"

"Few people remain out here in the country anymore as servants. Not when opportunities for harder work and more money are available in town. When the earl's uncle remade this abbey, his wife convinced him to fill it with people who had nothing else, and that their gratitude would fuel their service."

"She was right. No one could have found a finer, more loyal bunch of servants to staff a house."

He sighed, tapping the cover of the book. "It was wonderful while it lasted. Now we shall have to find something else."

"Death always leads to new life, and that will be true for the abbey. You will *make* it true. There are a wealth of hidden talents among the staff there, and you proved that when I needed help bringing life into those front rooms without spending a grand fortune. Perhaps it's time to release what the abbey once was and build it into something new — give it a second chance at life."

"No one will wish to spend money rebuilding that old relic when it looks the way it does."

"Perhaps you don't rebuild the ruined section. Haul it all away and make a big, glorious garden here in the center of the place.

See what sort of beauty can be brought to life."

He stared at me for long, silent moments, his tired old eyes warm and hopeful. Then a smile spread over his face like poured honey. "I do so wish you were remaining as our countess. You have a knack for bringing new life to things wherever you go, haven't you?"

I shrugged and smiled. "I am a rag woman. It's all I know."

"It's plenty." He looked about my small cell. "I feel as though I should arrange a place for you to sit and bring you tea."

"There's no point in serving me, Bradford. I'm not a lady."

He shrugged. "A habit, I suppose. It's all *I* know."

I squeezed his arm.

"I came here with a bit of news for you."

"Oh?"

He cleared his throat, shifting his shoulders as he tried to straighten himself against the cell's curved ceiling that was never built to hold a man of such height. "I'm honored to present you with the unofficial verdict of your trial. The most revered Prime Minister would like to offer you a choice in your future. You can remain here in Newgate, facing hard labor and the whim of whatever judge sitting at your trial, after which time you'll be released with neither debt nor opportunity, or you may choose to sail to Western Australia as a direct charge of Lord Darlington's and serve in the convict camps for six months' time."

"Australia!" I sank onto the cot in the corner. "I thought transportation had been outlawed."

"Certainly it has, thanks in part to Uncle Wells's work in Parliament, but all those convicts shipped there remain, many still serving sentences. The last such ship sailed over three years ago, but over a hundred thousand convicts have gone there over the years, and now they must be attended to. He's offering for you to work in the penal colonies, especially with the women. They need someone who can work with them without judgment."

"What sort of work?"

He shrugged. "Rehabilitation. A new life."

Renaugh. Renew. The word wafted through my mind with the gentleness of a spring breeze, but it was direct. Clear.

"You'll have a bit of time to think on it, as your trial —"

"I don't need time." I lifted my eyes to the servant. "I'll go."

He blinked his surprise. "Truly?"

I nodded as my mind spun with all the

ramifications of such a decision.

He studied me, his lips drawn down. "May I ask, my lady, what is it that draws you so to the rubble, so to speak, of humanity? I've seen you do it time and time again. Never quite like this, though."

I cast my gaze to the window, looking up to the thick, gray clouds barely visible through the bars. "We all bear little pieces of God's nature in us. When I look at a person — any person — that's what I think about. I cannot help but long to draw it out."

His eyebrows drew together. "You're even more than I thought you were as a countess, my lady."

I gave a wan smile. "May I ask one favor of you, Bradford?"

He nodded his assent.

I crouched on the floor and drew out the single object that remained in my possession — my own copy of *Jane Eyre.* Flipping to the thirty-eighth chapter of the beloved volume, I ran my finger over the single line I desperately wished to carry out in my own life. "I know it isn't likely, but if you should ever happen to see that second footman again, if he would come looking for me at the abbey someday, will you please give him a message and tell him where I am? It's very important."

His thick eyebrows ascended to his hairline. "The second . . . my, how interesting." A smile of understanding slowly lifted his features. "I do believe dear old Mrs. May was right — Adora *is* a real girl. Quite a girl, at that."

I wanted to laugh and to sob as I dipped into my story, telling him of Sully and how we passed coded messages even at the abbey, and I showed him my marked-up copy of Jane Eyre.

His face melted into a tender smile. "How very fitting for the two of you."

"Please, Bradford, if you would, give him one last message." I flipped through my book and pointed to a line that always affected my tender heart, and now even more so. "To be your wife is, for me, to be as happy as I can be on earth."

He closed his eyes and repeated the reference. "I shall write it down the moment I return to the abbey."

"Thank you ever so much, Bradford. And promise you'll write straightaway if you hear from him, any little mention. I need to know."

His eyes welled with pity. "That I will, my lady. Straightaway." He pinched his lips in the silence, clasping his worn Bible as he looked at me.

I turned away, unable to bear the sorrow in his long face that was only a fraction of what I felt inside.

"You deserve much better than the lot you've had, you know. How I do wish you could have a happy conclusion to your story."

"I may very well yet, even if it isn't what I imagined for myself." I rose and took his hand with a smile. "Don't fret, Bradford. My story is far from over." Yet instead of clinging to the pen and attempting to force its direction, I'd handed it fully over to God.

37

Being created in God's image means we bear traces of him. He is our truest identity.
∼ Diary of a Substitute Countess

"You'd best step back from there, miss."

Sea air brushed my face with its moist palm, soothing the damage done by that isolated prison cell. The salty air pulled away the odor of tightly packed bodies, carrying it out to the water.

"Yes, of course." I released the rigging and stepped back down onto the deck of the *Merry Rose,* my legs already wobbly with disuse. I couldn't wait to set sail, to be out in the middle of the water and making haste toward my new life. Despite the heaviness in my chest, there was a freshness to the day, a powerful sense of freedom around the bend. "Why don't you rest below deck and I'll find you later?"

The matronly woman tasked with mind-ing my compliance and my virtue glared at me, her lips turning down in a complicated twist of disapproval.

"No, I suppose that's not allowed."

She crossed her arms, then her attention pivoted to something across the deck that deepened her frown. "There's a man calling for you. Are you acquainted with him?"

I spun, my heart pounding, and caught sight of two arms waving overhead, a long coat flapping in the wind. I gasped and hurried toward him, weaving through the crowds on deck. I reached the earl and he took my hands, his face desperate and plaintive. "Come back to me, won't you? When your time is served, come back. Just send word and I'll pay your passage."

My stomach somersaulted, and I couldn't speak.

"At least write. Let me know you're safe."

I gave a nod. "As soon as I can."

Hope dawned across his countenance, spreading over his somber face. "Of all the people you've brought back to life, I was the worst before you came. I shall never forget you." He lifted my hand as the heavy winds whipped his hair over his forehead and placed a lingering kiss on my knuckles.

I smiled. "You are quite unforgettable yourself, Lord Enderly."

"Mitchell. Call me that."

I nodded again. "Goodbye, Mitchell."

With one long look, he released my hands and hurried back down the gangplank to the port where he blended into the waiting crowds. When the ship was finally readied and the crew began yelling for the departure, I clung to the side and watched the shore grow distant. The earl lifted his hand in one final wave, then he was out of view and I was on my way.

"You're still a prisoner, you know." My hired shadow eyed me as she approached, as if resenting the fact that I could walk about, unshackled, even as one under captivity. "How is it you came into the good graces of the Prime Minister, then?"

I took a deep breath of fresh sea air. "It's quite a long story."

Mitchell's face haunted my thoughts as I lay below deck at night on my cot, staring at the rough wood planks above me and feeling the vibrating groans of the great ship all the way through to my bones. I pictured his firm mouth, his chiseled jaw, those shadowed, piercing eyes.

Then I pictured Sully, and my whole being flooded with sorrow and desire. Would it take the entire trip to heal?

485

On the third day, a storm tossed the ship and a sailor fell from partway up a mast.

"You'd best see to him." Captain James pointed to the skinny lad, no more than seventeen, sprawled on the deck.

I ran to him and knelt before his form as he groaned in agony, clutching his arm. As one of the few women on board, I'd quickly become known for lifting up the downtrodden, and my help had been requested by the ship's doctor to aid in several injuries and sicknesses.

I held him still in the dripping rain while Dr. Phinneas tied the final strips of linen onto the splint, binding it to his arm. "Does it rain like this often?"

"Not lately, it hasn't. It's been drier than dry this entire summer. You'd be thankful for it if you were stuck in steerage, though. No one on this floating box has the chance to bathe, and this rain will be a blessing. Why, we even have one poor sap down there who cries out for rain at night. Over and over, 'Rain! Rain!' Keeps the others awake."

"Maybe *he* should be on deck." I grumbled in the spitting mist that soaked through my worn garments.

"Can't come up on his own. He came from the hulks, and they were none too kind to him there. Tried to be a hero for too many sickies."

My fingers curled harder around the boy's arm as my flesh crawled. "The one who called for rain? Who is he?"

The doctor shrugged as he dug through his bag with a frown. "He's here on some special provision from up high. The PM himself, I heard."

I sucked in a lungful of wet air. "I have to find him."

I bolted, but he grabbed my arm. "No you don't. You're not allowed down there with the men. Strict orders."

"Please, Doctor. You have to let me see him. I may know him."

He looked into my rain-soaked face, his eyes finally meeting mine, and what he saw there stilled him for a moment. "Very well. Sailor, I need you to go into steerage and bring someone up."

He described him and two sailors disappeared. I huddled under the loose rigging with a pounding heart and eyes focused on the hatch across the ship's deck as waves crashed into the side of the boat. Thank heavens the rain had chased my matronly shadow below deck, despite the rules, and I was free to relish this moment, in the hope so intense it might just knock me over. I waited endless minutes before two sailors struggled back up to the deck with a burden between them.

I blinked through the rain, then I saw it and wanted to weep — the blue cap. Just as it had appeared across the bridge and through the fog in Spitalfields, that bright wool cap signaled the arrival of the person most special to my heart. With a cry I jumped up and stepped over the injured sailor, watching that familiar figure in a gray shirt and suspenders rise onto the deck, each arm about another sailor. He tipped his dirty face up to receive the cool rain, that boyish delight overtaking his features. My hands flew to my mouth as I stood across the deck, but I couldn't move forward.

Sully craned his neck about and stretched his legs, then spoke to the two men who'd brought him. They said something back and pointed at me across the deck, and I waited, my heart in my throat. Then he turned and laid eyes on me, and time froze. He struggled to stand, and joy exploded in my heart. When the men who'd hoisted him scampered off, I walked toward him, giddy, trembling. The only thing between us now was the short distance across the deck. No secrets, no schemes. When a happy grin split his face, I launched myself across the last few feet with the abandon of an ordinary girl who loved an ordinary boy, and the freedom was wildly beautiful.

Weak as he was, he caught me up and held me close against his pounding heart, stumbling back to catch his footing. I clung to him, caught my breath, reveled in the reality of his presence as the rain and his eager kisses covered my face together. Words were too inconsequential in this most sacred of moments, so we said nothing. Being in each other's presence was enough.

Then as I moved back, his arms still firmly around me, that exultant celebration of friendship sparked an awareness of the deeper feelings that lay below, of which we'd only begun to speak.

I smiled up at him. "So the lad got his girl after all."

His eyes twinkled. "Did he, now?" His deep voice was raspy with his recent suffering.

"Oh yes, so very much." I buried my face in his chest, clutching his smudged cotton shirt and wondering why I ever wanted an adventure away from home, for nothing compared to the exhilaration of so precious a moment. His arms tightened around me, holding me to his rising and falling chest with all the fervor that had driven him to pursue me into this mess. When I felt him heaving for breath, I stepped back and eased him down to sit on the deck. He shoved his dark hair back with one hand, agony streaking across his face.

"What is it? What hurts?"

"I'll be fine."

My fingers gently prodded his chest and arms to find the source of the problem, but he moved them away. "I said I'll be fine."

"You're blessedly stubborn, Sullivan McKenna. Why in heaven's name won't you let me help you?"

"Because I don't need it."

"Nonsense. Don't be a fool."

"Please, just leave me be." He curled away from me, his pain evident.

Fighting back the hurt, I laid a gentle hand on his that was fisted against the deck. "Sully."

"I'm the rescuer, Raina, not you. What am I to you if not —"

I covered his lips with my fingers. "Everything."

He looked down as the rain cleared and distant thunder rumbled.

"Don't ever underestimate my love, Sullivan McKenna. It's there because of who you are, not what you do." The character, the very nature of this man, had drawn me to the true Rescuer, proved that sacrificial love was possible, and for that I would forever be grateful.

He looked at me, nostrils flaring, tears nearing the surface. He frowned and sniffed them away.

"This time maybe it's my turn to take care of you." I smoothed my hand along his cheek, and he leaned into it, closing his eyes. "I owe you that much at least."

He heaved a deep sigh and reached up to cradle my face. "I knew you'd be here. Just knew it."

"How did you know?"

"Darlington told me he offered you the same choice, and I knew you'd choose to restore the convicts."

"You did?"

He gave a slight shrug and a crooked little smile. "It's who you are. My *Renaugh.*"

I closed my eyes and grasped his dear hand, holding it to my moist cheek. What a blessed, blessed life I had been given. "And you came too."

"I'd follow you on any adventure." He smiled. "I cannot help myself. It's who *I* am." With an exhale of delight, he drew me close, his voice low and rough, and I curled into him where he sat. "You'll never be rid of me, Raina Bretton. Never."

"Promise?"

He tightened his hold, resting his head on top of mine, and for several silent moments we remained wrapped in the embrace. Finally he spoke into my tumbled curls, his breath warm against my wet scalp. "Raina?"

"Hmm?"

He pushed back and leaned his forehead against mine, those glowing eyes smiling into mine. "Can I kiss you now?"

Alive with eagerness at those simple words, I reached up and ran gentle fingertips along his face, smiling up into his eyes. "I suppose I've made you wait long enough."

He kissed my forehead like the seal of a promise, then brushed his lips down my face until they found mine and sank into the long, deep kiss that had been years in the making. It carried me away like the passionate, lilting melodies he drew from his instrument, the pure loveliness and harmony that spilled from his very being, and it intoxicated me with its depth.

From childhood chums to a grown lad and his lass, we'd been stitched together with years of love and honesty, sacrifices and invincible devotion, and his embrace felt like the culmination of it all. Intense and powerful, rich with sweetness, that moment was the first of many to come.

He released me and exhaled, smoothing my wet curls off my face. "So now you are finished with adventures?"

I nearly laughed at his hopeful face. "Hardly." I laid a hand on his chest and smiled. "Blessed are those who hand God the reins, for they shall find adventures. Only now, we'll have them together."

The moment we docked, I put pen to paper and explained everything in a letter to the earl. But to Bradford, I wrote only a single line.

And dear reader, I married him. ~ CB:JE 436

EPILOGUE

Addley Point, Australia, 1873

"You owe me a few moments alone today, Mr. McKenna." Wiping my sleeve across my moist forehead again, I tossed a basket of pruned branches across the aisle to him.

He caught it and raised his eyebrows with a little grin. "Aye, that so?"

"You've not forgotten our anniversary, have you, now?"

Dropping the basket, he hopped over the row of vines and slipped his arms around me. He leaned me back to steal a deep kiss, one that I sank into with delight. "How could I forget?" He whispered the words against my lips and righted me again as my head spun.

I caught my balance and covered both flaming cheeks with my hands. "No more of that out here, in front of everyone."

He walked backward a few paces, dipped a mock curtsy of obedience, and leaped over

494

to the next row with a firm hold on the post.

Two years into our life in Australia, we had fulfilled our sentences and worked harder than ever, but life was rich. Deep. We poured ourselves out onto these castoffs, helping to rescue and renew. Growing grapes and sugarcane and aiding these released criminals took every bit of strength and much of our time, especially in the fall, but we reaped great rewards. I winked at my husband and scanned the red kerchiefs bobbing among the rows, covering the heads of our many co-laborers. Many of them had earned passage here by committing petty crimes, and some none at all, but we delighted in our brood with pride. Over three hundred of them had passed through our farm, being trained and encouraged, then embarking on their second chance at life.

"It's all right, Missus." Sarah Jane Fowley approached, holding up her apron full of little sprigs she'd pruned. "Gives the rest of us something to hope for in a marriage."

I touched the girl's arm. "You'll find someone who fits you perfectly, Sarah Jane."

"That'll be a trick, finding a man who wants to love a pickpocket." She gave me a coy smile and moved on.

"It's part of your past, you know."

"Some parts of the past are simply who we are."

I turned at the quiet voice of Aster behind me, the former maid who had been sacked and transported after repeatedly lying to her mistress about tasks she'd overlooked or objects she'd broken. My heart squeezed as it always did when this girl, so characterized by her remorse, spoke of her own sins. Many hours and tears we'd spent sorting through her particular vice that she desperately wished to put behind her, despite its relentless hold on her that she felt would be a permanent fixture in her nature. Over time I'd seen the problem go from one that resided in her house to one that merely came knocking now and again, but she was only too aware of the times she'd given in.

I looked at her and brimmed over with the abundant grace that had been poured into me. "Do you know, I believe those children have been begging me to let you finish your story since sunup today. They love your tales."

She smiled shyly. "They come natural to me. I suppose it's the one good side to my affliction."

"You're brilliant at them too. Those children will remember the lessons wrapped in the neat packaging of your story far better than the sermons they hear on Sunday. There's much value in that."

"I suppose."

I put an arm around her. "You, dear girl, are a storyteller. It's who you are."

Her delicate brow furrowed. "I wish I weren't."

"You've always had a knack for spinning fiction, but what you once meant for deception is now a powerful conveyer of truth." I smiled. "That's God's redemption, you know." I spoke with the compassion of one who knew.

When the sun set over our very hot corner of the world and the laborers had all gathered in the big open rooms to consume the food we'd prepared, Sully and I finally slipped away and lay together on the flat roof of our bungalow, hands clasped.

"What should we name that one?" I pointed at a set of three bright stars in a row. "It needs a long name to cover that many stars."

"How about Agamemnon?"

"You're brutal." I laughed. "Those poor stars."

"Persephone?"

"What does that even mean?"

"Why does it matter?"

"It always matters." I closed my eyes and

pictured Uncle Wells just then. I owed him another letter soon. A few more weeks, and I could tell him our news. I shifted under Sully's hand that rested on my abdomen. "What do you think of the name Amethyst?"

"A bit pretentious, but I suppose it'll do. For a star."

I wasn't thinking of granting that particular name to a star. "Sully?"

"Hmm?" He lay with his eyes closed, tracing gentle circles on my arm in a way that still made me weak.

Before I could gather the right words, a door banged open and a voice erupted nearby. "You all up here?"

We scrambled to sit up and greet Amadeus Price, the longtime doctor of Addley Point and avid supporter of our mission.

"Well, look at what a year's done to you, Mrs. McKenna. How fine and bright you look, like a woman about to embark on an adventure."

I blushed at how close he was to the truth.

"Every day's an adventure with this one." Sully grinned at me.

"I was hoping to convince you to pull out your fiddle and give us a song, McKenna. Care to oblige?"

"I'd be honored, sir. Come down and I'll find me fiddle."

Moments later, I stood alone across a candlelit room full of the people who had become our family and watched my husband light up the house with his fiddle once again. Music poured into every crack of our bungalow and spilled out into the night, keeping time with the crickets. Everyone loved to hear him play, and none could keep from dancing. The happy crowd clapped and spun as his music overtook the room, yet I lingered in my little corner, watching with a smile.

The doctor approached again. "You truly do look different, Mrs. McKenna. You've always had a spark about you, but you look as though you're holding on to some lovely little secret."

I merely shrugged, answering with a smile. Certain secrets were meant to be savored with one's husband first.

He sighed. "I do wish you were able to be in England. The doctors there might have helped you where I failed. You both . . . you deserve children more than anyone. You deserve a good life."

"We have everything we need, Dr. Price, and I know one thing for certain." I sighed and watched Sully come alive with his music. "Much is uncertain in life, but with God, anything is possible."

DISCUSSION QUESTIONS

1. They say a house is always a reflection of its mistress. In what ways did Raina resemble the house while she was there?

2. Raina changed so much when she arrived at the abbey that she nearly believed herself to be an entirely different person. How do external things impact our identity? What would you say is the core of who you are?

3. In the beginning, Prendergast's offer seemed too good to be true, and later she thought the same of Uncle Wells. What is it that made those two offers so different, and how do they resemble offers made to us by the world, and by God?

4. What changes did you see in Raina when she began to "turn mirrors into windows" and focus on others instead of her own

self-image? Why do you think it is so important to look out instead of just looking inward?

5. Raina returns to the house after the fire and discovers God is still present in those abandoned rooms, even in the midst of their ruin. How does this parallel her life and her heart in that moment? What evidence have you seen of God in the midst of ruin?

6. What are the ways we see Raina rationalizing her part in the scheme? What do you think were her reasons, besides saving Sully? Which did you agree or disagree with?

7. What elements of Uncle Wells, particularly in chapter 25 and the scene where Raina reveals the truth to everyone, show us how God responds to us? What was most meaningful to you in what he said in those scenes?

8. What did you find meaningful in the longtime, often selfless love between childhood friends Raina and Sully?

9. How did a few of the people in the house

struggle with understanding who they were? How do you?

10. How does the following diary entry come into play throughout the house? "Just because it's who we have always been, it does not mean it's who we were created to be."

11. Did you feel the conclusion, with penalties for both Raina and Sully, was fitting? What did you find interesting or meaningful about the ending?

ACKNOWLEDGMENTS

This book was a total blast to write, and part of that is because of the people who joined me in the process. I had so much fun imagining possibilities and chasing down ideas with Susan Tuttle, Dawn Crandall, Stacey Zink, my dad Bob Davidson, my husband Vince, Crystal Caudill, Allen Arnold, Rachel Fordham, and many others. You all are phenomenal.

I thank God for taking me on an unexpected journey with this book when he made it clear I had the ending to this mystery — and answers to my deeper questions — totally wrong and that I didn't get it yet. I'm starting to now, and it's been a fun ride! No book ever has the same process when God is driving, and I love that.

I truly owe this story to my exceptionally wonderful team at Revell as well for pouring their energy into it and wrestling it into shape, sorting and sifting through my words and sewing up every plot hole with precision and beauty. Vicki Crumpton and Barb Barnes, extraordinary editors, constantly amaze me with both their intelligence and graciousness as we rewrite and polish together. The marketing team is powerful, talented, and fun. The entire group is a joy to know, and I'm thankful to be in your capable hands.

I appreciate my readers so much as well. You all make it exponentially fun to write, to twist the plot, to come up with surprising and nuanced scenes that will keep you reading. Your interactions and your enthusiasm have been an unexpected blessing — more than I can convey with words. I've discovered so many like-minded readers through this gig, and I treasure those connections.

Lastly, I'm very appreciative of my little brother, who has been an ongoing demonstration of what it means to figure out who you are and how to somehow turn that inward search into outward focus, others-centeredness, and servanthood. In a book about identity, you've been a great inspiration.

ABOUT THE AUTHOR

Joanna Davidson Politano is the award-winning author of *Lady Jayne Disappears* and *A Rumored Fortune*. She freelances for a small nonfiction publisher but spends much of her time spinning tales that capture the colorful, exquisite details in ordinary lives. She is always on the hunt for random acts of kindness, people willing to share their deepest secrets with a stranger, and hidden stashes of sweets. She lives with her husband and their two babies in a house in the woods near Lake Michigan and shares stories that move her at www.jdpstories .com.

The employees of Thorndike Press hope you have enjoyed this Large Print book. All our Thorndike, Wheeler, and Kennebec Large Print titles are designed for easy reading, and all our books are made to last. Other Thorndike Press Large Print books are available at your library, through selected bookstores, or directly from us.

For information about titles, please call:
(800) 223-1244

or visit our website at:
gale.com/thorndike

To share your comments, please write:
Publisher
Thorndike Press
10 Water St., Suite 310
Waterville, ME 04901